An author of more than ninety books for children and adults with more than seventy-five for Mills & Boon, **Janice Kay Johnson** writes about love and family, and pens books of gripping romantic suspense. A *USA TODAY* bestselling author and an eight-time finalist for the Romance Writers of America RITA® Award, she won a RITA® Award in 2008. A former librarian, Janice raised two daughters in a small town north of Seattle, Washington.

USA TODAY bestselling and RITA® Award-winning author **Marie Ferrarella** has written more than 250 books for Mills & Boon, some under the name Marie Nicole. Her romances are beloved by fans worldwide. Visit her website, marieferrarella.com

Also by Janice Kay Johnson

Hide the Child
Trusting the Sheriff
Within Range
From This Day On
One Frosty Night
More Than Neighbors
Because of a Girl

Also by Marie Ferrarella

Mission: Cavanaugh Baby
Cavanaugh on Duty
A Widow's Guilty Secret
Cavanaugh's Surrender
Cavanaugh Rules
Cavanaugh's Bodyguard
Cavanaugh Fortune
How to Seduce a Cavanaugh
Cavanaugh or Death
Cavanaugh Cold Case

Discover more at millsandboon.co.uk

BRACE FOR IMPACT

JANICE KAY JOHNSON

COLTON BABY CONSPIRACY

MARIE FERRARELLA

MILLS & BOON

First Published in Great Britain 2020
by Mills & Boon, an imprint of HarperCollins*Publishers*
1 London Bridge Street, London, SE1 9GF

Brace for Impact © 2019 Janice Kay Johnson
Colton Baby Conspiracy © 2020 Harlequin Books S.A.

Special thanks and acknowledgement are given to Marie Ferrarella for her contribution to *The Coltons of Mustang Valley* series.

ISBN: 978-0-263-28015-9

0120

MIX
Paper from
responsible sources
FSC C007454

FSC
www.fsc.org

This book is produced from independently certified FSC™ paper to ensure responsible forest management.

For more information visit: www.harpercollins.co.uk/green

Printed and bound in Spain
by CPI, Barcelona

BRACE FOR IMPACT

JANICE KAY JOHNSON

In memory of my dad, a noted Northwest mountain climber with many first ascents who shared his love of the mountains and wilderness with his children.

Chapter One

"This?" Maddy Kane balked like a horse that had gotten a good look at the rattlesnake coiled in the middle of the trail. Her feet said, *uh-uh. No way.* The rest of her was in complete agreement. "We're flying to the other side of the state in *this*?"

She'd vaguely noticed the airfield when she drove by and realized it was puny. Somehow she hadn't translated that into puny airplane.

Having lived in the small and remote town of Republic in eastern Washington the past year, she hadn't expected to board a Boeing 767 here, with only the one short runway and a few hangars by Lake Curlew. But considering she'd never flown in anything smaller than a 737—she thought that was the Boeing company's smallest plane—this Cessna didn't look much bigger than the really terrifying ultralight she'd seen once buzzing over a tulip field, the pilot sitting in what looked like a lawn chair beneath the wings.

Okay, this plane did have a cabin. Still.

The man next to her laughed, the skin beside his eyes crinkling. A United States marshal, Scott Rankin had been her handler throughout her ordeal. Really, her anchor. As horrific as witnessing the murder had been, thinking the killer would see her huddled only a few feet away, she'd never imagined the fallout after calling 911 and telling the detective everything she'd seen and heard. It had now been twelve months since she'd talked to her parents or sister or friends or the man she'd been dating. Supposedly, her law firm was saving her job, but she had to wonder. A year shouldn't seem so long, but she'd increasingly felt a kinship with Rip Van Winkle. In all these months she'd clung to the knowledge that Rankin was there, a telephone call away.

Graying but still broad-shouldered and strong in his fifties, he had shown her pictures of his wife, adult children and a new granddaughter. He'd been really kind to her. In turn, she'd cooperated with his arrangements. Until now.

How could he think this was the safest way to get her to Seattle, where she was scheduled to testify in a major trial that would begin ten days from now? *Safe* being a relative concept. So okay, flying commercial wasn't an option from this part of the state, but until he knocked on her door this morning, she'd assumed they would drive.

That was the moment he'd said cheerfully, "Nope, we're catching a flight."

Maddy had envisioned at least the kind of twin-engine passenger plane that carried twenty or thirty people. For one thing…there was a mountain range separating eastern and western Washington. A tall one.

She was already toting her bag when Rankin started across the pavement toward the little plane. "Come on," he said over his shoulder, "this'll be fun."

Oh, Lord. For a minute she stood there breathing too fast, until she realized she didn't have an option.

Reluctantly, she trailed him.

Another man had been circling the Cessna, doing

what she assumed was a flight check, which ought to reassure her. That meant he was safety conscious, right?

"I don't really like heights," she mumbled to Marshal Rankin's back.

The tall, lanky man doing the flight check straightened and, beaming at them, extended his hand. "Couldn't get better weather for the flight!" he assured Maddy and Rankin.

Sure. By the first day of July in this part of the state, *every* day was sunny and hot. Didn't mean there wouldn't be a lightning storm over the Cascades. A white-hot bolt from on high, and that little tin can would be zapped.

"You'll be able to get a good look at the Cascades," the pilot enthused as if he hadn't noticed her severe case of doubt. "Bird's-eye view."

Maddy squared her shoulders. This was happening, whether she liked it or not. And really, what did she have to fear, compared to the ten minutes when she'd had only a half-open bathroom door between her and a hit man who'd just murdered her new client? This was nothing; people flew in small planes all the time. A lot of people enjoyed it.

The pilot looked familiar, as most locals did. She didn't remember ever hearing his name, though.

When they shook, he introduced himself. "Bill Potter. You must be Cassie Davis. I know I've seen you around. And Mr. Rankin, I assume?"

"That's right," the man at her side agreed. "As I told you, Cassie is my niece. You'll have to excuse her anxiety. I saved the news that we were flying to be a surprise. A drive over one of the passes just isn't the same."

Until she stepped into that courtroom, she would remain Cassie Davis, divorced bookkeeper, instead of

Madeline Kane, never-married attorney-at-law. Supposedly, she and "Uncle" Scott were heading for a family reunion in Everett, a city only half an hour north of Seattle. She hadn't asked where she'd be staying. All she knew was that Rankin intended to keep her away from the courthouse until she absolutely had to show. She'd made it through the year in hiding; now she had to remain alive the last few days until she could testify.

The pilot lowered the big door on the hangar and locked it, loaded the two duffel bags in the rear of the plane, then asked her to sit in the back, Rankin in front beside him. "Got to balance our weight," he explained. Either he was really good at faking it, or he suffered from chronic good humor.

Or, heck, he loved to fly this plane and was brimming with excitement.

And she was being a crank.

So she smiled at him before she crawled over the front seat and buckled herself in, per instructions.

"This is a Cessna Skyhawk," Bill told her. "One of the safest planes you could fly in." He had been teaching lessons for something like the past thirty years in this and an earlier model of the Skyhawk, he added, while also offering charter flights.

She held on tight to the seat belt with one hand and the seat itself with the other as he taxied down the runway and the plane lifted into the air. He banked over Republic so she could get a good look at it, he told her over his shoulder.

Despite her queasiness, Maddy did gaze through the window at the town. People had been good to her here. It wasn't their fault she'd felt incredibly isolated. Living under an assumed name, she could never be honest with anyone about who she was or what life she'd actually lived. That meant being friendly without ever really making a friend. Still…as time passed, she'd felt safe.

Stepping into that courtroom, on the other hand, would be the equivalent of confronting a wounded grizzly.

"You okay back there?" Rankin swiveled in his seat beside the pilot and still had to raise his voice to be heard over the engine noise.

She summoned another smile. "I'm good." And… maybe it was even true, because as the plane leveled off, her anxiety lowered. If she didn't look out the window, she could pretend she was on a bus, say. That worked.

As a result she spent the first half hour brooding about the upcoming trial—and then the gap of time between the two trials. Rankin hadn't said anything about those weeks, except that she wouldn't be returning to Republic. Of course, she also couldn't resume her real life until both the hit man and the Superior Court judge who'd hired him had been convicted.

First thing to face was being "prepared" by the prosecutors. As if she hadn't prepped her share of witnesses for trial. Of course, her perspective as a defense attorney wasn't quite the same.

The buzz of the engine at last lulled her into letting go of the troubles that still lay ahead. The pilot yelled over his shoulder to tell her they were flying over the Okanogan National Forest, and would shortly cross the Pasayten Wilderness. She vaguely knew that it took in a swath of the drier eastern side of the Cascade Mountain range. Now she did look out the small window, seeing that sagebrush and juniper hills had been replaced with what she thought were lodgepole and ponderosa pine forest.

She gaped when she set eyes on the first pointy, white-topped mountains ahead.

Bill called out the names as they neared: Mount Carru, Blackcap Peak, Robinson Mountain. Maddy pressed her nose to the small window to see better. She was astonished by the amount of snow, given that this was July. Her awe grew as the snowcapped peaks became increasingly jagged, gleaming white in the sunlight. She could just make out deep cuts clothed in dark green between mountains. A long body of water had to be Ross Lake behind its dam. They flew low enough she could see the oddly opaque turquoise color of the water.

She flattened a hand on the cold window and stared in fascination. Ahead lay a range of mountains that made her think of a shark's teeth. And yes, in the distance was Mount Baker, a conical volcano like Mount Rainier, and Glacier, another volcano. How could she have grown up as close as Seattle and never visited these wonders? Even Washington's most famous volcano, Mount Rainier, seemed mostly unreal, floating in sight of Seattle. She'd never once taken a sunny summer day to drive up to Paradise and see the avalanche lilies in bloom.

She glanced at the marshal to see that he was watching her and smiling.

"This really is something, isn't it?"

"Yes!" It occurred to her belatedly that he might genuinely have been trying to give her a treat.

Oh, and the skinny lake below was called Diablo, according to the pilot, formed by a dam on the Skagit River. It, too, was that startling turquoise color. Over his shoulder, the pilot told her the coloration was the result of the powder from boulders that glaciers ground down. Ultimately, the glacial "flour" washed down the many creeks into the lakes.

They went right over the top of a mountain that was impressive enough, if not jagged like the ones ahead. Those made up the Picket Range, he told her, mountains that had names like Terror, Fury and Challenger, and for a good reason, from the looks of them. The deep valleys between had precipitous drops from the heights, trees clinging to the rocky walls. It was a wilderness that looked as forbidding as the Himalayas or the dense Amazon jungle.

Trying to drink in the beauty not so far below them, Maddy heard the murmur of the two men's voices but didn't try to make out what they were saying. She couldn't seem to tear her eyes off those particularly daunting peaks ahead.

A sudden hard *bang* made the whole airplane shudder. Fear electrified her nerve endings. It felt like a huge rock had struck them, but that couldn't be what had happened.

Clenching her seat belt and the edge of the seat, Maddy looked at the pilot, hoping to be reassured. In her oblique view, he radiated tension. But it wasn't he who riveted her horrified gaze. No, she fixated on the propeller as its blurring speed slowed, slowed...until it quit spinning altogether.

Before that moment of sudden silence, Maddy had never actually heard the thunder of her heartbeat before.

WILL GANNON HAD reached the summit a good ten minutes before, and still he turned in a slow circle to take in the most incredible panorama he'd ever seen. The Picket Range felt close enough to touch and menacing at the same time. One ice-and glacier-crusted spire after another. Mount Baker beyond, and was that a glimpse of Mount Shuksan? Mount Challenger to the north, Eldorado and Mount Logan to the southeast. Rocky ridges, plunging chasms, a sky so blue it hurt his eyes. And quiet. Most of all, he drank in the quiet and the solitude.

He'd chosen Elephant Butte to climb not because it was the best known of North Cascade peaks, or a mountaineering challenge, but rather because most climbers bypassed it. Even on a weekend like this, he could be alone. Later in the summer he might try to find someone who'd like to join him tackling a couple of the more impressive mountains, the ones he'd be foolish to climb alone, but right now what he needed was to pull himself together. After being severely wounded in an ambush in Afghanistan, he'd been shipped back to the States. Being a stubborn bastard, he'd been able to rehab physically. The crap he felt, that was something else. But this...*this* was what he'd needed. Peace and quiet. The vast beauty of nature.

He shook himself and returned to his pack, where he dug out the makings for the simplest of lunches: peanuts, beef jerky and a candy bar, all washed down with treated water. As pure as the sparkling streams looked and tasted, the water wasn't safe to drink without being purified.

He let his mind empty as the sun warmed his upturned face. Nights when he had trouble sleeping he could remember this. Replace ugly memories of gushing blood, missing arms or legs, sharp pieces of metal thrust like knives into bellies and chests and even faces or throats.

And crap, there he went again. He discovered that he'd closed his eyes, but he opened them again, looked at the spectacular scenery, heard the shrill whistle of what he thought might be a pika, a small mammal that lived among the rocks. It was answered by another, and Will blew out a breath. He was okay. This climb had been a good idea. He'd get out in the wilderness often until snow closed it to him, unless he wanted to learn to snowshoe.

Hey, maybe.

The time had come for him to decide whether to go back the way he'd come, the standard route along Stetattle ridge, or try a different and probably more difficult route. Will leaned toward the different route out of the backcountry. He wasn't in any hurry. He'd brought plenty of food if he ended up taking an extra day or even two, and if he hadn't, he could fill himself with the sweet blueberries ripe on low-growing shrubs at a certain altitude.

Reluctantly, he heaved his pack onto his back and adjusted the weight. Ice ax in hand, he started to pick his way across a patch of snow that began the slow descent. Far below amid a subalpine area of stunted trees and a bright patch of blooming heather, movement caught his eye and he paused. Was he about to have company? Damn, he hoped not. He wanted this day, this mountain, to himself.

Then he identified the patch of cinnamon-brown as a black bear, probably dining on blueberries, too. Not alone. He shifted his binoculars to see her cub. Smiling, he watched for a few minutes, glad his path wouldn't lead him too near to them. Getting between mama and her cub wouldn't be smart.

He'd let the binoculars fall and started forward again when he heard a faint sound that had him turning his head. A growl…no, a hum? It took him a minute to spot the small plane that must have come over Ross Lake and now passed north of Sourdough Lake. In fact, it was heading pretty well directly toward him, which disturbed him on a subliminal level—made him want to sprint to take cover.

He saw the moment the bear swung her head, too, in search of the source of that alien noise. A sudden sharp *bang*, although muted by distance, shot adrenaline through his body. What in hell…? Will lifted his binoculars again, this time to the plane, adjusting until he could all but see the pilot's face. Had the guy dropped some kind of load? Not the best country for retrieval, if so.

Frowning, he cocked his head and listened hard. No more irritating buzz. Oh, crap. The engine had shut down; the propeller no longer turned. The nose dropped. That plane was heading down. He watched in horror as it descended precipitously toward the steep, forested slopes beneath him.

"Start the damn engine. There's still time. Start it!" he shouted.

Following along with his binoculars, he saw the moment the plane hit the first treetops. Cartwheeled. Tore apart.

It might not be safe or smart, but the next thing he knew, he was running.

TAT-A-TAT, TAT-A-TAT, TAT-A-TAT.

Maddy tried to understand the staccato series of rapping sounds followed by silence, then a repeat. Strangely reluctant to open her eyes, she listened hard.

A harsh call. A trilling.

Something brushed her face. She jerked, and pain racked her body.

Have to see, have to see. Somehow she knew she really didn't *want* to know what had happened, but…

even aside from the pain, so diffused she wasn't sure what the source of it was, her head felt weird. So she slitted her eyes.

And let out a shocked cry. She was hanging upside down. And looking at a completely unfamiliar landscape. Ground that was tilted. Rocks, the rough boles of trees and feathery sweeps of green branches.

Wanting to retreat into darkness again, she squeezed her eyes shut, but a stern inner voice refused to let her go back into hiding. *Figure out what's wrong. Like why I'm hanging upside down like a bat settling for a snooze.* She'd have giggled if she hadn't known instinctively how much that would hurt.

All right, all right.

This time when she opened her eyes, she lifted her chin to look upward. It took her way longer than it should have to comprehend. A belt across her lap and shoulder held her in a seat anchored to torn metal. *Not a car seat*, she thought, puzzled. Was that…? It was… A wing—an airplane wing—was attached, stabbing toward the ground amidst the greenery.

Airplane seat belt, not car. It was all that held her from falling. A flicker of memory and she knew. *That's why I'm alive*, she thought in shock, trying to imagine the force that had torn the plane into pieces.

The Cessna. In a flood of renewed fear, she listened for voices, cries, *anything* to indicate one or both of the men were alive.

"Scott!" she called. "Bill!" Her "Anyone?" trailed off weakly.

She heard something; she just didn't know what.

Getting down had to come before anything else.

She could open the seat belt, but would drop what

had to be eight or ten feet onto her head. Even fuzzy-minded as she was, she knew that wouldn't be smart.

She tried to pull herself upward, grabbing a piece of the wreckage. Metal groaned, shifted, and Maddy froze. Her head swam, and she looked to see bright red blood running down her arm. She must have sliced her palm open. In the greater scheme of things, it didn't seem important. Being fuzzy insulated her. She found a more solid handhold—the side of the cabin, minus the window—took a deep breath and unsnapped the belt.

Her bloody hand slipped from the wreckage and she fell sooner than she'd planned, twisting to land hard on her butt and side. She skidded, bumping to a stop against a boulder. Pain engulfed her and she gritted her teeth against the need to scream.

When she was finally able to move, she wasn't sure she hadn't lost consciousness again. From the angle of the sun through the trees, it hadn't been long, though. Unless she'd lost an entire day? No, the blood on her hand and arm still looked fresh.

Sitting up proved to be an agonizing effort. The left side of her body must have taken the brunt of the damage. Either her arm was broken, or dislocated. Or it could be her collarbone, she supposed. And ribs, and hip. But when she ordered her feet to waggle, they did, and when she experimentally bent her knees, doing so didn't make her want to pass out.

Maddy continued to evaluate her condition. She had to wipe blood away from her eyes, which suggested a gash or blow up there somewhere. Her head hurt fiercely, making it hard to think. And yes, she had definitely slashed open her palm, although she was already so bloody, she could hardly tell where this stream was coming from. None of the blood fountained, though, just trickled and left smears, so she wasn't bleeding to death.

Or dying at all. She didn't think.

With her right hand she clutched the thin bole of a wispy, small evergreen of some kind and used it to pull herself to her feet. Then she turned slowly in search of the rest of the plane. Not the tail—she didn't care about the tail. The nose. The front seats, the two men. Logically, they had to be…somewhere in front of her.

Tat-a-tat, tat-a-tat, tat-a-tat.

Woodpecker, she understood. It kept tapping as she struggled forward, the sound weirdly comforting. Something else was alive, going about its business.

She glimpsed red and white between the trees, and tried to run even on the steep sideways slope. She fell to her knees and slithered downhill until she came up against a tree solid enough to hold her. As she pushed herself up again, an involuntary whimper escaped her. Her eyes stung—whether from blood or tears, Maddy didn't know.

This time she moved more carefully, watching where she put her feet, grabbing branches where she could for support. The rocky side hill didn't support huge trees. Maybe…maybe these had softened the landing.

And torn the plane to shreds, too.

She saw the other wing first. It had slashed raw places in tree trunks and ripped away branches. More metal lay ahead, another thirty or forty feet.

There she found Bill Potter, still in his seat as she'd been, but the way his head lay on his shoulder— Her teeth chattered as she made herself take a closer look. And then she backed away and bent over puking, snot and tears and blood mixing until she had to use the hem of her shirt to wipe her face again.

She called for Scott, listened. Did it again, and this time she heard a cry. *I'm not alone.* Whispering, "Thank you, thank you, thank you," she half crawled in that direction.

When she saw him, crumpled and twisted, her teeth started to chatter again. That couldn't be right. People didn't bend that way.

She had to scramble the last bit, the ground cold and sloping even more steeply here.

His eyes were open when she reached him, but beneath his tan his face was a color she'd never seen. His lips were almost blue.

"Scott," she whispered, not letting herself look at his lower body.

"Maddy." Her name came out so quietly, she bent close to hear him. Took his hand in hers, but his chilly fingers didn't tighten in response. Something else she didn't want to think about.

"I'll go for help," she said, unable to help crying.

"No." Suddenly, his fingers convulsed like claws, biting into her hand. His eyes held hers with fierce determination. "Not an accident."

That was something she hadn't yet let herself think. Even though she knew, she *knew*, Maddy heard herself saying, "What?"

"Bomb."

Chapter Two

As Maddy clutched his hand, Scott tried to work his mouth. "Can't trust marshals. Only people who knew."

"That you'd gone to get me and how we were getting back?"

"Yes."

"But…"

"Can't stay with plane."

"I won't leave you!"

"Have to." His voice had weakened. Blood bubbled between his lips.

"No—"

"They'll need to be sure you're dead. Someone will be coming." He stared at her with what she sensed took everything he had left. "Take coats, first-aid kit. Food. Run, Maddy."

Her hot tears splattered onto his face. He didn't seem to notice.

"Friend. Marshal. Ruzinski. Robert. Remember."

She had to lip-read now. "Robert Ruzinski," she repeated.

He made a sound that might have been confirmation. His lips moved again. "Trust him."

"Okay. But I can't leave you."

Staring into his eyes, she saw the very second *he*

left her. The tight clench of his fingers loosened. When she lifted her hand away, his arm flopped to his side.

He was dead.

She let herself cry for a few minutes before she made herself think through the cotton candy that seemed to fill her head.

Normally, she'd try to figure out whether there was some kind of beacon and how it worked. Or…would the radio still work? But as it was…

Run.

She didn't dare be found. Not yet. She had to hide. Stay alive until she could really think, evaluate her options. Right now she needed to scavenge what she could from the plane, or she wouldn't survive. She'd seen enough snow before the plane came down to know it must still get cold this high up in the mountains. And there might be some food. Something to hold water in. Yes, a first-aid kit.

Would she have phone reception? Maddy didn't remember seeing her purse. It could be anywhere. She'd look, but the phone, even if it was what Scott had called a "burner," would have GPS, wouldn't it? That might not be good.

Warmth, food, water, bandages—those were her needs. And also… She turned her head to the twisted part of Scott Rankin's body. If he carried a gun, she needed to take that.

The idea of groping his body felt like a hideous invasion. He'd want her to, though—she felt sure.

Shivering, Maddy knelt over him.

HE HAD TO be insane.

Will had had plenty of time to think about what he was doing, and how little chance there was that he'd be able to help anyone. People rarely survived that kind of crash. If anyone had miraculously lived, they might get a faster response from an activated beacon than from him. He'd known from the beginning that he'd take hours to reach the crash site.

But what if the plane didn't have a beacon? If the pilot hadn't filed a flight plan?

Straight lines in this country were rarely possible. No trail existed for him to follow. Instead, he'd reluctantly realized he had to drop from his current elevation of 7,380 feet on the summit and head southwest along the side of the ridge leading toward McMillan Spire. He had to stay above the tree line so he'd see the crash site. Then he just had to hope it would be possible to climb down to it.

This was *not* a recommended descent route from Elephant Butte. In fact, from what he'd read, he'd be facing brutal conditions. Chances were good he wouldn't have cell phone coverage once he dropped toward the Torrent Creek and Stettatle Creek drainages. Even as he jogged along a lengthy band of snow, using his ice ax to aid his balance, he debated whether he should call to report what he'd seen. Swearing under his breath, he made himself stop, lower his pack and dig for his cell phone, which of course wasn't easily accessed. He hadn't expected to want it.

And then when he did find it…he had no bars. Will dropped the damn useless thing back into a pocket that he zipped, then shouldered the pack again and set off.

The speed he tried to maintain was a lot faster than was safe.

Even as he thought that, his feet caught crumbling rock and skidded. He slammed the serrated end of the ax into a crack between boulders and felt the wrench on his shoulders as the ax held and one of his booted feet slid over a drop-off.

Swearing, sweating, he made slow, careful movements to get his feet back under him on a too-narrow ledge. The unwieldy pack didn't help; even though he'd eaten some of the food he'd carried in, it probably still weighed seventy pounds or more. Nothing he wasn't familiar with from deployments, but this was a different landscape. The weight shifted his balance, like a pregnant woman's belly shifted hers. He made his cautious and much slower way to another strip of snow, one of many that formed ribbons between stretches of tumbled rock.

Had to come up here alone, didn't ya?

Maybe this wasn't the right plan. He was strong. He thought he could make it back to Diablo by early nightfall, even though he'd taken two days to get up here. He could call 911 or find a ranger station, get a rescue helicopter in the air.

One that wouldn't be able to land in this mountainous landscape, Will reminded himself.

Still, if he ever reached the crash site, odds were he'd find a dead pilot. Given that this was Sunday, he might also find some climbers or hikers who'd been closer and had already reached the site.

He just didn't believe that. This was early in the season in the high mountains. A warm spring had opened the backcountry earlier than usual. A lot of people would have waited for the upcoming Fourth of July weekend. And even though people down at Ross Lake and hiking the Big Beaver Trail had probably seen the plane go overhead, if they paid any attention to it at all once it crossed the ridge, they'd have lost sight before it began to plummet. Climbers up McMillan Spire might have seen it, but they might just as well have not, too. No matter what, he was closer. Will had a bad feeling that, by sheer chance, he might be the only person who'd seen the crash.

He could do more to help survivors than almost anyone, too, although he regretted the limited medical supplies he carried. Still, as an army medic—former army medic—he'd seen and treated more traumatic injuries than most physicians. Death was all too familiar to him, but if there was any chance...

He groaned and kept moving.

IT TOOK MADDY half an hour and a panicky realization of passing time to realize the rear portion of the plane wasn't where she thought it should be. It should have broken off first and thus been behind where she'd regained consciousness hanging upside down. Every step hurt. Even the brush of hemlock or fir needles hurt. If she hadn't been terrified—*Run, Maddy*—she would have given up. But she couldn't, in case Marshal Rankin was right.

Holding on to a tree limb to keep from falling down the slope, she made herself remember when the plane first hit the treetops. As their trajectory slowed, she'd felt hope. And then a wing must have caught, because the entire plane swung around and then flipped. What came after, she knew only from seeing two large pieces of what had been a shiny, well-maintained and loved small plane.

So...other pieces could have been flung in almost any direction, couldn't they? She'd been lucky to find the nose of the plane so quickly. What she'd considered logic wasn't logic at all. The tail could have ended up somewhere *ahead* of the nose, or off to one side or the other. It wasn't as if chunks of airplane would have been shed in a straight line.

She paid attention to broken branches and scarred trunks. Raw scrapes in the gray rock. Her brain kept latching on to small, mostly meaningless details. What was that harsh call she kept hearing? Had the bang really been loud enough to have been a bomb going off? Could they have, oh, hit a big bird that fouled the propeller or the engine? No, Scott would have seen that; he'd been sitting in front, right beside the pilot. Of course he would. Then she started to worry about what kind of animals would be drawn by the smell of blood. Hadn't grizzlies been reintroduced into the North Cascades? What if the two men's bodies got *eaten*?

If her stomach hadn't already emptied itself, she'd have been down on her knees heaving again.

Even if she had the strength, could she bury Scott and Bill? Find enough rocks to pile on them?

Run, Maddy.

No. She had to leave the two men, as Scott had demanded she do.

Increasingly dazed, she came by pure chance on a duffel bag hanging above her. It took her a while to find a broken limb long enough to poke at it until it fell. She unzipped it and her heart squeezed in relief when she saw her own clothing. She wanted to hug the duffel just because it was familiar. Hers.

Instead, she made herself toss out everything that wasn't immediately useful. Shorts? Sandals? Gone. One pair of extra jeans she kept, because the ones she wore were so torn and bloody. Thin cotton pajama pants could be long underwear. She kept a toothbrush and toothpaste, but ditched shampoo. A shower was not in her immediate future. Socks—she'd need those. And thank goodness she'd brought her hiking boots. She'd almost left them behind, because she hadn't been a hiker until she had to fill long, empty weekends this past year. Now she took the time to sit down, change socks and laboriously lace up the boots with one hand. She wouldn't need her shoes.

She never did find Marshal Rankin's bag, but did finally locate most of the tail section of the plane. Packed in a compartment that hadn't broken open were two blankets, a pair of parkas, hats and gloves, a plastic jug full of water and a tool kit. Best of all was the cache of energy bars. They might have been in here forever, might be stale, but she wouldn't care.

Anxiety continuing to mount with her consciousness of time passing, she stuffed what she thought would be most useful into the duffel bag, finally discarding more clothes in favor of a puffy, too-large parka and the gallon of water. The shovel that unfolded…she couldn't think what she'd use it for, short of digging graves.

At last, she used one of the shirts to make a crude sling for her left arm, then slung the duffel as comfortably as she could—which wasn't comfortable at all—over her right shoulder.

Straightening, she looked around. She couldn't actually see enough through the trees to orient herself at all. Downhill would surely be easiest. She'd be bound to find a stream eventually. All that snow she'd seen from above must be melting, and the water had to go somewhere.

The flaw was that anyone in pursuit would assume she'd choose the easiest route. Which meant…she couldn't.

She'd go up.

HER ONLY CONSOLATION was that she lost sight of any evidence of the plane crash within minutes. Immediately, she began to second-guess herself. Maybe she would have been better off heading toward a lower elevation where the forest grew thicker, the trees taller. How would anyone find her there? She could huddle beneath some undergrowth until...

I die?

Her mind veered away from the bleak thought. She was panting as if she was at the end of an hour-long spin class, and she doubted she'd been on her way ten minutes. Although it might have been longer, or only five minutes. Time blurred. Each foot upward that she managed to haul herself required an enormous effort. She grasped rocks or spindly tree trunks and heaved herself up. A few times she turned to look back, but all she saw were trees and land that plunged sharply up and down. Weren't there supposed to be meadows in the mountains? Lakes?

The duffel bag grew heavier and heavier. Once she permitted herself to stop and take a few sips from the plastic jug and, despite a complete lack of appetite, eat half of an energy bar, hoping it would provide fuel to overcome her increasing lassitude. Her legs wobbled when she pushed herself to her feet again, but she scrambled upward over a rocky outcrop. Even with boot soles that had a deep tread, her feet kept slipping. If she wasn't on rock, roots tripped her. A few times she found herself crossing bands of snow. She felt too exposed in the open, but too tired to make herself go around.

Nothing in her head felt like an actual thought. She would stare at her feet until one of them moved. At her hand until it found a grip. Her world became the next step, and the pain that tore at her body.

Stop. Have to stop.

Another step.

She hardly noticed when her legs crumpled, when she crawled to the closest thing she could call shelter: a fir twisted by some natural calamity so that it grew nearly sidelong to the ground. Maddy squirmed until she felt almost hidden, and then she curled up, shaking.

WILL CONTINUED TO scramble along among the clusters of the highest, cold-stunted firs. He continuously scanned the trees downslope for any sign of recent scarring. He didn't have to pull out his GPS or compass; he could see over to a facing ridge, beyond which he knew was the deep drop-off into the Torrent Creek gorge. Ahead, water flung itself in a long series of waterfalls. Somewhere in his pack he had a map that would probably tell him what that stream was called.

He did pause now and again to check his watch, dismayed to see that several hours had already passed, and to use his binoculars to scan in a semicircle.

It was through the binoculars that he saw something off. An animal, maybe, but he didn't think so. The branches of a particularly oddly shaped alpine fir shook. There seemed to be a black lump, and a splotch of red. Part of the plane?

He altered his path with a specific goal now. The descent was damned steep, in places close to a class-three pitch. If he fell…no, he wouldn't even consider the possibility.

The closer he came, the less convinced he was that he'd seen a piece of metal. Somebody might have stowed a pack there with the intention of coming back for it—although this wasn't anyplace logical for a climber to pass through.

He was close when his feet skidded and he slid ten feet on his ass, swearing the entire way even as he employed his ice ax to slow the plunge enough to keep him from colliding with the boulder that lay ahead.

The tree shook. He regained his footing close enough to it to see that a woman huddled beneath the skimpy branches...and that she held a big black handgun in trembling hands. Aimed at him.

Will didn't move, barely breathed as he eyed the black hole down the barrel. "Would you mind pointing that away from me?" he asked.

It wasn't just her hands or the tree branches that shook. It was her whole body. He saw blood, a lot of it, and that she held the gun strangely, the butt almost against her sternum and resting on her other hand—which extended from flowery fabric wrapped around it. Brown hair formed a shrub around her face, poking out in places, matted with blood in others. Her face was a pasty white where it wasn't bloody. He wasn't close enough to see her eyes.

"You're hurt." He did his best to sound calm, even gentle. "Will you let me help?"

"I'll shoot you."

The words weren't really clear. He frowned, realizing her teeth were chattering like castanets. He knew shock when he saw it. Will felt something like exhilaration, because she almost had to be from the downed plane. A survivor, by damn. Although why hadn't she stayed with the wreckage?

"Please don't," he said quietly. "I don't mean you any harm. I was on the summit of Elephant Butte—" he nodded toward the mountain, not sure gesturing with his hands was a good idea right now "—and I saw a small plane crash. I thought I might be able to help."

She studied him, shaking and wild-eyed. "I won't—" chatter "—let you kill me."

Stunned, Will stared at her. "Why would you think—" And then, damn, he got it. "You think the crash wasn't an accident," he said slowly.

"I know it wasn't." The barrel of the gun had been sagging, but now she hoisted it again. "I knew somebody would come looking for me."

"That somebody isn't me. I'm a medic. I'm here in case somebody was injured." Will hesitated. "Can I set my pack down?"

After a discernible pause, she said in a gruff voice, "Okay."

He kept his movements slow. Lowered the pack to the hillside, laid the ice ax beside it and then squatted to make himself less alarming. He was a big guy, tall and broad enough to scare any woman alone in an alley—or on the side of a mountain. The two days of dark scruff on his jaw probably didn't help, either, or the fact that his face wasn't pretty at the best of times.

"Will you tell me what happened? Why you're scared?"

"Who—" mumble "—you?"

"Me? Ah, my name is Will Gannon. I got out of the military ten months ago, after getting hurt pretty bad." He hesitated. "I was shot, so you'll excuse me if I don't love seeing that gun pointing at me."

She looked down as if forgetting she held it. He hadn't forgotten for a second, given the way she was trembling. He hoped the trigger wasn't extra sensitive.

"Oh." She lowered the gun so it lay on her thigh, pointing off toward the southwest. "Sorry."

"Thank you." What could he say that would reassure her? "You're worrying me. I think you're in shock, and I can tell you've been hurt. I have some first-aid supplies in my pack, and I was a medic in the army."

"You promise?"

"Cross my heart." He cleared his throat, recalling the follow-up: *and hope to die.* Maybe not the best choice of words.

But she nodded. "Okay."

He took the chance to rise to his feet, pick up his pack and cautiously approach her. This time when he squatted, he was able to tip her face up and to the side so he could see an ugly gash running into her hair.

"Headache?"

"Yes."

Worse, her hazel eyes were glassy. On the good news front, she was conscious and coherent.

"You mind?" he said, closing his hand around the gun and easing it away from her. A Glock, which meant no safety. Not reassuring given that he'd have to carry it somewhere as he scrambled and fell down into the valley.

That worry could wait.

He kept talking to her as he unzipped the compartment on the outside of the pack that held what medical supplies he carried. First, he pulled out a package of sterile wipes. Once again gripping her chin, he cleaned her face, going through several of the wipes. Antibiotic ointment, gauze pad, tape. Then he asked, "Any other blows to your head?"

"Don't know."

He nodded and carefully explored, sliding his fingers beneath her hair and finding a couple of lumps. He'd have been surprised if there weren't any. Then he dug out a wool knit beanie with a fleece lining, and tugged it onto her head. The afternoon still felt warm to him, but she was shaking partly from cold.

"Were you the pilot?" he asked.

For a minute he thought she hadn't heard him, or was just shutting down. But then she said, "No."

"Was he killed?"

"Both dead. I was in the backseat."

"You're sure they're dead?"

A shudder rattled her. Her head bobbed, just a little.

"All right," he said calmly, "I need to look at your other injuries. Let's wrap something warm around you so you don't get chilled."

While a terrified woman was stripping, he meant. Yep, either that, or he'd be peeling off her clothes.

Chapter Three

Maddy couldn't look away from this stranger she had to trust. As out of it as she'd been, she wouldn't have been able to hold him off for two minutes.

A scar that started at one jutting cheekbone and ran over his temple marred Will Gannon's long, bony face. He had dark hair, shaggy enough to curl around his neck, and he was either growing a beard or just hadn't shaved for a few days. His eyes were light, though; gray or gray blue. Crow's-feet beside them made her wonder how old he was or whether he'd squinted into an awful lot of sunlight. He was tall—really tall, she thought— with the long muscles of a basketball player instead of the bulky, weight lifter kind.

As if his appearance or age mattered. But better to think about him than her situation.

He wanted to inspect all the places where she hurt. Since she hurt all over, was she supposed to take her clothes off?

"Do you…" She cleared her throat. "Do you have some aspirin or something?"

A smile did astonishing things to a face that had scared her at first sight. "I do. But I want to be sure I know about your injuries before I give you anything."

"Oh." If only she wasn't so fuzzy. And cold. "I'm

not sure. My shoulder or arm or something. And—"
she flapped her good hand toward her torso "—kind
of everywhere. Maybe my knee."

"All right. Can I look in your bag?"

She stared at him, puzzled. Without waiting for permission, he unzipped her duffel, sorted through the contents and pulled out a blanket he partly wrapped around
her, his enormous hands careful. Then he untied the
shirt she'd been using as a sling, and studied her T-shirt.

"You attached to this?"

"What?" She glanced down. "No." Too bad if she
had been. It made her shudder to imagine dipping it in
a sink filled with cold water. The blood would tint the
water red, not just pink.

When she looked up, she saw the knife that had appeared in his hand and shrank back.

"Hey." He waited until her eyes met his. "I need to
cut the shirt off you so we don't have to lift your arms.
I swear I won't hurt you."

Her teeth chattered a few times before she could get
her jaws clamped together, but she nodded and closed
her eyes, clutching one edge of the blanket. If he'd
meant to kill her, she'd be dead already.

A minute later he said, "Damn."

Her eyes flew open. "Damn?"

"The humerus is broken. Upper arm," he said absently. Fingertips slid along her collarbone, pausing at a
sizeable bump she could see when she craned her neck.
"Pretty sure the clavicle is, too." He sank back on his
heels, obviously thinking. "Let's pack your arm with
snow for a little bit before I put a splint on."

He had a splint? Did mountain climbers usually carry
things like that, or did he because of his medic training?

He had her lift her right arm, nodded in satisfaction,

and explored her rib cage, which even she could see was bruised, and suggested that her ribs might be cracked. "I'll bind them," he told her. "That should make you more comfortable."

A shot of morphine might make her more comfortable. Too bad she doubted he could produce anything like that from his pack.

Instead, he came up with two plastic bags, filled them with snow, wrapped each with what appeared to be one of his T-shirts and had her lie down. Then he placed one snow pack on her upper arm and had her hold it. The other he laid across her rib cage.

"I know you're freezing," he said apologetically. "These will help if you can hold out for a few minutes."

She gave a jerky nod.

He got busy untying her boots, pulling them off and easing her jeans down her legs, too.

She ought to feel self-conscious or unnerved, but she didn't. It was more as if she was standing behind an observation window, watching.

A big purple bruise showed on her kneecap, but the knee still bent fine and without significant pain. "I fell on my knees a few times," she offered.

One corner of his mouth turned up. "That'd do it. I think it's okay."

That was when she remembered she had a first-aid kit, too. When she told him, he found it in her duffel bag, opened it, grunted and closed it again.

"Nothing really helpful right now." He laid a hand on her calf. "You're cold."

Teeth clenched, she nodded. The heat of his big hand felt so good. She was really sorry when he removed it so he could explore the contents of her duffel more thoroughly. He pulled out the pajama bottoms and clean jeans, then gently dressed her in the two layers. Appearing unsatisfied with the couple of shirts she'd brought, he dug around in his own pack and pulled out a green flannel shirt. It might be way oversize on her, but the fuzzy flannel felt really good when he tugged it on her good side.

Kneeling beside her, he moved the ice on her arm once, finally deciding it was as good as it would get. The splint just looked like a roll of foam to her, but he adjusted it and closed the Velcro fastenings. He frowned when he sat back.

"I should splint your entire arm, but unless you're airlifted, we have to walk out of here. Plus, I don't want the weight of your arm hanging, given the break in the clavicle."

He used the knife on the flower shirt, making a simpler sling that went over the borrowed flannel shirt. Then he rolled the sleeves up half a dozen times, helped her sit up and gave her ibuprofen with water followed by a handful of almonds.

After he tucked the blanket back around her, Maddy saw his expression change, become flat, even hard.

"All right," he said. "You need to tell me what's going on. Why you're scared. And where the wreckage is."

Her fear blasted through that observation glass and was no longer nicely kept at a distance.

She grabbed his arm. "You can't use the radio or the beacon. If you won't promise, I won't tell you where it is."

His eyebrows rose at her challenge. "I found you. I can find it."

Oh, dear God, she thought suddenly. "Have you already called and told anyone what happened?"

His eyes narrowed. They were gray, she'd already

decided, clear and occasionally icy. "No," he said after a minute. "No coverage."

Maddy sagged. "A bomb brought the plane down. That's what…" She broke off, trying to think. How much did she have to tell him? Should she still be Cassie or give him her real name? What if he didn't believe a word she said? Not that he was the enemy; he'd been too kind, too gentle and too thorough with her. Still, he might talk to the wrong person. If she started lying now, would he know? Would he be willing to help her get out of this wilderness, just him?

He wouldn't if she lied, that was for sure.

So she took a deep breath, which hurt, of course, and said, "One of the men with me was a US marshal. He was alive when I found him. He said it had to be a bomb, and that meant he'd been betrayed by someone in his office. Not to trust anyone there. He said somebody would show up to be sure I was dead. And that I should run." Unable to read what this hard-faced stranger was thinking, she finished. "So I did."

And then she held her breath, waiting for him to insist the head injury had made her delusional.

WILL DIDN'T LIKE a single thing she'd said. If she hadn't been so obviously scared out of her skull, he'd have discounted a story so unlikely. Sure, he was climbing in the backcountry of the North Cascades when a bomb took down a plane carrying a now-dead United States marshal and a woman fleeing…who? What?

He muttered something under his breath he hoped she didn't make out and rubbed a hand over his face. He didn't care if he sounded brusque when he said, "You need to tell me everything."

Now she was unhappy, showing the whites of her eyes. Either deciding how much to say or dreaming up lies.

As he waited, he watched every shifting emotion on her pinched face. For the first time it struck him that she might be pretty or even beautiful when she wasn't injured and in shock. So much of her face was banged up, he wasn't sure, but...she did have delicate bone structure and big, haunting eyes, mostly green-gold. Calling them *hazel* didn't do the rich mix of colors justice.

She bit her lip hard enough that he almost protested, but then she started talking.

"My name is Maddy... Madeline Kane. I'm an attorney with Dietrich, McCarr and Brown in Seattle. I was sent to talk to a potential client at her home in Medina. Um, that's on the other side—"

"I know where it is," he interrupted. Medina was a wealthy enclave on the opposite shore of Lake Washington from the city. Was Bill Gates's house there? He couldn't remember for sure, but it wouldn't be out of place.

"While I was there, I had to ask to use her restroom. I wouldn't usually, but—" She shook her head. "It doesn't matter. The thing is, I heard the doorbell ring, and the client let someone in. She screamed. I started to come out just as she said, 'Please, I don't understand.'" Maddy's eyes lost focus as she went somewhere he couldn't go. "She was on the floor, trying to scoot backward. He... I only saw him in profile. He said she was a problem for Brian Torkelson. And then he shot her. Twice. It...was sort of a coughing sound, not very loud."

Suppressor. Tense, Will waited for the rest.

"And he said, 'Problem solved.' He started to turn, but—" She'd begun shivering again. "I stepped back, made it into the bathroom. If he'd walked down the hall—"

Will covered her good hand clutching the blanket to her throat with his hand. "He didn't."

"No." She looked away. "I keep having dreams where I hear his footsteps approaching."

"Yeah." If he sounded gruff, he couldn't help it. "That's natural. I have nightmares, too."

Gratitude showed in her eyes when they met his again. "Do you know who Brian Torkelson is?"

The name rang a bell as if he'd seen it in the news recently. But he had been making an effort since he got out of rehab *not* to follow the news, so he shook his head.

"He's—well, he was—a Superior Court justice here in Washington. Back when this happened, he'd just been appointed to become a federal circuit court judge, which is a big deal."

"But he had some dirty laundry."

"Apparently."

"And you're the only witness."

"Yes. I came very close to being run down in a crosswalk only a few days before Torkelson was arrested. It might have been an accident, but I don't think so. I ended up going into hiding. I've spent the last year in eastern Washington, living under a different name."

"Witness protection."

"I haven't talked to my family or friends in thirteen months. It's been hard, although at least I knew it wasn't forever."

"So Torkelson's trial is coming up."

She shook her head. "Not his. The hit man's." She

made a funny, strangled noise. "I can't believe I'm even using that word. But I guess that's what he is. I sat down with an artist, and the police recognized him right away."

"That can't be enough to convict him."

"The police watched surveillance cameras and those ones at stoplights. I'd gotten to the window to see him drive away. I couldn't see the license plate, but I described the car. It turned out the next-door neighbor had cameras, too. He's a big businessman who's really paranoid. Anyway, once they had a warrant, they got his gun."

"Ah." Hell. "So you'll have to testify in two trials?"

Looking almost numb, she nodded. And that was when she got to the kicker. The dead marshal had told her not to trust anyone in his office except a friend who also served as a US marshal.

"I think I can trust the two detectives I worked with, but word might get out. I'd rather hide until I can talk to Scott's friend."

This was a lot to take in, but Will was reluctantly convinced. "The handgun the marshal's?"

She bobbed her head, although doing so made her wince. "I thought I might need it."

"Have you done any shooting at a range?"

Maddy nibbled on her lower lip again. "No, I've always been kind of anti-gun."

Will's laugh didn't hold much humor. Man, he was lucky she *hadn't* accidentally pulled that trigger.

"Good thing I do know how to use one," he said. "I didn't see any extra magazines in your bag. Did you grab some?"

"No. I didn't think of it. I hated the idea of going through his pockets. It was all I could do to make myself unsnap his holster and take the gun. He had a duffel bag, too, smaller than mine, but I never found it," Maddy concluded.

"All right." Will rose to his feet, not surprised by the stab of pain in his left thigh and hip. It was sharper than usual, probably because he'd climbed a mountain this morning followed by the difficult traverse and downhill scramble to get here. He wasn't done for the day, though, not even close. "We need to move," he said. "I'd like to scavenge anything I can from the plane, and I want you tucked out of sight while I'm doing that."

And verifying the truth of her story, given how wild it was. He didn't really doubt her, but he wasn't good at trusting strangers.

"I thought…here…"

He shook his head. "Nope. I spotted you from a quarter mile away. We need to descend to better tree cover." Her attempt to hide her dismay wasn't very effective. "I'll help. I can carry you if I have to."

Her chin rose. "No. I got here, I can go farther."

BEING THIS HELPLESS was a humiliating experience. To begin with, she couldn't even put her own boots on this time, far less tighten the laces and tie them. Either the pain had caught up with her, or the cushioning shock had begun to wear off.

Oh, heavens—would she be able to lower or pull up her pants when she needed to pee?

Prissy, she scolded herself. Well, she came by it naturally. She loved her parents, but they had been older than her friends' parents, and acted like a much different generation, too. The idea of seeing nature in the rough wouldn't appeal to them, that was for sure.

She tried not to sound stiff when she thanked Will.

When he boosted her to her feet, she thought for a minute she was going to pass out. She tipped forward to lean against him, her forehead pressed to a broad, solid chest.

"Give it time," he murmured, his hand—an enormous hand—clasping her upper arm while his other arm came around her back. Maddy knew he wouldn't let her fall.

Finally, her head quit spinning and she forced herself to straighten, separating from him. "I'm all right."

They both knew that she wasn't, but she'd made it this far and she could keep on doing what she needed to.

"All right." His frowning gaze belied what he'd said. "Tell you what. I'm going to help you down then come back for my pack."

"I can carry mine—"

"Not a chance." He closed a zipper on her duffel and swung it over his shoulder. "Now, which way is the crash site?"

Turning her head, Maddy saw rocks and fir trees—or maybe spruce or hemlock, she didn't know—all set on a precipitous downslope. How on earth had she made it up here? "I…don't know," she said after a minute. "I climbed because I thought anyone who came to the crash site would assume I headed down."

"Good thought," Will agreed.

"I…don't know if I came straight up, or…" She couldn't look at him. His air of competence made her feel more inept. She couldn't even remember where she'd come from. "I'm sorry."

"No." His hand closed gently over hers. "You fell out of the sky. You hit your head and have broken bones. You should be in a hospital getting an MRI.

I'm amazed that you were able to get together the supplies you needed and haul yourself up this mountain."

"Is it a mountain?" She started to turn to look upward, but that made her dizzy again.

"Right here, just a ridge, but that way—" he pointed "—is Elephant Butte and beyond it, Luna Peak, and that way, McMillan Spire and… It doesn't matter. Mountains everywhere."

"I saw from the plane." Just before that terrifying *bang*.

"Okay, we need to move."

Maddy wasn't sure she *would* have made it any farther without his help. At moments he braced his big booted feet and lifted her down a steep pitch. Occasionally, Will led her on a short traverse, always the same direction, she noticed, but mostly they picked their way straight down.

The trees became larger, at times cutting off her view of the sky. Not that she looked. As she had climbing, she focused on her feet, on the next step she had to make—and on Will's hand reaching to steady her. Once they slid fifteen feet or so down a stretch of loose rocks, Will controlling her descent as well as he could. Then they went back to using spindly lower branches to clamber down.

When he stopped, she swayed in place.

"This will do," he said.

Maddy stared dully, taking a minute to see what he had. The trees weren't quite as stunted as they'd been above, but were still small. What he was urging her toward was a pile of boulders that must have rumbled down the precipitous slope any time from ten years ago to hundreds. The largest rested against another big one, framing an opening that wasn't quite a cave, but was close enough.

Without a word, she crawled inside, awkward as that was to do without the use of one arm and hand. By now, she hurt so much she had no idea if this was doing more damage. Mostly, she was glad to stop—to crouch like an animal in its burrow until coming out seemed safer.

Will squatted in front of her, arranging her limbs to his liking and nudging her duffel bag into place to serve as a giant pillow.

"I want you to stay low," he told her. "The rocks will keep you from being seen from above—the air or the ridge above—but if somebody happens to come along in the twenty yards or so below you, they might catch a glimpse. When I get back with my pack, I'll see what I can find to hide the opening."

Maddy nodded. "You'll be able to find me again, won't you?"

His smile changed his face from rough-hewn and fiercely male to warm and even sexy. "I will. I memorized some landmarks."

"Okay."

He reached out unexpectedly to stroke her cheek, really just the brush of his knuckles, before he stood. Two steps, and he was out of sight. She could hear him for a minute or two, no more—and she bit her lip until she tasted blood to keep herself from calling out for him, begging him not to leave her.

She hardly knew him—but somehow she had complete faith that he wouldn't abandon her.

WILL MOVED AS fast as he could. He didn't like leaving Maddy alone at all, but they'd need what he had in his pack. Fortunately, the ascent went smoothly, although his hip and thigh protested like the devil. Still, he swung the familiar weight of the pack onto his back, checked to be sure that they hadn't left so much as a scrap of the packaging that had wrapped the gauze pads, and retraced his steps. Given how he was tiring, he was glad to recover his ice ax to use for support.

This time during the descent he paused several times to scan the forest with his binoculars. Raw wood caught his eye, where it appeared the tops of trees had been sheared off. Yes.

From there, he calculated the route he'd take from Maddy's hiding place. He wished she was farther from the crash site, but still believed her hiding spot to be nearly ideal.

When he reached the rocks, he got hit by a jolt of alarm. What he could see of her face was slack, colorless but for the bruises that seemed muted in color since he left her. Was her head injury worse than he'd thought, and she'd lapsed into unconsciousness?

But then she let out a heavy sigh and crinkled her nose. She shifted a little as if seeking a more comfortable position.

Asleep. She was only asleep, and no wonder after multiple traumas.

She awakened immediately when he touched her, her instinct to shrink from him.

"You all right?"

After a tiny hesitation, she said, "I think so."

"Good. I'm leaving my pack here and going to the crash site after I cut some fir branches to cover the opening. Unless you need to, uh, use the facilities…"

She blinked several times before she understood. "No. I'm fine."

"All right. I'll be back as quick as I can."

Her hand closed on his forearm. "You won't call for help? Or…or let anyone see you?"

"No. I promise." He didn't know what else he could say. It was hard to believe anyone else would show up at the site but another hiker or climber who, like him, had seen the crash and come to help.

Relieved to be unburdened by the pack, Will sliced off a few branches to disguise the opening in the rocks, then left her. He kept to a horizontal path as much as he could. He hoped the crunch of his boots on the rocky pitch wasn't as loud as it seemed to him. When he paused to listen, all he heard was the distant ripple of one of the streams plunging toward the valley, a soft sough of wind and a few birdcalls.

He'd reached the first trees torn by metal, had seen a white scrap that could be from any part of the plane, when he heard the distinctive sound of an approaching helicopter.

Chapter Four

The roar of the rotor blades was familiar if discordant music to Will's ears. On deployments, he'd spent too much time in the air, often hoping to scoop up wounded men and lift away without being shot down.

He ducked beneath the low-growing branches of a hemlock. Chances were good this would be a search and rescue helicopter arriving at the site in response to a phone call from someone else who saw the plane going down, but Maddy's fear stayed with him. So did the US marshal's prediction. Even aside from Will's promise to her, he wouldn't have made contact no matter who showed up at the site. For now, Maddy had to disappear.

The helicopter remained out of sight, wasn't moving closer. Will needed to see it.

On this sharp incline, approaching without knocking rocks loose to clatter downward wasn't easy. He did his best, knowing the helicopter made enough racket to drown out most other sounds.

He progressed to what he estimated to be fifty yards, spotting other fragments of the plane but not the cabin or wings. Between one step and the next, the black helicopter appeared between trees. With no place to land, it was hovering, as he'd expected.

Will found cover again and lifted his binoculars.

From this angle, he was unable to read the FAA required numbers near the tail. He couldn't even be sure they were there. The windshield was tinted, allowing him to see the pilot but not his face. Wearing green-and-tan camouflage, another man crouched in the open door on the side. A rope ran from it toward the ground. The guy turned and seemed to be yelling something to the pilot. Then he lowered himself, swiveled and grasped the rope. Lugging a big-ass pack on his back, he slid down the rope as if he'd done it a thousand times.

Strapped to the pack was a fully automatic machine gun, an AK-47 or the like.

Will had a dizzying moment of seeing double. The other scene had different colors. Vegetation, uniforms, even the painted skin of the helicopter, were shades of tan and brown. At the sight of enemy combatants, adrenaline flooded him and he reached for his own rifle. When his hand found nothing to close on, he blinked. Damn. That hadn't happened in a while. He rubbed his hand over his face hard enough to pull himself back to the here and now. This wasn't Afghanistan, but it seemed to have become a war zone anyway.

He couldn't afford to flip out.

He continued to watch as another man reeled up the rope, waved, and the helicopter rose. It didn't swing around to head back toward civilization, however; instead, it continued forward, a little higher above the treetops but low enough to allow the men on board to search the landscape.

The thing wouldn't pass directly over him, but near enough. Glad to be wearing a faded green T-shirt, he pushed into the feathery branches of the nearest tree and compressed himself behind a rotting stump.

When he was sure the helicopter was receding, Will

held a quick internal debate. Forward or backward? Had
to be forward. He needed to know more about the men
who'd been left behind at the wreckage. He had to trust
that Maddy would follow his instructions, and that the
pile of fir branches he'd placed to hide her would look
natural from the air.

Two minutes later a raised voice froze him in place.

"Found the pilot."

Another male voice answered from a greater distance, the words indistinguishable.

So two, at least.

Taking the Glock from the small of his back, he
waited where he was, listening intently. The same two
voices called back and forth. He thought they might
have found the dead marshal, too, but couldn't be sure.
He wanted to do further reconnaissance, but knew he
couldn't risk it. Maddy wouldn't make it out of the backcountry without him, especially now that they had to
dodge two or more heavily armed soldiers.

Soldiers? No, they weren't that, he thought grimly.
Call them mercenaries. Killers for hire.

The marshal had saved Maddy's life by sending her
on the run. Now it was on Will to bring a seriously injured woman to safety despite the men who would soon
be hunting them.

MADDY AWAKENED WITH a start, staring upward at raw
rock and a crack of blue sky. Completely disoriented,
she didn't understand where she was. Pain pulled her
from her confusion. Staying utterly still, she strained
to listen. Was Will back? But what she heard was far
more ominous.

A helicopter.

Her panic switch flipped. Will had sent them to pick her up. He hadn't believed her. He'd betrayed her.

Run.

But he'd promised, and he'd made *her* promise to stay where she was. He hadn't said, 'Whatever you hear,' but that was what he'd meant.

Here, she was hidden. *Stay still. Stay still.* What if they'd captured him, or even killed him? She knew exactly what that looked like. Shivering despite herself, feeling like a coward, she nonetheless refused to believe they'd surprised Will. He'd said he was army. A medic, yes, but didn't they fight, too? Have the same training? She hoped he'd taken the handgun with him. At least he knew how to use it.

The terrifying drone grew louder and louder. Maddy forgot to blink, staring at the thin sliver of blue sky. When darkness slid over it like a shadow, the helicopter was so loud she pressed her good hand to one ear. It thundered in her head, but the streak of blue reappeared and...was the racket diminishing? She thought so.

Did that mean they hadn't taken any notice of the tumble of boulders that had made a cave?

What *had* Will done with the gun? Maddy tried to remember. Before, she'd believed she could shoot someone, and she still thought so. His pack was right there. She groped all the outside pockets but didn't feel anything the right shape. He wouldn't have just dumped it inside, would he? Even so, she unzipped the top and inserted her hand. The first hard thing she found was a plastic case holding first-aid supplies. Packets of what she guessed were food. Clothes—denim and soft knits, something puffy with a slippery outside. A parka. A book?

She gave up, lay back and waited, staring now at the opening she'd crawled through.

Once again time blurred—or maybe it had ever since the crash. Had that really happened today? Was she forgetting a night? Maddy clung to a picture in her mind of Will Gannon, alarmingly tall as he looked down at her. That too-bony face with a nose that didn't seem to quite belong, but eyes that were kinder than she deserved, considering she was holding a gun on him.

Hearing that deep, husky voice saying, *I was shot, so you'll excuse me if I don't love seeing that gun pointing at me.*

The relief of letting it sag, of feeling his big hand close over hers as he deftly took the gun.

Her head throbbed even as the pain radiating from her arm and shoulder worsened.

Please come, Will. Please hurry.

HE STOPPED UNDER cover twenty yards or so from the boulders to use his binoculars again. He could no longer hear the helicopter, but after a slow sweep he found it, deep down in the Stetattle Creek valley. Down there only fools would think they'd see anything from the sky; the Stetattle and Torrent Creeks ran through tangles of vegetation as thick as any jungle. When Will was reading about routes into and out of this wilderness, he'd seen several references to "bushwhacking."

If he could get Maddy down to that low elevation, they'd be hard to find. On the other hand, he didn't have a machete or any other tool that would be good for clearing their way.

He wondered if he wouldn't be able to find something like that in the airplane wreckage. Crap, he wished he'd beaten the damn helicopter there, had time to search.

Couldn't be helped.

He rose and scrambled the distance to the two largest boulders, steadying himself on other large rocks.

"Maddy? It's me."

The silence stretched. He was almost to the opening when she said, "Will?"

"Yeah, I'm coming in."

He parted the pile of fir branches and crawled between them. Same response he'd had earlier. Disliking the cramped space, he wanted to back right out. Tending to claustrophobia, Will had been especially unhappy when his unit was assigned to search caves in Afghanistan for the Taliban. Until today, he'd hoped he would never see a cave again.

Fortunately, this didn't quite qualify.

White-faced and tense, Maddy seemed to be holding herself together by a thread.

"Hey," he said. "You heard the helicopter?"

"It went overhead." She gestured upward. "It blocked the sky."

"Damn." He took her hand in his. "I'm sorry. Ah… hold on. Let me put the branches back in place."

Once he did, he found he could sit up and stretch out his legs if he didn't mind the top of his head grazing rock.

"Did you find the plane?" she asked anxiously.

"Saw a few pieces, but that's all before the helicopter showed up." He couldn't look away from her eyes that were filled with fear. "They didn't see me. The helicopter dropped two men. At least two," he corrected himself. "Only heard two voices. Your marshal was right. These guys look paramilitary and they're armed to the teeth. This was no search and rescue operation. The man I saw was carrying a heavy pack. They're prepared to hunt for you once they don't find your body."

Her eyelashes fluttered. He'd have understood if she had broken down, but she didn't. All she said was, "What are we going to do?"

"Not get caught," Will said flatly. "This is a vast wilderness. They're naive thinking they *can* track someone. Of course, they'll assume you're on your own, potentially injured, not equipped for such rough conditions."

"They're right."

Had he heard a hint of humor? Maybe.

But she was completely sober when she said, "I'm sorry I got you into this."

"I'm not sorry." Good thing he could be completely honest. "I always liked challenges." Medical school was the one he'd had in mind, not going to war in his own country, but he couldn't wish he hadn't found this woman.

Her smile shook, but it was real. "Thank you."

He smiled, too, and they studied each other openly, he aware of her vivid bruises, the swelling and wild hair, the dirt and scrapes, but also of her delicate beauty beneath. Disconcerted, he knew he had to shut down that kind of awareness. She needed a protector. Period.

"We need to stay here," he said. "At least for the night. The copter is still searching. At some point it'll have to go back to its base, wherever that is. Until it's gone, we can't risk making a move. I want you to rest up anyway. Get some food in you. Your knee might feel better by tomorrow."

"Okay."

Will suspected docility wasn't a normal part of her makeup, but was glad of it for the moment.

"I have a camp stove I can use once it's dark to make a real meal, but you need to eat right now." He dug in an outer pocket where he'd stowed snack food: peanuts, almonds, beef jerky and a bag of caramels.

She wrinkled her nose at the beef jerky, but accepted his water bottle, two ibuprofen and a packet of peanuts. Will found a spot where he could rest his back against a rock wall, and made his own selections for a midafternoon snack. Now that he'd stopped, he was even more aware of the fierce ache in his hip and down his thigh. With a few almonds in his stomach, he downed painkillers, too.

"You're hurt," she said unexpectedly.

"Not that serious."

"You said you were shot."

"Yeah." Will tried not to twitch. He'd done his time in counseling while he was in rehab for physical therapy, too, but he'd never been a big talker. "Just thought I'd take the edge off."

Even as she took a long swallow from the water bottle, her eyes stayed on him, but to his relief she didn't ask any more questions.

How COULD SHE feel so safe in such a strange setting, with a man she hardly knew? Maddy could only be grateful that neither her body nor her subconscious had any reservations about this man. Given the cramped space, they couldn't avoid each other.

The floor of dirt and rock was far from flat, of course; since it tipped downhill, once she and Will had finished eating, they stretched out side by side with their heads at the top of the slope. Still cold, Maddy wore the parka she'd found in the tail of the plane, while Will wadded his up under their heads. He made sure she wasn't lying on her more damaged left side. They had

to do a lot of squirming around until no sharp edge dug
into either of their hips or shoulders.

"Use me as a pillow," he suggested, holding out an
inviting arm.

As miserably uncomfortable as she was, Maddy took
him up on the offer. At first, she lay stiffly beside him,
trying to keep some space between their bodies, but he
finally exclaimed, "Damn it! Come here." He tugged
her closer and gently lifted her arm in the sling and laid
it on his chest.

The initial movement hurt, and she cried out, but
as soon as she let herself relax, relief washed over her.
The weight of her arm no longer tugged at the broken
collarbone.

"Better?" he murmured.

"Yes," she admitted. "Thank you."

He made a grumbly sound she took to mean he didn't
want her incessantly thanking him, but how could she
not?

She tried *not* to think about tomorrow, about more
scrambling on this mountainside, whether going up or
down—or sideways. Will thought her knee might feel
better, but didn't injuries usually hurt more the next
day? Stiffen up?

Well, they couldn't stay here, not for long. Even stepping outside this cubby beneath the boulders would
leave either of them too exposed. Her worry was how
drastically she'd slow their pace. The only positive was
that they wouldn't starve to death for a while—there
were those energy bars she'd stuffed in her duffel, never
mind what Will still had in his pack.

At a funny chirping sound outside, followed by a
shrill whistle, she stiffened and raised her head.

"Pika," he said. Since she'd never heard of any such

thing, he had to explain that pikas were brown mammals that looked somewhat like a rabbit without the ears and tended to live in rockslides. "They'll have dens down below."

"Like ours."

"Smaller." His voice conveyed a smile.

Sleep tugged at her even as she tried very hard after that to imagine herself home again, and was distressed because she had trouble pulling up faces from her former life.

She woke up enough to notice the light had changed. Of course it had; the sun would have moved across the sky. Okay, really the earth did the moving and the turning, but that was just a technicality. And why was her mind wandering like this?

Because pain was responsible for dragging her out of sleep. Distraction was a form of protection.

Also…she thought her leg might be lying across Will's. In fact, she'd practically climbed onto him.

Embarrassed, she started to shift. The white-hot stab of pain pulled a deep groan from her throat and had her seeing spots.

"Maddy?" His roughened voice was close to her ear. "You hurting?"

"Yes," she said. "Are we going to run out of painkillers?"

His "I hope not" failed to reassure her.

"Let me up and I'll get you some. Water and a bite to eat, too." He shifted her as gently as he'd earlier pulled her close, until he was able to sit up and root in his pack. It only took him a minute to produce the water bottle and three capsules.

She gulped them down without asking what she was taking. Without comment, he then handed her a small box of raisins. The sweetness with each mouthful was just right.

"I keep falling asleep," she said. "I never nap!"

"That's an expected symptom of both your injuries and the sheer trauma. You need extra rest to heal."

He had produced a watch at some point, so he was able to tell her it was nearly five o'clock.

She grappled with that. She, Scott Rankin and the pilot had left the small airport near Republic around eight that morning. It couldn't have taken them that long to get deep into the Cascade Mountains. An hour? Two? Of course, she had no idea how long she'd been unconscious, or how long she'd nodded off for when she first hid herself—or now. Still.

She said, "It won't be dark until something like nine."

He raised his eyebrows. "The sun goes down below the mountains long before it's close to sunset."

"Oh." Was that two hours from now? Three? Her bladder was beginning to nudge at her. Could she hold out even that long?

Something else. "Was the bomb on a timer, do you think? If it had gone off earlier…"

"Before you got deep in the mountains." He'd obviously thought about this. "It could have been on a timer, calculated to bring the plane down in the most rugged terrain, or triggered by a radio signal."

"What?" She stared at him. "I didn't see any other planes anywhere near."

"If that's how they did it, they knew the route your pilot planned to take. Although…" He frowned. "Do you know why you were so far north?"

"I think Scott was trying to give me a treat to take my mind off the upcoming trial," she said with difficulty. Having lost him, she realized that she'd come to think of the marshal as a friend. "It worked, too. I was dazzled. Until—"

"Then he must have told someone what he planned. I'd guess somebody was stationed down below to send off a signal once they saw the plane cross over into the most remote and rugged landscape. They could have been in Diablo or someplace along Ross Lake. Could have just pulled off Highway 20 at an overlook and gotten out of the car. No reason anyone would notice someone fiddling with his phone."

"No." She didn't know if it was worse to think the cold-blooded calculations had been made in advance, or that someone had tipped his head back and watched as the small red-and-white plane buzzed across the sky, then punched a combination of numbers to set off the bomb. He would likely have seen it start to plummet. Had he felt even a grain of conscience, or only satisfaction?

"They brought the plane down too soon," Will said, the set of his jaw hard. "Just a little farther and you'd have come down in the Picket Range. Seems to me, your path was taking you north, maybe toward the pass between Mount Terror and Mount Fury. The view would have been spectacular, and then you could have flown just south of Shuksan. The pilot probably wanted to give you an up-close view of some of the most awe-inspiring country in North America. If you'd hit the side of McMillan Spire or Mount Terror—" He broke off. "I'm not helping, am I?"

She tried to hold herself together. "I want to know. But… I'm not so sure it would have made any difference. The plane was torn to pieces, you know. It was sheer luck that my seat belt held and my section of the cabin got hung up on a tree."

"There wouldn't have been any trees at a higher elevation, say on a glacier. Only rock and ice and snow."

She closed her eyes. "I wanted to bury them. Or cover their bodies with rocks, at least. Leaving them there like that…"

"Was the smart thing to do." Once again he squeezed her hand.

Had Will been as caring with the horrifically injured soldiers he must have helped in Afghanistan or Iran or wherever he'd been? Yes, of course he had. By his standards she was barely banged up. She wasn't gushing blood, hadn't lost a leg or an arm or—an awful picture entered her mind: the grotesquely twisted bodies of the two men who'd also been on that plane.

Something else she shouldn't think about. Later, yes. Not now.

"He knew he was dying," she heard herself say.

"I'm guessing he held on for all he was worth until you found him."

How Will could pitch that deep, almost gravelly voice to be so comforting, she had no idea. Even the expression in his clear gray eyes was a kind of caress.

"He'd have known that if you were alive, your instinct would be to stay with the plane," Will went on. "Maybe activate the beacon, or call for help if you had a phone. He died knowing he'd given you a fighting chance. That would have been important to him, you know."

She ducked her head and nodded at the same time, hoping he didn't hear her sniffling. She'd done a lot of that in their brief acquaintance. He probably thought she was always weepy, which was far from the truth.

"Have you peed yet today?" he asked bluntly.

"How could I? You told me not to move."

He frowned at her. "Then you haven't had enough to drink." He thrust the water bottle at her.

"We'll run out."

"You brought a gallon from the plane. I can treat stream water as we refill both bottles."

Instead of glugging, she sipped. "I thought I should wait until dark to go out."

"Dusk is early here. You don't have to go far."

Maddy hoped she could be as matter-of-fact as he was about the call of nature. So what if he heard her?

"Is the helicopter still around?" she asked.

"I don't think so. I'm sure the men are, but I haven't taken the chance of searching for them with binoculars."

They talked quietly. She drained the bottle; he re-filled it from the gallon she'd lugged along with her. Eventually they ran out of impersonal things to talk about. She wanted to know more about him; natural, when she had to trust him, Maddy told herself, but was afraid her curiosity was part of her fascination with this man, a warrior and yet so gentle.

At her question he hesitated but told her he'd en-listed in the army right out of high school. "There was no money for college. It seemed a way out."

"Out?"

He shifted as if uncomfortable to be talking about himself. "I grew up in northern California. Up near Lake Shasta. There's not much money there. Tourism is the only industry, and the people who come mostly camp, maybe want to go out on the lake. We lived in an old trailer." Will fell silent for a minute, lines forming on his forehead. "I don't suppose it was anything like your background."

Maddy wanted to lie but couldn't. What was the point? "No, my mom's a school principal. Dad works at Microsoft. I know I was lucky." More than that, she realized. She'd lived in the protective bubble that privilege gave you until a gunman popped it in an instant.

"Will you go to college now?" she finally asked.

He gazed out at the darkening view across the V-shaped valley. "I got my degree while I served." His shoulders moved. "Part-time when I was in the States, some long-distance."

"You worked a lot harder for it than I did mine, then," Maddy said. "I had it easy." Funny, she'd never thought of it that way before.

He glanced at her briefly but turned his head away before she could meet his eyes. "That's one way to look at it."

The dry way he said that left her with no idea how to respond. He didn't give her a chance anyway.

"I'll take first turn at using the facilities. Then it's your turn," he said, and moved the branches at the entrance enough to crawl out. Despite his purpose, he carried both his binoculars and that ugly black handgun with him.

She couldn't decide if that was more reassuring, or worrisome.

Chapter Five

During his years in the military, Will had learned to set an internal alarm. Awake a couple of hours before dawn, he reluctantly edged out from under a still-sleeping Maddy. Last night he'd shifted the most important things to his pack, stowing nonessentials including extra clothes and the two books he'd brought to join some of what was in her duffel. He'd reluctantly decided to leave the duffel here. He needed a hand free to support her while he used the ice ax to stabilize them.

After lacing up his boots, he had pain pills and water bottle in his hand when he woke her.

Her moan worried him. He'd thought during the night that she radiated too much heat. He'd give a lot to be able to start her on antibiotics.

"Okay, sweetheart," he murmured, "have a bite to eat now."

Uncomplaining, she took the bag of granola he handed her and scooped out a handful. He heard her crunching as he wedged her feet into her boots, made sure her socks were pulled up so no wrinkle would give her a blister, and tightened the laces.

"How's the knee feel?" he asked in a low voice.

She bent and straightened that leg. "Sore," she whispered, "but not like my arm and shoulder."

"Good. When we stop later, I want to apply more antibiotic ointment on your gashes and replace dressings." He laid a hand on her forehead and winced. "I think you have a fever."

Her soft, huffing sound might have been a laugh. "Normally, I'd know because my joints would ache and I'd have a headache, but now…" She moved. Probably a one-shoulder shrug.

Will felt a violent dislike for what he was going to have to put her through. He needed to get her to a hospital, but wasn't so sure he dared even if—once—they reached his Jeep. He thought of a buddy, a doctor, who'd gotten out six months before he did. Javier would probably be willing to call in an antibiotic prescription in Will's name. That was the first essential.

When Maddy said stoutly, "I'm ready," he helped her scoot forward until they were in the open.

The moon had sunk low in the sky, but still cast a silver light across the landscape. That was good in one way, bad in another.

They parted to empty their bladders. By the time she fumbled her way back around the boulder, he'd settled his pack on his back, careful to stow the Glock in an accessible pocket. Not as good as a holster, but the best he could do.

Then they started what would be an agonizingly slow descent of a hillside that had Class-3 pitches—real climbs—here and there. He hoped the men hunting them weren't early risers.

MADDY RELEASED AIR in a slow hiss. How could she possibly do this? But with Will helping support her weight, she skidded down another rocky plunge until she could grab a tree limb.

The sky grew lighter by infinitesimal degrees, from that faintly moon-touched black to a deep gray, allowing her to see the closest trees and where she needed to put her feet next. She swore Will was part mountain goat, the way he picked his way along without dislodging small rocks or slipping. Maddy crunched and skidded on loose rocks, however hard she tried to be quiet. Her knee was both painful and stiff. The rest of her hurt so much that by the time the sky turned pearlescent with dawn she had become an automaton. Her head throbbed viciously, and agony radiated from what must be the break in her collarbone. Probably every movement scraped the broken ends together. Once, she surfaced to realize she'd closed her eyes, her only guidance the big hand on her elbow and an occasional murmur.

"Big step down here." Or, "There's a tree to your right. Grab hold."

Maddy forced her eyes open, feeling immediate alarm at how bright the sky was. The sun would surely be over the ridge in minutes. She and Will couldn't possibly have gotten far yet.

But she lost even that thought beneath the pain. Another step and she'd tell him she had to rest. Yet, somehow she kept her mouth clamped shut so she couldn't beg him to stop. He knew how much she hurt, and why they had to keep moving. A couple of times he'd made quiet, pained sounds after a whimper escaped her.

Maybe she'd rather die. The idea became increasingly enticing. She'd just lie down. It wouldn't be so bad, and Will could go on.

"I won't leave you."

She must have been thinking aloud. God, had she been begging, too, while she thought she was being stoic?

He spoke close to her ear. "We'll reach better tree cover soon. Just hang on, Maddy."

She wished he'd called her sweetheart again. She'd liked that. It sounded…tender.

Gunfire erupted, shocking her out of her dream state.

Will swore, picked her up and plunged downward. They fell onto their butts and rocketed down a drop-off at terrifying speed, ricocheting off small firs. Maddy thought she was screaming, but it didn't matter, did it? Not when the enemy already knew where they were.

They slammed to a stop against a larger tree trunk than any she'd seen. Dazed, Maddy saw Will assessing her before he pulled her to her feet again.

"We have to keep going."

"They're shooting at us."

"Yeah." He half lifted her again with an arm around her waist to lower her over another drop. "They were either out of range, or lousy shots."

The evergreens surrounding them were taller, she realized in what small part of her brain wasn't occupied by fear or agony. Unfortunately, the steep pitch hadn't eased into something a sane human being would consider for a grueling hike.

Will kept her going, the steady pressure of her hand relentless; the hard cast of his face merciless.

Once, she tried to sag to the ground, mumbling, "I can't…"

"You can." His arm felt like an iron bar on her waist as he refused to let her stop, or even slow.

She vaguely became aware that, while still heading downward, the route he'd chosen took them at an angle. Maddy slowly worked out that straight down would have been too obvious.

The sound of running water came from ahead.

"We'll stop here for a few minutes," he said, his grip easing as he lowered her to a seat on a slab of rock.

Maddy stared at the stream, if you could call it that when it looked more like a string of small waterfalls strung together.

"Runoff from the glacier on McMillan Peak." Will pressed something into her hand. A candy bar. He'd already ripped open the wrapper for her.

Once he was satisfied she was eating, he dug out the gallon jug and refilled it, dropping something in—a tablet? He put it away and tore open what she thought might be one of the energy bars from the plane.

"I could have eaten that," she said.

His sharp gaze caught her. "Sugar will give you a lift."

She nodded, not up to arguing. "Are they right behind us?"

"I don't think so. They were firing from well above us. I doubt they were willing to throw themselves down the mountain the way we did. Once we were out of sight, tracking us won't be easy, either. Ground is too rocky." He paused for another bite. "I'm hoping they don't have any backcountry experience. Bringing sleeping bags and freeze-dried meals doesn't mean they're good with rock pitches."

When he saw that she was done with the candy bar, he made her take some swallows from the water bottle. It tasted funny, probably from whatever he'd used to treat it.

Then he unbuttoned her shirt, peeled it off and examined both the splint and the lump on her collarbone that was the furnace forcing pain through all her ducts.

Gently putting her back together, he said, "I'm sorry I had to be so rough. You have a new raw place on your elbow—" he was looking at a tear in the flannel of the shirt as he eased it back on her good arm "—and a lot of new bruises."

"You're bleeding," she heard herself say.

Will glanced dismissively down at the trickle of blood coming from his skinned elbow. "It's nothing." He looked into her eyes. "Can you keep going? I could leave the pack and carry you piggyback."

And cover the same ground twice? Plus, increase the risk of being seen? "No. I can do it."

HE COULD HAVE killed them, throwing them down the mountainside the way he had. Forget bullets. What he'd done was crazy, especially hauling an injured woman along with him. This canyonside had stretches too steep to traverse, never mind descend at a run. What if he'd leaped off a pitch so steep he couldn't control the descent at all?

Eventually, as his pulse slowed and his hands steadied, Will watched Maddy.

People tended to lump together courage and heroism, but they weren't the same thing at all. The person who ran into a burning building to pull someone out often said, "I didn't think about the risks." Heroism was often impulse. Courage, in contrast, could be stoic. It was doing what had to be done, no matter the pain or personal suffering.

He had seen courage to equal Maddy's, but not often.

Reason said they needed to cover as much ground as possible, but when wounded, humans tended to have the same instincts as wild animals. Find a safe place and hide. That was what she'd done initially, and then it had been the best thing she could do. Now, when they needed to move fast, instead of reverting to instinct, she had trusted him absolutely. Will wished he deserved that trust. Truth was, they'd been damn lucky.

What grated him was that he'd known the bullets were falling short. Sure, they'd needed to open some distance between them and the gunmen, but they hadn't had to take what could have been a suicidal plunge. He hadn't quite flashed back to war, but he'd come too close.

Forget the self-recrimination, he told himself. *Focus.* He had to get them out of this wilderness before the hired killers spotted them again.

After studying his topographical map last night, Will had made the decision to take a southwest path in the general direction of Azure Lake, nestled below McMillan Spire, although he felt sure they were now at a lower elevation than the lake. If he'd taken them east, the drop toward the creek was less precipitous, but he feared it might be more open. With a little more luck, the men hunting them would expect them to go that way. With his chosen route, he and Maddy would have to struggle along Stetattle Creek for a greater distance, but they'd have a better chance of staying hidden in the thickets along the creek than they would on the steep drop from the ridge.

Maddy didn't argue, didn't question him, just stumbled along with his help. By early afternoon, though, she was even slower. Will had a bad feeling she was having to tell herself she could take one more step. That might be all that kept her going.

When she seemed to balk at one point, he turned to find her swaying, her eyes glassy.

They had to stop.

Will looked around. No talus slope, like the one where they'd huddled last night. With the drop in elevation, the fir and hemlock were tall enough to block any view from a distance, however, and an especially thick clump just below them drew him.

"Maddy, we'll spend the night right there." He pointed.

She followed the direction he pointed with a dull gaze, but nodded and managed to take the next step under her own volition.

The trick once they were enclosed in the grove was to find anywhere flat enough to lie down. Reaching for the sky, the trees grew at a sharp angle from the still steep mountainside. He spotted what he thought was a particularly wide trunk but then realized was two trees that had sprouted at nearly the same time and grown together. Dirt and crumbled rock had been dammed up behind the dual trunks. Will used the head of his ice ax to scrape out an area large enough for them both to lie down.

He could have gone on, but was still grateful to lower his pack to the ground, and grimaced at the stab of pain in his hip. When he checked the watch tucked into an outer pocket, he realized they'd started out almost ten hours ago. It was a miracle Maddy had stayed on her feet that long, particularly in such difficult terrain. He was forced to accept how slow their pace would continue to be, too. He could have whacked his way down to Diablo in a day, but with Maddy... He shook his head. They'd be looking at a minimum of two more days, maybe three, he feared.

As if she had no will left, Maddy had stopped when he stopped, not even sagging to the ground. He hastily spread his thin pad and atop it the sleeping bag, then gently guided her to sit down. Will dug painkillers and water out of his packet.

"Swallow these."

She stared at the three pills in her hand for a long moment before tipping them into her mouth and taking the bottle from him to wash them down.

"That's good. Those will help." He removed the water bottle from her hand and dumped some dried fruit in her palm. "Now eat."

He didn't see any more comprehension when she gazed at the dried banana and pineapple slices, but after a minute she did begin to nibble.

He followed that up with peanuts and more water. A hot meal would be good, but she needed sleep first.

Maddy moaned when he helped her lie down, pillowing her head on his balled-up parka and covering her with the blanket. She still looked so miserable, so he wadded up a sweatshirt under her injured arm, providing extra support.

Startlingly soon, her breathing deepened and evened out, and he saw that she was asleep.

HE TOOK THE chance of leaving her and climbed up to a crag he'd noticed earlier. Lying atop it, Will's view was still partially impeded by forest, but he scanned with his binoculars for any hint of other humans. A redtailed hawk swooped from above and disappeared into trees. Apparently having decided he was harmless, a chipmunk darted over the rock not five feet from him.

That was it. Will hated not knowing where the enemy was. He'd give a lot for a crackling voice in his ear offering intel, but he and Maddy were completely on their own. *You mean* you're *on your own*. He rejected the voice. She was out of it right now, but all he had to do was remember the way she'd faced him down at first meeting. Despite having survived the crash and suffering significant injuries, she had done a lot of smart things. He hoped like hell that, once she'd had some rest, they would be able to talk.

If her fever continued to mount… He shook off the worry. The same goal remained: get them off this mountainside, through the alder-and willow-choked jungle that protected the stream, to his Jeep parked in Diablo. Even if she was raving out of her head by then, could he risk taking her to a hospital?

Worry about that when it came.

He was trying not to doubt her story. Too much aligned with it, from the plane crash to her possession of a gun she didn't know how to use, and finally to the well-equipped men dropped from the helicopter.

Will thought he could keep her away from them. What scared him was the possibility she'd die from her injuries or a resulting infection before he could get her to safety. But in reality he had no way to call for a rescue helicopter anyway.

Right now he'd feel better to be watching over her.

MADDY SO DIDN'T want to wake up. She squeezed her eyes shut and tried desperately to call back the dream that had thinned like a cloud until it no longer had any substance.

The pain was white-hot.

But her nose twitched, because something smelled good, and despite the fact that her entire body hurt now, she was hungry.

With a groan, she pried open her eyelids, blinking several times before her eyes adjusted to a beam of sunlight that found her between tree limbs.

Just past her feet, Will was bent over the single-burner camp stove he'd used last night to heat water he added to freeze-dried meals. Last night's had been a chicken and rice curry, which had tasted wonderful. Or, at least, like real food. Tonight…

"Stew?" she guessed, her voice croaking.

He lifted his head and smiled. "Yep. I was about to wake you up."

"My stomach did it for you." She started the awkward process of sitting up.

Will immediately rose and offered his hand. As he tugged her up, she bit back a whimper.

"Why am I getting worse instead of better?" she exclaimed. "I hurt all over now. Even my stomach, but especially my legs and feet."

"You do have cracked or broken ribs," he reminded her. Then he grinned. "We started out at four this morning and didn't stop except for the one brief break until two. You know it's harder on the legs to go down than up."

She narrowed her eyes. "Are you telling me I'm sore because I'm in such lousy shape?"

Another grin flashed, making that bony, scarred face momentarily charming and sexy. "I'd never put it that way."

She wrinkled her nose, even though he was right. Even this past year when she'd taken up hiking, her two or three mile outings were more strolls than anything strenuous. She'd probably been more fit before, when she made herself go to the health club at least three days a week.

Smile lingering, Will handed her a pouch and spoon. "Fine dining."

"I'm starved," she admitted, and started eating. She was vaguely aware he was doing the same.

"How's your head?" he asked suddenly.

"Well, I have a headache, but…" It wasn't easy to separate out how her head alone felt. "It's better, I think." If only her thighs weren't screaming.

His relaxation was so subtle, she guessed he hadn't wanted her to know quite how worried he'd been.

"Does that mean I didn't have a concussion?"

"No, I'm sure you did, but apparently not severe. Which is fortunate, given our activities."

Running for their lives.

Maddy frowned. "Isn't it weird that they shot at us?"

"Yeah, I've been thinking about that." He balled up his dinner packet and dropped it into a zip-top plastic bag that held trash. "It's possible that, with high-end binoculars or rifle scopes, they got a good enough look at you to match up with photos. They might have seen the sling and your bruises. Plus, we were in the right vicinity, not that far from the crash site. That said, they had no reason to think there'd be two of us, and we mostly had our backs to them as we descended. They must know there are climbers in the area."

Feeling a chill despite the warmth of the afternoon, Maddy said, "Is it possible that they didn't want anyone who might conceivably have seen the crash site to get out and report it?"

His implacable expression belonged to the soldier he'd been. "That's my bet," he said after a moment. "If rescue personnel showed up and they caught a glimpse of a pair of mercenaries equipped with AK-47s, what're they going to think? And if they locate the crash and find one of the dead men was a US marshal, that would set off a serious hunt for the missing passenger. No, they need to—" He broke off, an apology in his eyes.

"Eliminate me," Maddy finished. "That's what you were going to say, isn't it?"

"And any witnesses."

"The trouble is, now they have to make *you* disappear, too."

His eyebrows climbed. "If you're thinking of apologizing, don't. I was where I needed to be."

How lucky had she been, to have Will Gannon come running to her rescue? A soldier, a medic and a man of honor.

"You'll have to let me thank you eventually."

He grunted. "Wait until we're back to civilization."

Maddy bent her head and finished her dinner. After disposing of the packet and giving him back the metal spoon, she said lightly, "I don't suppose you have any English breakfast tea in that backpack?"

"No, but I have coffee. Like a cup?"

"Are you kidding? I would *love* coffee."

Will laughed. "Won't take long to heat the water."

Two years ago she'd have disdained instant coffee. After all, there were at least two coffee shops on every block in Seattle, and coffee stands in most downtown businesses, too. This was only one of the many ways her life had changed.

In no time he handed over coffee that contained both sugar and creamer. Will sat beside her on the sleeping bag, his cup more a bowl. He'd offered her a choice of two candy bars, too.

"Was it Mary Poppins who could produce amazing things from her carpet bag?" Maddy asked.

The corners of his mouth twitched. "I'm sure I saw the movie, but I mostly remember the umbrella."

She couldn't resist singing, "Just a spoonful of sugar makes the medicine go down. You even had sugar."

Will chuckled. "Fortunately, I overpacked. I thought

I might stay an extra couple of days in the backcountry instead of heading right out."

"You're doing that, all right," Maddy murmured. "Only you're having to feed two of us."

The gray eyes resting on her were intent and...warm. "Food may get scanty by the end, but we'll be all right." He smiled. "I'll buy you a burger and fries on our way home."

The thought was lovely, but unreal. It might not be that many miles as the crow flies to the nearest burger joint, but she could barely walk. Still...it was something to hold on to.

"Where do you think those men are?" Maddy heard herself ask. "You don't seem worried."

In fact, Will's pose was casual, one long leg outstretched, the other bent. He hadn't yet hushed her, or kept his voice especially low. She knew the odds were slim that Torkelson's hired gunmen would either be able to track her and Will or happen to stumble on them, given the vast expanse of wilderness, but it wasn't that many hours since they'd been fired on.

All the tension his body didn't give away was in his eyes when they met hers. "It's time I show you where I think they are, and why we have a problem."

He spread out the topographical map, which clearly displayed elevation and how steeply it rose. Never having seen one before, Maddy watched closely as his finger tapped first on the summit of the mountain he'd climbed, then the approximate location of the crash... and finally their current location, at his best guess. And yes, experience with map reading wasn't necessary to see the problem.

Unless they were to do some serious scrambling and pass over a glacier at the foot of the sharp peak of Mc-

Millan Spire to descend into a different V-shaped creek valley, there was only one way out. Stetattle Creek.

Will put the obvious into words. "They don't know where we are now. But unless they're stupider than we can count on, they do know where we'll be soon."

Maddy couldn't tear her eyes from the map. "They'll be lying in wait."

Chapter Six

"What if we did go up?" Maddy asked, out of the blue.

It was several hours later, and they'd decided to hit
the sack, literally, given that their only bedding was a
single sleeping bag and one blanket. Since Will had
shown her the map and the hard reality ahead of them,
they'd talked about other things, quietly and with no
urgency. Nothing important, and yet the experience
had been strangely intimate. There'd been no pretense
between them, no game playing. Will recognized the
experience; nights before his unit was to head into the
kind of action some of them might not come out of alive,
they'd talked like this.

A sharp-edged memory popped up. Alan Todd had
described one night's spare meal and quiet conversation
as the last supper. Will wondered later if Todd could
have had a premonition. He'd died the next day, only
weeks before Will almost bought it.

He shook off the recollection. This wasn't like that—
except it was.

He didn't think either he or Maddy had said a word in
nearly an hour now beyond the practical. They'd shared
a cup of water to brush their teeth and, in her case, take
some more of his dwindling supply of pain meds. He
went one way, her another, for a few minutes of neces-

sary privacy. Now, although night hadn't fully darkened the sky, he had sprawled on his back and was helping Maddy arrange herself as comfortably as possible beside and on top of him.

Her softly voiced question followed a few gasps and small cries of pain as she slowly, awkwardly lay down. Will had had a broken collarbone once, and remembered well what the first weeks had been like. Add cracked or broken ribs, and lying down wasn't the relief you'd expect. At least last night they'd figured out the most comfortable position for her.

Once her broken arm lay on his chest and her head nestled on his shoulder, he said baldly, "You're in no condition to go mountain climbing. It could add two days to our trip, and a good part of that would be in the open, above the tree line. What if they're watching? Or the helicopter comes back for a flyover?"

She didn't say anything.

"Stetattle Creek will be hard enough to follow. Terror Creek is notorious. And if we made it, we'd pop out at Newhalem instead of Diablo where I parked my car. I could hide you and hitch a ride, I guess, but if those bastards got a good look at me—"

The way she sucked in a breath, he knew he didn't have to finish.

Truth was, he had enough worries about the Stetattle Creek route. The tangle of vegetation would be bad, and he had no doubt they'd also be swarmed by mosquitoes. They might have to cross back and forth over the creek if and when one bank was especially inhospitable, and how would Maddy do on slippery rocks or trying to edge across a fallen tree trunk? Bullets might come out of nowhere. And then, the last part of the route was on an honest-to-God trail that wasn't heavily used, but was promoted in the couple of guidebooks he'd seen. What would he or Maddy say to strangers met on the trail? Gosh, gee, had a little accident but she's fine? They'd remember her, talk about her in the campground or the store, maybe mention the green Jeep they'd seen the odd couple drive away in.

He and Maddy would not emerge from the wilderness unseen, which presented a danger as real as the ambush he had no doubt they would meet at some point higher up on Stetattle Creek.

Damn, maybe he should rethink this. But it didn't take a moment for him to know he'd made the only possible decision. Her fever hadn't climbed, but she was still too warm, which meant infection was working somewhere in her body. The fact that she'd be miserably sore tomorrow wouldn't help. And then there was the food situation. If all went well, they wouldn't starve to death, but his supply had dwindled alarmingly, and she needed fuel to overcome the pain.

As he lay there looking up, seeing bats darting against the deepening sky, she lay stiff until he lifted his free hand and smoothed her hair from her face, then kept stroking her, fingertips only, and carefully. Temple, cheekbone, the bridge of her nose and the uninjured side of her forehead.

She sighed and snuggled closer. Five minutes later he knew she'd fallen asleep, leaving him alone with his thoughts.

Fears and doubts raced like a hamster on a wheel. At the same time, he was distracted by the soft press of Maddy's breasts, the curve of her hip, the warmth of her breath in the V of his shirt. When was the last time he'd held a woman? Had to be months before he'd

come so close to losing his leg or even his life. She—
whoever she was—hadn't felt as good as Maddy did.

Funny to think that, considering her hair was still
matted, the left side of her face was garishly discol-
ored and swollen and she probably didn't smell sweet.
Since he hadn't had more than what his father called a
sponge bath in… Will had to think. Damn, had it really been five days? Well, he wasn't going to lift an
arm and do a sniff test. He did have a bar of soap and
a towel in his pack. Once they reached the creek, they
could both clean up. He hadn't brought so much as a
comb, but there'd been a brush in her duffel. He hoped
he had transferred it to his pack.

You want to die clean?

Irritated by the defeatist voice in his head, he returned to his original thought.

He liked sleeping with Maddy Kane. He'd like to
do more than sleep, once every movement didn't cause
her pain.

She stirred and gave a small moan. Will smiled
wryly, kissed the top of her head and closed his eyes.

MADDY SURFACED TO a gray dawn, the now too-familiar
awareness that if she moved it would hurt…and that,
once again, she was all but draped over an exceptionally solid male body.

His breathing changed almost as soon as she opened
her eyes.

"Morning, sunshine," he said huskily.

"That's me," she mumbled, struggling to remember
what day this was. Tuesday, she finally decided.

The muscular wall of his chest vibrated with a laugh.
"Speaking of sunshine, doesn't look like we'll have
any today."

She'd gotten so used to eastern Washington's drier, sunnier climate, the possibility of gray drizzle startled her. Getting wet was sure to make everything much worse. She didn't comment, however, because they had to move on. Whining was useless.

She did wince when she stretched her legs, hoping they wouldn't cramp. As soon as she was on her feet, she limped stiffly off to pee. When she returned to the camp, she found Will heating water.

He glanced at her with a smile. "I figured we could take the time for coffee."

"Bless you."

He skimmed her with an assessing gaze. "How are you?"

"Sore," she admitted, "but my knee feels better." She hoped that wasn't wishful thinking.

While they ate a hasty breakfast of granola and dried fruit, he told her about the time he'd broken his collarbone in a pickup football game on base. "Fortunately, I wasn't due to be deployed, or my lieutenant would have been seriously unhappy. It gets less painful as it goes, but I'm sorry to tell you it took months to completely heal."

"How does the bone ever knit when it's constantly being shifted?"

"Got me." He added powdered milk to her coffee and handed it over.

"So."

Will looked at her inquiringly.

"How are we going to avoid getting gunned down?"

"By moving slowly and doing reconnaissance."

"And what if they shoot some poor climbers on their way down?"

He shook his head. "This isn't a common route. I

think it was Fred Beckey, one of the great northwest mountaineers, who called whacking your way up or down the thickets in these valleys 'pure misery.'"

She digested that. "Are you telling me there's a better way?"

"From where we are now? No. To climb Elephant Butte, I came along the top of Stetattle Ridge from Sourdough Mountain. I could have followed another ridge from there to McMillan Spire. Otherwise, climbers in the southern Pickets sometimes drop down Terror Creek until it meets Goodell Creek, which leads to the Skagit River. That's the way we could have taken if we'd been willing to climb up and over. Stetattle Creek is doable, but not popular. Although I really wonder whether there's any difference."

She only nodded. What was there to say?

Will stared down into his coffee for a disquieting minute, then swallowed what was left and began to pack up.

Within minutes they were ready to go.

They might not have reached the "pure misery" part of the descent, but the still incredibly steep downhill pitch was torment enough for Maddy. She hadn't been on flat ground since the airport by Republic. The trees were now larger than the ones where the plane had come down, but otherwise every step was as difficult. She had to use her good hand to grab whatever branch or rock was available and slither or pick her way a few feet down. Will always descended first then turned to either lend her a hand or be ready to catch her if she fell.

Her arm and chest felt like…she didn't know. Burning embers. With her arm in the sling, it almost felt as if she were carrying the agony in the crook of her arm, something she didn't dare drop.

Her calf muscles and quads weren't happy with her, either. That, at least, was normal. She told herself to pretend she was pushing it on the elliptical in the gym, in those once-upon-a-time days when looking great in Spandex was a big part of her goal. Yes, her muscles had screamed then, but she'd never insisted they keep screaming until they became hoarse.

Every so often she saw a squirrel or a chipmunk, a quick dart, whisk of a tail, bright eyes watching these intruders in their wilderness. Will stopped her once with a hand on her arm.

"Listen."

Tat-a-tat.

"Woodpecker," she whispered. "That's the first thing I heard when I regained consciousness after the crash."

His gaze sharpened. "You were unconscious? For how long?"

"How am I supposed to know? It's not like I was paying attention to time anyway, and then after…my phone was gone."

Tat-a-tat.

"Sorry," he said. He squeezed her hand and started out again.

Until he paused to help her, she could only see his shoulders, the bulk of the pack and those long, strong legs. Lying down, she tended to forget quite how tall he was. At five foot seven, she wasn't short for a woman, but the top of her head barely reached above his shoulders.

Maddy wondered how much he chafed at their halting progress. She imagined him bounding downward—but he'd probably have taken a different route if he hadn't seen her plane go down and saddled himself with the injured survivor. Except she knew he'd meant it when he said, *I was where I needed to be*. Even... where he wanted to be?

As she tired, her thoughts bounced around as if they were in a pinball machine. What Mrs. Brophy would think when her bookkeeper didn't come back after the two-week "vacation." The view from her small office in the law firm in Seattle, including just the tiniest slice of the water. Her then-boyfriend reaching for her hand instead of Will. For an instant she was confused. Doug got manicures. He had narrow, elegant hands and absolutely no calluses. His hand didn't engulf hers the way Will's did, either.

Doug would have been no help to her at all in the wilderness with killers on her heels.

The word *killer* switched her to a loop she'd rerun thousands of times. The man standing over her terrified client, the big black gun. The *pop*, *pop*. How close Maddy had come to falling back. A face impassive but for a trace of disgust or irritation. The way his head came up suddenly, turned as if he'd heard her breathe, knew suddenly there was someone else in the house. If he'd looked for her, she wouldn't be here now. But then, two good men wouldn't have died horribly because of her, either.

Yes, but she wouldn't have had the chance to put him away for a lifetime, and maybe Torkelson, too. Having betrayed his office, he was almost worse.

"Doing okay?"

Will's voice jerked her from the dark memories.

"Peachy."

The cheek she could see creased with a smile.

Maddy's thoughts blurred as she plodded on.

Midday, she heard a waterfall. Maddy blinked and looked around, suddenly realizing that the vegetation

had changed. Deciduous trees—alders? Vine maples?—
were mixed with the fir and hemlock. Lacy something
draped from tree branches. She took another step and
skidded on what she realized was deep green moss covering a rock.

A firm grip on her upper arm kept her upright.

They stopped for a rest, drink of water and bite to
eat on a mossy downed log.

"It's going to be really slow going from here on,"
Will warned her. "We may get lucky and find a few
game trails, but mostly we need to stay up above the
creek, which is likely one waterfall after another for
this first stretch."

Another sound blended with the rush of water. She
cocked her head. "What's that?"

"A bird. Maybe a warbler? We'll see more of them,
and mammals, too. Deer and black bears are the biggest. Elk tend to stick to marshy land and meadows."

"Bears?"

He smiled. "I saw a mama and her cub eating blueberries before your plane went down. They didn't pay
any attention to me."

A branch rustled not far away and Maddy looked in
alarm to see a small bird sidling along watching them.
It had a creamy-white chest, brownish wings and back,
with black circling a yellow crown on its head.

"That's a sparrow, I think," Will said quietly. "There
are half a dozen kinds up here."

The bird flew away so fast her eye couldn't follow it.

"The vegetation is going to get thicker," Will continued. "Unfortunately, insects like these conditions, too.
Flies and mosquitoes will be the biggest annoyance. I'd
like to keep some elevation above the creek for now,
which may save us from getting sucked dry, but if we
find a pool, we might be able to wash up."

Maddy suddenly felt gross—sweaty, her hair greasy, what bare skin she could see on her forearms dirty and streaked with pitch where dried beads of blood didn't show new scratches. With deep longing, she asked, "You mean, actually get in the water?"

"Ah, probably not that." He leaned to scratch his back on a tree trunk. "This water is melt from the glacier. The temperature won't be much above freezing." A teasing light in his eyes, he added, "Depends on how tough you are."

She wrinkled her nose. "I'd love to get clean. I have to admit, though, that I'm the kind who inches into cold water instead of diving in and getting it over with."

He laughed quietly, stretched and shoved his arms beneath the straps of the backpack. "Ready?"

As they set out again, he said, "Let's keep our voices down."

Maddy nodded, the reminder making her skin prickle with apprehension.

WILL'S BEST GUESS was that the gunmen would be waiting downstream, closer to where Torrent joined Stetattle Creek, but he couldn't take anything for granted. First chance he saw, he wanted to cross to the other side, both because his topo map suggested the going might be easier and because the men might assume they'd stay on this side.

He stopped Maddy when he saw what he'd wanted: a large tree that had fallen across the stream just below a waterfall.

"Stay here," he said quietly. "Let me take a look around."

He scanned with his binoculars before moving, stopping when movement caught his eye. Identifying a river otter reassured Will. Would it be on the bank if it had seen or smelled humans too close? It obviously hadn't sensed him and Maddy yet.

He handed his binoculars to Maddy, murmuring, "Look right above the boulder across the creek."

She gave an almost soundless gasp when she saw the otter. "Two of them!"

Will took another look. Sure enough. As he watched, one slid back into the stream, followed almost immediately by the other. They hadn't moved as if they were alarmed, though.

He'd believed himself prepared for what they'd find in the V of the valley. Two minutes of trying to ease between tangles of alder growing out of rock changed his mind. Bulling through was probably the right technique, but that wasn't compatible with trying to go unseen. He thought he was doing pretty well until an alder caught his boot and sent him crashing down. As he braced his hands to jump up, something jabbed his face. Swallowing a profanity, he glared at the cluster of leaves edged with spines he recognized from a guidebook. The shrub was appropriately called devil's club.

He forged on until he reached the torrent of water bounding down what had once been a talus slope. When the tree fell, it had ripped its roots out of the soil. Already, lush vegetation had filled in the hole, which wasn't visible. An unwary step and he'd have gone down again. He believed in planning ahead, but didn't even want to think about what they'd do if he broke a leg.

Employing his binoculars again, all he spotted were a few birds. When a swarm of horse-or deerflies surrounded him and began biting, Will barely kept himself from swearing out loud. Swiping them off with one hand, he backtracked.

Sitting where he'd left her, Maddy didn't try to hide her relief.

"All clear," he said, "but it's hard going. Take each step carefully. The damn alders will try to trip you up, and there's loose rock hidden by devil's club."

Once they started off, he used his ice ax to point to the first spiny leaves he saw, in this case on a small shrub. Maddy reached out to touch and jumped when she found a spine.

"There'll be nettles, too. You'll want to keep your hand up so you don't brush it."

She nodded vigorously.

This time he separated branches and didn't shift his weight until he found solid footing. Then he turned and reached out for Maddy, who picked her way as carefully as he'd asked.

The roar of the falls grew louder in their ears. When the stream came into sight, he pointed out the log and the hidden pit below the mass of earth and roots.

He bent to talk right into her ear. "I'll cross first with the pack, then come back to help you."

She nodded.

Damn, he hoped the log wasn't slippery. They couldn't afford for either of them to fall, and she'd have a hell of a time scooting herself across on her butt with the use of only one working hand and arm.

Right beside the bank Will was able to step up onto the log. He moved one foot, then the other, experimentally. Not too bad. He bounced a little, finding it to be solid. Finally, he started forward cautiously. If crossing a pool, he wouldn't have worried about falling. The drop wasn't that far. Instead, below was a tumble of rocks and white water.

Once he stepped out over the torrent, water from the

falls misted him. He had to blink water away. The tree must have fallen this spring, he decided, or it would already be covered by slick green moss. As it was, Will made it over and stowed his pack in a dry place.

He crouched briefly to check that the Glock hadn't slipped too deep in the pocket to be easily available. Then he walked back across the stream with more confidence.

"That doesn't look hard," she said. "I usually have good balance. I even did gymnastics when I was a kid, balance beam included."

He grinned at her. "You mean, you could do a backflip on this thing?"

"No, but once upon a time I could have done a somersault and maybe jumped into a kind of split."

His sense of humor evaporated. "Well, don't."

She gave him an unreadable look, but let him help her climb up onto the log. Having decided to go first, he took her hand and put it on his belt. Satisfied when her fingers curled around it, he started forward.

He glanced over his shoulder a couple of times, worried about whether he'd shortened his stride enough, whether her head injury had affected her balance.

Even as he thought, *Pay attention to keeping your own damn balance*, one of his feet shot out from under him.

He teetered over the tumble of rocks and white water, knowing he'd pull Maddy with him if he fell.

Chapter Seven

Head bent, Maddy concentrated on her feet. This must be harder for Will, she couldn't help thinking, with his much larger feet. He walked with confidence, though, steadying her…until she felt him lurch. Looking up in horror she saw him stagger and flail his arms in a desperate attempt to regain his balance.

"Let go!" he roared.

Instead, she tightened her grip on his belt and leaned the other way as a counterbalance. She didn't let herself think about how much he outweighed her by.

The battle was brief. Swearing, he came upright and she did the same. Her pulse had skyrocketed and she gasped for breath. Neither moved for at least a minute.

When finally his muscles tensed, she felt it. As if nothing had happened, he took the next step. Like an echo, she did the same.

On the other side he hopped off the log and turned to reach for her. Water dripped down a face drawn tight with strain. His mouth was clamped shut, turbulence in eyes darkened to charcoal.

Hands at her waist, he swung her down but didn't release her. Instead, he just looked at her. Voice hoarse, he said, "I'd have taken you with me."

"I…didn't think," she admitted.

He shook his head. "I should say thank you, but when I think of you falling onto those rocks—"

She shivered at what had been a very real possibility. She didn't like imagining *him* hitting rocks, his body tossed by jets of white foam. "We're okay."

"Yeah." His hands slid up her back until his arms closed around her. She let herself lean on him, hear how hard his heart hammered. After a minute he murmured, "We're good."

Being so close to him felt good. Necessary.

But he drew a deep breath, let his arms drop and stepped back. "We need to keep moving."

Even as she regretted the space that had opened between them and the mask he'd drawn over his face to hide what he felt, Maddy knew he was right. She still felt shaky, but that was more likely because her muscles were rebelling against the past two days' exertions than as a reaction to the near-disaster, although she wouldn't swear to it. Neither cause kept her from walking.

Just ahead of her, Will plunged into a dense wall of greenery. Maddy hurried to follow, suddenly alarmed. If he got ten feet ahead of her, she'd lose sight of him.

Over the next ten minutes, as they shoved through alder thickets, sweated and swatted at insects, Maddy thought of that mountaineer's description: pure misery. And he, at least, hadn't also faced an ambush.

Jerking her hand away, too late, from a clump of nettles, she also envisioned Will's map. It was not encouraging to think, *We've barely started.*

WILL HAD NEVER been happier to see the trace of a game trail. At this point he didn't give a damn what animals used the trail, wearing down some of the low-growing plants and breaking whip-thin alder branches that would otherwise be trying to slap his face. Could be wolves, deer, bears or all of the above. A wealth of mammals made their homes in these mountains, including badgers, pine martens, minks and some of the big cats, which were unlikely to allow themselves to be seen. Like marmots and pikas, bighorn sheep and mountain goats stuck to the higher elevations, and he thought elk preferred marshy lowlands. There were undoubtedly beaver dams along the Stetattle—in fact, if he and Maddy were ever to get their bath, it would probably be in a pool behind a dam built of sticks. Some of those animals were nocturnal, which was just as well. Give him a bear any day over an annoyed porcupine.

Maddy tugged urgently on his shirt. "I hear something behind us."

He didn't waste time swearing. "This way." He urged her into a dense tangle of alder and devil's club.

She moved as fast as she could. When she tripped on a rotting, downed log, he rescued her from the fall but said, "Get down behind it."

Within seconds both sprawled flat amid ferns and lower branches of a tree with sharp needles. Will withdrew the handgun from the pack and raised his head, expecting to see armed Taliban slipping in near-silence through these woods.

He blinked. Wrong landscape. *Not Taliban.* He was disturbed by an expectation so vivid; the enemy soldiers had momentarily had real substance.

Will watched for any movement.

Like Maddy, he heard the rustling of branches first. Was that a camouflage uniform...? He expelled air in relief.

"Take a look," he whispered. "Quick."

Maddy carefully lifted her head, too. "Ooh."

The doe was followed by two fawns, spotted and with impossibly long, slender legs. Will bet they weren't more than a few weeks old.

"Those creeps wouldn't shoot her, would they?"

"Gunfire would give away their position. It would draw attention they don't want, too. Hunting and guns are illegal in a national park."

Her gaze shifted to the Glock in his hand. He smiled wryly. "Don't blame me."

The sound of her soft chuckle went straight to his groin. He almost groaned. "Can you go on for a while longer?"

Her "Yes" was clipped. Maddy rolled away from him.

Crap. He'd been curt, killing the mood. Just as well. He couldn't afford to let her get to him. His focus had to be absolute, getting Maddy out of the mountains safely his only goal. Later…

Not later. Never. The gulf between them was too wide, too deep. He'd grown up in poverty, she in privilege. He'd scraped out a BA from community colleges and online courses; she'd gone to Stanford and had a law degree. The men she dated didn't have ugly scars on their faces and bodies. They knew fine wines, the best restaurants, not the layout of cave systems where terrorists had set up camp. Will liked and admired Maddy—yeah, he wanted her, too—but she wasn't for him.

Game trail or not, their pace was painfully slow. They took a break for her to down more pain pills and for them both to eat or drink. He ate some nuts but skipped the candy bar. He hoped she hadn't noticed how few were left. Instead, he gave one to her while he ate a tasteless energy bar. Tonight would be their last hot meal, and it was a miracle he'd tossed more extras in than he'd remembered. By tomorrow night they'd be getting hungry. Nothing serious; they weren't that far from Diablo and the Skagit River.

Maddy needed the calories more than he did. The effort she was making despite fever and pain was taking it out of her. In fact, not more than an hour later he glanced back and immediately knew she was about to hit the wall. She'd dropped back and her eyes looked glassy.

When they came to a small stream, one of the numerous tributaries carrying snowmelt down to join Stetattle Creek and eventually the Skagit River, he decided the timing was perfect.

They crossed the stream on moss-covered rocks, more or less keeping dry, after which he led her upstream through the usual tangle until he found a mossy cove behind a cedar noticeably larger than any surrounding trees. A blackened scar on the trunk suggested it might have survived a forest fire that burned its compatriots.

Once again he spread the pad and sleeping bag before helping Maddy sit down. With a moan, she toppled onto her side, curling up.

Will laid a hand on her forehead. Speaking of burning. He needed to replace all her bandages to give himself a chance to search for obvious signs of infection. With nothing but soap and antibiotic cream, there wasn't much he could do, but that little would be better than nothing. For now, he'd let her rest.

MADDY COULDN'T SAY she felt better when she woke from her nap. Well…just lying down was a relief. She automatically turned her head until she saw Will partway around the tree sheltering them. Cradling a metal cup in his hands, he rested his back against the tree and sat with legs outstretched, crossed at the ankles. His brown hair was disheveled and the stubble on his jaw could now be described as a beard. His flannel shirt had tears, his jeans were dirty and his forearms and hands looked like he'd done battle with an annoyed bear.

Feeling a sting, she lifted her own arm. It was criss-crossed with angry scratches. More gingerly, she touched her cheek. Yep, face, too.

Will's head turned. "Nice nap?"

"I have no idea. It was more like lights out."

She loved the way his smiles both creased his cheeks and crinkled the skin beside his eyes.

"That was my impression," he agreed. "Lucky you weren't still standing up."

"I guess sleepwalking shows it's possible to do both things at the same time."

"Some soldiers will tell you they do it all the time."

She wanted to smile, but it was hard to move the muscles in her cheeks when her head ached the way it did. "I don't feel so good," she said after a minute.

"No," he said quietly, "you have a raging fever. Once you have a cup of coffee, I want to check all your wounds. We can clean up a little in this creek, too."

Without turning, Maddy couldn't see it, but she could hear a pleasant little ripple that was separate from the louder rush of Stetattle Creek.

"No dip in a deep pond?"

"Afraid not. Trust me, once you feel the temperature, you won't want to jump in."

The coffee energized her a little, and she popped some more pills.

Fifteen minutes later she discovered how right Will was. Still squeaking after yanking her hands out, she couldn't understand why the water was running and not frozen solid. Still, it was astonishingly clear and sparkled in the late-afternoon sun slanting through the tree branches.

She would have felt more self-conscious when she took her shirt off if Will's expression hadn't been so clinical. He examined her arm above and below the splint but decided not to take it off. He cleaned some grazes and gashes she'd almost forgotten about and then smeared ointment on them. After finding where the biggest lump had been on her head, he gave a grunt she took for satisfaction.

He removed her boots and socks himself, then helped her wriggle out of her jeans. That was when he saw something that made him mutter a sharp expletive.

Maddy twisted to try to see, too.

Even his gentle touch made her jump.

"It's infected, all right," he growled.

She couldn't get a good look at the spot she'd like to think was on her lower back but was probably actually her butt.

By the time he finished washing pus from what he said was an open cut, Maddy was gasping, her hands knotted into fists.

He must have said he was sorry ten times.

Eventually, he dug out clean jeans, shirt and underwear for her.

"I think you can do without these." He rolled up her pajama pants that had served as long underwear and stuffed them toward the bottom of the pack. Then he left her on the mossy edge of the stream to wash.

"Call if you need me. I won't be far."

Ice-cold water or not, it felt good to wash everyplace

she could reach. Although, wow, getting her hands on a razor jumped higher on her "I wish" list.

Still a few notches down from escaping a couple of merciless killers, of course.

As clean as she could make herself, she summoned Will, who buttoned the waist of her jeans and eased a T-shirt over her head and her splinted arm. He topped that with one of his sweatshirts, large enough to fit over the splint.

Squatting in front of her, rolling up the sleeves one at a time, Will once again demonstrated his extraordinary patience. His head bent, he concentrated on what he was doing, determined, Maddy knew, not to hurt her. How those big hands could be so deft and gentle both was a puzzle. She imagined him, suddenly, with a child. Watching him, she felt her heart cramp and her eyes sting. With the physical symptoms came the unsettling realization that she could love this man. Or maybe already did. Even the *idea* of saying goodbye to him was unimaginable.

If he didn't feel the same, she'd have no choice. She couldn't burden him with expectations he wouldn't want. Worse, he'd probably call what she felt *gratitude*.

Suddenly, she wanted to touch his beard. Find out whether it was wiry, prickly or soft. He probably wouldn't mind, but…

Sighing, she suddenly became aware that he'd rocked back on his heels and was looking straight at her, his expression quizzical. Blushing fiercely, she said, "Your turn. I'm, um, sorry the towel is so wet."

He only nodded. "Take it easy for a few minutes. I'll start dinner as soon as I'm done."

Maddy retreated to their campsite and sat on the sleeping bag with her back to him. She closed her eyes, listened for every tiny sound and resisted the temptation to peek.

WILL STUCK HIS head in the stream and used the soap to wash his hair. He did it as much to cool his over-heated body as because he cared whether his hair was grungy.

He'd give a lot to know what Maddy had been thinking to make her blush. Wondering was enough to tie his gut in a knot. It didn't seem to matter what he'd decided about the gulf between them. His body didn't want to hear it. And maybe he was wrong. Did any of those slick attorneys and businessmen in their custom-tailored suits *deserve* this gutsy woman?

Not in his book.

He did the best he could with the bar of soap and ice-cold water. Clean clothes felt good, although they'd be ripped, sweat-soaked and dirty an hour into their morning hike. Plus, it was his last set of clean clothes.

Will rubbed his hand reflectively over his jaw and neck. Damn, he did wish he could shave. He'd frequently let his beard go when on patrol, of course, but it invariably began to itch. He'd always scraped it off first thing.

Back at their campsite, Maddy sat unmoving. When she heard him, she burst out, "I wish I wasn't so useless."

"It's a miracle you aren't dead," he said brusquely. "Remember the part where you fell out of the sky?"

"Yes, but—" She pinched her lips together. "Never mind."

He crouched in front of her. "What's wrong, Maddy? What are you thinking?"

"I don't even know how to use a camp stove to heat

water! And if I did, I probably couldn't anyway with only one hand."

"That's not it."

She averted her face. He used his knuckles beneath her chin to turn it back.

"I'm mad," she said suddenly. "They stole my life! I've had no say in anything for a year now. Do you know what that feels like?"

"Yeah," he said drily. "I was in the military."

"You chose it!"

Had he? Sure, he'd signed the papers, but given the freedom she'd taken for granted, he'd have chosen college, not becoming an army grunt.

But he said, "Once you testify, it'll all be over." In half the time of a two-year enlistment. He rose to his feet, but before he could go to his pack she grabbed the leg of his pants.

"Wait."

He did just that.

"I'm sorry. I despise whining. Plus, I sounded like a spoiled brat. I'm...not usually like that."

Will couldn't resist the plea in her hazel eyes. He crouched again to put himself closer to her level and said, "You're entitled to some whining. The past year has to have been frustrating and frightening both, and now you've had an epically bad few days. It's taken a lot of courage to go on the way you have. Does it really matter if you can't boil water?"

"No," she whispered. "You're right. Ignore me."

He shook his head. "That's not gonna happen, babe."

"Babe?"

He grinned. "Thought that'd get to you."

As he set up the small stove, he gave the fuel can a

surreptitious shake. Not a lot left. Surely enough to boil water a few more times to make coffee.

Once he had it fired up, he asked for Maddy's menu preference.

"Pasta primavera," she said promptly.

While they ate, he asked her to tell him about the life she'd "lost"—although he didn't phrase it that way. He was curious, yes, but also needed to shore up his defenses.

She paused with her spoon in the packet. "Well... I had an apartment in West Seattle. Nice but not that fancy. I was lucky to find it given how expensive Seattle has gotten. At least I got to say goodbye to my parents, but I don't know if they are still paying the rent, or picked up my stuff and let the apartment go."

"Car?"

"Yes, because I needed it to see clients. I hardly ever drove it otherwise. Parking is hard to find, and you can get anywhere on the bus. There's a grocery store only half a mile from my place, and I like walking." She made a face. "I *used* to like walking."

Will smiled.

"I was seeing another attorney." She gazed into space for a minute then gave her head a shake. "I don't think it would have gone anywhere. I'm sure he's long since moved on."

"What if you get back and find he's been pining for you?"

"He won't be, but it doesn't matter. We had some fun, that's all. Anyway, I'm not the same person I was."

Will understood that. Her life had been flipped like a coin. Heads, everything was good. Tails, not so much. It was possible she'd slide back into her old life and gradually forget how it felt to be powerless, scared, on the run.

She could build walls, or she could just be one of those people who deep down believed their lives were meant to be shiny. Yeah, bad things had happened, but they'd been temporary. A nuisance, that was all. Forgettable.

But he didn't believe that, not about Maddy.

He got her talking about her law firm and the kind of work she did. Since she'd been a defense attorney, it was probably no surprise after her experiences this past year that she admitted to wondering whether she should shift to become a public defender instead, or even a prosecutor.

"Although the woman, Laura Bessey, who I'd gone to see…" She hesitated. "The one who was murdered. She was dealing with both threats and weird stuff going wrong. She'd been fired from her job for reasons she claimed were pure fiction."

"You're assuming Brian Torkelson was behind all of it."

"Given that she'd decided she had to tell someone that he'd raped her, yes."

"Eat," he ordered her.

She looked startled, but lapsed into silence as she finished her meal. "That was surprisingly good," she commented.

"These freeze-dried meals taste a lot better than they look." His stomach still felt hollow, though, and he wondered if hers did, too. "Dessert?" he asked.

"Cherry pie à la mode?"

He laughed. "Almond Joy or Butterfinger."

"Maybe later." She looked around. "It's so pretty here. So green. The way the light is filtered through the trees makes me think of stained glass."

"This is magnificent country. First time I've ever climbed in the North Cascades, but it won't be the last."

Sadness crossed her face like a shadow. "Bill—the pilot—was pointing out these incredible peaks with names like Fury and, I don't know, Terror. I suppose people do climb them."

"Yeah, I'm hoping to find a partner to climb with and tackle one or two of them. Not sure I should go alone."

"No." She fell silent for longer than he liked, crinkles forming on her forehead. "I was just thinking I might like backpacking or climbing—although no thousand-foot drop-offs, thank you—only then it occurred to me that maybe this isn't the best time to be talking about the future."

"When better?" Will cleared some gruffness from his throat. "We're getting out of here, Maddy. My word on it."

"You shouldn't say that." She seemed to be looking deep inside him. "And I shouldn't believe you. But… I do." More softly, she added, "Or at least, I want to."

"Hold on to that," he said quietly. He took her hand in his and discovered it was easier to be optimistic when they had a physical connection.

SOMEBODY CRIED OUT. Maddy reeled back at the hideous sight, an awful stench in her nose and mouth.

"I'm sorry! I'm sorry!"

"Maddy!" Big hands shook her. "You're dreaming. It's not real."

Not real? In the darkness, she couldn't orient herself. Where was she? Who—

Will. Of course it was Will waking her from a nightmare. Somehow she'd pushed herself to a sitting position, and his arm supported her now.

She shuddered and turned her face into his chest. He kept soothing her until she mumbled, "I dreamed

I was back there. At the crash site, where I found Bill and Scott. Only…only it was a day or two later and their bodies…"

"Maddy, they're dead. Unless a body is embalmed, that's what happens. Nature breaks down the flesh to return it to the earth."

The images from her nightmare were slipping away. "I know," she said after a minute. "I know." She swallowed. "Do you have nightmares?"

"I doubt there's a returning soldier who doesn't."

"So I have lots of company?"

"Yeah." Was that a smile in his voice? "You do. Including me. Now, lie down. You need your sleep."

"Okay." She tipped up her face impulsively to kiss his cheek. What she found was his mouth. Consternation mixed with excitement.

Before she could pull away, he'd lifted a hand to cup the back of her head.

"Maddy?"

That was all he said, but despite his hoarseness, she heard the question.

Chapter Eight

Her hand rose to his cheek, fingertips sampling his beard. Beard or no, Will felt her warmth. And her touch was answer enough, wasn't it?

He brushed her lips with his again, nibbled a little. She sucked in a breath and he took the chance to deepen the kiss. *Careful*, he told himself. He couldn't lay her down and expect her to take his weight. Even if she'd been uninjured and not half out of her mind with a fever…he couldn't take this that far. Not when she depended on him for her life. Not when he knew that what either of them felt right now might not be real.

But he savored this kiss, every quiver of her lips, the taste of her dinner and the mint of her toothpaste. Early Fourth of July fireworks. Will found himself squeezing her nape, so damn delicate. Deceptively delicate.

He lifted his head once so they could both breathe, then returned for more. Her response was eager as if she could keep kissing him forever. Will told himself he was good with that, except the bitter, too-proud kid he'd been started talking in his ear.

You roused her from a nightmare. Of course she's happy to kiss you! Great way to blot out the awful crap in her head.

The punch was a one-two.

Why wouldn't she kiss you? You've all but promised to die for her, if it comes to that.

The next time he needed oxygen, he kissed his way across her cheek, nuzzled her temple and laid her down. The inner voice was irritating but right. Anything like this had to wait.

"Sleep," he murmured. He didn't add, *Tomorrow is going to be a big day*, because that was a euphemism to end all euphemisms.

Tomorrow, he thought grimly, they'd likely come upon the surprise party. Given that they were massively out-gunned, their options weren't great.

When he stretched out beside Maddy, he noticed how stiffly she held herself. If she'd been able to turn her back to him, Will felt sure she'd have done it. He must have seemed abrupt, even to be rejecting her. Which, in a way, was what he'd done. For the best of motives. Somehow he doubted Maddy would see it that way.

Sleep wouldn't come easily. His empty belly alone wouldn't have kept him awake; he'd gone hungry plenty of times, both as a boy and as a soldier in the field. It was worries about tomorrow that held sleep at bay, along with second thoughts.

FERN FRONDS BRUSHING her face, Maddy sat hunched behind the roots of another fallen tree. This one might have fallen over the winter, or perhaps the year before. It hadn't taken long for the voracious vegetation to advance on the scar in the land. Nettles and devil's club seemed especially energetic.

Will had decided that today he'd scout ahead for each stretch then return for her. He'd done that twice already. She couldn't tell him how much she hated being left behind, or how afraid she was for him in these long interludes when she couldn't know what was happening to him. She clung to the memory of his kiss.

Infuriatingly, her arm and shoulder hurt worse when she sat still than they did when she moved. That probably wasn't really the case, but there wasn't much else to do but be aware of her body's complaints and listen for danger.

To top it all off, she itched fiercely beneath the splint on her arm, where of course she couldn't reach. Actually, she was afraid to move at all, partly because of the nettles. The back of her hand still stung from yesterday's carelessness. Mostly, though, she kept imagining watching eyes in the jungle around her. Every sound made her twitch. She listened for gunfire, knowing that even if Will managed to escape, it would take ages for him to make it back to her.

And if he didn't? What then?

He'd stuffed her pockets this morning with food: dried fruit, a packet of peanuts and two candy bars. He didn't say anything, but then he hadn't had to. He wanted to be sure she had something to eat if she found herself on her own.

A heavy rustling among the alders and willows downstream brought her head up. Whoever was approaching didn't care about alerting anyone nearby to his presence. Were she and Will that noisy when they were on the move?

Please let this be Will.

Somehow, though, she knew it wasn't.

Maddy sat frozen, waiting, her eyes straining for the first sight. Her heart thudded. They hadn't yet found so much as a hint of a game trail this morning, but whoever—whatever—this was seemed to be coming straight toward her.

A crash among the whippy trunks and branches shook the leaves. Maddy tensed. She could run—

The something coming was huge…and black. A black bear. Not a grizzly; they were brown, weren't they?

Should she stay still and quiet and hope it never noticed her, or make lots of noise to try to scare it away?

More of the surrounding foliage shook. The bear wasn't twenty feet away when it stopped and the huge head swung toward Maddy. The nostrils quivered and they stared at each other.

Unable to sit still a second longer, Maddy jumped up, waved her arm and yelled, "Shoo!"

The bear lumbered straight toward her, using its bulk to smash through the shrubs and small trees. Her head turned wildly. She couldn't run.

So she pressed among the tree roots, smelling the rank odor of bear even as it got so close she could see beady eyes and patchy fur.

At the last second it veered suddenly, continuing to crash away until Maddy heard a great splash. Bears probably didn't bother looking for fallen logs to cross a creek.

Her breath escaped in a big *whoosh* and her legs failed her. Butt in the dirt, she waited for her heartbeat to slow. Wilderness Girl she apparently wasn't.

Ten minutes later she heard someone/something else coming, but this one was a lot quieter than the bear had been. How he recognized where he'd left her, she didn't know, but by the time she made out Will, his gaze had already locked on to her.

"You okay?" he asked, sinking down beside her. His hair was full of twigs and leaves and debris and his arms and one cheek displayed new scratches. Sweat darkened his tan T-shirt and Maddy had no doubt the back of the shirt would be sweat-soaked, too, where he'd been carrying the pack. So far today he'd carried it with him during his reconnaissance, then stashed it somewhere for pickup once he returned with her.

Glad she'd had time to recover from the close encounter with the bear, she said, "Mostly. I had a scare when a bear passed only a few feet from me. I thought—"

In his usual calm way, he said, "Your typical black bear is as afraid of you as you are of it. Cubs can change that, but the one you met might have been male."

Her attempt to read his expression didn't get her anywhere, so she finally asked, "Did you see anyone?"

He shook his head, weariness or maybe frustration finally showing. "Nope, but I don't believe they've given up."

"Do you want something to eat?" She extended the first thing her hand closed on, a box of raisins.

"No, thanks." He grabbed a tree root and pulled himself to his feet. "Let's keep moving."

She got up and fell in behind him, grateful when he parted the springy alder branches and held them until she was through, but also feeling guilty. Because she was so awkward and slow, Will was having to hike three times as far as she was. For at least the hundredth time, she silently acknowledged how lucky she was that he'd been here when she needed him.

"WE NEED TO cross the creek here," Will said. "I made it without getting wet, but the rocks are slippery."

Maddy nodded stoically. The bank ahead of them rose in an impassible, rocky, alder-infested cliff.

"Step where I do," Will told her, even knowing he didn't need to.

The constant mist above the fast-running creek provided a perfect environment for moss. The lower in elevation they progressed, the richer the moss. A pretty emerald green, it covered rocks, swallowed downed trees and enveloped anything that held still long enough. And, damn, it was slippery stuff underfoot, especially when wet.

He must be getting tired, because his mind jumped to how it had felt to kiss Maddy. Naturally, a foot skidded and he ended up shin deep in ice-cold water. Grimacing, Will pulled his foot out, shook it and set off again. Fortunately, with daintier feet, Maddy was having better luck staying dry.

Will had almost reached the far side when he heard a distant hum. Airplane? He looked up but didn't see anything in the blue arch of sky except clouds gathering over the Picket Range.

The sound grew, and he knew.

"Helicopter!" He reached back for Maddy's hand. "Hurry!"

He splashed through water for the last few steps and thought she did, too. Almost immediately, they entered the familiar snarl of willow and alder and devil's club, but he wasn't convinced the cover was sufficient to hide them from above. Neither of them wore bright colors, but even the greens and browns were subtly wrong.

They ran, or as close to running as they could do. The noise swelled, a swarm of angry bees. It could be a sightseeing helicopter or a search and rescue one heading to pick up an injured climber. Will didn't believe it, though.

A thick clump of lush sword ferns ahead looked like their best bet. He and Maddy raced for it. At his direction, she wriggled among the ferns, lying prone, and

Will followed. He pulled out the Glock and rolled onto his back, parting fronds until he had a view that was barely a slit.

Not twenty seconds later a black helicopter flying dangerously low came into sight. At almost the same moment, a deer in a panic struggled past. A good decoy, he thought. The helicopter kept moving, staying low.

As the racket receded, he murmured, "They're getting nervous. They're afraid they've lost us."

"They might have expected us to get down the mountain faster."

All he could see were her boots. He reached out and clasped her ankle because he needed to touch her. "They have to know you're injured." Even if their enemy hadn't gotten a good look at the two of them fleeing the hail of gunfire, people rarely walked away unscathed from a plane crash, especially one that had killed the pilot and the only other passenger.

Maddy didn't say anything.

Will's mind kept racing. How had these men accounted for him? Did they think they'd been misinformed and really there'd been a third passenger? Maybe even a second US marshal? If that were the case, they'd expect him to be armed.

Impatient with himself, he realized they already knew that. They would have found Marshal Rankin's body and the empty holster.

Will was torn between moving on and waiting to find out whether the helicopter would turn right around and retrace its path. Depended on how sure the two hunters on the ground were that he and Maddy had come this way. They might fear Will and she had climbed over the flank of McMillan Spire and down Terror and Goodell Creeks, as he and Maddy had discussed. If she hadn't

been injured so badly, that might have been smart—
except he reminded himself of the scarcity of cover at
sub-alpine elevations.

He mulled over what the Forest Service personnel
would think about the black, unmarked helicopter scaring the crap out of the wildlife, and what they could re-
alistically do about it.

After venting a few words he should probably apologize for, Will said, "Let's keep moving. I left my pack
in a good place to stop for a bite to eat."

"Okay."

When she struggled to roll over, he took her hand
and pulled her to her feet. He didn't like that her face
was bone-white except for those too-bright red spots on
both cheeks. Fever. Even her hand was too hot.

Will liked even less knowing that despite all his
training, he couldn't help her.

As they resumed their trek, broken branches gave
evidence of the animals that had passed this way—
and possibly of the men he still expected to encounter ahead. Will kept the pace slow for Maddy's sake
and even his. He paused every few feet to listen, both
for the helicopter returning and for the two gunmen.
If they'd been hunkered down here for two days, they
might have grown careless. Careless enough to talk, to
set a fire to dry out the socks and pant legs they'd gotten wet when they slid on wet moss into the creek, tu-
multuous with snowmelt.

The sound he did eventually hear was one he'd expected. He'd left his pack close by where Torrent Creek
roared into Stetattle Creek.

His next task was to figure out whether there was any
easy way to get over Torrent, or whether they needed to
find a way to yet again cross to the other side of Stetattle

Creek. Shortly thereafter they'd come on Jay Creek and several others joining their waters to Stetattle, too. Each addition made their way more perilous—and, damn, he wished he didn't feel as if the two of them were obediently trotting like cattle into a chute.

AN HOUR LATER the helicopter did pass over them again. Will thought it hovered briefly a short distance downstream, but the density of the rain forest growth meant he couldn't see it. Had it stopped to drop off supplies? If so, had it flagged the trap he and Maddy were meant to spring?

Fueled by determination and probably not much else, Maddy kept going. They weren't more than a hundred yards from Torrent Creek when he led her deeper into the tangle to where he'd left his pack.

When he pulled out most of what he had left in the way of food, Maddy shook her head and said dully, "I'm not really hungry."

"Eat anyway." He handed her the water bottle. "Didn't I give you some raisins? Those should give you a boost."

A short one, about all sweets were good for.

For a moment she looked mulish, but after taking a long drink and returning the bottle to him, she produced the raisins and ate them slowly. Will confined himself to a small handful of almonds and a little bit of mixed dried fruit.

Then he pored over his contour map again. In theory, they'd reach this end of the Stetattle Creek trail in no more than an hour or two, depending on the difficulties they met during that distance. Unfortunately, from what he'd read in guidebooks, that didn't necessarily mean anything. In fact, it might not be possible to find any trace of trail there. It apparently wasn't maintained with any regularity. Only about the last mile, leading into the small town of Diablo, saw much traffic at all.

Still…if he were the gunmen, he'd set the ambush above Jay Creek, where the trail ended on the map. Hardy hikers must occasionally push on that far.

Will had no doubt these men would be willing to kill anybody who saw them, even a family. They must be aware that would make them hunted men, however. Most people would be missed almost right away.

Whereas if they could kill him and Maddy and carry their bodies even a few hundred yards from the creek, they might never be found. Will had registered for his climb, but would anyone really notice if he didn't reappear? Maybe after a while somebody would wonder about the abandoned Jeep, but that could take weeks. And Maddy had been on the plane that went down. If the pilot had filed a flight plan, there should already be a search in progress for the downed plane. If he hadn't, any search from the air would be happening well south of here. The route the small Cessna had taken deep into the North Cascades wasn't a logical one to deliver passengers to Everett.

When the plane was eventually found, rescue personnel would assume Maddy had lived but was direly injured and had wandered away. She could be anywhere. By that time—a minimum of a week after the plane went down?—the chances of her still being alive would be considered minimal.

It was just too bad that Judge Brian Torkelson's minions knew she wasn't dead.

Will especially disliked leaving Maddy this time, but he wanted to complete another leg of their hike out before stopping for the night. He shouldered his pack again and looked down at her. He'd swear she'd lost more weight than should be possible in a matter of only days.

She gazed up at him. "Be careful, Will."

She'd been sitting close enough to see the map as he studied it and would have reached the same conclusion he had: they were close to the spot where they were meant to die.

"I will." He hesitated. "If you want to lie down and rest, I can put a few branches on top of you."

"There's not much I could do if I were awake anyway, is there?"

No. He'd actually considered leaving the Glock with her, but remembered her holding it in shaking hands when he first came on her. All she had to do was panic and shoot a bear or deer and she'd give away their location.

He wasn't convinced she could pull the trigger to kill someone anyway.

If he, on the other hand, had a chance to take out one of the men, he wouldn't hesitate.

So he used his pocketknife to cut a few willow and alder branches, laid them gently atop her and said, "Sleep tight."

Walking away, Will wished she'd laughed. Her retreat into silence told him that either the pain was wearing her down, or the infection was gaining ground.

On his own, with no enemy between him and civilization, he could have pushed on and been in Diablo before dark. As it was, even if they could get past the gunmen, nothing he'd read about the trail made him think it was navigable by flashlight. Which meant another night.

When he glanced back, he discovered Maddy was already lost from his sight.

Will moved as carefully as he could, stopping every few strides to listen, to look. If he was right, the two men weren't mountain climbers or even necessarily hikers. They were probably ex-military, which gave them some skill, but not any level of comfort with a landscape so different from any in Iraq or Afghanistan.

Will could say the same about himself, except he and several high school friends had done some climbing up here and in the Olympic Mountains. They'd climbed Mount Shasta first, of course, the volcano in their own neighborhood. Then they'd done Mount Rainier. The summer after his high school graduation and right before he enlisted, they came up to climb Glacier Peak, the most inaccessible of the northwest volcanoes and possibly the toughest climb, too. They'd been lucky to hook up with a couple of men who actually knew what they were doing. Standing on the summit of Glacier had been one of the more exhilarating moments of Will's life.

Maybe that was what he was doing up here in the North Cascades: trying to recapture remembered happiness. Except that this time he hadn't climbed with friends or even strangers. He'd have said he was best off on his own…until he'd found Maddy.

He watched for a chance of crossing Stetattle along here, but could see that wasn't an option. The land on the far side climbed too steeply from the creek. That meant they instead had to cross Torrent Creek…which would be an ideal place to set a trap.

When he knew he was getting close, Will left his pack behind and bent low as he crept forward, trying not to so much as shake the leaves. Long training and experience allowed him to become a ghost. He was hunting. His sharpened senses threw him back until momentarily the where and when blurred in his mind.

But the nonstop roar of the waterfalls that made up Torrent Creek as it plunged from near the summit of Elephant Butte pulled him back to the present. When the white water tumbling over rocks came into sight, he lifted his binoculars and began his search.

A tiny movement, a glint of something metallic, gave them away. He zeroed in on them, wishing he was looking through a rifle scope rather than binoculars. No such luck, and they were well out of range of a handgun.

Wearing the green camouflage that blended eerily well with the lush surroundings, they had set up above a fallen tree that made a convenient bridge across Torrent Creek. From where Will crouched, it appeared to be the *only* way to cross.

One of the two men lay on his belly with his AR-47 on a bipod. Behind him and screened by a few twisted alders and what might be a cedar, the second man sat with his back to the trunk of a large fir. His hands moved… He was eating. Will couldn't quite tell what. His own stomach cramped but his awakened rage made it easy to ignore his physical needs.

These men were prepared to kill a courageous, smart, sweet woman who'd done nothing wrong. No principles involved, no issues of national security, nothing personal at all, just a paycheck. That, or they actively enjoyed hunting their fellow humans. With no conscience, no empathy, the type sometimes made good soldiers—unless an occasion came when they had to depend on their own judgment.

Will had never trained to be a sniper, never wanted to be one, but he'd just changed his mind. Too late.

Now came the hard part: finding a way around the ambush…or a way to take out the men.

Chapter Nine

Maddy started awake, gasping from some horror already dissolving as most dreams did. Opening her eyes to find branches in her face added a jolt, too, until she remembered where she was and why. Then…then she felt as if they were a cozy comforter Will had tucked around her.

She hurt so much. Maddy hadn't said anything to Will, because she heard the rattle of the remaining pills in the bottle each time he doled out painkillers. They were almost gone. He hadn't been taking any that she could see, and she suspected he hurt, too.

If only she had a watch or her phone so she'd know what time it was and how long Will had been gone.

Instead of sitting up, she stayed where she was, curled on her side. She could see where Will would emerge when he returned.

Although she drifted some, she didn't think it was more than another ten minutes or so when he did appear. To her surprise, he still carried the pack.

"You didn't leave it?"

"I want to stay here for the night." His expression was very closed, but anger leaked through.

Pushing branches away, Maddy squirmed until she

could push herself up to a sitting position. "What is it? Did you see them?"

In the act of unzipping his pack, he flicked a glance at her. "I did. They're set up just across Torrent Creek where it enters Stetattle. They found the obvious place to cross and assume we're dumb enough to use it."

"What are we going to do?"

The gray of his eyes had chilled, leaving her in no doubt that the soldier had taken the forefront. "I scouted farther up and found another way across. It's…not easy to get to, and scary as hell. The log isn't more than about ten inches in diameter. We'll have to shimmy across on our butts, and, damn, I wish I'd brought a rope."

"Okay," she said, refusing to surrender to fear. Or maybe she was just too tired, hurt too much, to be bothered by the possibility of an awful outcome.

Will studied her broodingly. "We'll see how you feel tomorrow. There is an alternative."

His grim tone awakened apprehension in her. "What is it? Are you…you won't leave me and go for help, will you?"

"No, although that might be smart." He frowned. "Which reminds me…" Suddenly, he began digging in his pack. He came up with a smartphone. "I wonder… hey, look at that. About time the damn phone isn't just deadweight. I might be able to make a call."

"You can't!" she exclaimed in alarm.

"Wouldn't it be better to trust some search and rescue people than die?" he asked harshly.

"You think Torkelson doesn't have someone watching for anyone carried out of the park?" she scoffed. "It's not that hard to get to someone in the hospital, and that's assuming they're not waiting at the trailhead to gun me and everyone else down."

He stared at her without blinking for at least a minute. Then, muttering something she was glad not to have heard, he dropped the phone, scrubbed both hands over his face and let his shoulders sag. "I do know that. But you have a fever, we aren't eating enough and every step must hurt like hell. Now I'm telling you we have to climb an extra thousand feet or so, scoot on our butts over a raging torrent, then whack our way across a steep downslope to get behind these—" He swallowed whatever he'd meant to call them. "Oh, and assuming we succeed, we then have several *more* miles of bushwhacking and river crossings to go."

"I can—"

As if she hadn't opened her mouth, he shook his head and said, "Maybe plan B makes the most sense."

Bothered by his expression, the way the muscles in his cheeks and jaw had tightened, Maddy asked, "And what's that?"

"I cross without you, circle behind the bastards and kill them."

"Execute them."

His eyes no longer gave away any emotion at all. "If all goes well."

Feeling semi-hysterical, she said, "You mean, if they don't see you in time to kill *you*."

"That would be the downside." He didn't shrug, but he might as well have. *Hey, no biggie,* he was saying.

Spitting mad, she snapped, "You think I don't *care* if you die?"

"It's been my worry all along that if anything happens to me, you're screwed."

"I should just worry about myself? Like you don't *matter*?"

Now he looked faintly wary. "I didn't say that."

"You did! I'd rather die myself than have you do something that…that stupid!"

He blinked a couple of times. "We're at war, Maddy."

"Maybe we are, but we both have to make it out of here. Besides…"

His eyebrows climbed. "Besides?"

"To kill two men you don't know from behind seems wrong. I mean, this is America. You fought for the rights we believe in, for due process."

His reaction was somewhere between pity and a sneer. "In battle you don't give someone a chance to say, 'Oh, sorry, didn't really mean to shoot you.' Not when their damn gun is pointing at your head. Those two SOBs already tried to strafe us. Now they're set up in a blind waiting for us to walk into range. When I saw them, one lay in classic sniper position with his rifle positioned on a bipod. What do you think, I should shout across the river, 'We'll give you a chance to do the right thing and pack up and leave'?"

When he put it that way, Maddy felt foolish. Of course he was right. She realized that what bothered her wasn't so much the idea of bloodshed as it was what summarily killing those two men would do to Will. He hadn't said so, but he'd come back from war injured badly enough to need many months of rehab. He could well be dealing with some PTSD. He maintained internal walls that had to be hiding something. And now, thanks to her, he was thrown back into battle.

She didn't want to be the reason he had to kill.

"I've made it this far," she said, chin up. "I feel lousy, but I'm not on the verge of collapse. I can climb, and crossing the creek on a skinny log will probably be harder for you than me—"

"Except that you'll be doing it one-handed."

Holding his gaze, Maddy made sure he saw her determination. "If I have to, I'll take my arm out of the sling. It won't kill me."

"Not a good idea."

Eyes locked, they held a stare, neither wanting to back down. In the end, Will relented.

"We'll try it your way."

"Thank you."

He grunted and said, "Let me fire up the stove to heat water for coffee. I'll make sure we have enough for a morning cup, too. I want us to make an early start."

Maddy nodded, even as she couldn't help thinking sleep wouldn't come easily tonight given the worries that were bound to get in the way.

DEEP SHADOWS REACHED them long before sunset. Will had earlier laid out the pad and sleeping bag. Maddy and he sat on it, her cross-legged, him with long legs outstretched. Clouds blocked the moon and had him grumbling about the possibility of rain. Naturally, he had a tarp folded in his pack, which he took out in case of need.

Dinner consisted of a few nuts and a candy bar for her, an energy bar for him. Maddy had a suspicion he hadn't fairly divided the nuts, and called him out on it.

Those broad shoulders lifted. "I've gone without food plenty of times in my life. You're more vulnerable right now. I'll stay strong for a few more days."

She wanted to object, but couldn't. Her stomach was already taking sharp exception to the news that a nice stir-fry or pizza or a juicy hamburger weren't forthcoming.

"You know," he remarked, "if I took those two worthless bastards out, we could raid their packs for food."

The thread of humor in his voice sparked hers.

"Okay, that's tempting…but no."

"Yeah, thought you'd say that."

The night wasn't entirely silent. She could hear the creek, rustles all around them. Bats darted into sight and out of it as fast. Mosquitoes whined and she or Will would slap irritably at them. A series of hoots almost had to be from an owl. Once a darker bulk waddled by not ten feet from them.

"Porcupine," Will murmured.

She held her breath until it was gone. "Thank goodness we haven't met up with one."

"They're nocturnal."

"Oh." Maddy was beginning to realize how ignorant she was about everything from the geology of these mountains to the birds and flowers, mammals and fish that made their home here. Today she'd noticed mushrooms beneath trees and she'd caught sight of a lizard. Except for the flies and—whack!—the mosquitoes, she didn't even recognize the insects.

Once it was safely dark, she said, "You don't have to answer, but… I was wondering if you have PTSD."

Will didn't move for a long time. She couldn't even hear him breathe. At last he said slowly, "Sure, to some degree. Most of us who've seen much combat probably do. I'm holding it together, if that's what you're asking."

"No." Maddy reached out blindly to lay a hand on his arm. "I wondered, that's all."

He covered her hand with his. "I've needed more solitude and quiet than usual. I don't love cities. That's… something I'll have to get over if I go—"

Despite the way his hand tightened on hers, she asked, "Go where?"

"Oh, maybe back to school. I haven't decided."

His tone held a warning. He didn't want to tell her his plans. That stung, since he knew everything about her. She had to remind herself that he had no obligation to balance the scales. He'd jumped in to save her life, not to become her best friend or more.

And that, Maddy knew suddenly, was why his retreat hurt. She was falling in love with this man, and obviously the feeling wasn't reciprocated.

She started the laborious process of getting up. "I think I'll brush my teeth now."

Without argument, he reached for the pack where he kept their toiletries.

HOLDING MADDY IN his arms, Will looked up at the canopy of trees and the complete darkness beyond that told him clouds still blocked the moon. He wasn't at all sleepy.

Part of his tension had to do with Maddy, who he suspected was pretending she was asleep. The few last words they'd exchanged had been practical. Once they'd arranged themselves on the pad, covered by the open sleeping bag, she'd said, "Good night," which he'd echoed. Nothing since.

He knew what she felt like asleep, and this wasn't it. He also knew he was responsible for her withdrawal. Kissing her had scared him. Even thinking about telling her his plans—better labeled as hopes—stirred up his insecurities.

If he couldn't get over his inferiority complex, he'd have to walk away from her once he knew she was safe to go on with her life. Was that what he wanted?

No. And yes. He couldn't stand hearing condescension or the wrong brand of kindness from Maddy, of all people.

"You okay?" he asked softly.

"Mmm."

Will smiled. Stubborn woman was giving him the silent treatment, which he deserved.

"I'm sorry," he said a minute later.

Sounding sincere but frosty, she said, "You have nothing to be sorry for."

He was still smiling, he realized. Maybe that was what pushed him over. "I'm hoping to go to medical school. I've been studying for the MCAT."

"Will!" She lifted her head, although he knew she couldn't really see him. "That's wonderful. The years as a medic have to be a big plus."

"I hope so," he said a little stiffly. The training had been far more extensive than even a stateside paramedic received. In the midst of battle, military medics had to act without concern for their personal safety. With even a field hospital often hours away, they sometimes even had to perform rough and ready surgery.

"Are you already set on a branch of medicine?"

He hesitated. "No. Maybe trauma, but—" He'd seen too many broken, bleeding bodies already "—I like the idea of family medicine. Being the first line of defense."

"I like that." She laid her head on his shoulder again and wriggled a little as if burrowing in closer. "You'll be an amazing doctor. I can give you a testimonial."

Will chuckled. "I'll keep that in mind. Now, go to sleep."

Good advice.

Actually, once he knew she slept, he allowed himself to drop off, too.

Barely past dawn, they each had a cup of coffee— a little weak, since he was running out—and ate the last of their food. He gave her the last painkillers, too.

If they could get around the trap, he could carry her if he had to.

Not *if*, Will told himself. When. A positive attitude worked.

Even so, today was their fifth day.

Half an hour of bushwhacking brought them within twenty yards or so of where he'd crouched yesterday and spotted the gunmen. During the hike he'd made the decision to leave his pack behind. He'd take the few essentials in it—his car keys, phone, wallet, binoculars and the Glock as well as the ice ax, while making absolutely certain there wasn't anything left that could be used to identify him. He asked Maddy if she was especially attached to anything. She pondered and shook her head. If they were stuck out here for another night, he might be sorry, but he needed to be able to help her and to move quietly and swiftly.

Leaving her, he crept forward again. The sky was still pearly, but damned if the men weren't in position and appearing alert. He studied them carefully, in part to be sure they were the same two he'd seen. He'd worried all along that there could be more than two. If he was right in thinking the helicopter had stopped to hover near them yesterday, it could have been dropping off more troops.

Personally, if he'd been setting up this op, he'd have left one man in position where they were while having the other work his way up that side of Torrent Creek in case his quarry did exactly what he and Maddy intended to do. His gut said these two were overconfident, smugly certain the woman injured in the plane crash and whatever man accompanied her wouldn't have the backcountry expertise or the stamina to overcome the challenges.

He went back for Maddy, and they began the tortuous trek up the steep slope above the creek plummeting down from the mountain above.

MADDY DIDN'T KNOW how she could go on. She'd quit caring if she lived or died. She thought she'd have collapsed long since if she hadn't assured Will she could do this. Pride. What stupid motivation.

If it works...

She reached for a sturdy alder branch, drew a deep breath and heaved herself up. Her chest and shoulder exploded with pain. In the distant reaches of her head, she knew that every time she used her arm to pull herself upwards, she did bad things to the broken ends of her collarbone, even if the damage was on the other side of her chest. In between, the agony would subside to a dull ache, but this...

I can't do it. I shouldn't have said I could.

He'd given her the last ibuprofen this morning, only two pills.

Will paused and turned back, the worry on his face giving her the strength to reach for his hand and let him hoist her the next few feet.

Same result: pain that felt like a knife thrust into her shoulder and twisted. Her vision dimmed, but she focused on his eyes, as dark as charcoal right now.

He knows.

"We're almost there," he said in a low voice. "You're doing great. Five more minutes."

Five more minutes. She couldn't do this.

Yes, she could. *Five more minutes.* She took his hand again.

A branch whipped across her face. Maddy knew

without touching her cheek that she was bleeding. At least it hadn't struck her across the eyes.

Five more minutes.

"Almost there."

If she could just *rest*.

"We're here, sweetheart. We can take a break."

His tenderness made her eyes sting. With an arm around her waist, he lowered her to sit on a rock. It was a minute before the pain abated enough for her to take a look at the log lying across the head of a viciously foaming cataract. If she fell…well, the first rocks she'd hit were only about ten feet below, but then she'd be bounced—or swept by the white water—down another ten feet, and another.

Scary. Wasn't that the word Will had used?

Normally, she'd be able to stroll right across it, if only it wasn't soaking wet.

Close behind her, Will was scanning the other bank through the binoculars. Not looking entirely happy, he slung the strap across his body again.

"Looks like we're alone up here."

She nodded, because it seemed like the thing to do.

He growled suddenly. "I'd give anything to be able to rope you up while you cross."

"What about you? You're so much bigger. What if—" Maddy couldn't finish.

His mouth twisted into a smile. "I'll be okay. Promise."

She tried to smile, too, when she wanted to grab hold and never let go. She didn't know why he hadn't kissed her again, but…

His head bent to hers. "How about a kiss for luck?"

Unhesitating, thankful, Maddy lifted her face to his. The kiss was achingly gentle, heart-wrenchingly sweet.

She forgot the pain, forgot what lay ahead of them, lost herself in a kiss nothing like any she'd experienced. When it ended, she barely held back from saying, *I love you.* This might be the right moment…but it could as well be the worst of moments.

INCHING ALONG THE log that lay over Torrent Creek was the most hair-raising thing Will had done in a long while, and that included some journeys through dark, narrowing sandstone caves, crouching behind a tree or rock formation half his size as a troop of Taliban wound its way past only feet away from him.

This was damned uncomfortable for a man, besides. He'd never had a problem with heights, but he was going to make an exception for this. The idea of slipping off, not being able to catch himself, hearing Maddy's cry…

He forced himself to concentrate on what he was doing.

He'd like to feel relief when he reached the other side, but his tension only ratcheted up. Watching Maddy scooting over the skinny log above the torrent, only able to use one hand to propel herself, was going to be one of the hardest things he'd ever done.

He blew out air, rolled his shoulders, finally taking a minute to search the overgrown creek valley through the binoculars. Nothing stood out.

Didn't mean he could relax.

He had to hold on to his self-control with both hands when he called over the roar of falling water, "Your turn."

It killed him just watching how long it took her to rise to her feet. She stumbled once reaching the bank. Will closed his eyes. He would do *anything*…but couldn't help at all.

She straddled the log the way he had, scooted forward two or three times then stopped and worked the sling past her elbow, slipping her arm out of it. He kept his mouth clamped shut. Whether she could stand the pain if she had to clamp hold with both arms, he didn't know, but having the arm free if she started to slide was smart.

Maddy winced as she cautiously straightened her injured arm before pulling it back against her body. Still, with just the one hand on the log, she scooted forward again, and again.

Will stood on the bank, his hands flexing into fists, loosening, knotting. He'd have paced, except he couldn't take his eyes off her.

Spray shimmered on her hair. She didn't look at him at all. Instead, she stared at the log just in front of her with burning intensity.

"Come on, come on," he chanted under his breath. "You can do it. Keep going. That's it."

She passed halfway. A moment later she wobbled, reached out with her injured arm and steadied herself. He thought she cried out, but he couldn't hear her. She immediately bent forward, cradling her arm.

Shuddering, Will felt rooted where he was. His knuckles ached and his fingernails bit into his palms.

"Keep going. Please. Keep going."

Maddy never looked up. Just slowly straightened, stared fixedly ahead of herself and resumed inching forward.

The moment she cleared the bank, he snatched her up into his arms.

Chapter Ten

Will thought they were at an elevation of between fifteen hundred and two thousand feet. Maddy wondered why he cared. They were slipping and slithering along a side hill that wasn't as steep as where they'd been when this all began, but was difficult going anyway. Especially since she so often had to grab a branch for support, wrenching her torso and collarbone. Even so, it was initially a relief compared to their trek straight uphill.

Fifteen minutes along, her thigh muscles and ankles began to protest. The positive was that they were moving slowly. Will obviously intended to be ultra-careful.

They had barely exchanged a word since they left Torrent Creek behind. Maddy knew they were passing right above the murderous pair still lying in wait, maybe as little as five hundred feet separating them. If one of them decided to scout around…

She clenched her teeth to keep any gasps from escaping.

They came to yet another creek carrying snowmelt from above. It wasn't as wide or powerful as Torrent Creek, but Will left her to hunt for a safe way to cross. They ended up descending to a place where they could scramble over on mossy rocks. One of her feet got soaked, as did one of his. She dismissed the squishy feeling as a minor discomfort.

Sometime in the next hour, Will began angling them downward. Instead of the miserable creek-bed jungle they'd previously beaten their way through, this was a magnificent forest. Maddy recognized big-leaf maples mixed into evergreens, including a few massive trunks of ancient trees. It was so green everywhere she looked. Moss grew everywhere, and lacy swags of pale green and gray draped from branches. Lichen, Will told her.

They were so close. She'd looked at the map enough to know they would meet up with the Stetattle Creek trail anytime. And yes, Will had read that the upper half or more wasn't maintained, but at least there'd *been* a trail there once upon a time. That had to be better than the completely untamed wilderness they'd been crossing, didn't it?

They ended up finding a remnant of the trail by accident. This time it was Will who lost his footing. Swearing, he skidded down a sharp drop-off and, from her perspective, thudded to a sudden stop.

"Hot damn," he said. "It's flat here, Maddy. See if you can get down on your feet instead of your ass like I did."

There were purple berries on one of the shrubs. She reached out without thinking, made herself ask, "Will? There are berries here. Are they edible?"

"Purple?"

"Yes."

"Huckleberries. Good eating."

Maddy picked and stuffed several handfuls into her mouth before cautiously picking her way down to him, where she found him doing the same.

"We'd probably better not have any more." The hand

that reached for her was stained purple. So was hers, for that matter. "Don't know how much our stomachs can handle. Besides…"

Besides, they were so close to escaping.

Without a word, she set off behind him.

WITHIN MINUTES THE trail vanished, having clearly fallen victim to a washout. Will had to lead Maddy up a sharp climb before angling back down again. Another creek emerged from a sharp cut in the slope. This time he and Maddy simply scrambled through it, past caring about wet boots.

He started paying attention to the sun. More hours had passed than he'd realized, which lessened their chances of meeting a party of hikers coming up from Diablo. Will really didn't want anyone else to set eyes on Maddy.

As they kept moving, he became increasingly wary, stopping her at regular intervals to listen and look, both ahead and behind. Anyone pursuing them would expect them to pop out in the tiny hamlet of Diablo. Given how major the operation was that had been set in motion to find her, Will expected that someone would be hanging out between here and the parking lot, waiting for them.

Twice more they had to detour around stretches where the trail was missing, a tree had fallen or a rockfall presented an impassable obstacle. Eventually, the trail began a series of switchbacks taking the steep drop back to the creek. Maddy plodded along, looking at where she was placing her feet. She never lifted her head, even when a doe splashed through yet another tributary right in front of them.

But damn, she was still walking. The strange swelling in his chest, Will finally identified as pride. She'd insisted she could do this, and she had.

Almost.

Just as he started to feel complacent, he heard a voice, followed by a younger, excited one. He turned his head. There.

He grabbed Maddy's arm and steered her up and over a giant fallen tree, rotting and moss-covered. Beyond was a lush cluster of ferns and the hated devil's club. Will coaxed her into lying down but hadn't gotten that far himself when a man and two boys appeared on the trail.

Will smiled and nodded.

"Whatcha doing?" the younger boy asked.

"Having a snack," he said, picking a few berries to demonstrate.

"Oh. Dad, can we…?"

"They're thicker just a little ways up the trail," Will put in. He held up his hand in illustration. "I just decided to grab a last few."

The man, balding and wearing running shoes, said, "Come on, boys."

"There's a landslide and some washouts ahead," Will warned. "You can get around them, but it's a scramble."

With a thanks, the small group moved on. The minute they were out of sight, Will helped Maddy back to her feet, over the log and down the trail.

Even over the gurgle of the creek, he heard the sound of a car engine.

He kept her behind him along the last, short stretch until buildings came into sight. The whole way, his hand hovered over the butt of the Glock. He had to find a place to hide her while he went to get his Jeep.

He spotted what appeared to be a garage. He could drive right up to it.

He steered her around behind it. "Okay, honey, I want you to wait here for me. I'll get the car and come back for you."

Comprehension was slow in coming, but finally she nodded.

To cheer her up, he said, "There's nowhere to eat in Diablo, not even a store, so it's just as well we don't want to hang around anyway. The first real town we come to that has a drive-through burger joint, we're stopping." He didn't mention that it would be some miles. On the map, Newhalem looked like a town but was really just housing for National Park Service and Seattle City Light employees. He was pretty sure there was nothing like a restaurant there.

Maddy's lips were cracked. Damn it, had she been biting them? But those lips also curved. In a croaky voice, she said, "I want a root beer float."

Will grinned at her. "You can have anything your heart desires."

Her eyes more alert, she said, "I'm okay. Go."

Hating to leave her, Will did anyway, strolling as if he wasn't in any hurry at all. A man sitting in an SUV seemed to be watching him...or happened to be idly gazing in his direction. Hard to be sure, but what could he be waiting for? Will nodded in a friendly way then let his own gaze wander.

The hair on his neck prickled when he saw a beefy guy wearing camo cargo pants, a dark green T-shirt and boots striding across the narrow bridge that led into town. The guy looked him over but seemed to dismiss him when Will veered into the parking area and unlocked his Jeep.

Will hated situations like this. He'd lost track of days, but he knew there were too many people around. With this having been the Fourth of July weekend, the campground and trail around the lake were undoubtedly still packed. Plenty of people would have taken a week off. This time of year, climbers and hikers came and went constantly. He hoped he didn't stand out.

If a watcher had noted the Jeep sitting here for over a week and then saw a man who wasn't carrying a pack strolling out of the forest and hopping in, that might catch his attention. Especially when that man didn't head over the bridge to the highway, but instead drove back to the trailhead.

Couldn't be helped—but he'd keep the Glock close at hand.

MADDY HEARD VOICES and car engines, but didn't see anyone as she waited. Still, she felt exposed. She let herself lean on the clapboard wall, but not sit. She knew how hard it would be to get up again.

The growling sound of an engine coming closer made her feel like a rabbit that unexpectedly found itself in the open when a coyote prowled toward it. *Please be Will*, she thought.

It was. He startled her by coming an unexpected way around the building.

He said only, "Let's get out of here," and hustled her into the backseat. "Lie down. I'm going to throw some stuff on top of you."

She crawled in, and seconds later was buried by what she thought was a parka and a blue tarp. A thump was the descent of a boot right beside her head. She couldn't tell where the other boot went.

"Keep down until I tell you otherwise," he said tersely.

The door slammed. The driver-side door opened and closed, and they were moving. They stopped briefly—

"Bridge is narrow," he said, voice low. "I'm letting a camper cross."

Rattling as they passed across the bridge, then the smoother whir of tires on a highway.

"Stay there for a few minutes," Will said, his tone normal. "I want to be sure no one follows us."

A part of her wanted to sit up and *see*, but the motion of the vehicle and the hum of the engine also made her sleepy. She blinked awake when Will said sharply, "Maddy! Are you okay?"

"I…" She worked her mouth. "Yes."

"I think you can sit up if you want."

"I'm kind of comfortable," she admitted.

He laughed. "Okay. Tell you the truth, I'm afraid we won't find a drive-through until we get to Rockport, and that's, I don't know, fifteen, twenty miles."

"Okay," she mumbled, and went back to sleep.

She woke up again when they reached the town of Rockport, but at his suggestion stayed where she was while he went through the drive-through and asked for three cheeseburgers, three orders of French fries, a Coke and a root beer float. Only after he paid, collected the food and pulled out did she untangle herself from the debris on the backseat and sit up.

She'd barely gotten a quick view of lake, trees, mountains, when Will snapped, "Get back down. *Now.*"

Without hesitation, she followed his order, yanking stuff over her with her good hand. "What is it?" she whispered.

"I recognize the SUV behind us." He swore. "I didn't see it when I pulled into the eatery, but if he was hanging back…" Pause. "I think I'll eat and dawdle along, see if he won't give up and pass us."

Her stomach growled and her mouth watered at the smell of burger and fries and the sounds of Will eating, but she lay still, her pulse racing. To get so far and then be caught. They couldn't be so unlucky, could they?

The minutes ticked by. Then, "Yep, there he goes," Will said, but tension remained in his voice. "He took a good look at me as he went by."

"He can't know it's you."

"No, there's no way they got much of a look at me the one time we know they saw us. I'm not wearing the same shirt, and I have plain brown hair. I just hope he's satisfied that I'm alone."

"Can I sit on the floor back here and eat?" She sounded pitiful and didn't care. "I'll duck further down if you tell me to."

"Yeah."

Given the length of his legs, it wasn't surprising that his seat was pushed back so far. Maddy squeezed herself onto the floor on the passenger seat.

Will handed back a bag, then the tall cup with her float.

The salty French fries she crammed into her mouth might taste better than anything she'd ever eaten.

WILL MANAGED TO down his double meal with no trouble even as he kept a sharp eye out during the remainder of the drive, especially when he reached the turn-off from Highway 20 in Concrete. He was renting a log cabin in what seemed like the middle of nowhere, just the way he'd wanted it. Now he didn't love the fact that his cabin was at the end of the road, with no neighbors near enough to hear or see any visitors. Fortunately, he hadn't yet changed the address for his driver's license or car registration from the barracks at Fort Lewis, the army base by Tacoma. He'd be surprised if somebody hadn't noted his license plate number, probably along with others. He couldn't think of any way they'd track him by it, though. Even the army didn't know where he was.

Relaxing, he said, "You can get up if you want. We're almost home."

His home, he reminded himself, not hers. A successful Seattle attorney wouldn't want to live in the back of beyond, even if the commute was possible. Which it wasn't. No, he was giving her temporary refuge, that was all. He couldn't afford to get any ideas.

He heard her struggling to get back up onto the seat. There was a silence as she looked around.

"This doesn't look any different than it did up there." Her surprise was obvious.

"No, my cabin is just outside the Mount Baker National Forest. I don't know if this is technically rain forest, but it feels like it. The things draping from tree limbs are a form of lichen like Old Man's Beard. Takes a really wet climate for them to survive. Looks like someone toilet-papered the trees and no one bothered to clean up, but they grow from the branches. Sort of a moocher, I guess."

"Like me," she said, so softly he suspected he wasn't meant to hear.

The comment gave him a pang. Maddy was no user.

"I don't know about you," he said, "but I'm looking forward to a shower. Wanna race?"

Caught in the rearview mirror, her smile was weak but present.

She'd stiffened up, accepting his help to climb out of

the Jeep. Her head turned as she took in the open forest, the green light filtering through high fir, cedar and
hemlock boughs, the peace. The only sound was the ripple of a small creek that the back deck looked down on.

"It's beautiful." Her voice was hushed in keeping
with the atmosphere.

"I think so," he agreed.

He unlocked the front door and led Maddy in. The
space was open, the only walls enclosing the bathroom.
Steps almost steep enough to be a ladder led up to a loft,
where he slept. A cast-iron stove sat in front of the river
rock chimney. Hewn of fir, the kitchen cabinets fit with
the glossy log walls and small-paned windows. Will was
going to hate to leave this place when the time came.

He nudged Maddy straight into the bathroom and
sat her down on the closed toilet seat. There he helped
her strip to bra and panties, trying desperately to look
at her from the perspective of a medic, not a man who
wanted her.

It didn't prove to be as difficult as he might have
thought, not once he got a good look at how battered
she was. She'd acquired plenty of new bruises, as he
probably had, too. The lump on her collarbone had en-
larged and felt hot to the touch. The gash he already
knew was infected was violently red around the edges
and filled with pus. The only good news he could find
was that the bumps on her head were gone.

His close inspection, he noticed, had brought pink
color to her grimy cheeks. Pretending he didn't realize
she felt self-conscious, he said, "Okay, pain meds, then
shower. If you need help washing your hair, give me a
yell. While you're in there, I'll find you something clean
to wear and a real, honest-to-goodness sling. I'll call my

doctor friend for an antibiotic prescription, too." He sat back on his heels. "You up to this?"

She might look like hell, but she managed a smile. "A shower? Are you kidding?"

He laughed, shook out a couple of the strongest pain pills he had and gave them to her with a glass of water. Surreptitiously, he pocketed a couple of them himself. His hip and thigh throbbed.

While she downed her pills, he set out a pile of clean towels and shook out the bath mat before turning on the water and waiting until it reached a reasonable temperature.

Once he left her alone in the bathroom, Will groaned. He couldn't afford to picture her naked with water sluicing over creamy skin and feminine curves. It helped to remind himself the water was also sliding over a lot of black-and-blue skin, not to mention the virulently infected slice on her hip.

He rubbed his hand over hair made stiff by the bar soap and sweat, and leaned against the kitchen counter while he scrolled to his buddy's number.

"Javier? Will Gannon."

"Will? Damn, it's good to hear from you! How are you?"

He downplayed his physical and emotional issues for his former teammate and, as soon as he could, said, "I have a situation. I'm hoping you'll help me out."

As he'd expected, despite jeopardizing his medical license, Javier Sanchez promptly agreed to submit a prescription for a powerful antibiotic in Will's name to a pharmacy in Sedro-Woolley. Will had opted against the one here in Concrete. Better not to be seen so close to home right now.

MADDY WAS CAREFUL not to give away how much she dreaded being left alone. She understood Will's reasoning; in a small pharmacy like the one in town, he'd be recognized. People might wonder why he needed the antibiotics. Better for him to go somewhere only the pharmacist would see his name, and he'd be forgotten the minute he walked away. He'd decided to do a major grocery shop while he was out, too, and he'd pick up some basic clothes for her, as well, even if he had to drive into Burlington, the next town down the highway.

She helped make a list of her sizes and preferences. Somehow she wasn't surprised to learn he wasn't much of a salad eater, but he promised to pick up a long list of fruits and veggies.

Finally, he looked at her, creases deepening between his eyebrows. "We need to get in touch with your contact at the marshal's service. I'll pick up a burner phone while I'm shopping because I don't want to use my own. Might be better if I make the call from a location away from the cabin, too. Let's hope he isn't off taking a two-week vacation."

The struggle to survive had required all her inner resources in recent days. His reminder brought it all back in a rush, from the shooting to all the consequences that followed.

"If they really were friends, I bet he'd have ditched his vacation to get back."

Will conceded her point with a dip of his head.

"I guess there's no reason to wait," she said, although she felt a cramp of anxiety. What if Scott was wrong about this friend of his? Who would be more likely to have known the details of his plans for picking her up?

"I remember the Robert part."

"Robert Ruzinski."

"And he's a marshal, too."

"That's what Scott said."

Will kept watching her, making her wonder if she was succeeding in hiding all her worries.

"Do you know something about this Ruzinski?" he asked, confirming her suspicions. "Had you ever heard the name before?"

Maddy shook her head. "All I know is that Scott said to trust him, and no one else."

"Okay." He didn't move. "What's worrying you?"

"Can we really trust anyone in the marshal's office?"

After seeming to ponder he said, "I don't think we have a good alternative. You seem to have trusted Rankin."

Past a lump in her throat, she said, "Yes."

"Then I think we need to keep trusting him. Our only alternative is to turn to the Seattle PD detectives who worked the crime."

"What about the FBI?"

"Would they even have jurisdiction?"

"The fact that Torkelson was up to be a federal judge might give them the excuse they need," she suggested.

"That's true." Will hesitated. "Your call."

Maddy remembered the awful last moments with Scott, the way his fingers had bit into hers. His intensity. The moment when his hand fell away.

He'd called Robert Ruzinski a friend as well as a fellow US marshal. His dying words were, *Trust him.* How could she do any less?

She had to clear her throat. "Let's take a chance on Marshal Ruzinski. Although…won't he want to talk to me?"

"Eventually." Will's voice turned steely. "When I trust him."

She offered a wobbly smile. "I'm so lucky to have you."

He brushed that off, as he had all her thanks. A minute later he pocketed the lists and left, after instructing her to keep the doors and windows locked. He approved her plan to nap.

It was all she could do not to roll her eyes like a teenager. She didn't, because he was all that had stood—and probably still did—between her and an assassin.

The sound of the Jeep engine receded, leaving her in a silence that wasn't as soothing as it should be. She'd been fixed on the single goal of getting out of the mountains where she could recover physically. It was weird now to realize how little thought she'd given to all the future steps. Part of that, it occurred to her, was that she'd had to give her independence, every meaningful choice about her life, even her *name*, into the keeping of the US Marshals Service. She'd had no choice but to become a passive participant in the plans. Once in Everett, Scott would have set up meetings with the prosecutorial team, arranged for transportation to the courthouse, armed escort inside. Now...

How could she safely meet with this Ruzinski? What would he want from her? Would Torkelson's minions dare attack her when she arrived at the courthouse? And...what would she *wear*?

Even knowing how silly it was to obsess over something so unimportant, she looked down at the navy blue sweatpants that stayed up only because of the drawstring, and that she'd be tripping over if she hadn't rolled up the legs half a dozen times. No panties beneath, and no bra until she could wash both. T-shirt sized for a man with formidable shoulders, which meant it swamped her and hung to midthigh.

She could hardly stop by her apartment—former apartment?—to pick up suitable clothes and heels for her court appearance. She didn't dare call her mother and have her mail an appropriate outfit.

Humor came to her rescue as she tried to imagine Will shopping at Nordstrom for a stylish business suit.

Surely, if he'd lend her his credit card, she could buy what she needed online.

Chapter Eleven

Will had belatedly realized that he could have accomplished all his errands at Fred Meyer, if only he'd
thought to ask Javier to send the prescription here. As
it was, he picked it up in Sedro-Woolley, then continued
down Highway 20 to Burlington, a small city straddling
I-5, the major north-south freeway connecting California, Oregon and Washington to Mexico on one end and
Canada on the other.

He'd never had a reason to shop for women's clothing, which made this a first. Picking out jeans, shorts, T-
shirts and a sweater for Maddy was no problem. Socks
and flip-flops, he could handle. The lingerie department
was another story. Feeling conspicuous, he struggled to
choose a bra and panties. Since he didn't want to linger, he went for items as close as he could get to what
she'd been wearing.

He picked up a hair dryer, brush, elastics and gel,
too, although he had to wing it where the gel was concerned when he couldn't find the brand she'd suggested.
Groceries came next, then the phone with a charger.

Once he'd stowed his bags in the rear of his Jeep, he
figured the Fred Meyer parking lot was as good a place
as any to charge the phone and make the call.

Frowning as he noticed the time, Will feared the man

might have left the office for the day. He might have to try again in the morning.

It took some doing to reach a real human being, but she listened to his request and said pleasantly, "I'll connect you to Marshal Ruzinski, sir."

He got even luckier when his call was answered on the second ring by a brusque voice. "Ruzinski here."

Amazing.

Now was when it got tricky.

Will had decided to go for blunt.

"I'm calling on behalf of Madeline Kane. Marshal Rankin told her to contact you."

The long silence didn't surprise him. Nor did the cagey response.

"What do you know about Ms. Kane?"

"I'd rather not say yet. Marshal Rankin told her that they had to have been betrayed by somebody within your agency. He said she could trust you. No one else." He paused. "Can she?"

Another silence ensued.

"Give me fifteen minutes," he said abruptly. "I'll call you back."

Satisfied, Will moved the Jeep to the Haggen parking lot half a mile away. He opened the back hatch, rummaged in the bags and came up with a package of Fig Newtons. Good to indulge his sweet tooth while he waited.

When the phone rang, the number that came up was unfamiliar. Will answered with a "Yes?"

"I'm calling from my car using a burner phone. I always keep a few around," Ruzinski said. "Now, tell me what you know."

As uneasy as Will was, they'd made the decision to trust this man. That started now.

"I know that Marshal Rankin had gone to fetch her. They were to stay in Everett, or so he said. She's the prime witness in a trial that starts next week. The small plane crashed in the North Cascades National Park. It broke apart. The pilot was already dead when she found him. Rankin wasn't. He had time to tell her it was a bomb, that she needed to hide."

"She wasn't injured?"

"She was. She has a broken collarbone, humerus, possibly ribs. She was concussed and had multiple gashes and horrific bruising. She is, however, alive and prepared to testify."

Ruzinski swore softly. "Scott and she just disappeared. He drove over the mountains to get her, and that was it. A chartered plane had disappeared. No one has spotted it. That's all we could learn."

"I can tell you where to find the wreckage and the bodies. It's possible the wreckage has been tampered with—say, proof that there was a bomb wiped out. I doubt there was any reason for them to have done anything to the bodies."

"They?" the marshal echoed.

"Black helicopter, markings covered. It dropped two men wearing camouflage and outfitted with heavy packs and machine guns. It appears their task was to find Maddy and make certain she never made it out of the mountains."

"And how do you know all of this?" Ruzinski asked with deep suspicion.

"I found Maddy," Will said simply. He explained that he'd intended to scavenge from the plane, but the helicopter beat him there. "I've been out of Army Spec Ops less than a year. I'm a medic," he added. "I was up there climbing alone when I saw the plane go down."

He summed up the rest of the story in as few words as possible: the shooting, the ambush laid for them at the Torrent Creek crossing. The multiple days it took him and Maddy to make the trek out because of her injuries.

"Ideally, she should get X-rays," he concluded, "but we can't risk taking her to a hospital. I've…acquired some antibiotics to knock out the infection, which is her first hurdle."

"You want me to find a place for her?"

"No." Any offer like that was off the table. "She'll stay with me."

"Good." The marshal's relief was apparent. "You can keep her until the trial?"

"Yes."

"The prosecutor will want to put her through some prep before then. Let me think about that. I'll need to talk to her, too."

"We can arrange that," Will agreed, having expected the demand.

"I need to know who you are, too."

He was less enthusiastic about this, but had assumed he'd have to put his name out there. He'd worry more if he believed he could be found. He'd paid cash, six months up front, for the cabin, for no particular reason. The owner was a guy in his sixties, a Vietnam War vet who'd recognized what Will was going through the minute he'd seen him. At the moment the only snail mail he received was addressed to "occupant." He paid his bills online. The utility company was his only concern.

"Will Gannon. William Bradley Gannon. I should warn you that everyone from the driver's license bureau to Mastercard thinks I still live in the barracks at Fort Lewis."

"And you don't."

"Nope."

"That's fortunate."

"Do you have a plan yet?"

Ruzinski wanted to start by finding the wreckage. Will did his best to pinpoint the location and added, "The plane did some damage coming down. I'm sure the pilot did his best to reach an elevation with smaller trees to break the force. Should be visible from the air."

"All right. I'll get search and rescue out to find it, and bomb experts to examine what's left of the plane. I'd really like to recover the bodies. Scott and I have been close friends for a lot of years."

Hearing the grief, Will held his tongue.

"I'll speak to the prosecutor, too, but only her. Officially, I heard about a crash, but don't know if it was the plane Scott chartered or not, and if so whether there's any chance of survivors."

"You trust her?"

"I do. She's good. They start jury selection Monday, you know. She seems confident they can convict Mooney—he's the guy who did the hit—even without Maddy's testimony, but Torkelson is another matter. My call will make her day. Maybe even her year."

Will smiled. "You should know that Maddy is a remarkable woman. She told me what happened. I don't think she needs a whole lot in the way of prepping, especially given that she's an attorney herself."

"Never hurts to plan for what the defense will throw at her."

"Only if we can assure her safety."

"Can I call you at this number?"

"Better if we set up a time and I call you."

They settled on two days hence, eleven in the morning. Call over, Will did some meandering through Burlington until he found a big green dumpster in an alley. He wiped the phone clean with the hem of his shirt, dropped it on the pavement and stomped on it before tossing it in the dumpster.

A glance at his watch told him he'd been gone longer than he'd intended. Urgency to return to Maddy thrummed inside him.

He kept a sharp eye on the rearview mirror during the drive and, because there were several cars behind him when he reached Concrete, he continued on a couple of miles until he could turn into a driveway framed in dense foliage. He waited until he heard no traffic, backed out and got back on the highway, eastbound now. No one was behind him; no one appeared interested when he turned off the highway this time.

MADDY HAD NO warning before the front door opened. Her heart came close to stopping. She hadn't heard Will's Jeep—her gaze swung wildly. She could go out the back door—

"Maddy?" he called.

"Will?" His name came out in a near whisper.

Apparently too quiet, because he roared, "Maddy?"

"Here!"

He strode into the kitchen and his eyes locked on to hers. His face had been honed by some tension. "You scared me," he said.

"I didn't hear your Jeep. I thought—" Without thinking, she flew into his arms.

They closed hard around her. "Log walls are good insulation."

"Oh," she mumbled against his chest. "I'm sorry, I—"

"Hell with it," he interrupted.

When she lifted her head in surprise, his mouth closed over hers, hot and hard. The kiss seemed to explode. His tongue drove into her mouth and she met it with her own. Her body became hypersensitive. Her palm rested on his chest and she felt the hammer of his heart. His hand wrapped her hip, his fingers digging into her buttock. The ridge against her belly had her rocking, pushing herself up on tiptoe as if she was climbing him. He nipped her lower lip and she did the same to him. He broke the kiss long enough for them both to gasp for air and then bent to reclaim her mouth.

Or so she thought. The heat in his eyes didn't diminish, but they narrowed slightly. She saw his internal struggle on his face. Finally, he rested his forehead against hers.

"Damn. I didn't mean to…"

His withdrawal stung. She didn't want to hear why he shouldn't have kissed her.

Maddy lifted her hand away from his chest and stepped back. Given no choice, he let his hands drop. They stared at each other for a searing moment. Maddy was overwhelmed by everything she felt: desperate passion, an unfamiliar bone-deep hunger, light-headedness, an echo of the fear that a stranger had entered the house, and so much anger.

"You've been through so much," he said slowly.

"Think of the damage you might have done," she said, her flippancy slicing like a knife. She hoped. "With me so enfeebled and all."

"You've had a raging fever for days," Will snapped. He sounded really mad. "Broken bones. And me? I was about to set you on the table and—" Color streaked the jut of his cheekbones.

For an instant all she saw was herself, stripped of

the sweatpants—and that wouldn't have been hard to do, especially since she had no panties beneath them— lying back on the kitchen table, legs spread. Will standing between them, ripping at the snap and zipper on his jeans...

She blinked a couple of times. She'd melt where she stood if she let herself take the fantasy any further at all.

As an excuse to turn away from him, she opened the refrigerator and grabbed a soda. "Forget about it." Without letting herself look at him, Maddy went to the living room and plopped down on the sofa. There was only silence behind her.

Will took his time but did follow her. Instead of going to his usual spot at the other end of the sofa, he handed her a pill bottle and then chose a chair.

"Quicker you start on these, the better."

"I hope they work fast."

"I talked to Ruzinski."

"He believed you? I mean, about me?"

"He had to. I knew too much." Will reported most of the conversation virtually verbatim, or so she guessed from shifts in intonation.

"So he didn't want to put me in a safe house or something."

"No, I think he was relieved to be able to leave you with me. Who could he trust? I blindsided him. Now he has to look at everyone in his office and wonder."

"Unless jury selection drags, I should be testifying next week." She could hardly believe the time had really come.

"They sound like they're on schedule."

"Wait, didn't you buy groceries?"

"Crap!" He shot to his feet and jogged out the front door. "What am I thinking?"

HE'D LET A stew of lust and fear, frustration and anger
do his thinking for him, that was what.

Damn, he loved kissing her, but he was still brooding
when the two of them sat down to dinner. He'd fallen
on her like a rabid wolf. He was still ticked that she'd
taken offense at his apology. Had he *ever* discounted
her intelligence or her strength? No. So what was her
problem? He hadn't been rejecting her! All she'd had to
do was look at him to see how aroused he was.

Will tried to shut down that kind of thinking. His
meal sat untouched in front of him. Maddy was talking,
wondering if she could safely call her parents.

"I don't know," he said. "We'd better ask Ruzinski.
If there's any chance their phone has a tap on it…"

"But all that would give them is a phone number,
right? If I use one of those prepaid phones, how could
that hurt?"

Surprised, he said, "Your parents still have a land-
line?"

"Well…they did a year ago."

"I doubt they'd have dropped it given that they're
probably desperate to hear from you," he said thoughtfully.

"I'm sure they wouldn't."

She looked so eager, Will hated to shake his head,
but he did anyway. "We're talking to Ruzinski Saturday. After a year…"

Maddy made a face. "What's another day anyway?"

A few bites later Will said, "You're close to your
parents?"

"Yes. Less so to my sisters, just because our lives
have diverged." She frowned at him. "What about you?
You haven't mentioned your mother. And is your dad
still in California?"

"Mother took off when I was ten. She called and sent birthday cards, that kind of thing, for a few years, but the intervals got longer and eventually…" He shrugged. The hurt had dulled to nothingness, but the contrast to her family life held its own brand of pain. "My father is still in the same run-down, single-wide trailer planted on a piece of dirt in a park with a couple of rows of others just like it. No," he corrected himself, "some look worse, but a few have a woman who likes to have flowering baskets or even tries to grow roses. Nobody living there has any money or the slightest hope of that changing. They get by."

Maddy listened with crinkled brow and eyes that showed compassion. "Do you see him?"

"Sure." Will smiled crookedly. "We get along, more or less. I just didn't want to stay in the area. Too easy never to leave."

"I understand that." Her smile betrayed something he didn't understand. "I guess I never really tried to leave home."

"You went to Stanford."

"Then came back to Seattle. Safe in the nest." As if to end the conversation, she pushed back her chair and rose with her dirty dishes in hand.

He didn't let her reach the sink before he shoved back his chair violently. "That's ridiculous! Our lives were *nothing* alike. Why wouldn't you want to stay close to home?"

She set down the dishes then faced him. "That's what I always told myself, but you make me wonder if I shouldn't have…stretched a little more. You know?"

"You're trying to turn this around," he accused.

"What do you mean?"

Will would swear she was genuinely puzzled. He

just shook his head. He didn't have to remind her that her life had changed in a big way this past year. She'd *stretched*, all right, to survive a plane crash and a grueling trek out of the mountains.

EITHER THE CONVERSATION at dinner or the kiss had changed something between her and Will. Clearly, he was ashamed of his background, but call her naive, because she couldn't see why. All she knew was that he'd been keeping his distance in the past day and a half. So obviously so, she'd retreated, as well, not talking much or even looking at him when he was likely to notice.

Maddy's stress level would have been climbing anyway. Her appearance in the courthouse was barely a week away, if that. Did the defense have a clue that anything was wrong? Or had the man paying them have hinted that oh-so-conveniently she wouldn't be able to appear?

No, she didn't want to believe that. The firm hired to defend hit man Kevin Mooney was a respectable one, so far as she knew. One of the associates was a friend of Maddy's from law school. If they understood that the major prosecution witness had been threatened or killed to prevent her appearance, surely they would have refused to continue defending Mooney.

On Friday Will left CNN running all day long, although he jumped channels when local news came on. As tense as she felt, she became a news junkie right alongside him. At least the local politics gave them something impersonal to talk about during meals.

That, and her delight that her temperature was normal after only twenty-four hours on the antibiotic. Much of her headache and general achiness went away with the fever.

The evening local news featured the discovery of a Cessna Skyhawk that had crashed in the North Cascades National Park. Maddy straightened, clutching her broken arm, her gaze riveted to the television.

A news anchor, tone grave, said, "We've received confirmation that this is the plane reported missing after departing on a charter flight out of a small airfield near Republic in eastern Washington." Footage of the short runway and the hangars flashed on screen before returning to the solemn news anchor. "Authorities also confirmed that they have recovered two bodies from the wreckage, one of whom was the pilot." He talked about Bill Potter and there was a brief interview with his grieving wife. Finally, the anchor concluded by saying, "Authorities are withholding the name of the second victim, likely because they haven't yet been able to notify the next of kin."

The anchors behind the news desk talked briefly about how shocking it was that it had taken so long to locate the plane after the pilot's wife raised the alarm. This was one of the risks taken when the pilot didn't file a flight plan, they agreed.

One turned brightly to the camera. "Next, we'll be talking to—"

With a stab of his thumb, Will turned off the television.

Maddy wanted to feel numb. The crash had happened a week ago. She'd *been* there. *Bang*. Watching in horrified incredulity as the propeller slowed, stopped turning. Still staring at the darkened TV screen, she saw the surreal scene when she regained consciousness and discovered herself to be hanging upside down. The blood dripping from her sliced hand. The struggle on the steep mountainside to find pieces of the plane. Bill Potter. Scott—

She swallowed and closed her eyes. No, she wasn't numb, even though at the same time it all felt unreal, as if it was part of a movie they'd been watching.

"Are you all right?" Will asked quietly.

A cushion separated them on the sleeper sofa that had seen better days.

"Yes. It's just…" Just what? She shook her head.

"They aren't still lying out there waiting to be found."

Typical Will, to sound so gentle even though he'd been remote since yesterday.

"No." She was squeezing the hand emerging from the splint and sling. "I'm glad." When he didn't comment, she turned toward him. "There was nothing about a bomb."

"I'm going to guess the 'authorities'—" he smiled crookedly "—are withholding a few tiny details. It's also possible, as I told Ruzinski, that the men who dropped from the helicopter did some housekeeping, so to speak."

"It would have been hard to be thorough given how far-flung the pieces were." She was proud of how coolly she said that. As if she hadn't been part of the debris. Hadn't seen how violently the pieces of the small plane had been distributed.

To her astonishment, Will reached out and laid his hand over hers. "You're going to hurt yourself."

"What?" She glanced down. "I'm okay."

"No, you're not." He shifted over to the middle cushion and wrapped his arms around her.

For a moment Maddy stayed stiff. He'd been so clearly determined *not* to touch her; why was he doing this?

But temptation overcame her. No, she wasn't all

right. *She* was about to shatter, and heaven knew where the debris would fall. It had to be the sitting and waiting, almost worse than everything that had come before. With a gasp she fitted herself against his solid body, laid her cheek on his shoulder where she'd so often found shelter during their days fighting to survive. She even let herself slide her unbroken arm around his torso. Except for clenching his shirt in her hand, Maddy collapsed.

She didn't cry, didn't even feel the urge. She needed human contact, that was all—except she knew better. She needed Will. She felt dumb now, having dreamed he felt something for her, that maybe in the future they could explore having a relationship. Well, his recent cool distance told her clearly that wasn't happening, but if he offered comfort, she'd accept it.

They stayed like that for a long time. Maddy focused on his steady breathing, the strength enclosing her, until she felt ready to stand alone again.

Then she carefully withdrew, smiled pleasantly without quite meeting his eyes, and said, "I can relax a little bit when we have a plan. Fingers crossed Marshal Ruzinski *has* one."

"Anxious to get back to your life?"

Maddy had a one-shoulder shrug down pat. "Something like that. It would be good to get an X-ray and maybe even a real cast, to start with."

"I'll second that."

When she headed for the bathroom, he stayed where he was. She had a feeling that a brooding gaze followed her.

Chapter Twelve

Will didn't like making the call from his house, but he liked even less the idea of taking Maddy anywhere. She'd have to go out eventually, but right now it wouldn't surprise him if men weren't still cruising Highway 20, maybe asking questions anywhere they could. They might well know that a guy who seemed to be alone in a Jeep had stopped at the eatery in Rockport and bought three cheeseburgers, all with fries, and two drinks.

If they knew that much, it meant Will should stay home, too.

In the end, he chose the better of two options, neither of which made him happy. It helped that Maddy had believed wholeheartedly in Scott Rankin, and Will had gotten a good feeling about Ruzinski in their initial conversation.

So Saturday he and Maddy sat on the back deck overlooking the creek, water splashing over rounded rocks. The shade of the trees, a mix of deciduous and evergreen, kept the deck cool even with midday approaching.

Ruzinski answered on the second ring.

"Will Gannon again."

"Good. Do you have her with you?"

"I do."

"May I speak to her?"

"Sure." Will handed over the phone.

"Marshal Ruzinski? I'm Maddy Kane. I… I want to tell you how sorry I am your friend died protecting me. He was really good to me." She listened for a minute, then said, "Almost the last thing he told me was your name. He called you a friend and said to trust you."

Quiet for another minute or two, she blinked a few times, trying to keep herself from crying if Will was any judge. Finally, she nodded. "Sure. We can put the phone on speaker."

Will took it from her and did so, laying it on the rustic cedar table between their chairs. "Marshal, I'm hoping you can tell us what was found at the crash site. We saw the news, with no mention of bombs or US marshals."

"And we want to keep it that way," he said immediately, "until the trial if at all possible. Ah…investigators found enough remnants of the bomb to verify its existence. They aren't yet sure whether it was triggered by a timing device or a signal sent from the ground."

Will reached over the table for Maddy's hand. She grabbed on tight.

"If it was a timing device, that means they knew how long it would take for the plane to pass above inaccessible country," Maddy said. She succeeded in sounding matter-of-fact, as if the explosion and crash of the Cessna were mildly interesting, how it was brought down an intriguing puzzle. As if she hadn't known the dead men, hadn't been injured, never had nightmares about the moment when the plane fell. Only the strength of her grip on Will's hand said otherwise. "What if the pilot had circled to show me something scenic and we'd come down where there were plenty of people to see and come running?"

"Well, there aren't a lot of those in that country, but at this time of year, Ross Lake and Diablo would have been busy, so yeah, that would have been risky from the bombers' point of view. That's one reason we suspect a radio signal was sent."

"Someone could have been hanging around at a picnic area or campground by either lake," Will agreed. "Watched the plane pass by overhead, waited until he knew it was almost to the Picket Range, where no more than a handful of climbers were likely to be near." He paused. "If I were them, I'd have had a timer on the bomb, too, in case they *didn't* see it."

"That's our assumption," Ruzinski agreed.

"You know that Scott surprised me with the flight over the North Cascades because he thought I'd enjoy it, don't you?" Maddy asked.

"I did know," Ruzinski said after a moment.

"If there's any possibility someone triggered the bomb from Diablo or Ross Lake, that means they knew his intentions, too. That's…not the kind of thing that would have been in a file."

"No, it isn't," the marshal agreed, a hard, angry note in his voice. "He had other friends in the office. Scott was well liked. I can't see him telling many people, though. It's not real pleasant right now, when I have to wonder about everyone I see."

Will leaned forward. "You aren't there right now, are you?"

"Of course not. I'm sitting on a park bench." He paused. "Just so you know, we take pride in having never, in our history, lost a protected witness who followed the guidelines. I don't believe a marshal betrayed

Scott and you. He could have been overheard talking, had his phone tapped… I don't know, but you can be damned sure I'll find out."

Will believed him.

Ruzinski cleared his throat. "In the meantime, I have no choice but to turn to the FBI for additional security getting you to the courthouse."

"Who knows that Maddy is alive and still prepared to testify?" Will asked.

"Only the lead prosecutor, Cynthia Yates, and the special agent in charge at the Seattle FBI office. The three of us have agreed to keep the information close. Ms. Kane—"

"Maddy, please," she interjected.

He continued, "Maddy, Ms. Yates wants to meet you in person to discuss your testimony and what the defense might throw at you. All she's telling the others in her office is that she's confident that, with the evidence they have, Mooney will be convicted."

Will mulled that over. If that was true, why risk Maddy to put her in the witness box? Despite his doubts, he decided not to voice them for now.

"How are you doing physically?" Ruzinski asked. "I'm trying to think how we can get you into an ER."

"I'm much improved." She sounded as determined as ever. "The antibiotic is working. My bruises and gashes are healing, although my face may still scare people."

"That's fine by me," he said.

She laughed. Will felt a clutch of serious pride in her. No thugs, however lethal, could stop her.

"Where's the judge?" he asked.

"Torkelson? He was arrested based on what Maddy told the detectives, but he walked out on bail within twenty-four hours, of course. No surprise, he's denying the accusation to anyone who'll listen. He looks real noble when he talks about his long career standing up for justice and the law."

Maddy didn't quite hide a faint shudder.

"Mooney?"

"Still behind bars. The detective in charge of the investigation feels confident he has him solid. Stupid of him to have kept his gun. Of course, it will be open and shut when you testify that you saw his face. From what I hear, Detective Saunders and Ms. Yates have been trying to flip Mooney. He's been offered a tempting deal if he'll name the man who hired him, but so far Mooney has stayed mum. He likely knows about the plan to knock you out, Ms. Kane. Er, Maddy. If you hadn't been able to testify, Torkelson would have a good chance of wriggling out of this. Mooney might be afraid of him, or has been offered a different kind of deal. Once he sees you walk into that courtroom, he may see things a little differently."

"We can only hope." She gazed toward the creek and the leaves dancing in a breeze. "I won't be safe until Judge Torkelson is convicted."

"Right now all we can do is take the next step."

"And what is that, Marshal Ruzinski?"

"Sitting down with Cynthia."

The two men plotted a meet, Will hating even the idea of it but understanding the necessity. The location was theoretically secure. He'd borrow a vehicle; he and Maddy would come up with a disguise for her. Cynthia Yates would walk into her office building as usual but leave surreptitiously with some help from an FBI agent.

At the end Ruzinski said, "Use this number if you need me. Otherwise, we can connect again after you've met with Cynthia Yates."

Maddy said hurriedly, "I'm wondering if I can call my parents."

The pause lasted long enough to tell her what he was going to say. "I'd rather you didn't. I know it's hard on them and you, but remember that they never knew where you were taken or that the plane crash had anything to do with you, so they aren't suffering any new anxiety. They don't expect you to reappear until you're scheduled to testify."

"I know that, but…"

"Somebody may be watching them. If they see open joy and relief, they'll know you're alive and secure enough to be able to call."

She opened her eyes, but he kept talking, sounding regretful. "I don't think we can rule out the possibility of an assault on them in an attempt to find out your whereabouts. Unfortunately, my resources are too limited to allow me to put a 24/7 guard on them."

"And if you did, anyone watching would know why you had."

"I'm afraid so."

"Okay," she conceded.

With the call over, Maddy mentioned her need for an outfit to wear to court. "I'm hoping you have a credit card I can use," she said tentatively. "Of course I'll pay you back once—"

"Don't be ridiculous," Will said curtly. What had she thought, he wouldn't loan her a little money? Or did she suspect he might be flat broke, maybe not even qualifying for credit? That thought irritated him even more. "All you had to do was ask."

"Why are you mad?" Her expression was not friendly.

"I'm not mad."

"You are."

"I'm not—" He cut himself off. Clinging to his pride was one thing; childish behavior another altogether. Will squeezed the back of his neck. "I have plenty of money to lend you whatever you need."

Her glare became bemusement. "I never doubted you do. Why would you think…?" She gave a disgusted huff. "I suppose this is more of the 'I'm servant class, you're privileged' crap."

He stared at her. "Crap?"

"I could call it worse."

His lips thinned, but he shook his head. "No need. You're right. I stumble over my pride occasionally."

"With everyone?" She tipped her head. "Or is it just me?"

"With—" Damn, he had to be honest. "Mostly you," he admitted.

"But…why?"

He'd either hurt her feelings or she was just flat-out perplexed. A burn under Will's breastbone told him he needed to bare himself. God knows she'd trusted him enough times.

"Because you've gotten to me." He sounded hoarse, and wanted really badly to look away from her wide, astonished eyes. "It's hard to imagine a woman with your background and education would have any interest in an unemployed former soldier with a bum hip and leg."

"That's how you see yourself?" She stared at him in obvious bewilderment. "That's ridiculous! Anyway, you said you plan to go to medical school."

"I didn't say *plan*," he corrected her. "I said I'll be applying. But you must know what the competition is like. I may not be accepted anywhere. Then I'll get a job like any other grunt."

Maddy's expression changed. He didn't like to think that was pity he saw.

"You expect to fail?"

He hesitated. Truth was, he'd always been a pretty cocky guy. Mostly, he did believe in himself. It was Maddy who scared him. She was class, he was—

Yeah, that wasn't like him, and he didn't enjoy the feeling.

"No," he said. "I have top-notch grades. I'm hoping the on-the-job experience as a medic makes up for the fact that my degree isn't from a blue-ribbon university. I've been studying hard, and I'm doing really well on the practice MCATs I've taken."

The Medical College Admission Test was notoriously tough, so yeah, he was proud of himself.

Her expression warmed. "They'll be impressed because getting a degree was a lot harder for you than for the typical kid who goes straight off to a four-year school with mommy and daddy paying the tuition." Her forehead crinkled. "You won't be able to start for another year, though."

He rolled his shoulders. "Rehab took everything I had. Then there was the hit of being invalided out of the service. You know it can happen, but that doesn't mean you're prepared. I needed time to…reintegrate, too."

She nodded.

The silence that followed wasn't a comfortable one, even for her, Will thought. Maddy didn't look at him, which had him feeling sick. She hadn't reacted to what he'd said about his feelings for her. Somehow they'd ended up talking about his ambitions instead.

He needed to let it lie. She was stuck with him for the foreseeable future. Why put her on the spot and make their relationship awkward? He'd done enough damage by backing away.

He started to stand. "I'll make sandwiches for lunch."

Maddy laid her hand atop his on the arm of the Adirondack chair. "No, wait. I...have something to say first."

MADDY DIDN'T EVEN know why she felt so shy, but she did. Maybe because Will wasn't like any man she'd ever dated. She'd never felt like this, either. And yes, he'd hurt her each time he withdrew. But she couldn't let this chance pass by. He'd told her how he felt, and she could do that much, too.

Of course, her cheeks were probably flaming red.

His eyes met hers. She knew he wasn't calm only because the muscles in his forearms were rock hard, tendons and veins standing out as did the small bones on the backs of his hands.

"I knew you were attracted to me." Maddy knew her smile was a flop. "I couldn't understand why since I've looked pretty awful since we met with me holding you at gunpoint." She lifted her fingertips to gingerly touch the side of her face that had been a mass of bruises and cuts. She was healing, but knew fading colors and scabs remained. *Okay, quit procrastinating.* "What you said, um, implies a lot more than that."

"I meant to."

Wincing at his flat tone, she gathered her courage. "Well, I'm interested in you, too, and that's true whether you get into medical school or not. I just never thought you—" Words died as she watched his shifting expression.

"Why?" His puzzlement was plain.

"Oh, come on! I know I've been a burden. And do

you have any idea how guilty I feel? You've risked your life for me, over and over. And even though you've been really nice about it, I assumed you'd be glad to unload me as soon as you could."

He swallowed. "I've been dreading the day you leave. I keep telling myself I like being alone, but that's a lie. You…brought me back to life."

"Oh, Will."

She started to rise. So fast she didn't see it coming, Will scooped her up and sat back down with her in his arms. His mouth found hers, both of them made clumsy by need, but it didn't matter. They bumped noses, clanked teeth, but finally found the right angle and the kiss became astonishing: urgent but tender, too; sweet even as need rose. Each time they needed to breathe, they'd look into each other's eyes.

Eventually, a groan rumbled in his chest and she felt a tremor in the hands cradling her head.

"I want you so damn much, but we can't do this. And please don't get mad at me."

Mad? Oh. He'd said the same another time, and she'd stupidly felt rejected.

"I really do feel a lot better overall. If that's what you mean."

Eyes as dark as charcoal searched her face. "You can't tell me you don't still hurt."

No, she couldn't, but today it had been mostly when she got careless in how she moved. "We could, well, find a way." Now her face burned. "Except I'm not on birth control."

"That I can take care of. But…you're serious?"

Maddy squirmed a little for the pleasure of rubbing herself against his powerful thigh, not to mention the ridge against her hip. "I can't think of anything in the world I'd rather do," she confessed.

The sound he made inhuman, Will surged to his feet holding her as if she didn't weigh a thing. He strode across the deck, shoved open the French door with one shoulder and carried her into the living room where he came to a stop.

"Damn. The sofa bed is miserable."

It wasn't so bad for her, probably because she did weigh a lot less than he did but also because she draped herself over him when they slept. Right this minute she didn't think she'd so much as feel the bar that seemed to be right beneath their hips.

"I can climb up to the loft."

"Do you need the bathroom?"

Maddy laughed at his chivalry, unromantic as it was. "No, I'm good." Then she frowned at him. "You didn't say whether you have condoms."

"Picked 'em up when I shopped on Thursday." He crossed the living room in two or three strides and set her on her feet halfway up the steep staircase to the loft. As she climbed, Will kept a hand on her butt, either to boost her or because he was gently squeezing and enjoying it.

He wasn't the only one.

Under a pitched roof, the loft had the same wood floors that could use a refinishing, a queen-size mattress and springs that sat on the floor, a dresser, a small wood stool that obviously served as a bedside stand and a low bookcase.

Within moments Will had yanked the thin blanket and top sheet from the bed. "Maddy. Are you sure?"

She nodded shakily.

"Then lift your good arm." As he had other times, he

carefully removed her T-shirt, leaving her breasts bare. Staring, he cupped her breasts to gently rub until she moaned and arched. Still without looking away, Will ripped his shirt over his head and tossed it away before reaching for the button at her waist. He peeled her chinos and panties down her legs, Maddy stepping out of them and her flip-flops at the same time.

Squatting, Will wrapped his hands around her ankles and slid them up. She shivered when he reached the sensitive skin behind her knees. Her breath hitched when calloused fingers stroked over the inside of her thighs. He leaned forward, breathing in her essence, kissed her and then exploded to his feet. Maddy vaguely heard the twin thuds as his shoes hit the floor or walls, who knew? His pants and stretch boxers were gone as fast.

Maddy reached for him and splayed her fingers on his chest. He was...spectacular, those long muscles well-defined, his belly flat and hard. While he stood completely still, she bent forward to rub her cheek against the soft hairs on his chest and explore his contours with her fingertips, finally licking the small hollow at the base of his throat, just because it was there and looked so vulnerable.

He tried to take over then, lifting her and laying her back on the bed before he came down beside her. Always so careful not to hurt her. Knowing he'd never forget made something squeeze hard in her chest. He kissed her breasts and drew each nipple in turn into his mouth, the suction compelling her hips to rise. She wanted his weight on her, to be able to wrap her legs around his waist, feel him deep inside her. Maddy struggled to remember why he still held himself separate.

Her wandering hand touched thick scar tissue. Will

returned to kissing her, but she pushed him. "Wait! I need to see—"

"What?" He lifted away in confusion, but Maddy was focused entirely on the scars, some surgical, some from torn flesh, that covered his right hip and reached down his thigh.

She'd known, but seeing it was different. "Oh, Will," she whispered. She stroked the damaged area before looking up in chagrin. "Does that hurt? When I touch you?"

"No." He sounded ragged but cleared his throat. "To tell you the truth, the skin is mostly numb there."

"Oh." She lifted her hand.

He captured it and laid it back where it had been. "Touch me. Anywhere you want. I like it."

"Me, too. I mean—"

Will grinned. "I know what you mean."

Maddy loved what the smile did to that craggy, scarred face. She loved the way he touched her, too, and kissed her, and whispered how beautiful she was even as he had to work around her splinted arm, broken collarbone and gashes. She could hardly wait for the day when she didn't look like she'd been in a plane crash.

She saw him grope beneath the stool and come up with a packet. Lost to sensation, she rubbed against him, hardly aware he was putting the condom on.

Will suddenly rolled to his back and displayed his upper body strength by picking her up again and turning her to straddle him. Eyes betraying desperation as great as what she felt, he said, "Let me know if you hurt."

Hurt?

She took him in, riding him, grateful that he helped pace her with his grip on her hips. Sounds she didn't even recognize kept escaping her. When pleasure seized

Maddy, she cried out Will's name—and heard her own as part of a groan when his body bucked as if he had no choice but to follow her.

Chapter Thirteen

The next day after dinner, Maddy sank onto the sofa and cuddled up to Will. "Happy?"

Closing his arm around her, he said, "I'm happy." Which was a major understatement. "You?"

"Of course I am." But her very stillness spoke of the black cloud that hung over them both. This was Wednesday. A week from now or less, she'd be testifying. "Except… I wish we didn't have to do that thing tomorrow," she added.

The *thing*. Drive almost a hundred miles to Bellevue, where the prosecutor would meet them at a borrowed house. Will would have liked it better if they'd planned to meet halfway in between Seattle and Concrete—Everett came to mind, since that was where Scott Rankin had intended to hide Maddy until the trial. But Cynthia Yates had claimed an extremely busy schedule that allowed no time for long drives. Admittedly, in a matter of days she would be starting jury selection for a major trial. She had also refused to do the witness prep over the phone, claiming she never went to trial with a witness she hadn't met with, face-to-face. She sounded annoyed that Maddy had been yanked into hiding before they had a chance to talk.

Will didn't get the feeling she took the danger to

Maddy anywhere near seriously enough, but Maddy's determination to do what was asked of her hadn't faltered despite his frustration and fear. This was the first time she'd expressed any worry, although he had been well aware that she wasn't either blithely certain of her safety or in complete denial. He'd awakened her from two or three nightmares a night. She was trying to hold in all her stress.

"If anyone knew where I am," she said slowly, "we'd know."

Translation: they'd be dead.

"So there's no reason the drive should be a problem," Maddy continued. "I don't really see why we even need to switch cars."

They had both been enjoying an interlude. It was time to lay out his biggest worry to her. If everything turned to shit, he needed to know she'd follow orders and react fast.

So he said, "I agree. I don't think we'll be followed. My real concern is that Yates will be. These guys knew she was prosecuting this case long before she walked into the courtroom today. I did some research on Torkelson. You know he was a prosecuting attorney himself before he was appointed to the bench? He knows how it works, how she thinks."

Her muscles tightened. "They're watching *her*. That's what you're saying."

"Yeah." Lay it out there, he told himself. "The judge in particular would know she always meets with witnesses before putting them on the stand. It's unrealistic to believe she can get out of the building unseen. Even if there's a parking garage, they could put people in it watching for her. Even in the building itself. I had the feeling Ruzinski didn't like this plan, either, but felt we had to cooperate."

Maddy pulled away from him, turning on the sofa and tucking one leg under her so she could see his face. "Really? I didn't get that."

"I didn't have the impression you were paying much attention."

Obviously chagrined, she said, "You're right. I wasn't offered a voice in making the arrangements, you know. Still, I should have listened."

"You had a lot to think about." He leaned forward to kiss her lightly, then smiled. "It's also possible he was chafing at having to turn to another agency to do what he can't."

Maddy chuckled. "It can't be comfortable for him to have to admit the marshal's service needs help protecting a witness under *their* care."

"Nope."

He waited while she thought it over. "So we're just going to walk—drive—into a potential ambush?"

"I'll approach with great care. You need to be ready to jump when I say jump."

"Haven't I always?"

"Yeah," Will said gruffly. "You have. I have the feeling you aren't usually a docile woman, though, and the better you feel, the more likely you are to want to think for yourself."

Maddy frowned at him. "Thinking for myself doesn't make me stupid, you know."

"That's not what I—"

She cut him off. "I'd have died if it weren't for you. *You've* kept me alive. I promise to jump when you say so."

Will slid a hand around her nape and squeezed. "You're right. I'm sorry. I'm just, uh…"

"Worried."

Scared out of his skull, actually, but he wasn't going to say that. He wouldn't quit being scared even if tomorrow's expedition went like clockwork. The trial had to take place at the courthouse, and he had no doubt at all that they'd be ambushed there. It would be their last chance.

Of course, a second trial was scheduled to begin in late August, and Maddy had to testify in it, too. Will was less concerned about that one, because she'd already have described in court what she saw and heard the day her client was gunned down. Shutting her up after that wouldn't help Judge Torkelson.

Which didn't mean Will intended to relax one iota until Torkelson was convicted and led away in cuffs.

"How about we put it out of our minds for the rest of the day," he suggested.

A smile quivered on her mouth. "That's a lot of hours to fill. I wonder what's on Netflix?"

"Netflix isn't quite what I had in mind." Will traced the curve of her lips with his forefinger. When she nipped it, his body jolted. "You know, the fit is tight here if we don't pull out the bed, but if I spoon you from behind…"

Just like that, he was painfully aroused. And even more so when he saw her eyes darken and her lips part.

"That sounds interesting," she said huskily. "I'm betting you don't have a condom handy, though."

With a groan, he let his head fall back. Then he eased himself to his feet. There was no way around it. "Close your eyes, count to twenty and I'll be back."

Maddy's chuckle followed him up to the loft.

IT WAS NOT a fun drive.

At least once they were on the freeway and Will was confident they weren't being followed, he let Maddy sit up. Naturally, he'd consigned her to the backseat so that she could dive for cover beneath the familiar blue tarp if need be. She fastened her seat belt, glanced at the back of Will's head and some of his stubborn jaw and angular cheekbone, all she could see, then looked out the window just as they drove over the Skagit River. It was more impressive than she'd have expected, broad and running high, deceptively placid except for the ripples of current.

She could only remember traveling this far north once, when she and Doug had gone to La Conner for a weekend getaway. They'd been chattering, and she hadn't paid that much attention.

Doug. She hardly thought of him. They'd been seeing each other for nearly a year before she witnessed the shooting that changed everything, and yet Maddy could barely picture his face. How much had he been told about her disappearance? She wondered how quickly he'd moved on…because she felt sure he would have.

A better question was why she wasted so much time on a tepid relationship.

The freeway briefly followed the river as it looped south before it curved west again. Once Mount Vernon fell behind them, the land was flat and mostly agricultural although she saw a plant nursery, wine grapes and a sign advertising rides in hang gliders.

Maddy was not in any hurry to fly again. *Never* sounded good.

Once they crossed another river, the Snohomish, traffic increased and the surroundings were urban. First Everett, then Lynnwood where Will exited. This was where they'd leave the Jeep and borrow a car from a friend of his for the last leg of the trip.

Will didn't tell her to hide, but he didn't introduce his friend, either. The two talked briefly on the front porch of the modest rambler and the guy handed over the keys with only one curious glance her way. Will carried the tarp to the silver Toyota Corolla and said, "I'm afraid you need to stay in the back."

She got in and shook out the tarp so she could squirm under it quickly. Will drove a circuitous route out of the neighborhood, his gaze turning frequently to the rearview mirror. Apparently satisfied, he got on Highway 405, which led south down the east side of Lake Washington.

The more familiar the sights became, the more nervous Maddy got. She'd grown up in Redmond, bordering on Bellevue. They'd be passing within half a mile of her childhood home. She felt an ache to hear her parents' voices, hug them.

Not helpful.

"We're coming up on the exit," Will said. "I want you out of sight."

"Okay." The tarp crackled as she lay down on the seat and drew it over her. Knowing how close they were, she felt suddenly claustrophobic. "Um…will you talk to me?"

"When I can."

He complained aloud about hitting a red light every block, about the traffic near Bellevue Mall, then grew quiet for a few minutes. "Why here?" he said almost beneath his breath. "Nobody in the prosecutor's office should earn enough to run in these circles."

From that, Maddy deduced that they were still heading straight for the lake. He was right; homes here started over a million dollars. Prices on waterview or waterfront property climbed sharply from there.

Her nerves tightened when he turned at last, and turned again. His phone buzzed.

"Yeah?" A moment later, "We're getting there. I don't like this." He listened again, said, "Okay," then, in an entirely different voice, "You okay, Maddy?"

"Yes. Are we almost there?"

"Yeah. I'm circling a few blocks, mapping the fastest way to get out of here if we need to."

"Do you see anything to worry you?"

"More parked cars than I like. All nice ones. I guess no one here drives an eight-year-old Jeep."

"No, but neither are you at the moment."

"At least this car is still shiny." After a minute he said, "What did you drive?"

"Would you believe a Honda Civic?"

"No BMW or Land Rover?"

She laughed, even though she knew he was trying to distract her from the building tension. "Nope."

The phone buzzed again. Will didn't bother with a hello. He listened, then said, "Be ready."

"Who was that?"

"The FBI agent. That was his all clear."

"But you don't buy it."

He didn't answer. Didn't have to answer.

No, HE WASN'T any more convinced this was safe than he'd been when he and the marshal first discussed it. Will wished he knew whether this FBI Special Agent Moore was seasoned or a rookie. He sounded too casual.

The garages and parking on this block were in the alley running behind the homes. Turning into the alley, Will wished he had eyes in the back of his head. He didn't like being boxed in. He'd have more options if he'd parked at the curb and they'd entered the front door. Moore was right that they'd draw less attention this way—but who cared what the neighbors thought?

The big shiny black SUV parked next to the third garage on the right looked government even if the license plate didn't say so.

His gaze flicked from the rearview mirror to each side mirror, back to the front, then rearview. He wished he was driving a Humvee.

No other vehicles appeared. He braked but didn't turn off the engine. There was zero movement until the garage door rolled up, revealing a parked Lexus and a workbench and lawn mower.

He said quietly, "Don't sit up until I come around the car to let you out. Stay close to me. Got it?"

"Yes."

Leave the key in the ignition, he decided. He didn't pull the emergency brake on, either.

They should have supplied her with a Kevlar vest. Will was angry at himself for not asking. For all they knew, he was unarmed, depending entirely on the single agent who stood inside the garage. He hadn't told Ruzinski that he had the dead marshal's handgun. He'd give it back eventually.

At least Special Agent Moore had his weapon in his hands and appeared alert.

Will's skin crawled as he got out, slammed his door and walked around the front of the Corolla. How many times had he felt this, when he *knew* they were being watched? It was quiet. Too quiet. His every instinct told him to jump back in the damn car and step on the gas. Get out of here. But he acknowledged that his combat senses were still raw. Maybe he wasn't ready to be thrown back into this kind of situation.

Or he should listen to instincts built on experience.

He scanned the entire alley, rooftops, fences. He couldn't relax, but had to open the back door for Maddy to wriggle out, hampered by the arm in a splint and sling.

"Keep low," he murmured.

Her hair ruffled, she crouched next to the fender.

"What's taking so long?" the agent asked from behind him. "Get her in here."

Will ignored him. Talking to Maddy, he said, "All right, scoot behind me and stand up. Put your hand on my back so I know where you are."

She did exactly as he asked.

"We're going to back up," he said in the same quiet voice. "You take a step, wait for me to take one."

Feeling as if every hair on his body bristled, Will heard the soft scrape of her foot moving backward on asphalt. He moved his right foot back, keeping his weight on his stronger side.

"Another—"

A tiny rattling sound was his only warning before the gate almost directly across the alley burst open and a man in black stepped out shooting.

The first shot pinged off the roof of the Corolla and passed within inches of his head.

"Drop!" he yelled.

Maddy did so without hesitation, crawling by him for the shelter of the car.

The second shot came from higher and went over the car. A sharp cry from behind told Will the agent was down.

He started shooting. The closest man jerked and fell

forward. Will could barely see the flattened form of the gunman on the roof of a garage they'd driven right past, but he took some shots as he flung open the back door for Maddy.

"In, in."

She scrambled, he slammed it and duckwalked around to the back bumper. It was farther from the driver door, and he counted on his choice being unexpected.

One look over his shoulder. Moore had pulled himself to the front corner of the garage where he was partially sheltered by the back end of the Lexus. Blood soaked one thigh of his pants, but he held his gun in firing position. His eyes met Will's.

His lips scarcely moved as he said, "I'll provide cover. Get her out of here."

Crouching, Will counted a few seconds, leaned his head around the bumper for a quick glimpse then came out shooting. And, hell, he had to leap over the prone and unmoving body of gunman number one. Kept shooting until the magazine was empty, leaped into the front seat. Started the engine, thrust the gearshift into Drive and slammed his foot down on the accelerator. The small Corolla rocketed toward the side street.

ALMOST AS SCARED as she'd been when that propeller quit turning, Maddy hated being blind. She heard the door being opened, felt the car rock when Will flung himself in. She kept waiting for another gunshot, to hear a guttural sound when he was hit. The Corolla would swerve, smash into a garage or a parked car. If he was killed—

Don't think it.

How could she not, after he had once again put his

body between her and danger? He'd been *prepared* to take a bullet. For her.

The car swayed through another turn, after which she thought it slowed.

"Is anyone following us?" she asked.

"Not yet." Will sounded grim.

Another turn, and she heard his voice.

"Ruzinski." Pause. "Blew up in our face. Two gunmen were waiting. The FBI guy is wounded. Maddy and I got out. Car suffered a lot of damage. I'm looking to ditch it." A long silence. "Yeah, it's missing a couple of windows, got some interesting dents. I'd get pulled over for sure." Then, "Uh-huh, I can do that. Thanks."

Assuming the conversation was over, Maddy asked, "Can I please sit up?"

"I don't see why not. We're going to drive half a mile, a tow truck will pick up the car and Ruzinski is coming for us."

Relief rushed through her as she emerged from beneath the tarp. A mole sniffing the air. "Are you hurt?"

"No. Agent Moore was shot, but should be okay. We'll find out."

Dazed, she said, "You were right."

"I shouldn't have agreed to this in the first place." His steely voice made it plain that his cooperation would be hard won in the future. "We should both have been wearing vests."

"Vests?"

"Kevlar. Bulletproof." He shook his head, his eyes meeting hers in the rearview mirror. "It was a miracle neither of us took a bullet. More so that a tire didn't get shot out."

"Maybe they aren't that smart," she ventured.

"No. I recognized one of them."

"But not the other?"

"He was up on a roof. Couldn't see him well enough."

Her pulse was only now slowing. "They quit shooting." *Are they dead? What will happen to the bodies?*

"The one in the alley was down. I don't know if I killed him or not. The one on the roof... Not sure. Moore and I were both banging away at him. If we pinged him at all, he may have dropped his rifle. The roof was pitched enough, it would have slid away."

And dropped into somebody's yard. Remembering the barrage of bullets, Maddy could only imagine how many bullet holes residents would find in fences and garage siding. And maybe in a roof?

She hadn't been paying attention to their route, but now Will steered into a parking lot at a lakefront park, driving to the far end and backing into a slot so that he could see who was coming.

Then he reached for the gun he must have tossed on the passenger seat, dug in a pocket and changed magazines.

"How many bullets does that hold?" Maddy asked.

He glanced in the rearview mirror again. "Thirteen, one in the chamber. Remind me to give you some basic lessons before our next exciting outing."

Her laugh might have been just a little hysterical. Will grinned because he'd gotten what he had been aiming for.

"Ah, listen." He opened the glove compartment and took something out. "I need to take the license plates off."

"Because they'd lead to your friend," she realized.

"Nope. Because they don't belong on this car." He got out, stuck his head back in and added, "Paul collects license plates. That's one reason I called him. These are BC plates. He'll want them back even if there is a bullet hole or two."

"He's not going to be mad about the car?"

"Nah, he'll get it back in pristine shape. This auto-body place does a lot of work for local LEAs."

LEA. She considered that while Will crouched first behind the back bumper then the front. She'd heard the acronym before… Law enforcement agencies. That was it. What, was the guy who owned the shop a retired cop?

Will reappeared in the door. "Ruzinski is here."

They transferred to an older Blazer or Explorer or something like that. Maddy, of course, was consigned to the backseat. She was beginning to get annoyed by the assumption she wouldn't have anything worthwhile to contribute. She reminded herself that she'd have her chance when she made it into the courtroom.

The marshal glanced at the license plates Will set down by his feet, raised his eyebrows but didn't comment.

For some reason he didn't look quite like she'd expected. He was thin, taller even than Will, she thought, with short blond hair spiked with silver, and blue eyes. Except for crow's-feet beside those eyes, his face was as smooth as that of a man decades younger than she somehow knew he was.

Two blocks away from the park, he glanced at Will. "I hear you were armed."

"You talked to Moore? Is he okay?"

"Sounds like. Said he bled like a stuck pig."

After a pause Will said, "I was carrying. Did you really think I'd risk Maddy in a setup like this if I wasn't?" His voice crackled with anger. "Depending on someone I've never worked with before? Who was there *alone*?"

"Calm down. I didn't think that. But there is a dead

man in that alley. I need to know where those bullets came from."

He'd killed for her. And yes, he must have killed before, but Maddy didn't like knowing this violence had been committed on her behalf.

"I have Scott Rankin's Glock. Maddy grabbed it for protection," he said tersely.

Ruzinski was quiet for a minute. "I tried to educate myself about your background, but I couldn't learn much but that you were army."

"Delta Force."

The marshal's eyebrows climbed. "On leave?"

Will shook his head. "I'm out. Humpty Dumpty and I have something in common."

"Couldn't put you back together again? Looks like they came close."

"Good enough, but not up to active-duty demands."

"I see."

Delta Force. She'd been even luckier than she knew, Maddy realized. What she couldn't understand was how Will had reconciled being a healer with the violence he must also have committed. It was telling that his goal now was to become a family doctor. He had to be looking for peace, finding a place he could help instead of harm.

And yet he hadn't hesitated to jump into the mess her life had become.

My hero, she thought, knowing quite well what he'd say to her calling him that.

Chapter Fourteen

Will hoped recriminations had been flying between the FBI and the Seattle City Attorney's office. When Yates, who he had learned was a senior deputy prosecuting attorney, called Maddy Thursday evening after the debacle, Will eavesdropped unashamedly, even though he could hear only one side of the conversation. Even so, he could tell that Cynthia Yates started with a shovelful of apologies.

Leaning against the kitchen counter, arms crossed, he watched Maddy's reaction.

From her place at the kitchen table, she rolled her eyes toward Will and said repeatedly, "Thank you, but you don't need to—yes, I understand. No, I don't think we can discount the resources a former judge commands. It does make me nervous about reaching the courtroom safely." She listened some more, expressed more understanding and finally said, "Why don't we just get down to business?"

She had displayed more patience than Will felt. He'd expressed his reservations about the meet loud and clear. Ruzinski claimed to have shared them, but had he really? Who knew?

Apparently, the FBI agent had been discharged from the hospital after only one night's stay but with his femur shattered. He'd be on disability for several months. Will and Maddy would certainly be dead if they had trotted on into the garage as ordered.

Will had never had trouble following orders within his unit, but he'd since had an attitude adjustment. No more.

He didn't listen closely as the two women had an intense discussion about courtroom tactics, what to expect from counsel for the defense and the judge. Maddy had appeared before her on a couple of occasions and had strong opinions on the woman's particular areas of tolerance and, on the flip side, her biases. During this call, Maddy didn't docilely listen; she sometimes argued, sometimes stood firm, sometimes acquiesced. She had strong opinions and didn't back down unless Ms. Yates had solid reasons for a strategy.

The Maddy of today didn't have a lot of resemblance to the injured, feverish survivor of a plane crash, but she hadn't lost the quality that enabled her to survive: determination.

While the women talked, Maddy took extensive notes on Will's laptop, her fingers flying. Watching her, he smiled.

When he heard her say, "I'm going to speakerphone," he tuned in.

"I'm sure you'll be in discussions with the Seattle PD and courthouse security about your arrival next Monday, but I want to reassure you—"

Will cut the woman off. "We won't be reassured until we've safely reached the courtroom. I'm assuming your office hasn't anything to do with those arrangements?"

"Only in the sense that we're aware of what's happening and offer our assistance where necessary."

"Ms. Yates, I encourage you to take security measures yourself. If you were to be killed, it seems likely the trial would be postponed."

Silence told him he'd surprised her.

"That's possible," she said after a minute. "But postponement wouldn't help the defendant's cause."

"Forget Kevin Mooney. The former judge is clearly a ruthless man who will do anything at all to avoid going to trial. As multiple attacks on Maddy make plain, he wants her dead. A postponement would give him more time to find her."

"Very well," the DA said stiffly. "I'll relocate for the rest of the week and will request personal security until the trial ends."

"Good."

He let the two women wind it up. Torkelson would likely appear before a different judge on his day in court, but this trial could in effect convict him. Considering he'd ordered the original murder to cover up a rape, it was his bad luck that neither he nor Mooney were likely to get much sympathy from the female judge, female prosecutor and female primary witness.

Tough luck.

After Maddy hung up, Will said abruptly, "Are your parents planning to attend the trial the day you're testifying?"

"I'm sure they are."

"If their lives were threatened…"

"I'd do just about anything," she finished, stricken face giving away how hard she'd been hit. "I should have thought of that sooner."

"Somebody should have," he said grimly. "From the minute the marshal's office knew a bomb had brought that plane down, I'd have expected security measures to have been ramped up to DEFCON one. Why hasn't that happened?"

"I...don't know."

"You get a sense of anything off with Ms. Yates?"

"No." She started shaking her head. "No."

"Okay."

Maddy was the one to say, with clear reluctance, "Marshal Ruzinski?"

Will went with his gut. "No. I think he's focused on finding the leak."

"So what? You think Torkelson might have a hold on some police officers? Courthouse security?"

He blew out a breath and scrubbed his hands over his head. "Yeah, I guess I do. The man was a prominent local judge. He could make or break people's lives. It's pretty clear he lacks a conscience or any kind of morality. Sociopaths can be CEOs of a Fortune 500 company...or an attorney or superior court judge. We don't know whether he preyed on just one woman, your client, or whether he's bought off or intimidated a bunch of women. From his point of view, his career and life were going just fine until the one woman decided to speak out. First, he blamed her, then you. I don't trust even round-the-clock security for your parents, I'd like them to fly out tonight. London, the Caribbean, doesn't matter. What's important is that they go off the grid when they get there. Find a place to stay that accepts cash and doesn't insist on getting a name."

The way Maddy had blanched worried Will, but even if he could, he wouldn't take back his suggestion. The stakes were high, the man set on stopping Maddy intelligent and remorseless.

"Let's go for a drive," he said.

Maddy didn't argue.

WILL DROVE ALL the way to Bellingham, not far from the Canadian border, before he pulled into a vast parking lot in front of a shopping mall.

Then he took a phone out of the glove compartment and handed it to her. "Call them."

Maddy nodded.

His steady gray eyes held hers for a long moment before he smiled, bent his head and kissed her. The kiss was quick, but also tender and possessive. She tingled all over by the time he opened his door and got out.

"You can listen if you want," she said.

"You deserve a few minutes with them. Just be sure nobody says anything too specific. I'm calling Ruzinski." He slammed the door and walked around to the front of his Jeep, where she could see him lifting another phone to his ear. Typically for him, he didn't stand still. He paced with seeming idleness as he talked, but never going far from the Jeep. She had a feeling he was aware of every car in their vicinity that had a person waiting in it, every shopper heading toward the mall entrance or returning to a car with full bags.

He also looked incredibly sexy, his jeans well worn to conform to his butt and the long muscles of his thighs, his brown hair rumpled, strong forearms bared by the T-shirt. Maddy had never been involved with a man who had anywhere near his physical presence.

She gave herself a shake, dialed her parents' phone number and stared down at it for a minute. She'd missed them so much, hated knowing how scared they must have been about her. Then she pushed Send.

"Hello?"

"Mom?"

The sound her mother made might have been a sob. "Maddy? It's you?"

"Yes." When she tasted salt, Maddy realized she was crying. She had to say, "Just a minute," and juggled the phone while she swiped away the tears. "I'm sorry."

Her father must have picked up an extension, because it was him saying urgently, "Maddy? You're all right?"

"I'm fine, Dad." She took a deep breath. "Mostly."

"Mostly?" Mom. "What's that mean?"

"I don't know if you read about the small plane going down in the North Cascades."

They had, and were horrified when she told them about the bomb. She didn't linger on the ordeal getting out of the mountains, but gave a quick summation.

"You know I'm supposed to testify Monday."

"We didn't know what day for sure, but we'll be there."

"No, that's the thing. Will—he's the ex-army Delta Force guy who found me up there and got me safely out of the mountains—he thinks you could be in danger. There have been other attacks. I won't go into that right now, but he wants you to pack and go somewhere tonight. Get on a plane and wherever you go just use cash. It'll only be for a week or two."

After a long pause, her father said, "You're right. We have to remove any chance we could be used to influence you. We could go to—"

"No! Don't tell me. If your phone is tapped…"

She heard her father breathing. Or maybe both of her parents, synchronized.

"Understood," he said finally. "We'll do that. As long as you have someone…"

"I do." Maddy had to clear her throat and repeat the words. "I do. Will has been amazing. I trust him."

Her voice must have softened, because her mother said, "Like that, is it?"

Her lips trembled on a smile. "Yes. Maybe. I don't know." Her face was wet again. "I love you. Please stay safe."

"You, too," her father said gruffly, and she ended the call.

After mopping her cheeks with the hem of her shirt, Maddy lifted her head to see that Will had come to a stop right in front of the car where he could watch her. She couldn't seem to draw a breath. She could only look at him and hope she wasn't imagining what she thought she saw in his eyes.

And that he didn't take a bullet for her and die.

WILL TOOK HIS time making love to Maddy that night. They could explore each other's body in between quiet talks tonight and every night to come. He pretended the days weren't counting down.

He found Maddy endlessly fascinating, starting with that supple body and feminine curves, with the way she responded to his touch—and the way she touched him.

But it was more than that. He'd liked women he'd been involved with before, but nothing he had felt measured up to this. He wanted to know everything about Maddy. How had a beautiful woman who'd grown up in privilege become so tough and principled? Why did she regret not having broken more of her ties to home? What did she imagine she'd have done with her life if she hadn't become an attorney?

What would she think about moving to Houston or Los Angeles, Cincinnati or Atlanta, depending on where he was accepted to medical school?

Maybe most important, he needed to find out what happened when she was no longer living in fear for her life, depending on him for her safety. She might see him differently then, start noticing that he had an ugly scar on his face and worse ones on his body, that he knew more about primitive living in the bone-dry mountains of Afghanistan than he did fitting in with people his age in a sophisticated American city. She'd discover that he wouldn't have a clue how to pick from a wine list at a fancy restaurant, that most nightlife held no interest to him even if he could stand the crowds and the noise and flashing multicolored lights.

Deep in his heart, Will didn't believe any of that would make a difference to her. Going through what they had together, he and Maddy knew each other better in barely over a week than most dating couples would in a year or more. Stress and danger did that to you—taught you whether someone had the qualities that meant you could rely on them, now and forever.

With an effort, he pushed all that out of his mind. Their first lovemaking was slow and emotional. Then came fast, even desperate. He woke up once to find her rubbing against him. Come morning, his body spooned hers, and he slid into her from behind for another tender lovemaking. He wouldn't mind waking up like that every morning for the rest of his life.

Getting dressed, starting the coffee and scrambling some eggs while Maddy wrapped a plastic bag around her arm and showered, Will glanced involuntarily at a calendar that had hung in this kitchen when he moved in.

Five more days.

THE GOOD NEWS came from Ruzinski, who called Friday to let them know that a clerk in the marshal's office had been arrested for selling info about Rankin's plans for Maddy. Once accused, the clerk had crumpled and admitted that she'd overheard him talking to the pilot when he booked the charter. Ruzinski was confident she'd acted alone.

He also informed them that a female Seattle PD officer who resembled Maddy enough to pass as her from a distance agreed to serve as a decoy. She would be escorted into the courthouse the way a protected witness normally would be. Will guessed there was a tunnel directly from the jail, or it would be via a loading dock or something like that. He didn't ask, and Ruzinski didn't volunteer the information.

Ruzinski did admit to being bothered by the courthouse security liaison's insistence on knowing Will and Marshal Ruzinski's plans. The guy didn't like it when Ruzinski refused to share how they intended to reach the courthouse. It was possible the security liaison felt he was being kept from doing his job—but it was also possible he needed the information for another reason altogether.

Ruzinski and Will had already made the decision to trust no one. They'd considered calling the detective who arrested Kevin Mooney and would also be testifying. He almost had to be trustworthy. But there were risks. He might trust somebody whose integrity had been bought. He wasn't a direct threat to the judge, but his testimony was critical to convicting Mooney. If he and Maddy both were killed, Mooney would walk. No, best if he, too, knew nothing about how Maddy was to get safely into the courtroom.

If Ruzinski and Will didn't involve anyone else, they had two options: take her in through a tunnel from the county admin building across Fourth Avenue from the courthouse, or walk in the main entrance. Either way, they'd have to stand in line like everyone else to go through airport-like security.

Ruzinski liked the first option, Will the second. He'd have to turn in his gun before entering the tunnel, leaving Ruzinski the only one of them armed. If a cop or guard had been turned, the tunnel could be a trap. Put someone ahead, someone behind, and they'd have no escape. Plus, they'd have to get safely into the administration building in the first place.

His suggestion to stroll right in the main entrance might be the most unexpected but had its own downside if they drove themselves. The closest parking lot was a block away. He shook his head at the idea of them standing to wait for lights to change so they could cross streets. At least a *moving* target was harder to hit.

"Better," he had said to Ruzinski, and with Maddy listening in, "we take a bus, a taxi or an Uber. We could be dropped off right in front."

"That's the busiest entrance. There can be long waits until you go through security."

"Maddy isn't likely to testify until afternoon. How much line would there be once the morning rush has passed?"

"She'd stand out less if she arrived at the same time as employees and jurors," the marshal argued.

"Late morning we could get her inside a lot quicker."

"You picturing a disguise?" Ruzinski asked.

"Of course I am. She could be—" His gaze touched on her breasts. Not a man. "An old woman. I'm her dutiful son."

"And I'm the old man," Ruzinski said drily.

Will grinned despite the serious subject. "When the shoe fits."

Maddy laughed.

The marshal grumbled, "Tell her I heard that."

Laughter sparkling in her eyes, she said, "A little hair dye and *he* could be my dutiful son."

"Sure."

"What if we were a trio of old people?" Maddy suggested.

"Why would one witness, juror, whatever, bring two other people along? I think Ruzinski should be arriving separately. Just happen to be ahead or behind us in line."

"I agree," the marshal said. "Crap. You know witnesses who have been threatened are safely brought in and out of the courthouse all the time. Maybe we should trust the usual protocols. Maddy isn't the first one I've worked with who was threatened, you know."

On a bite of anger, Will countered, "So far, she's narrowly escaped death three times, and then there was the ambush we evaded. And the ultimate defendant isn't a crooked businessman or money launderer. He's a superior court judge."

"Was. But you're right. I'm just frustrated. Wait a minute. Could we bring her in by helicopter?"

Maddy must have heard that last word, because her eyes widened, and not in a good way.

All Will had to say was, "Bomb, remember?"

Ruzinski swore.

Maddy spoke up. "One of the men in the alley escaped. They know I have a broken arm. How are we supposed to hide that?"

Good question.

MADDY DIDN'T EVEN hear what the Uber driver and Will were saying. She sat in the backseat of the silver Toyota Prius, gazing out the passenger window at a wet, gray day. Raindrops slid over the glass.

Only a year ago she'd belonged here in downtown Seattle. She might know some of the men in well-cut suits and women in heels carrying umbrellas as they navigated the steep, rain-slicked sidewalks. Her law firm was in the building at the corner ahead. She could go in, take the elevator to the fifth floor and stroll in. Would anyone recognize her in the thick makeup? Would they recognize her without it? How much turnover in personnel had there been in the past year?

She'd always assumed she would go back to work there, as if the slice of time she'd been away was nothing. Vacation. What she hadn't imagined was the changes in herself she only now began to recognize.

I don't belong.

Her strange mood today might have something to do with the sense of alienation, Maddy recognized. The long-awaited day was here, and she felt fatalism instead of fear. Which might be best, if it didn't slow her reaction time.

Will might be talking to the Uber driver, a prematurely balding young man, but really he was keeping an eye on her.

The rain was a stroke of luck, allowing Maddy to wear a calf-length, enveloping raincoat that hid both the splint on her left arm and the bulky Kevlar vest that Marshal Ruzinski had supplied. With a forest green hooded slicker over his own vest, Will looked thicker through the waist and chest than usual, which fit with his drastically aged face. Meeting him for the first time, Maddy would have sworn he was in his sixties, courtesy of salt-and-pepper hair and lines skillfully applied by the woman who'd done their makeup. Her own face was equally strange to her.

Maybe that last, astonished look in the mirror had given rise to her peculiar mood.

She heard Will say, "I didn't realize the hills were so steep here. Why don't you go around the block so you can drop us right by the entrance? My wife needs hip replacement surgery."

The driver obediently took a left on Cherry Street, his eyes meeting Maddy's in the rearview mirror. "My dad had the surgery six months ago. I'd swear it took ten years off his age."

Her lips curved on command. "I'm looking forward to not living with constant pain, I can tell you." How true.

"I can imagine."

Two right turns, and they passed the small city park where she'd sat on a bench and eaten lunch a few times during a break from a trial. Almost there. Her pulse jumped.

A last right, onto Third Avenue, and the Uber driver steered them to the curb in front of the main entrance.

Will's phone buzzed. He took it from his pocket, read a text and, expression never changing, held out his phone so she could read it, too.

Decoy under attack. Shots fired.

They thanked the driver and exited onto the sidewalk, Will first then Maddy. He tucked her close to his side, his head turning. The sidewalk was busy despite the rain.

A taxi pulled up behind the Prius and a man got out. Dismissing him, Maddy worried. Where was the marshal?

"We're ready," Will said in a low voice. "Let's move."

Ready? Maddy felt a shock as she sneaked another look at the stranger from the taxi. Not a stranger. Ruzinski.

He didn't so much as glance at them but, as planned, fell in behind them as they started toward the doors.

Maddy had taken only a few steps when she heard a horribly familiar coughing sound. At the same moment somebody bumped her from behind.

Ruzinski had fallen to the sidewalk and wasn't trying to get back up. The gun he must have had in his hand skittered a few feet across the concrete.

Without thinking, she bent to pick it up.

Chapter Fifteen

People screamed and ran, knocking each other over and confusing the scene. Unbelievable that these bastards were willing to gun down innocent passers-by. With the assailant using a suppressor, Will had barely heard the first shot. Not until a woman five feet beyond Maddy went down, blood blossoming on her pale blue suit jacket, did Will know shots were still being fired.

That might have *been* Maddy, if she hadn't unexpectedly ducked.

Weapon extended, Will swung in a circle, almost straddling her, waiting for her to rise. Where was the shooter? Damn it, *where*? His gaze flicked from face to face. Men of all ages, several more women. Panhandler…with cold eyes and a handgun spitting bullets. Probably not alone, but one at a time.

Will fired. Once, twice, three times. The gunman slammed back against the gray wall of the courthouse.

"Will!" Maddy screamed.

He spun. The bullet slammed into his chest, dead center. More shots hammered his torso. He reeled, stumbled back. Saw Maddy on her knees, gripping the marshal's gun with both hands, which meant she'd ditched the sling. This shooter wore a black balaclava and leaned out of a taxi that had pulled up behind Ruzinski's.

Will kept pulling the trigger, but he was going down. Leaving Maddy—except she was firing, too, nothing on her face he'd ever seen. God, please don't let her kill an innocent. Don't let her die.

His head hit the pavement and the lights went out.

ASTONISHINGLY, HER HANDS were steady. If there was any pain from her broken arm, she didn't feel it. Maddy aimed low; this past week she'd done internet research that told her the kick would push the gun up. He was firing, too, but her focus narrowed to *him* in an instant of surreal clarity. When she pulled the trigger, the recoil was greater than she'd anticipated, but she'd hit him. He slumped, hanging out the car window. The gun he'd held fell.

Something stung Maddy's arm. Had she been shot? But who—

There. The driver of that same taxi had opened his door and was firing over the roof. Afraid she'd miss and hit someone in a passing car or on the opposite sidewalk, she hesitated.

Behind her at least two voices yelled, "Put the gun down! Put the gun down!"

Guards? Would they shoot *her*? She flung herself flat, cheek pressed to the gritty concrete. A man crawled over her and, panicked, she started to scramble away.

"Maddy, it's me!"

Ruzinski. Thank God he wasn't dead, although blood darkened his raincoat and dripped onto her.

She heard more gunshots but had no idea who was shooting now.

Will. Oh, dear Lord, was he dead? Terrified, she knew *he* would have thrown himself over her if he wasn't badly injured, at least.

"Put the gun down!" a man yelled right above her. She saw the blue-uniform-clad legs. A police officer.

Suddenly, her hands trembled viciously. Another hand closed over hers and gently removed the gun, laying it on the pavement. A foot in a shiny black shoe appeared in her limited vision and edged the weapon out of reach.

She closed her eyes, gripped by shock. But... "Will," she mumbled.

Ruzinski rolled off her. He was swearing, a litany that seemed to punctuate the moment.

Somewhere, a woman still screamed. Somebody else was sobbing. Sirens screamed, too.

Maddy had to know. Cradling her injured arm, she awkwardly pushed herself to her knees. She must have skinned them, because they burned fiercely. She rose until she was kneeling and could turn in place.

Will.

There he was, a few feet away. Dead or only unconscious. She crawled to him. He lay on his back, his face slack.

"Will," she whimpered. "Will, open your eyes."

She wrenched open his raincoat but didn't find any blood. A pulse throbbed in his neck and he was breathing.

"Ma'am, out of the way," a man said. Wearing a uniform, he crouched to assess Will's condition. A paramedic, whose sharp eyes lifted to her. "You're injured, too."

She shook her head. "I'm just scraped up."

"You have blood all over your raincoat."

Maddy looked down. "Oh. No, that's from him." She gestured. "He's a US marshal."

The man yelled, "Higley, over here!"

Within seconds he slid a brace around Will's neck and he and a second paramedic, a woman, shifted Will onto a stretcher. Moving fast, they lifted him and started toward an aide car.

"Wait!" Maddy tried to stand. "I need to—"

"Ma'am, let me check you over." Another uniformed woman with kind eyes reached for the buttons on Maddy's raincoat.

Two others worked over Ruzinski. Face creased with pain, he rolled his head toward her. "You okay?"

"Yes. I think so." Actually, she hurt a whole lot, but that was because her battered body had once again been assaulted.

"Then get inside and do what you came to do. Put that scumbag away," he said fiercely.

The ambulance with Will inside pulled away from the curb. Maddy wanted desperately to run after it, but Ruzinski was right. This had all been about keeping her from testifying.

The closest EMT helped her to her feet. "You're in pain. You need to go to the hospital. Here. You can ride with—"

"No." She pulled away. "I'm a witness in a trial. I have to get inside. All I need is to clean up."

"I'm sure your testimony can be pushed back…"

"Then we'd have this to do again." She fully looked around for the first time. Ruzinski was now being loaded into another ambulance. A bloodstain marked where the woman had been shot and fallen. Other people sat, faces gray with shock as paramedics worked over them. Handbags, briefcases, coats, umbrellas and women's scarves littered the sidewalk, abandoned where they'd fallen. Police cars and ambulances jammed the street, so many lights flashing Maddy's eyes were dazzled. More cops than she'd ever seen at one time interviewed stunned people who were lucky enough to be uninjured.

The Uber driver who'd delivered her and Will was one of those. Even as he talked, his head swung toward her and their gazes met. She wanted to say *I'm sorry, we used you*, but at least he was unhurt.

Just once she looked at the body half hanging out of the taxi. The man she had killed.

Then she asked the EMT beside her, "Will you help me?" She began hobbling toward the entrance.

"Ma'am, you should—" He gave up and put a hand under her elbow to support her. Once she was inside, Maddy thanked him and groped in her pocket for the latest phone Will had given her.

Before she had a chance to dial, a woman emerged from an elevator. Gaze intense, she hurried toward Maddy.

"WELL." HEAD TILTED to one side, Cynthia Yates assessed Maddy. "That's an improvement."

They were in a restroom on the same floor as the designated courtroom. On a first-name basis now, they'd been in here for half an hour, delayed because once Maddy gingerly removed the dirty, bloody raincoat, balled it up and shoved it into the trash, she realized a bullet had grazed her upper arm. That was what had stung.

While Cynthia disappeared in search of a first-aid kit, Maddy managed one-handed to peel off ruined tights and the bloody, ripped blouse, then washed her scraped knees and hands. Then she washed the stage makeup from her face, leaving it stark.

After returning with supplies, Cynthia applied copious antibiotic ointment to the ugly graze and then wrapped Maddy's arm with gauze. More ointment on her raw palms, more gauze. Maddy winced as she donned a borrowed white blouse and tights. She let the DA brush her hair and apply light makeup.

Supporting her broken arm with her opposite hand, Maddy grimaced. "I don't know what happened to my sling."

"How about some more gauze?" the other woman suggested, brandishing the roll.

"I'm starting to look like a mummy, but why not?"

"Not a mummy, a zombie."

She would have laughed if the ache of fear hadn't held her in such a tight grip. Why hadn't somebody called to tell her about Will's condition? Ruzinski... well, he might be in surgery, she realized.

"I think this is as good as it's going to get," she said, studying herself in the mirror. Aside from her eyes, she looked fine. Good, really, now that the bruises were gone. Only her eyes betrayed the craziness inside her, the shock and fear and anger.

Cynthia's phone buzzed. She glanced at it. "Good timing. We're ready for you."

Maddy closed her eyes, drew a few deep breaths and sought composure. So many people had sacrificed so she could do this. She wouldn't let them down.

The restroom door had just closed behind them when her phone rang. Maddy snatched it from her pocket and answered.

"Will?"

"Yeah." His voice sounded as if it had been scraped over gravel, but was so welcome. "You okay?"

Maddy blinked back tears. "Basically. What about you?"

"The vest stopped a few bullets. I have a cracked

sternum and cracked or broken ribs. Mostly, I knocked myself out when I went down. They won't let me go yet." He paused. "I'm sorry. I wanted to be there for you."

"Oh, Will." She stopped in the hall and turned away from the prosecutor. "I made it here only because of you. This part, I know how to do."

"I guess you do."

Behind her, Cynthia said, "Maddy, we need to go."

"Kick butt, sweetheart," Will said. "As soon as I can break out of here, I'll come get you."

"Okay." *I love you.* But she had no idea whether he'd want to hear those words.

The hall had emptied while they were closeted in the restroom. The click of their heels seemed to echo.

A guard opened the heavy wooden door for them to enter. People in the galley automatically turned to see who was coming in. Attorneys on both sides did the same.

No, they weren't all attorneys. The man she'd seen murder her client had turned, too, to see her stride in, his face frozen with shock.

Surprise!

WILL GAVE SERIOUS thought to getting dressed and walking out. Not like anybody could stop him.

Impatience eating at him, he waited, though. He'd had an MRI and wanted to hear what, if anything, they'd seen. Brain damage wouldn't help him get accepted to medical school. The last time he'd pushed the little button to summon a nurse, she patted his hand and said, "Just a few more minutes."

Damn, he'd wanted to see Maddy on the stand, staring that son of a bitch in the eye.

There wasn't any way someone could have smuggled a gun to the defendant, was there?

No. Besides, after the scene outside, the bailiff and every armed officer in the courtroom would be hyperalert.

He had to quit worrying...but where in *hell* was the doctor?

THE COURTROOM LOOKED different from this perspective. *Get used to it*, Maddy told herself. After all, there was another trial to come.

Any other time, she might have been nervous, but anger was her predominant emotion. A few weeks ago, seeing Kevin Mooney's face might have rattled her. What she saw him do was terrible beyond any other experience in her life. But hey, now she'd experienced plenty of other violence. All, of course, because of what she saw that day.

Defensive counsel, a man Maddy didn't know, objected to the sling she wore. "If she's attempting to draw sympathy..."

A gleam of delight lit in Cynthia's eyes. "Your honor, we're certainly prepared to explain how Ms. Kane came to be injured."

The judge tipped her head to study the attorney. "You'll have your chance to ask questions. I'll allow it if you choose to pursue that line of inquiry."

Cynthia calmly led Maddy through the day she'd witnessed a murder. The second best moment came when Cynthia asked, "Do you see that man in the courtroom today?"

"Yes." Maddy pointed. "Right there."

The best moment? When she was asked if the gunman had spoken. Maddy said firmly, "Yes, he did. Ms.

Bessey was begging. She wanted to know why he was going to kill her. His exact words were, 'You're a problem for Brian Torkelson.'" The courtroom was utterly silent during her pause. "Then he shot her."

The opposing counsel's attempt to shake her went nowhere. Her previous courtroom experience gave her the confidence to take her time before answering questions, ensuring that she spoke clearly with no digressions that could weaken her testimony.

Somehow it was no surprise that he didn't raise the subject of her sling. He might not know about the bomb or the ambush in Bellevue that left an FBI agent badly injured. She'd prefer to think he didn't. However, she'd seen a woman hustle into the courtroom to pass a note to him, likely informing him about what had taken place out front only an hour ago. He couldn't risk letting the jury hear about it.

The judge thanked her for her testimony and Maddy rose, surprised to find that her legs weren't entirely steady. Unwilling to meet her eyes, the defendant stared down at papers on the table in front of him.

Maddy walked out.

THE RELIEF ON Maddy's face when she saw him loosened the knot in Will's chest.

He hadn't been happy to spot her standing alone in the lobby. What were these people thinking? But as he strode toward her, a guard materialized to intercept him, backing off only when she said his name and rushed forward.

He didn't care where they were. He pulled her into his arms, his kiss fueled by all the tumult the day had set loose in his chest. He needed to know she really was all right. This was the only way he could reassure himself.

He did hold on to enough awareness of his surroundings to know they had to get out of here before this could go any further. Also, he had to deliver one piece of irritating news.

He gave their pulses time to slow before he said, "I've been asked to bring you to the police station. They need to interview you."

She gripped his hand. "You'll stay with me?"

"I'm going to guess they won't let me sit in on the interview, but I'll be waiting."

"Um…how did you get here?"

Will grinned. "I went for variety and hired a taxi."

Maddy laughed. "Just think, what if the same Uber driver had come to pick you up?"

"If I were him, I'd be taking the rest of the day off."

She made a face. "I'd suggest *we* do, except by the time we get home it'll be evening." Her expression changed. "That is… I guess I shouldn't assume I can keep imposing on you—"

Will scowled. "Of course you're coming home with me."

Did his cabin feel like home to her? Man, he wanted to think so.

Not the moment to have that talk, he reminded himself.

Fortunately, the Seattle PD detective who interviewed Maddy knew the backstory and, after hearing her side of what happened upon their arrival at the courthouse, assured her there'd be no repercussions for shooting a man who'd clearly been trying to kill her.

During the taxi ride back to Northgate, where Will had left his Jeep, Maddy told him the detective had congratulated her on her skill with a handgun. She smiled impishly. "I shook him up a little when I told him I've never fired one before."

Once they'd been dropped by his Jeep, parked in the transit lot at Northgate, Maddy insisted on driving.

"I'm fine," he said automatically. "Your arm is in a sling."

A steely look in her eyes, she held out her hand for the keys. "If your Jeep had a manual transmission, that might be a problem. As it is, I can drive with one hand. You, though... Major narcotics? Head injury? MRI? You were *unconscious*, Will."

Feeling chagrined, he dropped the keys into her hand.

Once on their way, she asked about Ruzinski and any other victims from this morning. "I saw that woman with blood all over her chest."

"She went straight into surgery and is still in critical condition. Two other bystanders are, too, not to mention the injured from the decoy team." He hesitated. "Including your replacement. A bullet grazed her head, but she'll be okay."

Maddy absorbed that. So many people, injured and dead, to keep her silent.

"I saw Ruzinski in recovery before I left," Will added, "and he asked about you. His wife and an adult son were there by then. The surgeon told us he expects a complete recovery."

"So nobody died."

"Two of the bad guys are dead, one also in critical condition."

Her fingers tightened on the steering wheel. "Which one lived?"

"The one I shot. He posed as a homeless wino."

"Oh. I saw him when we got out of the taxi."

"He's the first one who started shooting. Goes without saying that the detectives and FBI agents who showed up at the hospital really want him to survive. One more nail in Torkelson's coffin."

"This guy might not know who had hired them."

"Possible, but we can hope. Now, tell me how it went in court."

She did.

"Too bad the guy didn't ask you about the broken arm."

Maddy laughed again. "Cynthia was hopeful, but I think by then he'd heard about the shoot-out in front of the courthouse."

A phone rang. He immediately identified it as the one she had been carrying. Since she didn't have a spare hand, Will answered.

"Mr. Gannon?" It was Yates herself. She asked to speak to Maddy, and when he explained that she was driving with only one usable hand, she said, "I have good news. During a recess Mr. Mooney's attorney approached us. He's willing to accept a plea in exchange for us taking the death penalty off the table. He'll go for a life sentence with a possibility of parole. In return, he'll testify against Torkelson."

Will grasped the consequences immediately. "Eliminating Maddy won't save him anymore."

"Unless Mr. Mooney were to be killed, but we're asking for solitary confinement until Torkelson is convicted."

"That's excellent news."

He repeated what she'd said aloud for Maddy's benefit.

"Oh." She went quiet for a minute. "He won't dare go to trial now. Everything would come out. The bomb on the plane that resulted in a US marshal's death, the men who tried to hunt us down, the assault intended to prevent me meeting with Yates, and the last-ditch attempt today. He'll go for a plea."

"Don't suppose he'll fare well in prison," Will said with satisfaction.

"No. It's all over."

She didn't seem to want to talk after that. What could he do but let her have the space she needed to come to terms with what had to be an emotional crash after a year of unstoppable tension? The news was good, but still unsettling.

She'd want to go home, he realized. Her parents would need to see her. After today's spectacular events, her law firm was sure to welcome her back with open arms.

Will's mood plummeted as the miles passed.

SHE DIDN'T NEED him anymore. The realization shocked Maddy. Perhaps she should be glad, and she was in one way; if they had any kind of future, it had to be as equals. In another way…she hadn't expected the end to come so abruptly.

It wasn't a sure thing that Torkelson would take a plea…except she knew it was. He'd be foolish to risk a trial, and that was one thing he wasn't.

Maddy had expected to have more time with Will. More idea of how he felt about her.

When they let themselves into his cabin, she sneaked a sidelong look at him to see that some of the creases in his face had deepened. He might just be preoccupied, she decided, but what was he thinking about? Getting his life back?

"I can hardly wait to get out of these clothes," she

said. He only watched as she scooped undergarments, shorts, T-shirt and flip-flops from the small pile of her belongings.

She shut herself in the bathroom and changed, her mind on him the whole time.

Talk to him? Wait until he said something? Cheerily announce there was no reason she couldn't go stay with her parents now?

Maddy felt sick when she emerged from the bathroom.

Will stood right where she'd left him. "I'll miss you," he said.

She bit her lip and nodded. He looked so much like he had that first day, when he'd come upon her. *Déjà vu*, she thought. "This feels—"

"I don't want you to go," he said gruffly. "I know you're probably eager to get back to work, but…maybe we could figure something out."

Her eyes stung. She started forward, wanting his arms around her, but she remembered all those cracked or broken bones and stopped.

"I don't want to go," she admitted. "I've been hoping—"

"God." Two long strides, and he swept her into an embrace. "Damn, Maddy. The whole way back all I could think was you'd be in a hurry to go home."

She lifted her head to smile shakily. "You know I haven't lived with my parents for a very long time. And my apartment was never exactly home." She swallowed. "You are."

He kissed her almost clumsily, desperation allowing for no gentle preliminaries. Maddy held on as tightly, tangled her tongue with his, nipped his lip, wrapped a leg around his. Oblivious to their surroundings and the fact that they were clothed, she tried to pull him closer. She needed him inside her. *Now*.

They stripped each other. He was sane enough to don a condom before they made hard, frantic love on the sofa. Maddy wasn't sure she'd have noticed if he hadn't.

They ended with her sprawled atop him, her arm in the way, of course. She lay savoring the long, muscular body near hers, the gradually slowing beat of his heart. The groan when she shifted her weight.

Horrified that she'd let herself forget his injuries, she tried to lift herself off him, but Will held her in place.

Finally, she whispered, "I was afraid you still thought you weren't good enough for me."

He groaned again. Before she could worry, he said, "We need to buy a new sofa."

Maddy burst out laughing. "That's one of the few really great pieces of furniture I have."

"Good," he said, a smile in his voice. His hand slid down her back, his fingers delicately exploring her string of vertebrae. "We need to talk about how we can make this work."

"I suppose."

They got dressed and jointly started dinner, since there wasn't much she could do with only one hand. She did most of the talking, telling him she didn't want to go back to work at the same firm, and maybe not at all as a defense attorney. "I think I'd like to become a prosecutor. Everything that's happened has changed my perspective. Not just that. It's changed *me*."

The knife he'd been using to dice a bell pepper still in hand, he kissed her lightly. "Meeting you has changed me."

Neither of them said *I love you*. They didn't have

to. She knew, and thought he did, and really, what was the hurry?

"You'll come with me to meet my parents?" she asked. Seeing his expression, she added, "They'll like you. I promise."

He had her when he said, voice rough, "Maybe we can take a week or two to go to Lake Shasta, too. Meet my dad. And did I ever tell you I worked one summer for a place that rents houseboats? We could do that."

"Yes." What could be more perfect than a week on the water, just the two of them? She held up her hand, forefinger and thumb almost touching. "First time I set eyes on you? I was *this* close to just shooting you, you know."

He only laughed. "And I was so sure you couldn't hit me if you tried."

Maddy raised her eyebrows. "Now you know not to underestimate me."

Smiling, Will laid down the knife and used both hands to cradle her face. "Never," he murmured. "That's one mistake I'll never make."

* * * * *

COLTON BABY CONSPIRACY

MARIE FERRARELLA

This 300th book is dedicated with love

To my wonderful readers,
Without whom I would still be working as
a health insurance claims adjuster,
Dreaming of becoming a writer;

To
My fabulous editors, especially Patience Bloom,
Whose fear of being buried alive in stacks of
Proposals had them finally deciding to take a
chance on me;

And
To
Charlie,
Who was, and is, my inspiration for every single hero
I have ever written about.
I couldn't have done it without you, honey.

From the bottom of my heart,
Thank you!

Prologue

They enjoyed being in control; they always had. Even back in the early days, alone and struggling to make ends meet, a day-to-day world nothing if not hopeless and bleak, they'd *dreamed* of being in a position when they would finally be in control.

Slowly but surely, they had worked relentlessly toward reaching that goal, moving from stepping-stone to small stepping-stone until finally, *finally* arriving at a place of authority. When they finally controlled people who didn't even realize they were being controlled.

I am that good, they thought with a self-congratulating smile.

And this, *this*, they thought, looking at the email draft on their laptop, was going to be the ultimate achievement, the crowning glory. Because when this email went out and at long last set this greatest plan in motion, they were going to be in control of not just a person or a small group of people but of a large, thriving company.

An entire, billion-dollar company.

It would be, they thought with a smug, self-satisfied smile, like going from presiding over a tiny cottage in the forest to ruling over a giant kingdom.

My giant kingdom.

Oh, there would be a figurehead to front the company, but *they* would be the one who told that figurehead what to do, what to think. *They* would be the one in charge of everything.

As it should be. After all, who better to control all those employees? Who was more deserving to reap all those rewards?

They laughed to themselves.

"Why, *me* of course. I'm the most deserving person I know," they announced to the surrounding darkness of the small office where they presently oversaw the organization they had created and molded out of nothing.

Taking a deep breath, they pulled back their shoulders and focused on the task at hand. The shadowy figure reread the words that had been typed and then retyped so many times since this idea had begun to take its final shape.

This had to be perfect.

The email had to sound coherent. To read as if it was written by an intelligent person—but not by someone who was overly intellectual. Or that some delusional, misguided person had written it.

Above all, it could not come across as if it was a hoax. It had to read as if every word was nothing but the absolute truth.

They wanted the message to read as if the person who wrote it was cool, calm and just a touch superior. *Because I am*, they thought. *Superior to the lot of them. And more than just by a touch.* Because once they acted on this knowledge, it would be the beginning of their downfall.

It might take a week, or a month or even a year—although they doubted it would take that long—but they *would* definitely fall.

A smug smile curved their lips as they relished the thought and looked forward to the day all of this would come together.

For what felt like the hundredth time, they scanned the words on the computer screen. Words they had been tweaking and tinkering with for what felt like an eternity now.

They would really love to sign a name to the email, but in order for this to work, to avoid intense scrutiny and questioning, the source generating this had to be thought of as anonymous.

One last time, they read each word very slowly.

To: Colton Oil Board Members Listserv
From: Classified
Subject: Colton Oil CEO Ace Colton is NOT a real Colton

Ace Colton, born 40 years ago on Christmas Day in Mustang Valley General Hospital, was switched at birth with another newborn baby boy in the nursery. This shocking truth can be confirmed with a simple DNA test that will prove Ace is not a Colton by blood. Since the Colton Oil bylaws state the CEO must be a biological Colton, Ace must be ousted. I will provide you with no further information, but rest assured this bombshell is the tip of the iceberg.
Good Day

As their eyes rested on the last word, they felt their smile widen, even more smug and far more self-satisfied than it had ever been.

"Perfect."

Now there was nothing left to do but send this email to all six members of the Colton Oil board—and then sit back, calmly waiting for the fireworks to start going off.

With a mixed surge that was composed of equal parts excitement and confidence, they handed the computer over to their tech expert. This trusted employee had organized the logistics of this mission and would continue to monitor it. They pressed Send.

"And now it begins!"

Chapter One

Marlowe Colton had always thought that one of the perks of being the president of Colton Oil was having her very own private, luxurious en suite bathroom installed within her rather cavernous office.

An en suite bathroom where she was currently having her very own private nervous breakdown as she stared at a small white stick that had the audacity to mock her with a glaring pink plus sign.

Her breathing grew shorter and more erratic as she continued to stare at the awful, incriminating stick. Her stomach kept tightening until it had twisted itself into a hard, painful knot.

Marlowe realized that she was sweating even as she felt a cold chill shooting down her spine and passing over every part of her body.

And the nausea was back. In spades. Any second now, she was going to throw up.

Again.

"No, you're a Colton," she told the unusually pale blonde looking back at her in the mirror. "You're not going to throw up. You're not!" she insisted.

Marlowe blinked back tears. They weren't tears of

joy, or tears of sorrow. What she felt stinging her eyes were angry tears. Angry tears that were aimed at no one but herself.

How *could* she have let this happen? One stupid moment of intoxicated but entirely willing weakness and longing and now here she was, in the throes of morning sickness.

It wasn't possible.

It *wasn't*.

And yet the stick in her hand told her it was all too possible.

It was a reality.

The white stick had come out of the discarded white box that was now haphazardly sitting on the edge of the sink. The pharmacist had assured her that this product was supposed to be the best, the most accurate pregnancy test on the market. She truly doubted that it had made a mistake.

Besides, if she was being completely honest with herself, the thought that she was pregnant had been in the back of her mind for the last six weeks. Ever since she had lost her head and her iron grip on her emotions by succumbing to the sexy, dark good looks and charms that she had been all but bred to hate. Because the man on the other side of that bed six weeks ago had a father who hated her father, and that feeling was very, very mutual.

What in the name of all that was good and proper had she been thinking? Marlowe silently demanded of her reflection.

That was just it—she *hadn't* been thinking. For once in her career-driven life, she hadn't been thinking at all, just feeling. Or at least *telling* herself that she'd been feeling. Feeling an overwhelming attraction to a man she had viewed as the enemy for as far back as she could remember.

This was what came of trying to behave civilly toward someone who she had been taught did not deserve to be treated with any sort of respect.

All of her life, Marlowe had done exactly what was expected of her—and then some. She was a Colton, and Coltons were supposed to behave a certain way. At least Payne Colton's daughter was supposed to behave in a certain way.

She closed her eyes, fighting another strong, rising wave of stomach-lining-destroying nausea as it tried to claw its way up her throat.

If only she hadn't gone to that stupid energy conference…

Or, at the very least, if she hadn't spent so much time arguing with Bowie Robertson, president of Robertson Renewable Energy Company, over proposed pipelines and the environmental consequences they could have. The argument went on and on relentlessly until everyone else at the conference had withdrawn for the night. That left just the two of them to continue the argument on their own.

How heated words had somehow given way to splitting a bottle of champagne—or had that been *two* bottles?—she still really wasn't clear about. But somewhere along the line, their different philosophies and the eternal ongoing rivalries that defined their lives had just somehow managed to melt away, leaving nothing to get in the way of a very real and exceedingly strong attraction that had mysteriously taken root and been growing between them for who knew how long.

Marlowe could remember only bits and pieces of their night together after that. One of those bits and pieces had included a very strong desire to be, for once in her life, swept away, for the space of at least that one isolated evening.

An evening that became free of thoughts about rivalries, corporate profits and even the ever-increasing concerns about green energy being a threat to her family's oil company.

Just one carefree evening, that was all she had wanted, Marlowe thought.

And now this stick and its menacing, mocking pink cross were exacting a price for those frivolous few hours of passion she had spent.

A price she had never, even in her wildest dreams, been prepared to face up to and pay.

That wasn't to say that she didn't want children. She did, Marlowe thought. She *did* want children. But just not *now*.

And definitely not with *him*.

They hadn't even spoken a single word to each other since that fateful night, as if silence was actually an acceptable way of denying that those few hours of unabashed passionate consorting—of wild, consensual *lovemaking*—had ever happened.

But not talking about it, not acknowledging that it took place, was *not* a way of wiping that night's existence out of the annals of time. The pregnancy test clearly testified that it had happened, she thought ruefully, frowning at the offending mark on the white stick.

And that, in turn, had most definitely produced a consequence. A very big consequence.

Marlowe felt her throat closing up. What the hell was she going to do now?

The question throbbed insistently over and over again in her brain. But no matter how many times she asked herself, she came up with the same answer.

She didn't know.

She had absolutely not even a *glimmer* of an idea what she was going to do about this.

The only thing that she *did* know was that her father was going to see this pregnancy—and how it came about—as nothing short of a personal betrayal of him of the first order.

"I wasn't thinking of you at the time, Dad," Marlowe whispered to the man who wasn't there in person but was somehow always around Colton Oil headquarters in spirit. Payne Colton was the reason behind everything she did.

The truth of the matter was that her father had always been a very strong presence in her life, influencing, in one way or another, her every move, practically her every thought.

But not that night.

That night the intrusive spirit of Payne Colton had been utterly absent. At least, he had been by the time she and Bowie Robertson, drunk on champagne and each other, had gone up to her suite at the Dales Inn.

The Dales Inn was the only hotel in town, and coincidentally it was also where the green energy conference was being held.

To someone viewing this from the outside, with everything that was going against them—feuding fathers, rival companies—that night she and Bowie might have come across as a modern-day Romeo and Juliet. Except, once the dust had settled again, they were much more like the Hatfields and the McCoys, but with the Coltons focusing on drilling oil wells and the Robertsons worrying about environmental impact.

She sighed, holding her head with one hand. There was no happy ending in sight here.

But then, she remembered, there hadn't been one for Romeo and Juliet, either.

Her head was really beginning to hurt, Marlowe thought. And it didn't exactly help her condition any to have both her desk phone and the cell phone she had left next to it when she'd walked into the bathroom ringing like crazy now. The phones sounded as if they were jointly heralding the end of the world and doing so just slightly out of sync.

Maybe they were, she thought darkly, still staring at the offending stick.

"Why don't they shut up?" she cried, helplessly putting her hands over her ears.

As if that would stop the noise, Marlowe thought angrily.

She rose to her feet—her legs felt oddly shaky, she realized, holding on to the wall for a moment to get her balance—and opened the bathroom door and glared accusingly at the offending phones.

If they were *both* ringing like that, something had to be very, very wrong, she thought.

Something other than an offending white stick with its glaring pink cross.

Taking a deep breath, Marlowe made her way over to her wide custom-built desk. Part of her was hoping that the ringing would abruptly stop by the time she reached the phones.

No such luck.

Braced for almost anything—after all, the worst possible thing had already happened, she reasoned—Marlowe picked up her multiline desk phone. Thinking it was one of the company's many administrative assistants on the other end, she said tersely, "Okay, this had better be good."

"On the contrary," she heard her father's deep voice rumbling against her ear, "this is very bad. And where the hell have you been? Why aren't you answering your phone?" Payne Colton, chairman of the board of Colton Oil, demanded angrily. "Your damn phone's been ringing off the hook. Why were you just ignoring it?"

"Dad?" Marlowe said shakily, still looking at the stick she was clutching in her hand.

Payne snorted. "Well, at least you still know who I am," he retorted in disgust. "Did you forget your way to the boardroom?"

"What?" What was he talking about? It was after five o'clock. There was no meeting scheduled this late, at least none that she recalled. "No," she responded after a beat.

"Well, that's good, because that's where the rest of us are, sitting around that big old table and twiddling our thumbs, waiting for you to make an appearance." His voice hardened. "I sent you a text," he snapped, the fury he was feeling now more than evident in his voice. "Didn't you see your email?"

No, Dad, I didn't see my email. All I see is this big, ugly white stick that's about to topple my whole world, Marlowe thought numbly.

"Well, Your Highness, we're still all waiting for you to deign to put in an appearance," her father was saying while she was having her crisis. "So read that email I forwarded to you and get that skinny behind of yours in here. Pronto! Do you hear me?"

Hovering over her laptop, Marlowe hit a key. The screen that was currently there gave way to another one that contained her corporate email. She scrolled up the page to the latest message to see what had set her father off like this.

Her mouth dropped open when she got to the subject line.

She reread the words twice.

"Oh my Lord!"

Her father took her shocked response to mean she had looked at the email. Or at least she had seen enough of the email to shake her up, which was good enough for his purpose.

"All right, get in here *now*, Marlowe!" Payne screeched. "I'm not going to ask you again."

Marlowe's knees were shaking so badly, she had to sink down into her chair. This had happened to her twice in the last fifteen minutes, she thought, feeling as if she was completely losing her grip on the immediate world.

Despite her father's voice reverberating in her ear with his loudly shouted demands, Marlowe opened her email, hoping that maybe the contents weren't as bad as it initially seemed.

It was worse. Marlowe's head was suddenly filled with a swirling kaleidoscope of memories, all grounded in her childhood. Adventures and events that she and Asa, whom everyone called Ace, had shared as children. Ace was her big brother. He was a big brother to *all* of them, even to her adopted brother, Rafe. Ace didn't care. He treated Rafe just like he was a *real* brother.

That was just the way that Ace was.

Marlowe looked back down at the email's subject line.

That was absolutely absurd, she thought. Who would *say* such a crazy thing? Who would even come up with such an idiotic idea, she silently demanded, stunned beyond words. Maybe this was the work of some competitor in an attempt to disrupt the company.

"Marlowe? Marlowe, are you there?" Payne Colton's deep voice thundered, bringing her back to the moment and her suddenly cold and incredibly inhospitable-feeling office.

It took her a second to focus and come around. Thinking took another second. "Yes," she said, breathing heavily, "I'm here, Dad."

"No," her father corrected her sharply, "you're *there*. I need you to *come here*. *Now!*" he declared. "Can you do that for me?" he asked his daughter sarcastically. "Can you hightail it out of your overdecorated office and get yourself to the boardroom *five minutes ago*?" Payne shouted.

It wasn't just Marlowe's knees that were shaking now—it was all of her.

With effort, she gripped the armrests of her chair and literally hauled herself up to her feet. Testing the strength of her legs for a second to make sure that she wouldn't just fall flat on her face with the first step she took, Marlowe slowly moved her hands away from the armrests. By now her heart was pounding against her chest like a drumroll.

"I'm coming," she told her father in what seemed like a whisper.

"What did you just say?" Payne demanded angrily. "I can't hear you!" he declared like the marine drill sergeant that all his children, at one time or another, had felt he was.

Marlowe took a deep breath, filling her lungs with air before she repeated the words. "I said I was coming."

"Then get here already!" Payne snapped.

The next moment, the connection was abruptly terminated. Only her father's disapproval and anger lingered in the air around her like a dark, malevolent cloud.

This wasn't happening, Marlowe silently insisted as she closed down her laptop.

That done, she raced out of her office. None of it, she tried to console herself. None of this terrible stuff was happening. Not this hateful email and not that positive pregnancy test.

It was all just a bad dream, and any second now, she was going to wake up, Marlowe promised herself. And when she did, all of this was just going to be an awful, fading memory.

Her high heels resounded, clicking rhythmically against the highly polished marble floor as she ran down the corridor to the Colton Oil boardroom. The staccato sound seemed to mock what she had just told herself.

Her heart fell with a thud as she reached the open boardroom door.

It didn't look as if she was going to wake up from this one after all.

Chapter Two

It was almost surreal that after all these years of being on the opposing side of every argument, Bowie Robertson couldn't seem to be able to get thoughts of Marlowe Colton out of his head. The simple truth of it was that he hadn't been able to stop thinking about the Colton Oil president for the last six weeks.

At first, it had been because the woman was single-handedly responsible for what was admittedly the greatest night, bar none, of his thirty-two-year-old life.

Granted that, for years now, he had been very aware of the fact that Marlowe Colton, with her shoulder-length mane of whitish-blond hair and a figure that wouldn't quit, was drop-dead gorgeous. But he had also viewed the woman as the personification of an ice queen. An ice queen with nothing but cutthroat ambition running in her pretty veins.

He had been completely blown away to find out that the total opposite was really the case.

Yes, he had had a great deal of champagne to drink that night, but even an entire river of alcohol wouldn't have been able to drown his brain to the point that would get him to believe something that wasn't really true. He would have to have been beyond utterly drunk to believe that what had actually been a sow's ear had transformed into the proverbial silk purse.

No, he wasn't suffering from some sort of delusion; that had actually happened.

But as enchanted as he'd been by the slightly vulnerable, passionate, warm, funny woman he had made love with in her oversize hotel bed, the cold reality was that it had turned out to be just another illusion, a sleight of hand with no staying power once it was viewed in the light of day.

In fact, he had discovered that Marlowe actually *did* care about the environment and that she had set up awards for Colton Oil employees who created sustainable technologies and were working to make the family business more eco-friendly. That notably went against her father's narrow-minded view, but once he had left her room and was on his way back to his own world, Bowie quickly found out just how cold and vicious Marlowe Colton could really be.

A few short hours after they had spent what he had viewed at the time as an exceptionally passionate night together, Bowie found himself to be a marked man.

Marked for death.

There had been two attempts made on his life in breathtakingly short order. Right after he had left the hotel, someone driving a black SUV tried to run him over. When that attempt hadn't been successful because he had managed to get out of the way just in time, someone tried to shoot him.

The sound of a gunshot had been so benign that at first he thought it was a car backfiring—and then he saw the hole a bullet had made right through the car window that was less than a foot away from where he'd been standing.

The two incidents, so close together, were just too much of a coincidence for Bowie to merely shrug off. It *had* to have been because of Marlowe—or someone acting on that she-devil's orders. It was too much of a coincidence that, right after he'd slept with the enemy, someone tried to kill him…right?

He speculated that the reason for the attempts on his life—the *failed* attempts, he gratefully amended—were twofold. One, the woman had obviously let her guard down that night, and since he was the one who had witnessed this drop and been on the receiving end of the consequences of that action, she undoubtedly didn't want him telling anyone about it. The only way to ensure that didn't happen was to have him eliminated.

Why had she gone to such drastic lengths? She had also shared something with him that, in hindsight, would probably be considered a company secret. She was going behind her father's back and looking into ways to make Colton Oil more eco-friendly. She hadn't told Payne yet because she had nothing tangible to present to him, but it wouldn't be long. All this was told to Bowie in strictest confidence. And even though he had promised to take that to his grave, Marlowe had obviously decided to hasten that scenario along and kill him. While he didn't think her so-called "secret" was a big deal, she obviously did.

Maybe, given time, he might have just chalked up these feelings as unnecessarily paranoid. After the second failed attempt on his life, he had deliberately kept his distance from Marlowe, avoiding all forms of contact and definitely not calling her. He even made sure to have a security detail around him at all times.

But now, six weeks after their one wildly insatiable night of passion—as well as the two subsequent attempts on his life that had occurred—a third attempt had been made just that morning.

This attempt had borne fruit. It hadn't wounded him, but the bullet that had been fired killed his security guard.

A second bullet had narrowly missed hitting Bowie himself.

It was now painfully obvious to Bowie that lying low and avoiding contact with Marlowe wasn't working. And ignoring the source of the problem was *not* making the problem go away.

So, focusing on that, he decided that it was time for him to confront Marlowe before another attempt was made on his life. Or before anyone else wound up paying the ultimate price by being on the receiving end of a bullet that was meant for him.

Out of respect for the night they had shared, he'd wound up behaving like a coward, not confronting Marlowe about their time together and the subsequent attempts on his life. That in itself was something that, to Bowie, was even worse than death.

Death was quick and final, but the label of being a coward carried with it a stigma that could haunt him until the end of his days. He was *not* about to allow that to happen.

It was time, Bowie decided, to confront the lioness in her den and get this whole thing out in the open.

MARLOWE ENTERED THE BOARDROOM, crossing the threshold on legs that still didn't quite feel as if they belonged to her.

She was no longer clinging to the hope that this was all just a bad dream, but she had to admit that the scenario still didn't feel as if it was real.

Marlowe took in the immediate scene within the room. Her father was right. The rest of board was already there, and they were obviously waiting for her.

Looking around, she quickly scanned all their faces. Her father; Ace; her half sister, company attorney Ainsley; and CFO Rafe all looked to be stricken to varying degrees. The only member of the board who did not look stricken was Selina Barnes Colton, the company VP and director of public relations, and coincidentally, her father's second—and mercifully *ex*—wife.

Not only was Selina *not* stricken looking, but if Marlowe hadn't known any better, the auburn-haired viper seemed to be almost gleeful about this potentially dire situation threatening to unravel right before them.

Marlowe had never liked Selina. None of her siblings ever really had, she'd discovered years ago. But truthfully she had never disliked the snide, smug woman more than she did right at this very moment. Why her father insisted on keeping his ex-wife not just with the company but actually serving on the board, giving her an equal voice when it came to decisions, was totally beyond her.

The air in the boardroom was exceedingly tense. Out of the corner of her eye, Marlowe could see that her father was waiting for her to take her seat, so she did.

Only then did Payne speak. The anger vibrating in his voice was impossible to miss.

"Now that we're all here, let me take this opportunity to say that this email, sent by a quivering coward who didn't even have the nerve to sign his own name, is a complete and utter fabricated lie. It's obviously a pathetic stunt pulled by some spineless, sniveling jackass who is trying to derail our company in any possible way that he can."

Listening, Rafe could clearly barely contain himself. "Of course it's a lie," he cried, agreeing. "But how can it possibly be able to derail a billion-dollar company? Even if what this jerk is claiming *was* true—which it isn't—who cares?" he demanded. Rafe glanced at the man who was the center of this ridiculous email. "Ace is a Colton, blood or not. Right?" he said, looking at Payne.

To Rafe, it was a rhetorical question that didn't even need or expect an answer.

But the opportunity was far too good to waste, so Selina was more than happy to offer an answer to her former stepson's question.

"Not to throw water on your theory," Payne's ex-wife murmured in a just barely audible voice. "But you, Rafe, of all people, being adopted the way you were by Payne and his kind late first wife," Selina continued, her voice fairly dripping with a false sweetness as she circled back to her point, "should know that blood is *everything* when it comes to being a Colton."

Although there was a smile on the woman's face, her eyes were cruel and ice-cold, looking not unlike those belonging to a cobra just before its fatal strike.

"What are you talking about?" Rafe asked. "What is she talking about?" he repeated, turning toward the other people on the board for an answer.

When his gaze landed on Ainsley, the woman shifted uncomfortably. Marlowe knew the last thing Ainsley would want to do was side with Selina, especially against someone she actually considered family. In this particular case, however, as odious as it seemed, apparently the law was on the woman's side.

Clearing her throat and avoiding looking at either Ace or Selina, Ainsley told the others, "The reason it would derail the company is because on page one, paragraph two of the Colton Oil bylaws, it clearly states that the company CEO must be a Colton by blood only."

Okay, enough was enough. Incensed, Ace shot to his feet.

"This is crazy," he declared, using, Marlowe thought, the exact same phrasing she had when she'd seen the results of her pregnancy test.

This was crazy. They couldn't oust Ace from the board, Marlowe thought. He belonged on it.

And yet…

"This ridiculous email is a lie," Ace was saying. "A total fabrication meant to send shock waves through our entire company and undermine its very structure. I'm a Colton! I was born a Colton and I'll always *be* a Colton." He looked at his father. Though it wasn't in his nature to ask for any sort of help or backup, this one time he made an exception. "Tell them, Dad."

It wasn't a plea, it was a request for the older man's verification about his birthright.

Payne nodded so hard, his thick silver-gray hair shook and fell into his eyes.

"Of course it's a lie!" he declared with a fierceness that defied opposition. "Ace is my son. I was right there, in the delivery room, the day that he was born," Payne said, looking directly at his oldest son. "Of course, he wasn't quite this big at the time," he added with a small, dry chuckle. "As a matter of fact," Payne recalled, "he was pretty frail. Everyone in the hospital, myself in-cluded, thought it was a Christmas miracle that he even survived. But he *did* survive. Not just survive—he man-aged to *thrive* almost overnight," Payne recalled with a nearly tangible wave of nostalgia. "And now just look at him!" the family patriarch cried.

It took Marlowe a moment to realize that his small trip down memory lane had been received with surprise by the others around the conference table.

This was part of the narrative that hadn't been pre-viously broadcast. This was the first she'd heard that Payne and Tessa's big, robust firstborn had been born a sickly infant whose chances of making it through the night had been regarded as slim to none.

Despite their obvious surprise, only Selina picked up the thread that had been dropped.

"A Christmas miracle?" she asked in a slightly mock-ing tone. "Really? Or did you or your first wife at the time deliberately decide to switch that sickly, frail baby with a healthy newborn?"

Payne's face immediately turned a vivid shade of red.

"How *dare* you insinuate," Payne screeched, "that either I or Ace's mother could do something so repre-hensible as—"

He couldn't even bring himself to finish his sentence, he was so incensed.

Everyone suddenly started talking at once, their raised voices drowning one another out as each tried to make his or her point.

Despite the turmoil going on in her head and her life, Marlowe's inner instincts took hold. Before she even realized what she was doing, she was on her feet, her raised voice louder than anyone else's as she attempted to calm them down.

"People. People!" she cried even louder. "Calm down!" she ordered in a semi friendly, albeit very authoritative, voice. "Of course this is all a huge mistake. My big brother is a Colton. He always has been—in his heart as well as in his blood. You know that," she insisted. "And, like this awful email said, one simple DNA test will prove that."

"You're right," Ainsley said, adding her voice to back up her younger half sister. She glanced at Ace. "I'll go with Ace to make sure he gets a test fast and have that test expedited as quickly as humanly possible. It'll cost a fortune," she said before Selina had the opportunity to raise an objection concerning the cost of having the test results delivered so quickly, "but it will definitely be worth it. Especially when you think of it how it will prevent certain chaos if the press ever got hold of this."

Selina raised and lowered her shoulders in a careless, dismissive shrug. "It's only money, right?" the woman said scornfully.

"Yes, it is," Marlowe replied. "And it's not *your* money," she deliberately added, knowing that was the sort of thing that would really irritate the hateful woman.

Selina's eyes narrowed, her pupils like two laser pointers as she glared at Marlowe. "To prevent anyone from contesting the results and saying that they were deliberately manipulated to give the results *we* were all after—" her tone placed quotation marks around the word *we* "—shouldn't there be a disinterested third party present to act as a witness—just to keep everything honest?" she concluded sweetly.

"You're absolutely right," Payne said. It was obvious that agreeing with his ex-wife was costing him. "Any suggestions?" he asked the others, deliberately ignoring Selina as he looked around the table.

But Selina refused to be ignored. "How about—" the woman began, only to be drowned out by Ainsley, who spoke over her.

"I can ask Chief Barco to come along and serve as a witness to the whole procedure, from the initial taking of Ace's blood to every single step taken in order to get to the end result." Only then did Ainsley look at Selina. "Will that satisfy you, Selina?" she asked the woman.

"Absolutely," Selina replied smugly. "I'm just trying to make sure that everything's aboveboard so that no one can say the results were manipulated or doctored," she told the rest of the board.

Marlowe kept her expression neutral even as she glared at Selina. They all knew that the only one who would claim that the results were "doctored" was Selina. Selina was clearly the enemy in their midst, but they were going to have to deal with that if the company was going to continue to survive the way it had all along.

Marlowe made a silent pledge that it would, if she had anything to say about it.

For the time being, focused on fighting for the company—and her brother—all thoughts of the earthshaking test in her office were temporarily pushed into the background.

Chapter Three

Marlowe quickly made her way back to her office. She was a woman with a mission. The crisis surrounding Ace and whether or not he was truly a Colton—a ridiculous question at best—had, however temporarily, displaced her own personal drama. After all, it wasn't as if *that* problem was going anywhere, at least not without some sort of intervention on her part.

And besides, there was still a chance, albeit an increasingly slim one, that it was some sort of mistake, or glitch, and she really was *not* pregnant. But pregnant or not, she would tackle that problem later. Right now, she had to join the rest of her family and *do* something about this terrible, unfounded rumor before it made the rounds. It needed to be disproved and stopped at its source.

Which meant finding out just who this so-called "anonymous" sender was who had emailed that hateful message to all six of them. Getting to the bottom of this was going to require some expert online sleuthing by someone who was far savvier than she was when it came to technology.

And Marlowe knew just whom to turn to. The reigning expert, as far as she was concerned, was an IT specialist who was already employed by Colton Oil and was currently working right here in the company's headquarters.

If *anyone* could get to the bottom of all this and track down just where this heinous email had originated, it was Daniel Okowski. Not only was Daniel good at his job, but he was also decent and loyal. Marlowe knew that she could trust the IT director to keep the subject matter he was going to be investigating quiet, just as she was confident that once he *did* find out who was responsible for sending this email, he wouldn't make that information public, either.

Picking up the telephone receiver, Marlowe was about to call Daniel when the cell phone that she'd left on the side of her desk beeped, informing her that she had a text.

Her first inclination was to ignore it. She just didn't have time to handle yet another new crisis. One more thing and she was in danger of having a real breakdown.

Her deeply imbedded work ethic trumped her survival instinct, and Marlowe looked down at her phone screen, bracing herself.

The text was from her administrative assistant, Karen. Marlowe didn't even bother reading it. Karen was not the type to bother her unless it involved something important.

Taking a deep breath, Marlowe pressed the number that directly connected her to Karen. The second her assistant picked up, she told the woman, "I'm kind of busy right now, Karen. Can this wait?"

"I don't think he wants to wait, Ms. Colton," the assistant whispered nervously into her phone.

"He?" Marlowe questioned. But even as she asked, her sixth sense, ever alert for the next pending disaster, caused her stomach to suddenly plummet to her knees.

Still, she told herself that she could be wrong, which was why she asked, "Just what 'he' are you referring to, Karen?"

The next second, rather than hearing Karen's voice giving her an answer, Marlowe saw her door being slammed open. Bowie Robertson came barging into her office, loaded for bear. He had no sooner entered the door than the door banged shut behind him, the sound reverberating throughout the office and echoing menacingly in her head.

"*Me*, Marlowe. Your assistant is referring to me," Bowie declared angrily.

A beat behind, Karen appeared directly behind the man who was currently behaving like a raging bull. Her normally efficient assistant looked extremely fearful and was all but quaking in her shoes.

"Do you want me to call Security, Ms. Colton?" she asked, her eyes furtively glancing in Bowie's direction, then looking away again.

Yes, I want you to call Security, Marlowe silently answered her assistant. But saying that out loud would make Bowie think that she was afraid of him, and she would rather die than have him believe that. She wasn't afraid of anyone, she thought fiercely.

So instead Marlowe tossed back her head, sending her blond hair flying over her shoulder. Her brown eyes, shooting daggers, met Bowie's green gaze dead-on.

"No, not yet, Karen," she told her assistant. "You can go. But stay close to your phone," she cautioned the young woman.

Looking somewhat uneasy, Karen never took her eyes off the back of the intruder's dark head as she slipped out Marlowe's office. She eased the door closed behind her.

The second her assistant had left, Marlowe turned her attention back to the man she regarded as a detestable, unwanted invader. She was now all but shooting bullets at him.

"What the hell do you think you're doing, barging into my office like this? Who the hell do you think you are?" Marlowe demanded hotly of the man she held responsible for the personal minidrama she was going through.

Bowie clearly was in absolutely no mood to back away, no matter how much she yelled. "I'm a man who's done hiding!" he shouted right back at her.

Marlowe stared at him. That made absolutely no sense to her. Bowie was just tossing about meaningless words. Why would he be in hiding?

"Hiding?" she repeated. "Hiding from what?" Marlowe demanded, both confused and enraged.

Bowie's eyes narrowed. "Don't play dumb with me, Marlowe. It doesn't suit you," he said bitingly. Then, because she continued to look like she didn't understand what he was saying, he snapped, "Hiding from your goons." Like she didn't know that, he thought.

"Goons?" she repeated, still just as lost as she had been a moment ago. "What goons? Did you fall on your head, Robertson? What are you *talking* about?" she asked, growing angrier by the second.

So she was going to play it dumb, was she? Okay, he'd spell it out for her, even though he was certain that she wasn't ignorant of the reason that he had come looking for her.

"The goons that tried to run me over and who shot at me—*twice*," he emphasized. "The second time they went target shooting, they killed my bodyguard and, incidentally, just narrowly missed me. *Now* do you know what I'm talking about?"

This had to be an act, Marlowe thought. Nothing more than an attempt to throw up a smoke screen for some unknown reason. The man was crazy.

Furious, she shouted at him, "You are totally delusional!"

"Yeah, well, there's a body lying on a slab at the morgue who begs to differ with you," Bowie told her in disgust. "Why don't you have one of your minions call up the medical examiner at the morgue and ask if he just did an autopsy on a Miles Patterson?" he suggested. "I bet the answer's going to be yes."

He looked absolutely serious, Marlowe realized, beginning to feel uncertain. But how in heaven's name *could* he be? She hadn't sent anyone to shoot at him or threaten him in any way.

Marlowe glared at the impertinent man. If *anyone* was going to do something to this raving lunatic, it would be her, she promised herself.

And she'd do it with her fists, Marlowe thought.

"*You* are insane," she accused.

"No," he contradicted, "I *was* insane to ever allow

what happened between us to go as far as it did. But what's done is done," he snapped. "It's in the past, and I'll be regretting it for the rest of my natural life.

"But I'm here to tell you that you don't have to worry. I don't know what kind of people you're used to dealing with, but I'm not about to take something that was told to me in confidence and spill it to anyone willing to listen. You said it was a secret when you told me, and unlike you people," he said, encompassing her entire family, "when I make a promise, I *keep* it. So call off your hired guns, Marlowe, and just let me go on with my life in peace."

She looked at him as if he were babbling in some foreign language she couldn't begin to identify.

"What the hell are you *talking* about?" she demanded, growing steadily angrier and more frustrated with every second that went by.

Bowie stared at her, incredulous. How far did she intend to carry this charade?

"So what?" he asked. "You're telling me that you're going to continue playing dumb?"

"I am *telling* you that I don't have the faintest idea what you are carrying on about," Marlowe informed him, exasperated. She was *not* buying into this act of his, and she was insulted that Bowie would even *think* that she would.

His eyes pinned her where she sat. "You mean to tell me that you don't know that someone's been trying to kill me ever since I left your hotel room at the Dales Inn six weeks ago?" Bowie questioned angrily.

Marlowe looked at him, stunned and momentarily speechless that Bowie could actually believe she was some sort of black widow, femme fatale capable of "mating" and then killing the man she'd just had sex with.

That was totally bizarre.

Of all the images she'd ever had of herself, that wasn't one she'd even remotely *ever* entertained. She'd never thought herself capable of doing something like that. She *knew* she wasn't glamorous enough to pull it off.

Nor would she want to. Behavior like that was vapid and empty, and completely devoid of any sort of moral scruples. None of that would ever come even close to describing her.

Pulling herself together, Marlowe found her tongue. "Again, I have no idea what you're talking about. *None,*" she emphasized. "I don't even remember what this 'secret' was that I was supposed to have told you."

The second the words were out of her mouth, Marlowe's eyes grew large as it occurred to her that she had another problem on top of the one she was already aware of. Oh God, what was this secret she'd told him, and how was this going to blow up in her face?

The suspense and anticipation threatened to eat away at her stomach lining in record time.

"You don't remember telling me anything," Bowie said in a mocking tone. "You honestly expect me to believe that?"

"I can't help what you believe or don't believe, but that's the truth," she insisted angrily.

"No, you're lying," he accused, standing firm. "It's too much of a coincidence that right after you told me your precious secret, people started aiming their cars at me and shooting at me." His eyes darkened. "Our families have been rivals practically since the beginning of time, and I should have had my head examined for going against everything that made sense and thinking that I could have misjudged you. I should have kept my distance from a viper like you the way I always have."

Marlowe glared at him, furious at what Bowie was insinuating. Furious with herself for ever letting her own guard down and allowing him to get close enough to really complicate her world.

Furious with herself for *ever* thinking that he could be capable of being a decent human being…even though he was the father of her child.

Staring at the ruggedly good-looking man now, Marlowe couldn't help wondering if he—or maybe someone in his family, if not the entire lot of them—could be behind that awful email that had thrown her own family into such turmoil.

"Well, you didn't keep your damn distance, did you?" she all but spat out. "And pretty soon everyone's going to know that."

He stared at her, completely at a loss as to what she was saying to him. The woman certainly spent a lot of time babbling, he thought, irritated.

"*Now* what are *you* talking about?" he demanded. "I don't speak gibberish."

Marlowe glared at him. "Neither do I," she shot back at this interloper.

"Then what the hell are you *saying*?" he asked.

He wanted it spelled out? All right, she'd spell it out for him. She was through being patient. "I'm saying that our families are going to have to find a way to tolerate one another."

"And why, pray tell, would they want to do that?" he asked, really wishing that in the middle of all these hot words that were flying back and forth between them he didn't find this woman so damn attractive that his toes all but curled.

Why couldn't he find her the least little bit repulsive, or ugly or even off-putting? Hell, he'd really settle for off-putting.

Instead, while shouting at this woman he was convinced was trying to have him killed, all he could think of was the way her mouth had tasted that fateful night. How soft her skin had felt beneath his hands and how much he *still* wanted to make love with her.

He had to be out of his mind, Bowie thought. That was the only explanation he could come up with. Maybe she had slipped him something that night, something that was now making him behave like a mindless, lovesick loon.

At least he was managing to cover that part up, he thought thankfully.

His question rang in Marlowe's ears. If she had an iota of sense, she would have just let the subject drop, or answered him with some mindless bit of trivia that said nothing. She could just accuse his family for being underhanded and causing all this havoc in her own family.

She could say *anything* but what she knew she'd wind up saying in response to his question.

"Our families are going to have to figure things out, because in seven and a half months there's going to be a little human being with both Colton and Robertson blood running through his or her veins," she said from between gritted teeth.

Dumbstruck, Bowie stared at Marlowe. When he finally recovered the use of his tongue, he could only inanely echo, "What are you saying?"

"What I'm saying, Einstein," she answered sarcastically, "is that our temporary truce that night resulted in a permanent baby. I'm pregnant, you idiot!" she shouted at him.

She felt angry that she was trapped in this situation. Angry that it had ever happened. And most of all, angry that out of all the men in the world who could have been the father of her child, it had to be this Neanderthal.

"You're lying," Bowie accused numbly. She *had* to be lying, he told himself. She *couldn't* be telling him the truth.

But the expression on Marlowe's face gave him very little hope.

"I really, really wish I was," she told him, meaning her words from the bottom of her heart.

Bowie's stomach twisted in a knot, coming perilously close to making him throw up.

"You're pregnant," he repeated.

She blew out a frustrated breath. "That's what I just said."

It wasn't sinking in. He felt like a drowning man fighting like crazy to keep his head above water. "And it's mine?"

"Yes, it's yours, damn it."

He didn't remember forming the words until they finally emerged. "How can you be sure?"

There was fury in her eyes, and for a moment, he was

certain she was going to *really* blow up. But somehow, she managed to keep herself under control.

"Count yourself lucky that the handgun my father gave me for my fourteenth birthday is in a lockbox and not in a drawer in my desk because I have a license to use it and if it was the latter, right now I would be sorely tempted to use it on you. In the long run that would be preferable to having you as the father of my baby, but there you have it. You *are* the father of my unborn child, and that's a horrible fact we're both stuck with."

Her eyes grew very, very dark as she added, "And to answer your question as to how I know you're the father of this child, I know because I haven't had the time or the inclination to sleep with anyone in months, so unless this baby is the result of some sort of spontaneous generation, you, Bowie Robertson, are the father." Her eyes narrowed as she concluded, "Deal with it!"

Chapter Four

Marlowe looked at the silent man sitting directly opposite her.

Tall, dark and handsome by anyone's standards, Bowie Robertson's complexion had suddenly turned very, very pale right before her eyes. If it hadn't been for the change in his color, she would have thought she was witnessing, up close and personal, one of the finest acting performances of her life. But to her knowledge, no one could turn that pale at will. Which meant that her news had caught Bowie totally by surprise.

Well, that makes two of us, Robertson, Marlowe thought.

She almost felt sorry for him, considering what he was probably going through—the key word here being *almost*, Marlowe thought, because *she* was the one who was pregnant, not him. "Wow," Bowie murmured, more to himself than to Marlowe. The thought of having fathered a child left him numb. He had no idea how to deal with it. He had never even thought of himself as a father. Unable to deal with it, he pushed the thought into the background for the time being.

"I believe that sums it up as good as any word."

She agreed sarcastically, then switched gears as she demanded, "Now what was that secret I told you?"

Bowie blinked, scrutinizing her more closely. She was being serious, he realized. "You mean you really don't remember what you told me?"

Marlowe liked to think of herself as a patient woman, but after all the things that had happened today, she was utterly out of patience and dangerously close to another out-and-out display of pure, unadulterated anger.

"No, I *really* don't know what I told you," she snapped, enunciating each syllable.

Bowie continued to stare at her. If what Marlowe was saying was true—and she really didn't know what secret she had shared with him or that she had even disclosed *any* company secret while in the throes of their lovemaking—then she couldn't be the one who was trying to have him killed. She would have no reason to want to eliminate him.

So who the hell was trying to kill him?

The attacks had started shortly after he had slipped out of her room at the Dales Inn. Had someone—either there or just outside the hotel—seen him leaving the bar with her?

Or maybe these attempts on his life didn't even have anything to do with him spending the night with Marlowe. All right, then what? Why would someone be trying to kill him?

His mind was a total blank.

Marlowe noted that Bowie's brow was completely furrowed and he had a very strange expression on his face. So strange, in fact, that she couldn't even begin to fathom what was behind it.

"What is it?" she asked.

Her almost melodious voice broke through the fog around his brain. For a second, he thought she sounded genuinely concerned. So much so that he forgot to keep his guard up against a woman he had been indoctrinated his entire life to regard as someone who came from the enemy camp.

His guard down, he said aloud the words that were currently buzzing around in his head. "If you're not the one who hired someone to kill me, then who the hell did?" he said, totally exasperated.

She had no idea, nor the will, at this moment, to figure it out. Maybe she hadn't even told him anything of importance that night and he was just yanking her chain.

"Well, it's not that I wouldn't love to help you find an answer as to why someone is supposedly using you for target practice," she said flippantly, "but I'm kind of in the middle of a crisis of my own right now."

"You mean something else besides suddenly finding yourself pregnant with the enemy's child?" he asked her cryptically.

Marlowe raised her chin defiantly. "Yes, other than finding myself pregnant." She bit off the words, skipping the rest of his description. The fact that it was his baby only added to her feelings of being overwhelmed.

"So what's this other big crisis of yours?" It seemed to be the right question to ask, Bowie thought, given the situation.

"I can't tell you," Marlowe said. When she saw him raise a quizzical eyebrow, she did offer one piece of information. "It's not just a company crisis…it's a family crisis, as well."

The moment she said the last words, she suddenly covered her mouth with her hands, horrified, as she rolled her eyes. That was too much. Annoyed with herself, she dropped her hands from her face and blew out a ragged breath.

"What is it about you that keeps making me blurt things out like that?" she demanded accusingly, glaring at Bowie.

"Then you *do* remember what you said to me?" he asked her.

"No, I don't," she answered, frustrated, "but apparently you seem to have that kind of effect on me." Marlowe was angrier with herself than she was with him. She should have never had that champagne that night at the inn. Then none of this would be happening.

Belatedly, she thought of where she had been about to go when Bowie had suddenly come storming into her office. Nothing had changed. She still needed to see Daniel and talk to him about trying to track down the person who had sent this email that was causing such shock waves to go ripping through her family's lives.

"Look," she told Bowie as she rose to her feet, "I really have to go right now—"

Bowie followed suit, standing up, as well. He followed her to the door. "To handle that company-slash-family crisis, right?" he assumed.

"Something like that," she replied noncommittally. "But I'll be in touch later to arrange a meeting between us. Somewhere private," she added, "so then we'll be able to talk."

"All right," he agreed. "I'll wait for your call." His tone made it clear that if it didn't come, he would be back to see her.

By now they had walked out of her inner office. Karen looked apprehensively at the heads of the two most influential energy companies in Arizona. "Is everything all right, Ms. Colton?" she asked nervously, her eyes darting toward Bowie and then back again.

Marlowe wasn't in the habit of wearing her emotions on her sleeve, but just for a second, she was tempted to say "No, Karen, it's not. It's so far from being all right, it might never be right again." But she managed to suppress the urge as well as the words. Instead, she said, "Yes, Karen, everything's fine. Thank you for your concern." She swept past her and headed toward the elevator.

Because his legs were longer, Bowie easily matched her quick stride step for step until they reached the elevator. He was going out while she was going up, so he paused for a moment before leaving the building.

Whispering into her ear, he told her, "You lie like a pro."

Stunned, she demanded, "Excuse me?"

"Just now," Bowie explained, nodding his head toward the office she'd just vacated. "When you answered your assistant's inquiry, you told her that everything was all right, but you told me that you were in the middle of a crisis."

"There's no reason for Karen to know about that." Her eyes narrowed as she looked at him just as the elevator arrived. "There's no reason for you to know that, either, but you seem to have this strange power to make me lower my defenses and say all manner of things to you that I shouldn't."

"I'll do my best to use that power wisely," he told Marlowe with just the faintest hint of a smile curving his lips. "Don't forget to call and tell me the time and place that we'll be meeting," he reminded her as the elevator doors shut, removing her from his view. "Or I'll be back," he called out, raising his voice, although he doubted that she could hear.

Marlowe uttered a few choice words in response to his parting ones, but the doors had closed by then, sealing her off from him.

It was just as well, she thought. Why had she ever even *bothered* to talk to the man at the conference? Yes, what came afterward could easily be described as the best, the most remarkable night she had ever spent in her life. But at what price? Marlowe asked herself. And could she really say that it had been worth it?

In view of the present situation, she couldn't honestly say yes. But then, she couldn't really say no, either.

With all these diametrically opposed thoughts going on in her mind, Marlowe felt as if her head was liable to explode at any moment.

She knew she was dangerously close to being on overload, with just too many shocking pieces of unsettling information bouncing around in her brain, all accumulated in such a short amount of time. She didn't feel able to sort them all out without drowning in words and feelings.

C'mon, Marlowe, get a grip. If you fall to pieces, everyone else will, too. You have got to get it together! For everyone's sake, she admonished herself.

Marlowe realized as she quickly walked down the long corridor that she was consciously or unconsciously pinning all her hopes on Daniel, fervently trusting that somehow he would come up with something, preferably the name of the person who had sent them that unnerving email. She was convinced that he had it in him to save the day.

The boyish, studious-looking IT director was only six years older than she was, but in her opinion, he looked younger. Despite his looks, however, he possessed a razor-sharp mind, and if there was *anyone* who could unearth the name of the person sending them this awful email, it was Daniel.

His door was wide-open, and she knocked on the door frame as she crossed the threshold into the office. It looked like the other two people who were part of his department had already left for the night and that Daniel was just about to leave the office himself.

"Daniel?" she said, walking toward his desk. "Do you have a minute to talk?"

Whatever humorous retort he was about to offer instantly faded without a single syllable even partially emerging when he saw who was approaching him.

"For you, always," the tall, thin man told her. Rather than just paying lip service for the effect it had, she knew Daniel truly meant what he had just said. He felt boundless loyalty to the family that had taken a wet-behind-the-ears computer science graduate and placed him in a department where he worked in positions of respect and power, something he had never experienced before.

In return, Daniel had gone to great lengths to show

them that he was worthy of the faith and trust they had placed in him. Even so, he never took anything for granted. She knew for a fact that there were a lot of other people in his graduating class who were still struggling to pay off their school loans, while he was able to move around completely debt free because the Coltons had been willing to take a chance on him.

"Something's come up," Marlowe began, trying to find just the right words to use in order to present and explain the dilemma that they all—especially Ace—found themselves currently facing.

"Please, have a seat," Daniel said, gesturing toward a chair that was facing his desk.

At first, Marlowe looked almost hesitant to sit down. But then she finally did, sinking into the chair almost in slow motion.

"Go on," he urged.

After a beat, Marlowe took a deep breath. "Maybe it would be easier if I just showed you, Daniel," she said, because saying the words just might have made her choke, she thought.

"Whatever works for you," Daniel responded amicably. He waited for Marlowe to make the next move or say the next thing.

He watched in silence as Marlowe dug into her skirt pocket and pulled out her phone.

Marlowe forwarded the anonymous email and looked at the explosive piece on the screen in front of Daniel.

"This was sent to all six board members a few hours ago," she told the IT director. At least she assumed that was the timeline, although for all she knew, her father had been aware of this email's contents longer than that. She had no idea how she knew, but she just had a feeling.

She fell silent as she allowed Daniel several seconds to read the words.

Once he had finished reading and then rereading the email, Daniel raised his eyes to meet hers. "Is this on the level?"

"Whoever sent it seems to think so," she answered grimly.

"Do you know who sent it?" Daniel asked next.

Marlowe shook her head. "No. That's where you come in, Daniel," she told him. "I was hoping that you could track down whoever sent this to the board and find him for me."

"You said him—we're sure it's a he?" Daniel questioned.

Sighing, she shook her head again. "Daniel, at this point we're not sure of *anything*."

"Okay," Daniel said, taking the information in stride. He approached the problem from another direction. "You said this just came in?"

This time Marlowe nodded. "From all indications, late this afternoon. My father was the one who notified me," she added. "Do you think you'll be able to track this email back to its source and find out who sent this abomination out?"

"And you have no idea who might have sent it?" he questioned.

"Not even a clue," she answered him flatly. "Daniel, it's extremely important that you get us a name as fast as possible. This needs to be nipped in the bud before it somehow gets leaked to the press." She caught herself gripping the armrests and forced herself to make her hands go lax. "I don't have to tell you that we don't need that sort of publicity getting out."

Daniel nodded, his unruly dark brown hair falling into his eyes. He combed his fingers through it, absently brushing it aside from his black-framed glasses. His attention was completely focused on his boss. "Understood," he replied.

She was struggling to project the picture of confidence, but at the moment, given everything that had toppled down onto her shoulders, that was definitely not easy.

"Do you think you can do it, Daniel?" she pressed.

"I can certainly try," he answered cautiously. She knew he didn't like making promises unless he was 100 percent certain that he could successfully deliver.

"But can you do it?" Marlowe asked again, *needing* an affirmative promise from him. "You're the best in the business, Daniel, and if you can't do this…" A note of hopelessness filtered through her voice as it trailed off.

"Ms. Colton, you have to understand that a search for something this heinous could very well involve the dark web, and that's a great deal trickier to navigate than the regular web. They don't call it the dark web just to create an aura of mystery. The transactions carried out on *this* part of the internet are way more difficult to pin down. I would be remiss if I wasn't being honest with you, Ms. Colton," he confided. "The truth of it is that you might never find out who sent this email."

"But you *will* try to, right?" She was aware that she was practically imploring Daniel at this point.

"That goes without saying, Ms. Colton," he told her.

"I will use every trick in the book and lean on everyone I know to help me uncover just who sent out this piece of unfounded propaganda."

She knew he was doing his best to comfort her, but she had one more request. "Can you do all that without telling them why?"

Daniel smiled at her. "The people I deal with are accustomed to these sorts of nefarious transactions. Don't worry, Ms. Colton. If it can be done, I'll do it," he promised, "and no one will be the wiser."

"That's good enough for me," she told him, rising to her feet. "And when you do find out, call me, Daniel. Night or day, call me," she repeated.

"I'll be sure to do that, Ms. Colton," he promised solemnly.

Chapter Five

Well, that didn't exactly go as planned, Marlowe thought as she left the IT director's office.

She supposed that part of her disappointment was tied to the fact that she had begun to expect nothing short of miracles from Daniel. Marlowe had always had a great deal of respect for the man's abilities. The problem was that she had gotten those impressive abilities confused with his ability to do *anything* when it came to the internet.

Truthfully, until he had mentioned it, she hadn't even thought about the dark web. To her, the internet was the internet, whether it was "dark" or not.

If anyone *could* make some notable headway there, it was Daniel. Especially since she had made him realize how important finding whoever had sent out that email was to her. To the family.

Still, Marlowe was definitely not looking forward to telling her father that, rather than "mission accomplished," there was a chance, albeit it a slim one, that it might turn into "mission impossible."

She sighed. There was nothing to be gained by putting this off, so she went back down to the boardroom on the off chance that her father was still there. This was the kind of message that she preferred delivering in person rather than over the phone.

As she made her way down the corridors, the area felt oddly empty at this time of the late afternoon. Unless faced with a deadline that necessitated working overtime, most of the Colton Oil employees had gone home for the day. Even the lights seemed dimmer than usual, somehow, although none had been turned off yet.

Drawing closer to the boardroom, Marlowe heard the sound of raised voices. Or at least one raised voice. It didn't take much for her to recognize that the one she could clearly make out belonged to her father.

There was no doubt about it. No one could project his voice—or his emotions—the way that her bombastic father could.

Knocking on the door, Marlowe didn't wait for a response but opened it and walked right in.

Payne Colton immediately swung around. "What?" he demanded, abruptly curtailing the supposedly encouraging words he was imparting to his firstborn, Ace. However, coming from Payne's mouth, even encouragement came out sounding like he was venting his anger.

Ace Colton wasn't the target or the cause of that anger, but given the scope of his father's displeasure, Marlowe could imagine he felt as if he might as well have been.

All of his children had decided long ago that Payne Colton's ways took a lifetime to get used to—and even then it wasn't always easy.

Marlowe mustered the best smile she could at the moment and told her father, "I just thought you'd want to know that I put Daniel Okowski on the trail of our anonymous emailer."

The silver-gray mane bobbed up and down in approval. "Good. What did Okowski say? How long before he has some answers for me?"

The fact that her father had placed himself rather than her as the key player in this wasn't lost on Marlowe, but then, he did own the company, and anything that affected the company affected Payne Colton directly, so she wasn't about to quibble. It was a given, she thought, resigned to the fact.

"That's just it, Dad…" she began slowly, attempting to hedge her bets, only to have him break in and interrupt her.

"*What's* 'just it'?" her father demanded. "C'mon, girl, speak plainly. It's way too late in the evening to be playing riddles," he thundered.

"Let her talk, Dad," Ace requested patiently.

Payne glared at his oldest son. He'd never liked being interrupted. "I *am* letting her talk," Payne retorted. "It's not my fault that she doesn't talk fast enough, and when she does talk, it comes out in circles." His eyes shifted back toward his daughter. "Well, go ahead. What is it you're trying to tell me?"

Marlowe picked her words slowly, never taking her eyes off her father's face. "Daniel said that navigating the message might have links to the dark web. That is tricky, and there's a chance that we might never find out who's responsible for sending that email to us."

"What do you mean by never?" Payne demanded, exasperated.

"Exactly that," she responded. "Those were Daniel's words, Dad. Not mine. I guess he means that it's a lot more complicated than any of us might think," she began, only to be cut off again.

Payne laughed. It was a nasty sound with no mirth attached to it.

"Don't be so naive, little girl. Money can buy anything. It can damn sure get us those answers we're looking for, so we can fight even dirtier than this guy who's hiding behind his anonymous email. I'll just give Okowski a bunch of money to wave around, and you'll be surprised how fast those 'dark web' doors will fly open for us," he informed Marlowe and Ace with utterly unshakable confidence.

"I certainly hope you're right, Dad," Marlowe said. Her eyes darted toward her half brother. "For everyone's sake."

"Of course I'm right," Payne retorted. Marlowe saw that her father was dead serious as he added, "I'm always right."

Marlowe only wished that she had even half of her father's confidence.

"I'm going to go back to my office and talk to Okowski about that added incentive I'm giving him," Payne told his children. He held up the cell phone he had in his hand. "Keep these close in case I have to call you about any further developments." And with that, he walked out of the boardroom.

"Why don't you go home, Marlowe, and get some rest," Ace suggested kindly.

She looked at him sharply. "Why would you say that?" she demanded. Did her brother suspect something?

"Well, I hate to put it this way, but to be honest," he said in a kind voice, "you look terrible."

She was instantly defensive, but the feeling quickly subsided. Ace was just watching out for her the way he always did. "Funny you should say that. I *feel* terrible," she admitted.

"Are you sick, Marlowe?" he asked, concerned.

No, I'm pregnant.

But Marlowe didn't feel up to sharing this news with her family just yet, so she merely said, "Just about this situation." Then, because it was in her nature to be the family cheerleader, she said, "Don't worry, Ace. None of us are buying into that ridiculously fabricated claim in that email, and Dad's behind you a hundred percent. We're going to get to the bottom of all this," she promised him with feeling.

"I'm not worried," Ace told her. "Just mad that this is taking away precious time from the work we *should* be doing." He looked at her more closely. "Now go home and get some rest," he repeated, kissing the top of Marlowe's head. "That's an order."

Though it was strong, she resisted the urge to wrap her arms around Ace and cling to him the way she used to when she was little and felt as if the whole world was closing in on her.

Ace would never judge her, never indicate that he thought it was a sign of weakness for her to display a need for comfort. But she knew that if she did that now, Ace would sense that there was something wrong other than the fatigue she was claiming. He would start asking her questions, and she wouldn't be able to lie to him. She never had, but she couldn't burden him with this, either. He had more than enough to deal with without taking on her problem, as well.

So instead, Marlowe flashed a smile at him. "Sounds like good advice, although I really am fine," she assured him.

He nodded, clearly glad she wasn't fighting him on this. Seemingly as an afterthought, he told her, "Call me if you hear anything."

"You, too," she told him.

Ace grinned at her, that same warm grin that he usually flashed. She knew he was doing it for her benefit, and she appreciated it.

"Count on it," he said.

Somewhat heartened, Marlowe left the building and got into her car. But instead of going home—a home she shared with all of her siblings as well as her parents, as the house was large enough to accommodate all of them without having *any* of them running into the other members—she made the decision to go to her *other* dwelling.

She had purchased a condominium in downtown Mustang Valley. It was located at the very base of the mountain. She used it only whenever she found herself working late and didn't feel up to undertaking the drive home.

No one would bother Bowie and her there, Marlowe thought. That meant they could talk in private, although very honestly, aside from asking him a few questions about the allegations he had initially made, she didn't know what she was going to say to the man who had turned her entire world upside down by impregnating her.

She wasn't even sure at this point just what she planned to do about that pregnancy.

Turning on the car's overhead light, she took out her phone and sent a text to Bowie.

If you still want to talk, I'll be at my condo in half an hour. She then texted Bowie the address. Finished, she tucked away her phone and started up her car.

She'd lied about when she expected to arrive home. The condo was only ten minutes away from Colton Oil's headquarters. But she wanted the extra time to change her clothes and try to unwind from this overly stressful day before she had to face Bowie again.

The traffic was light. She arrived at the condo in eight minutes rather than ten.

Parking her car in the underground parking structure, she took the elevator up to her condo. The moment she walked inside, she stepped out of her high heels. The entire trip from her door to her bedroom, she shed one article of clothing after another.

By the time she had slipped into her jeans and her oversize, baggy sweater, Marlowe felt like an entirely different person.

Her stylish high heels were replaced by fuzzy socks with corgis pictured on the front of each. She did *not* look like the high-powered president of a major oil company. Instead, with her perfectly styled hair now pulled back into a jaunty ponytail and all of her carefully applied makeup completely wiped away, she knew she looked more like a teenage version of herself.

Marlowe looked into the mirror, doing a quick survey of herself. For at least the rest of the evening, she had effectively gotten rid of "corporate Marlowe." Or at least the aura of that persona. She had transformed into just a young woman who had unfortunately made a very bad misstep in the heat of passion.

She'd completed her transformation just in time. The condo doorbell rang.

Habit had Marlowe glancing at her watch. Apparently Bowie Robertson had a thing about punctuality. She had said thirty minutes, and damn if he wasn't here exactly thirty minutes after she'd sent her text to him.

Leaving her bedroom, she went to answer her door. She supposed there was something to be said about punctuality, Marlowe thought.

Still, mindful of the fact that she *was* home alone and there was someone out there sending an anonymous email meant to throw her family's life into total chaos, Marlowe took her small, unloaded handgun out of its lockbox and brought it with her as she went to answer the door.

"Who is it?" she asked a second before she looked through the peephole.

Bowie Robertson was standing on the other side of the door, suddenly feeling tenser than he could remember feeling in a very long time. He had no idea what he was going to say to Marlowe, or even why he was actually here. Everything seemed as if it was completely jumbled up.

"Guess."

Marlowe couldn't decide whether or not the voice she heard was friendly or ominous. Had Bowie come here to talk to her or to threaten her? She wasn't sure, but she squared her shoulders, determined to meet this challenge head-on. She was a Colton, and Coltons were never afraid.

Her hand closed over the small weapon in her pocket.

"Well, it's too damn early for Santa Claus, so I'm guessing that this is *not* the answer to my prayer," she said, flipping the two locks on her door and pulling it open with her free hand.

She saw Bowie's gaze land on the handgun she had removed from her pocket.

"Did you invite me over to shoot me?" he asked her, staying exactly where he was.

"No," she answered. After a beat, she lowered the weapon in her hand. "After what you said about someone trying to shoot you, I thought it wasn't a bad idea to keep my gun handy when I opened the door to my condo." She nodded over her shoulder, silently inviting him in before telling him, "Come on in, Robertson."

Bowie stepped over the threshold cautiously. "You know how to use that thing?" he asked, nodding at her lowered weapon.

"My father took me to the shooting range the day he gave me this gun for my fourteenth birthday. I can shoot the top feathers off the head of a turkey at twenty paces," she informed him proudly. "I could give you a demonstration if you'd like," she offered.

"Sorry," he quipped, "I left the turkey at home."

"You could do in a pinch," she told him. "All you'd have to do is hold up a few feathers in your hand and I can shoot those."

"Tempting, but I'll pass," Bowie told her. "My luck can only hold out for so long," he added, doing a quick survey of her immediate living space. "I don't intend to push it."

Once inside her condo, and with her weapon tucked away back in its place, Bowie sighed audibly.

"You look different," he told her.

"Nothing gets by you, does it?" Marlowe quipped. "Do you want something to drink?" she asked. "I've got a fully stocked bar."

Marlowe was still waiting for him to answer her. "Robertson, you're staring," she said.

"Sorry. I've never seen you look like a civilian before," he told her. His face softened a little. "You look nice."

That surprised her. She had never been complimented before when she looked like this, and she had no idea how to respond, so she didn't. Instead, she went back to her original question.

"I asked you if you wanted something to drink."

He shrugged. "Sure. I'll have whatever you're having."

"I'm not having anything," she told him. "I'm pregnant, remember?"

And the reason he was here, the attempts on his life and all that entailed—including an unknown source, now that Marlowe denied having anything to do with it—instantly came crowding back into his brain.

"Oh, right," Bowie murmured. "For a second, I just forgot." And was trying to forget, despite everything, just how much he still wanted her.

Chapter Six

"All right, let's get down to business," Marlowe said, sitting down on her sofa and approaching this new problem logically. "Who would want you dead?"

Her blunt question threw Bowie. He'd thought that she had asked him here to talk about what they were going to do about the condition she suddenly found herself in. That and perhaps even touch on the night they had spent together, when he had gotten to see a completely different Marlowe Colton than the one the rest of the world—including him, up until then—was acquainted with.

But since she was asking about the attempts on his life, he was willing to address that first. Bowie sat down on the other end of the sofa. He had been giving his own dilemma a great deal of thought since he had confronted Marlowe in her office earlier. As a result, he had come to a new conclusion about it, a totally different one from the one that Marlowe was suggesting.

He started out treading lightly. "While it's true that I have made some enemies in my energy dealings, so have you," he pointed out.

"No argument there," Marlowe acknowledged.

But before she could continue, Bowie advanced his theory a little further, getting to the heart of what he believed.

"I think that this would-be killer is somehow connected to you or maybe to Colton Oil."

Marlowe's face clouded up. "So we're back to you thinking I hired someone to kill you? Is that what you're saying?" she asked incredulously.

"No," he corrected her, "what I'm saying is that these attempts on my life somehow have something to do with you, because someone started targeting *me* only after I spent the night with *you*."

"You mean you think that someone's watching me?" Marlowe demanded, clearly doing her best not to show Bowie how much the very idea of what he was suggesting unnerved her.

Bowie shrugged. "I honestly don't know," he admitted. "But it does make sense in a way. All I do know is that no one took a shot at me or tried to run me over before you and I spent the night together."

Marlowe thought of the anonymous email that had been sent to all six members of the board. Was that somehow connected to these attempts that had been made on Bowie's life?

Maybe Bowie *was* onto something, she thought, although she was not about to tell him about that. She had absolutely no intention of divulging anything about what was going on in the company unless it turned out to be absolutely necessary.

For now, she just shrugged, doing her best to seem casual. "Maybe you were just lucky before."

"Yeah, maybe," he agreed, although it was obvious

from his tone that he didn't really subscribe to that theory. "All right, then why don't we get down to it and talk about the elephant in the room?" he proposed.

Marlowe stiffened, instantly knowing what he was referring to. She felt heat rising up her neck to her face, inevitably turning it to a reddish hue. She was far more comfortable talking about gunmen, hired or crazed, than she was talking about something that was so utterly personal.

But she had been the one to initially blurt out the news to him, so she couldn't very well just fluff Bowie off or shut him down now.

"What about it?" she asked stiffly, her voice devoid of all emotion.

"What do you want to do about…it?" he asked her point-blank.

"You mean you don't have any suggestions?" Marlowe asked sarcastically. After all, she would have thought that an opinionated man, such as he was, would try to impose his will on her, especially since the child was half his. Or at least she *assumed* that was the way he would think of it.

"Oh, I have plenty of suggestions," Bowie assured her.

Big surprise. "I thought so," Marlowe retorted.

She'd pegged him right, she thought. But for some reason, she didn't find that nearly as satisfying as she would have thought she would. As a matter of fact, as she examined her feeling, she was rather disappointed that he was like that.

"But," Bowie went on to say, "it's your body. So ultimately, the decision is yours."

That he was capable of that sort of thinking caught Marlowe totally off guard. Was she actually wrong about him?

"Then you don't care what I do about this baby?" Marlowe asked, trying to get a handle on how he really felt.

"I didn't say that," Bowie pointed out. The fact of the matter was that he clearly did care. Cared a great deal, Bowie thought. "But I'm not the one who has to go through this."

Bowie meant the pregnancy and birthing part, but Marlowe immediately jumped on a different interpretation entirely.

"You're damn right you don't." She couldn't begin to think about everything that was involved, the huge changes that she was going to have to make in her life. Her head began to swirl. "I don't know the first thing about being a mother—" she began in exasperation.

"Most first-time mothers don't," Bowie told her, staying way calmer about this than she could currently appreciate. "From what I hear, it's a learning process that goes on indefinitely." His eyes pinned her down. "You *are* aware of the fact that perfect mothers don't just fall out of the sky, instantly doing the right thing, right?" he asked.

Did he think she was an idiot, or was he just getting his jollies talking down to her? Marlowe fumed, instantly taking offense.

"I'm a workaholic," she reminded him. "How can I possibly juggle those two entirely different roles, being a mother and Colton Oil president, and not doing a horrible job of both?"

Bowie opened his mouth, apparently to answer. Fired up, Marlowe just went on talking.

"I've always been the best at everything," she informed him, not boasting but just stating a fact. "But this…this is something I don't know if I can pull off," she admitted, and that really worried her more than she could express.

Bowie was quick to jump in, making the most of the fact that she was taking a breath. In the handful of run-ins they'd had, he had never seen Marlowe anything but confident. That she was actually having doubts made her all too human in his eyes.

And oddly enough, he liked this version of her. Liked the fact that she was being vulnerable.

And cute as hell, he thought, his eyes once again skimming over what she was wearing.

"Sure you can pull this off," he told her. "You can do anything you set your mind to. Being a mother isn't any different from being the president of Colton Oil— except that there aren't any diaper changes involved in the latter."

"Very funny," she commented, visibly trying very hard not to laugh at the scenario he'd just painted.

His eyes held hers. "And I'll help."

Marlowe suddenly fell silent. She looked at him as if he had just lapsed into a foreign language she was completely unfamiliar with.

"You'll help what?" she questioned.

"With the baby. I'll help," he repeated. He slid in closer to her on the sofa. "We'll do it together. If you decide to have this baby, then you can count on me being there for you and the baby every step of the way," Bowie assured her, his tone completely serious.

It took her several moments to finally get the words out. "You mean it?" she asked.

Bowie smiled at her. It was a warm, comforting smile. "Cross my heart," he said. And then to get his message across, he did just that. "Scout's honor."

"Since when were you a Boy Scout?" she asked.

But oddly enough, she wasn't belittling him or even scoffing at his answer. She was, Marlowe realized, incredibly touched and unbelievably grateful for his offer.

Bowie's reaction to the news when she had told him had been a complete surprise. So many men would have immediately claimed that the baby wasn't theirs, and yet he had taken the news, once the initial surprise had worn off, in stride.

And unlike what so many partners, especially casual ones, would have said, his response was different. They would have said, "You're on your own, honey." Or just told her to "get rid of it," washing their hands of the whole thing.

But Bowie hadn't. He wasn't behaving at all the way she would have expected that he would. Instead, he was assuring her that he would be there for her, ready to hold her hand, to help in any way she needed. To do anything she asked of him.

Marlowe felt tears filling her eyes. She immediately willed them away. There was nothing she hated more than women who broke down in tears.

And she was strong, Marlowe silently insisted. She *was*.

But strong or not, she felt so grateful for Bowie's

closeness, grateful beyond words to have someone to share this completely unexpected, overwhelming responsibility with.

At that moment, she felt not only incredibly thankful to him, but, in addition, she felt closer to Bowie than she ever had to another living soul.

Feeling utterly vulnerable, Marlowe rose to her feet. Bowie rose with her. They were standing inches apart.

Less than inches.

Bowie put his hands on the sides of her shoulders, drawing her closer still. They were all but in each other's shadows.

Marlowe could feel herself leaning into Bowie, and she felt that he was doing the same.

Her breath caught in her throat, and her heart rate suddenly launched into double time as she leaned in even closer to him than she'd been a second ago.

He was going to kiss her, and she desperately wanted him to, she thought. There was absolutely no alcohol involved this time, and she still really, really wanted to kiss him.

To have him kiss her.

And then, without any warning, it happened.

Just as their lips were a fraction away from meeting, a gunshot echoed as a bullet came crashing through her window. It shattered the glass and came so close to Bowie's head that, for one awful, awful moment, she was convinced that he had been shot.

That he had been killed.

Time froze even as he fell on top of her, his body covering hers.

It was the pounding beat of his heart that alerted her he was still alive.

Bowie was apparently trying to shield her with his body the second he'd heard the gun discharge.

The weight of his body on hers had knocked the wind right out of her.

Terror had done the rest.

Bowie stayed exactly where he was, immobile except when he evidently raised his head to conduct an up close inventory of her condition.

"Are you hurt?" he asked, his voice thick with emotion.

"Other than having all this heavy weight on my body, I think I'm fine," she told him, struggling to remain positive. But that immediately gave way to fear. "Someone just shot at you," she cried.

"I know," he told her. "I was there. Except that I think it was at *us*. Or at you." But they could sort that out later. "Are you sure you're all right?" he asked.

"I will be as soon as you get off me," Marlowe told him. "You really are heavy."

Unlike when they had made love and he had taken care to balance his weight on his elbows, she remembered. Today, he'd been too concerned with protecting Marlowe from the shooter to take any other precautions.

"Sorry about that."

Bowie quickly drew himself up to a sitting position. They were both behind the sofa where he had dived, taking her with him.

They were still there, taking care to remain out of range of whoever had done the shooting.

A thought suddenly occurred to him as he looked at her, horrified. "I didn't hurt the baby, did I?"

Despite the situation, she found his concern incredibly sweet. "From what I remember from my high school science class, the baby is currently the size of a pea, if even that big, so I'm guessing she or he is all right."

Bowie blew out a long breath. "Well, that's a relief."

Since there were no more shots, Marlowe ventured out from behind the sofa before he could stop her. "Are you out of your mind?" he demanded, making a grab for her.

"Shooting's stopped," she told him. "I guess he quit while we were ahead," she quipped. Marlowe looked up toward where the bullet had shattered the glass. "Where did that shot come from? It couldn't have been the street," she guessed. The angle was all wrong.

Bowie rose cautiously to his feet. Marlowe was right. Whoever had shot at them was gone.

He took a closer look at the hole the bullet had made. "My guess is that it came from the building across the way."

Marlowe said the first word that came to her mind. "A sniper?"

"As good a term as any for now," Bowie answered. He looked at her again. This time, he frowned. "You sure you're all right?" he asked. "You're shaking."

Embarrassed that he had noticed, Marlowe did what she always did. She took refuge in anger. "Someone just took a shot at one of us. Of course I'm not all right. I want to fillet that SOB."

Despite the seriousness of the situation, Bowie couldn't help laughing. "You really are one tough woman, aren't you?"

"I have to be," she admitted, being more honest with him than she had intended to be. "Otherwise, I'm going to fall all to pieces." Marlowe realized that he had taken out his cell phone and was calling someone. "Who are you calling?" she asked.

Heaven help her, her suspicions about Bowie were back. Was he calling whoever had fired at them to tell the hired gun that he'd missed his target—her?

"The police," Bowie answered. "Someone just took a shot at one or both of us. Who should I be calling?" he asked her.

But before she could attempt to answer him with an offhanded remark, Bowie held up his hand and put the phone on speaker. Someone picked up on the other end of the line.

"911. What is your emergency?" a woman's voice asked.

"Someone just took a shot at us through the window. Could you send police officers to Ms. Marlowe Colton's residence? No," he told the dispatcher who told him she was taking down the information, "not to the family residence. This happened in her condo right here in town. Yes, that's right," he said, "that's the address." He verified the address that was already registered with the police. "Thank you." Closing his phone, he told Marlowe, "They'll be here in five minutes."

"I really wish you hadn't done that," she told Bowie, less than happy that he had taken this initiative.

"Why?"

"Because now the police are going to notify my father," she told him. "And all hell is going to break loose."

Marie Ferrarella

Wait, please don't tell Chief Barco about this, because the police are going to do it my way. In their official time. And all hell is going to break loose.

Chapter Seven

"Wait, let me understand this," Bowie said, putting his cell phone back into his pocket. "You're Payne's daughter. Wouldn't he want you to be safe?"

"I'm his daughter," Marlowe agreed. Bowie had gotten that much right, but not the rest of it. "That means that, if at all possible, he'd expect me to handle this situation on my own. Quietly."

Bowie shook his head.

"Your father's as bullheaded as mine is," he commented, surprised at how alike two men who professed to be sworn enemies could actually be.

Blowing out a breath, she said, "I guess you're right."

She'd no sooner said that than there was a knock on the door. Marlowe audibly caught her breath as she exchanged looks with Bowie.

"I really doubt that a hit man would knock on the door," he told Marlowe. Still, he knew it didn't hurt to be cautious. Moving her behind him, Bowie made his way to the door. "Who is it?" he asked, one hand on the doorknob.

"It's Chief Barco," the gruff voice on the other side

of the door answered. "I just got a 911 alert transmitted to my radio. Are you all right, Ms. Colton?"

Marlowe moved Bowie out of her way and opened the door. A sense of relief went through her as she looked up at the tall, slightly paunchy but commanding fifty-two-year-old police chief. She'd never been so happy to see the bald-headed man before in her life.

"I'm fine, Chief. But the bullet came really close to Bowie over here." Saying that, she turned toward Bowie, and for the first time since the incident occurred, she saw that there was blood at the very top of his ear. He *had* been grazed. "Your ear," she cried, her eyes widening. "You're bleeding."

Bowie ran his finger along the region where she seemed to be looking. There was just the slightest trace of red on his fingertips. He shrugged as if this was no big deal.

"I've done worse shaving," he assured her.

"You shave with bullets?" she asked Bowie sarcastically, attempting to cover up her initial horrified reaction.

"Let me get this straight," the chief said, slightly confused. "You two were together when this shooting happened?"

Like everyone else in Mustang Valley, the chief knew the Coltons and the Robertsons to be sworn enemies. Finding them together must have seemed rather odd.

"Yes," Marlowe answered for the both of them. "I'll show you where the bullet came from." She led the chief to the window.

The chief studied the shattered glass closely. He frowned at the hole and looked around the area for signs of more damage. But for now, the window seemed to be the only casualty.

Barco turned toward Bowie. "Do you have any idea who might have wanted to see you dead, Mr. Robertson?" he asked him.

Marlowe spoke up, interrupting the two men. "Robertson seems to think that I was the target."

The chief's frown deepened. This surely did not fall under the heading of "good news" in his book. "And why is that?" he asked.

"Well, for one thing, it's her condo," Bowie answered before Marlowe could say anything further.

"You do have a point," the chief allowed. "Any other reason for you to suspect that Ms. Colton was the intended target?"

Bowie was forced to shrug, at least for now. "Fresh out of ideas, I'm afraid," he said.

When the chief looked toward her for her input, Marlowe shrugged her shoulders, as well. "Other than the usual crazies who resent my family, I haven't a clue," she confessed.

The chief made a few notes in his battered notebook, then closed it, tucking it back into his jacket pocket.

"I'll have my people ask around, see if anyone saw or heard anything unusual," he told Marlowe. "I can post one of the officers outside your door if that would make you feel safer, Ms. Colton," he offered.

Marlowe smiled. "Thanks for the offer, Chief, but doing that would be cutting down your force by a third," she told him.

The entire Mustang Valley police force was small, but then, considering how quiet the town usually was, only a few law enforcement officers were more than adequate to keep the peace.

As if to contradict the thought, just then the front door, which Marlowe hadn't bothered locking when the chief came in, flew open, rattling the beveled glass in the upper portion of the door so hard, for a moment it seemed in danger of breaking, as well.

"Marlowe, are you all right?" her father demanded as he came storming into the condo. He was closely followed by Callum, his son and Marlowe's twin.

"Are you hurt?" her brother asked at almost the same time.

"I'm fine, really," Marlowe assured both her father and her twin.

Both men stopped dead the next moment as they realized that Marlowe had more than just the chief with her and that the other man standing next to her was *not* part of the police force.

Payne suddenly looked as if thunderbolts were about to come shooting out of his eyes. "What the hell is Franklin's whelp doing here?" the senior Colton demanded, glaring at Bowie. "Is he the one who tried to shoot you?" Payne shouted, pulling himself up to his full height.

"Now, calm down, Mr. Colton," Barco began in a soothing tone. His words had absolutely no effect on the oil baron.

Marlowe moved in between her father and Bowie, predominantly to keep her father from doing something that they would all wind up regretting rather than to protect Bowie.

Even at sixty-eight, Payne Colton was no one's idea

of an old man. On the contrary, her father was still a force to be reckoned with and exceedingly imposing in his own right.

"No, Dad," she insisted, "Bowie didn't try to shoot me."

"Then what the hell is he doing here?" Payne demanded. "Are you spying on us, boy? Doing some recon for your old man because he's just too weak and afraid to do it himself?" With each word, Payne only succeeded in working himself up more and more.

She could tell Bowie was having trouble holding on to his own temper, but losing it would only make a bad situation worse.

"No, sir—" Bowie answered politely, only to have Payne cut him short.

"Well, you can tell that coward who sired you he knows what he can do with his precious company, and I'll thank him not to send his boy sniffing around my daughter, if he knows what's good for him." Drawing back his shoulders, the senior Colton gave the illusion of towering over Bowie, even though they were actually about the same height. "Because if he crosses me, your father's going to get a hell of a lot more than he *ever* bargained for, you hear me?" Payne demanded, all but shouting the question in Bowie's face.

This was going to turn into a really bad situation faster than she had ever bargained on, Marlowe thought. Chief Barco was a nice man, but he was basically afraid of her father. It was up to her to put a stop to it before it got really ugly, Marlowe observed.

"Dad," she said, raising her voice. But her father either didn't hear her or didn't want to hear her, because he went on shouting and threatening Bowie.

"Now you get your sorry butt out of here, boy, if you know what's good for you." Bushy silver eyebrows drew together in an angry wave. "I am *not* going to ask you nicely again," Payne warned in a menacing tone.

"Dad—" Marlowe tried again, raising her voice even louder. She got the same result she had the first time. Her father continued to deliberately ignore her.

Payne turned toward his son. "Callum, get him out of here," the Colton patriarch ordered, "before I do something that I am going to really regret."

"Mr. Colton," Barco said, trying to interrupt Payne, who paid even less attention to the chief than he did to his daughter.

Marlowe was well aware that her father's threats were far from empty. She was also aware of how quickly they could escalate. Sticking two fingers into her mouth, she whistled loudly, which forced all the men in the room to focus their attention on her.

"Nothing you can say right now is going to keep me from throwing this whelp out to teach him some respect for his betters—" Payne began to tell his daughter, not even looking at her.

"Well, you had better learn how to hold on to your temper, Dad," Marlowe informed him, shouting the words at Payne.

"And just why the hell would I do that?" Payne demanded angrily, glaring at Marlowe.

"Because Bowie's the father of your grandchild!" she answered in a voice that all but shook the ceiling tiles loose.

It also stunned the other three men in the room. And even Bowie looked surprised that she was breaking the news this way.

"Say what?" Callum responded, the first one to recover.

Payne blanched. "He's the *what*?" he asked almost at the same time.

"The father of your grandchild," Marlowe repeated, enunciating each word. She saw the shock on her father's face and sincerely wished she could have given him the news a different way. But her father never made anything easy for her. "I'm pregnant, Dad, and you and Franklin Robertson are going to have to find a way to deal with that and learn to stop fighting!" she cried, her voice sounding almost hoarse.

Callum looked at her, wide-eyed. He asked, "Is it true, Mar?"

"Trust me," Marlowe said wearily, "I wouldn't make up something like that."

Chief Barco slanted a look at the Colton men, as if unsure if he should be congratulating the parties involved, or just holding his peace. Instincts apparently had him opting for the latter.

But Payne was not about to willingly accept this situation, not without registering his intense dissatisfaction and contesting the matter.

Glaring at Bowie, Payne angrily demanded, "Did you force yourself on my daughter? Because I swear if I find out that you did—"

Marlowe blew out an angry breath. As if she didn't have enough to deal with, she had to smooth her father's ruffled feathers. "Nobody forced themselves on any-

one, Dad. You know me better than that," she told him.
"I would have gutted him before I let that happen." She
drew in a fortifying breath, then said, "It was mutual."

Disgust, anger and disappointment all took turns
washing over Payne's rugged face. He glared at his
daughter. "How could you?" he accused.

Marlowe squared her shoulders. "I'm a grown
woman, Dad, as well as your daughter. I think you already know the answer to that," she told him, doing her
best to hold it together and not fall apart in light of his
heated disapproval.

The disappointment she saw in her father's eyes cut
her to the quick, but she wasn't about to show him that
by flinching or apologizing. It was already hard enough
for her to try to deal with what she had done in the heat
of the moment—and the consequences that single action had produced. Attempting to atone for it for her
father's sake was out of the question.

Payne turned on his heel and marched over to Bowie.
For one tense, horrible moment, Marlowe was afraid
that her father was going to punch the other man out—
or at least try to.

There did appear to be an inner struggle going on.

But then Payne growled, "If I hear even a hint that
you're not treating her exactly the way my daughter
deserves to be treated, I will hunt you down no matter
what rock you're hiding under and gut you like a pig."
Payne then turned toward Callum and issued an order.
"Let's go. I'm through here."

But Callum had never acted like his father's lapdog,
and Marlowe knew he was not about to start now. "I'll
be there in a minute, Dad," he said.

Payne fumed. "In some places this would be called consorting with the enemy," he angrily informed Marlowe's twin.

"And in some places it's called being a family," Callum countered.

Payne said something that was biting as well as callous under his breath just before he walked out, slamming the door in his wake.

"I'd better go, too," the chief said to nobody in particular. Whenever he was around Payne Colton, he took all his cues from the man.

"Thanks for coming so quickly," Marlowe said.

"Of course," the chief responded, and then he left, as well.

Callum looked at his sister. "He'll come around, Mar," her twin promised.

"You're a lot more optimistic than I am right now," Marlowe told her brother.

Callum turned toward Bowie. "You really think that bullet was meant for my sister?" he asked Bowie.

"I do," Bowie answered, evidently prepared to be peppered with more questions.

Instead, Callum told him, "Then take her up to our cabin in the mountains, but make sure that you're not being followed when you go. If you are followed by someone looking to take either one of you out, the isolated location will only act against you."

She had never taken to having other people make decisions affecting her. "Callum, I can't go with him to our cabin," she protested. "There's too much to do. That email—" Marlowe began.

But her brother immediately cut her protest short.

"Listen, you have just one major thing to focus on right now—this baby that you're carrying. You need to make that a priority in addition to work. Work will go on whether or not you're there. Maybe not as well," he allowed, "but it will go on. However, there is no question that this baby needs you, and it needs the healthiest version of you that you can possibly provide—because without you, that baby *won't* be able to go on."

Marlowe shook her head. "But, Callum, there *is* a crisis and—"

"And I will handle it for both of us," he assured her. "The rest of the family is all joining forces to try to get to the bottom of this. Now I know you're really good, but you have to admit that even you don't equal the five of us. So go to that cabin with Bowie and take care of my niece or nephew for the next couple of days until things calm down a little—and that's an order," he told her. "Do I make myself clear?" he asked his sister.

"Perfectly," Marlowe answered just before she threw her arms around Callum and hugged him for all she was worth. "You're the best."

"I know," Callum answered with a grin.

"But you will call me if you hit a snag?" she asked, watching her brother's face for her answer.

"I won't hit a snag," Callum told her.

"That's not what I just asked," Marlowe pointed out with a touch of exasperation.

"Yes, I will call you if I hit a snag," Callum told her in a singsong voice.

She still had her doubts, but for now this would have to do. "All right, then, you'd better go and join Dad in the car. You know how surly he gets whenever he's kept waiting."

Callum laughed. "You're preaching to the choir, Mar. That man's picture is in Wikipedia with the word *surly* written right under it." He turned toward Bowie. "I never thought I'd hear myself say this, but if you need anything at all involving my sister, give me a call."

Bowie nodded. "Consider it done."

For a split second, Callum locked eyes with the other man. The silence hung heavily between them. And then Callum said, "I'd better."

Marlowe knew that was as close to a threat as he would allow himself to utter. And then he left.

"Are all you Coltons always this charming, or is it just me, bringing out the worst in you?" he asked Marlowe, following her to her bedroom as she went to pack an overnight case.

"You really want to know the answer to that?" she asked him.

"No, on second thought, maybe I don't," Bowie answered.

"Wise choice," she told him, nodding her head. She closed the lid on the suitcase and snapped the locks shut, secretly marveling at how oddly final that sounded.

Chapter Eight

Marlowe found the silence in the car almost deafening. Bowie had insisted that they just take one vehicle to go up to the cabin: his. Marlowe had let him win that argument, even though she didn't like being chauffeured around. Moreover, she liked the control of having and driving her own car. But she could even put up with that if she had to.

What she couldn't put up with was this oppressive quiet that was beginning to burrow its way under her skin. Marlowe had to admit that it was quickly getting to her.

Just as she reached over to turn on some music, Bowie stopped her cold with a question. "So what's this that's going on with your family?"

Marlowe dropped her hand in her lap. The question, coming out of the blue, completely stunned her. She hadn't been prepared to field anything like this.

"What do you mean?" Marlowe asked. Even she had to admit that her voice sounded rather stilted to her own ear, not to mention that her mouth had gone dry.

"I'm not sure if it was Callum or you, but one of you said something about there being a major crisis that needed handling," Bowie said. He glanced in her direction. "*What* major crisis?"

Marlowe's protective barriers immediately fell into place. When unarmed, she had always felt that denial was the best way to go. "I don't know what you're talking about."

Yeah, right, Bowie thought.

"C'mon, Marlowe, you're way too smart to play dumb," he told her, and then he added the crowning touch. "That doesn't look good on you. Why don't you tell me what's wrong, and maybe I can help."

For one moment, Marlowe wavered. She really wanted to be able to tell him. For possibly the first time in her life, she found herself wanting to share her burden with someone rather than just shoulder it on her own the way she always did.

But the truth was she didn't know if she could afford to share it with Bowie—because this could all be just a ploy on his part to get information out of her so he could, in turn, score points with his father.

Despite the fact that she had told her father that he had to find a way to bury the hatchet when it came to Bowie's dad, she herself trusted Franklin Robertson just about as far as she could throw the man—which meant not at all.

Marlowe looked at him, unable to sublimate the suspicion in her eyes. "Just how do I know that I can trust you?" she asked Bowie bluntly.

Bowie laughed under his breath. "We're totally traveling off what's considered the beaten path in order to get to a cabin hideaway in the mountains. As far as I can see, there isn't a snowball's chance in hell that we're being followed—as per your brother's instruction. If you don't already trust me, then you seem to be willingly setting yourself up for a world of hurt," he told her.

"Now, you don't have to trust me if you don't want to," he continued. "I can respect that. But if you'd like to talk about whatever it is that's clearly bothering you, I just wanted you to know that, at least while we're out here, I'm here for you."

"Oh, you mean like a Boy Scout," Marlowe mocked, worried that she might have made a major mistake in trusting Bowie. Maybe she should just find a way to boot him out of the car and then drive quickly back to the family house.

"No, like the father of that baby you're carrying," Bowie reminded her. "And, to answer your question," he said, "yes, you can trust me."

"No," she replied pointedly, "my question was how do I *know* I can trust you. After all, someone did just try to kill me, thanks to you."

There was nothing on the road up ahead, just as there hadn't been for miles now, so Bowie spared Marlowe a long look. "Because I said so," Bowie answered.

She felt anger crease her forehead. Did he think she was that gullible? "And I'm just supposed to take your word for that, is that it?" Marlowe asked. For all she knew, he might have told people at his company what she had shared with him in confidence. What if her father found out? Would he accuse her of siding with his enemy in this eco-friendly war that was being fought between the two companies?

"Yes, you are," he told her firmly. "Because I don't

lie." His eyes met hers before he looked back at the road again. "My word is my bond."

"That all sounds very noble," she told him in a mocking tone, telling him just what she thought of his declaration.

"It also happens to be very true," Bowie replied simply.

The truth was that she wasn't sure if she could trust Bowie or not, but she knew that she really, really wanted to. She had already trusted him with her body. If their relationship was going to progress any further, for the sake of their baby, she was going to have to find a way to trust with the rest of her.

Drawing in a deep breath, Marlowe forced herself to dive into the deep end of the pool. She told him what he wanted to know.

"All six members of the board of Colton Oil—my father, Ace, Ainsley, Rafe, my father's ex-wife, Selina, and I—were all sent identical emails earlier today," she informed him grimly.

"I'm guessing that the email didn't say you were all winners of a clearinghouse lottery," Bowie said.

"You'd be correct," she answered, her tone utterly gloomy. "The email claimed that my brother Ace wasn't really a Colton or my father's son. It went on to claim that Ace was switched the day he was born with another male baby born the same day at Mustang Valley General Hospital."

"Switched at birth?" Bowie repeated. "You're kidding, right?"

Marlowe blew out a frustrated breath. "I only wish that I was."

"Even if he *was* switched at birth, which seems pretty improbable to me, what difference could that possibly make? Unless there's something you're not telling me," Bowie qualified. "Ace was still raised as a Colton, which in my book makes him one." Like Rafe before him, apparently Bowie didn't see what the fuss was about.

"Unfortunately, that's not enough," Marlowe told him, her voice a mixture of sadness and anger. "It clearly states in the company bylaws that the CEO of Colton Oil must be a Colton by blood only. If this crazy claim for some reason turns out to be true and not a hoax, I'm not sure what we're going to do," she confessed.

And therein obviously lay the problem, she thought.

Bowie said, "Changing the bylaws comes to mind."

Marlowe blinked, stunned by Bowie's suggestion. "Excuse me, but have you *met* my father?" she asked. "He'd sooner topple Mount Rushmore than change the company bylaws." Despite herself, she was already picturing the chaos that would result once news that Ace wasn't really a Colton became public. "I don't know what this is going to do to the company, to our family—"

"Aren't you jumping the gun a little here?" Bowie asked. "You're already assuming that this crazy claim is true, and it could just be someone trying to undermine everything that your family's worked so hard to build. You know, there's a simple way to clear all this up," he told her.

She knew what he was going to say. The same thing that had been suggested in the email. "I know, I know.

A DNA test," she said flatly. "We've already agreed to have Ainsley take Ace in for one first thing tomorrow when the lab opens. Chief Barco said he's willing to go with them to bear witness to the whole process. Drawing the blood, sealing the vial, everything. That way, he can attest that everything was aboveboard if anyone should contest the results—provided that the test results point to Ace being the genuine article."

"How would you feel about that?" Bowie asked her.

Marlowe shifted uncomfortably in her seat. "Feel about what?"

"What if the test results come back and they point to Ace *not* being an actual Colton," he told her. "Would that change anything?"

"Of course it would change things. It would change everything," she cried. Hadn't Bowie been paying attention? "I already told you, he couldn't be on the board, and—"

"No," Bowie said, cutting her short, "for you. Would it change anything for you? Would you suddenly see Ace differently if the blood running through his veins wasn't that of a genuine Colton?"

"No," Marlowe informed him indignantly. "Of course not. I wouldn't see him any differently than I do right now."

"Then that DNA test really doesn't matter," he told her. "Ace will still be your brother whether or not Colton blood is running through his veins. Besides," he continued, "it's not the blood that makes you family. It's the day-to-day living and what's involved in that day-to-day existence that does it.

"Now, don't buy trouble," Bowie advised. "If something bad is going to find you, that'll happen soon enough. Until it does, just go on with things as if everything's all right."

She was oddly heartened by his words, but she wasn't about to admit it. Instead, she told him, "You sound like a fortune cookie, Robertson."

"It'd have to be a pretty big cookie to accommodate all that writing," Bowie said, visibly amused. "In the meantime, do you or your family have any idea who sent this bundle of enlightening information to all of you?"

Well, she'd already told him this much, so she supposed there was no harm in telling him the rest. "I put our IT expert on it, but he told me not to get my hopes up that we'd get an answer. He feels that it came through the dark web, and some of the dealings there might never be unearthed."

"Maybe I can help," Bowie offered.

Marlowe turned toward him, stunned. "You?" she questioned.

"Don't sound so surprised," he said with a laugh, appearing to take no offense.

Since she was being honest, she told him, "I admit that I am a little." Maybe he had misunderstood her. "This is the dark web I'm talking about." His expression didn't change. Marlowe began to entertain hope. She had to ask, "Do you know your way around the dark web?"

Bowie laughed softly under his breath. "Let's just say that I know people who know people who might be able to help out in this case."

"You are just full of surprises, aren't you?" Marlowe marveled.

"I'd like to think so. In the meantime, it looks like we've arrived at your designated castle, Your Highness, safe and sound," he added, looking in his rearview mirror for the umpteenth time.

"Time to play house," she said flippantly. The next moment, she realized what that had to sound like. "I mean—" Her voice failed her as she turned a rather bright shade of scarlet.

"I know what you meant," Bowie told her, gallantly taking her off the hook. "You go inside. I'll get your bag," he said.

"I can carry my own bag," she informed him, following him to the trunk of his car.

He popped open the trunk and pulled out the suitcase before she could reach for it. "Will you relax and stop seeing everything as a challenge to your authority, or position or whatever?" he said. "Learning how to accept help is every bit as important as offering help to someone else."

She rolled her eyes impatiently. "You know, you really should start writing down all these golden gems of yours, Robertson. Maybe even put them all into a gift book."

Taking the suitcase, he went toward the cabin. "Please relax a bit, Marlowe. You could probably use the rest. I know I certainly could."

Her eyebrows drew together as she fisted one of her hands at her waist. "Is that an insult?" she asked, her back already going up.

"That's just an observation," Bowie informed her calmly. "I promise you'll know if I'm insulting you. For now, all I'm trying to do is get a truce going—between us, and then, hopefully, between our two families." Opening the front door, he deposited her suitcase just inside the cabin. His mouth curved into a grin. "How'm I doing so far?"

Marlowe sighed. Maybe she was being too touchy. "Apparently a lot better than I am," she answered honestly.

Bowie stood in the doorway, facing out. She could see the cabin was elevated enough to give him a decent panoramic view of the immediate area surrounding it. "I'd say that it's safe to assume nobody followed us," he told her.

Clearly satisfied, he stepped back inside, then closed the door and secured the locks.

"Just in case," he explained, then proceeded to tell her why he had made sure that all the locks were in place.

"Now what?" she asked, looking around the spacious cabin. From where she stood, she could see the entire living space all at once, except for a bedroom that was in the back. But the way she felt right now, having had that bullet come so close to Bowie *and* to her, Marlowe sincerely doubted that she would be able to ever sleep again.

Bowie had a different take on the situation, however. "Now you do what your brother suggested you do," he told her. Bowie evidently knew better than to use the phrase "told you to do."

"Easy for him to say," she commented.

"No, I really doubt that," Bowie contradicted. "I think he knows that asking you to do something is far from easy and far from a guarantee that you would actually do it."

Her eyes narrowed. "Just what are you saying?" she demanded.

"Only what we both know to be true," he answered. "You're a very strong-willed woman who isn't about to obediently comply with something unless she really wants to."

Marlowe pursed her lips. "Laying it on a little thick, aren't you, Robertson?"

"Maybe," he allowed. He raised his brows as he asked, "You buying any of it?"

He suddenly looked so boyish as he asked her that question that Marlowe found she was having a problem keeping a straight face.

"Maybe," she answered, parroting the word he'd used back to him. It suddenly felt as if it was getting warm in here, she thought. Marlowe changed the subject. "How long do you think we're going to have to be here?"

"Spoken like a prisoner who's ready to fly the coop at any second," he commented.

She raised her chin. "I just like to know what I'm in for and what's ahead of me."

"Maybe what your brother had in mind," Bowie suggested delicately, "is for you just to kick back for a bit and let things unfold naturally."

She shook her head. "Nope, that doesn't sound like Callum," she answered.

"All right, then, how does a couple of days sound to you?" Bowie asked, his eyes on hers.

"Today counts as one day, right?" Marlowe asked.

Bowie glanced at his watch. It was almost ten o'clock

in the evening. "If you think that two hours compose a day, then yes," he answered, "today counts as one of those days."

"Good," she pronounced, looking satisfied that she had won.

Chapter Nine

"Well, at least we won't be starving anytime soon," Bowie announced, looking into the surprisingly large modern refrigerator in the kitchen. "Looks like it's been restocked recently." He looked over his shoulder toward Marlowe. "There's a pretty good selection of steaks, eggs, a few fruits and some vegetables just waiting to be turned into a home-cooked meal."

He closed the refrigerator door and crossed back to her. "I know it's kind of late, but you probably haven't had anything to eat for hours. Can I interest you in some dinner?"

The second Bowie mentioned food, Marlowe felt her stomach lurching. She pressed her palm against the swirling area, praying she wasn't going to throw up.

"I don't think so," she told him. "The idea of eating anything right now..." Her voice trailed off. The next second, her eyes widened as she drew in her breath. "Oh no, it can't be."

"Can't be what?" Bowie asked, concerned. The horrified note in her voice had gotten his complete attention.

Marlowe didn't answer. Her stomach was letting her

know just how unhappy it was. She could feel herself beginning to perspire, despite the cold temperature outside.

She looked around frantically. She hadn't been here for so long that she'd forgotten where the bathroom was located.

Bowie immediately knew without being told what she was looking for. He had noticed the bathroom while checking out the Colton cabin to make sure no one was already there.

"This way," he said, quickly leading the way to the rear of the cabin. To make sure she was following him, Bowie took hold of her elbow, guiding her in the right direction.

The moment Marlowe sighted the door, she yanked away her elbow and pushed past Bowie, barely slamming the door behind her just in time.

Bowie leaned against the door frame. "Anything I can do to help, Marlowe?" he offered. "Hold your hair out of the way, give you moral support?" he asked, saying the first things that came to his mind because he was worried about her. He thought that she'd looked positively green just as she'd slammed the door.

Marlowe didn't answer him, but he was fairly certain he detected a subdued retching noise coming from the bathroom. Looking at the closed door, Bowie shook his head. Marlowe Colton had to be the only woman he knew who would deliberately try to keep the sounds of her physical misery a secret.

Feeling bad for her, Bowie decided to remain where he was, waiting for her to pull herself together and come out. He was ready to offer assistance any way he could should Marlowe realize that she wanted it.

Or needed it.

When he no longer heard anything coming from inside the bathroom, Bowie put his ear against the door, straining to make out any sound coming from the other side. By no means did he want to invade her privacy, but at the same time he found himself worrying about Marlowe—and the baby she was carrying.

His baby.

Yes, it was early days as far as that was concerned. He'd known about this for only a number of short hours, but being pregnant was obviously creating havoc for Marlowe, and he felt protective toward her and their child.

"Marlowe?" he called to her, knocking on the bathroom door. "Are you all right in there?" When there was no answer, he decided that he had been considerate of her sensibilities long enough. Coddling her wasn't getting him anywhere.

His hand on the doorknob, he turned it. "Marlowe, I'm coming in there," he announced. But as he began to open the door, it was suddenly opened from within and Marlowe emerged, her face slightly damp from what he assumed was the water she had splashed herself with, most likely trying to freshen up.

"What are you getting so excited about?" she asked indignantly. "I'm fine."

He looked at her more closely. "You have morning sickness."

"You have your time confused," she informed him coldly. "It's nighttime, not morning."

"And morning sickness is just a term to describe the nausea that being pregnant sometimes ushers in," he countered, refusing to be baited and get annoyed.

"And you're an expert on that, I take it," she retorted.

It occurred to her, completely out of left field, that she didn't even know if Bowie had a wife stashed away somewhere, or maybe a fiancée. For all she knew, the man had mistresses tucked away everywhere. She knew absolutely nothing about Bowie's private life, nor had she wanted to—until just now.

What if she'd gone to bed with a married man? Or with someone who was just interested in nothing more than a one-night stand?

If it turned out to be the latter, it almost seemed like poetic justice, seeing as how, at the time it had happened, she hadn't exactly been interested in establishing a permanent relationship, either. She had wound up going upstairs with him strictly for pleasure—something she wouldn't have allowed herself to indulge usually.

But there was something about mixing champagne with equal doses of Bowie that had blurred all the lines for her. It had made her behave like someone she didn't even begin to recognize.

"I read a lot," he said in response to her snide question about his being up on the symptoms of morning sickness. "I also read that crackers and soda water sometimes help you feel better."

Marlowe was really skeptical about that. Right now she was feeling miserable, and all she wanted was to retreat and pray that exhaustion would just take over and blanket her.

Bowie answered her glibly, "But the article did say that the prospective mother might react badly to attempts to help her and behave like an angry wet hen."

"A wet hen?" Marlowe echoed indignantly.

"An *angry* wet hen," he deliberately corrected.

For some reason, the fact that they were having this discussion about the condition of a hypothetical chicken managed to hit her funny bone and she began to laugh.

The sound of her laughter coaxed laughter out of Bowie. His laughter fed hers and vice versa. They laughed until her sides literally ached and she couldn't laugh anymore.

When she stopped laughing, allowing an exhausted sigh to escape, she looked at Bowie, feeling contrite.

"I suppose I should apologize for being so short-tempered," she told him.

"You can if you want to, or we could just forget about it and you could go to bed." He clearly had already surmised that she was having a hard time of it, and he apparently wasn't interested in any apologies.

For the first time, she looked around the room and spotted the bed.

She felt a wave of heat wash over her. Did Bowie intend to sleep in it with her, perhaps even have an encore of that night they had spent together six weeks ago?

"What about you?" she heard herself asking nervously, although she tried her best not to show it.

Bowie seemed rather unfazed by the question. He answered her as if it was already a given. "I'm going to take the couch."

She peered out of the bedroom, looking into the living area. "It's not very comfortable," she commented.

"That's okay," he said, unconcerned. "I don't intend to be very comfortable."

Marlowe looked at him, wrinkling her forehead in confusion. What was that supposed to mean? "I don't understand."

"Well," he told her matter-of-factly, "if I get comfortable, I just might wind up falling asleep on the couch."

"And you don't want to?" she asked him, still confused.

He laughed quietly. "It's pretty hard to stand guard if I'm sleeping."

"Wait." He wasn't making any sense, she thought. "You said no one followed us."

"And from what I saw, they didn't," he agreed. "But even so, I don't want to take any unnecessary chances, and I've always been a firm believer in being safe rather than sorry."

Marlowe sighed wearily. "More sayings for that book," she said more to herself than to him.

"Maybe," he allowed with an engaging grin. "But that doesn't make it any less applicable to the situation," Bowie told her. And then he advised, "Get some rest." Before she could protest, as she was so very capable of doing, he winked at her and said, "Remember, you're sleeping for two."

Did he mean she was sleeping for him as well, because he couldn't, or was he referring to the baby as part of that "two"?

Marlowe stood in the bedroom after he closed the door behind him and sighed as she shook her head. She didn't want to be beholden to Bowie, didn't want him making any sacrifices for her.

And yet…

And yet the very fact that Bowie was doing all this created warm and fuzzy feelings inside her.

Feelings she admitted to herself that she had never experienced before. Oh, she'd had her share of boyfriends, and she'd had flings. But none of those boyfriends or the flings could have been termed to be the least bit serious. They certainly never even once came before her job. That was a contest that had never taken place.

None of her so-called relationships ever lasted, and she had never felt as if she was missing anything whenever those relationships had run their exceedingly short courses and quietly faded into history.

She certainly had never, ever felt as if she was falling for someone…

Marlowe blinked as the words startled her, popping up in her head completely unbidden—like a comet streaking across the sky.

She wasn't falling for him; she was just tired, Marlowe told herself.

Tired and imagining things.

Still, she had to admit that part of her stomach's rebellious upheaval was due to something other than strictly this so-called morning sickness that Bowie claimed to be such an expert about.

Falling for Bowie, she thought as she sank down on the bed.

Her.

With him.

No way.

That had to be some sort of a mistake, right? Of course right, she told herself.

Even so, the very idea seemed to waft through her brain, teasing her, whispering insane words.

Would it be so very wrong if you were right about that?

"Damn it, Marlowe, you're just overtired. Get some sleep!" she ordered herself.

That turned out to be a great deal easier said than done.

But somewhere along the line, with all that tossing and turning she did, she must have fallen asleep. Because sometime in the morning she found herself being teased awake by the scent of eggs frying and something she identified as bacon after a moment.

For a split second, the scent was tempting.

And then her stomach kicked in, rebelling and reminding her that food and she were not friends right now.

Instead of going out to the kitchen, she found herself communing with the commode again.

Finished being sick, she got back up on her shaky legs. That made twice in less than twelve hours, she thought wearily.

Marlowe went out of the bathroom and sat down on the edge of the rumpled bed, waiting for her stomach to settle down.

"We're not off to an auspicious start, you and I, baby," she murmured under her breath, addressing the tiny being within her body.

And that was the moment she suddenly knew—knew that she was going to have this child, keep it and be a mother. As good a mother as humanly possible.

Nothing else seemed remotely imaginable.

Marlowe knew her decision would probably infuriate her father. He undoubtedly expected her to sweep what he viewed, at best, as an "unfortunate circumstance" out of her life. After all, this baby was half Robertson, and Coltons wanted to have nothing to do with Robertsons. Payne had said that so many times over the years that she had lost count.

"Wrong, Dad. We do now," she said, addressing her absent father.

Preoccupied with her thoughts and with this decision she had just made to keep the baby, Marlowe jumped when she heard the knock on her bedroom door.

"Marlowe, can I come in?" Bowie asked, waiting for her permission.

Part of her would have expected Bowie to come barging in, the way he had into her office. That he didn't surprised her—and, she had to admit, pleased her.

Bracing herself, Marlowe said, "Okay. You can come on in."

Bowie opened the door, but rather than walk right in, he peered into the room, checking to see if she was alone. "You had me worried. I thought I heard you talking to someone."

She felt embarrassed that Bowie had overheard her. Rather than explain what she'd been doing, Marlowe said, "No, just to myself."

She had a defensive look in her eyes, Bowie thought, so he tactfully retreated and changed subjects. "I made breakfast."

That was the last thing she was interested in. Her stomach was knotting up again. "I hope it's something you like to eat, because I'm not hungry."

Bowie frowned. That wasn't what he wanted to hear. "You have to eat," he told her.

"Later," Marlowe answered, putting him off. "I'll eat later," she promised. "I never eat first thing in the morning."

"You didn't eat last night, either," Bowie reminded her.

"So now you're the food police?" she asked with a trace of annoyance.

"No," he answered patiently, "just someone who knows that you need to keep your strength up."

"My strength is fine, thank you," she answered curtly, then immediately felt guilty about the tone she had used. She hadn't meant to lose her temper. He was just trying to be thoughtful, she told herself. "I'm sorry, this whole situation has me on edge. I don't mean to be taking it out on you."

"Well, that's good to know. By 'whole situation,' do you mean this business with the email, the shooter or the pregnancy?" Bowie asked.

"Yes," she answered glibly. When he looked at her quizzically, Marlowe told him, "All of the above."

Bowie sat down on the bed next to her and put his arm around Marlowe's slim shoulders. There was nothing sexual in the gesture. She sensed his only intent was to try to offer her some measure of comfort and support.

"You're not alone in this," he told her quietly. "I intend to be with you on this new journey every step of the way."

She turned her head slightly to look at him. "You mean with the baby?"

"With the baby, with finding out who sent this email

to your family and with discovering who the hell is using either of us or both of us for target practice," he concluded.

Hearing him say that made Marlowe feel infinitely better.

And a great deal safer, she realized.

With a relieved sigh, she leaned her head against Bowie's shoulder.

Just having him there beside her like that succeeded in making her feel that all of this would eventually somehow be resolved.

"Thank you," she murmured so quietly that at first he thought that he had imagined it.

She felt Bowie smile against her head.

"Don't mention it." He rose to his feet, extending his hand to her. "Now come into the kitchen and keep me company," he said.

She was glad he refrained from asking her again to have something to eat.

She would do that all in good time. He just had to be patient. It was, she thought as they left the room, a learning process.

Apparently for both of them.

Chapter Ten

Bowie watched as Marlowe moved around the kitchen, cleaning up and in general being what to him seemed very domestic. If anyone had asked him, he would have had to admit that he hadn't thought Marlowe had it in her. Maybe once, as a lark, but definitely not twice.

But there she was, cleaning up again, not just after lunch, but after dinner, as well. A dinner she hadn't really bothered to eat because she still wasn't able to keep much down.

When Marlowe caught him watching her, she guessed what was on his mind. "I don't like sitting still, and I don't like leaving a mess."

"Well, it's not like it's exactly your mess," Bowie pointed out. "Seeing as how you didn't really have anything to eat so far, except for a couple of pieces of dry toast."

"And tea," she reminded him as she rinsed off a plate. "Don't forget the tea." Trying to find a way to help her soothe her stomach, Bowie had managed to scrounge up half a box of herbal tea bags from the pantry. He boiled water in a pot and then made her a large mug. "I had no idea you had all these hidden talents."

Joining her at the sink, he took the towel from her and began to dry the dishes she had finished washing. "Dunking a tea bag into a mug of boiled water isn't exactly a hidden talent," he said with a dismissive snort. "It's more of a wrist exercise." He held out his hand to demonstrate. "A very slow wrist exercise," Bowie emphasized before continuing to dry the dishes.

"Still, I do appreciate the effort," Marlowe said.

Bowie laughed. Finished with drying the dishes, he retired the dish towel on the side of the sink. "Yes, now I'll have to rest my wrist for the rest of the evening." His expression turned serious. "Sorry you didn't have any of the steak."

She shrugged his apology off. "I'm not. No reflection on your culinary skills, but the very smell of that steak sizzling tonight was almost enough to send me back communing with the porcelain bowl."

He couldn't picture having to live that way. "I hope for your sake this morning sickness of yours doesn't last too long."

"That makes two of us," she replied, "although I've heard of women feeling like this for the first five months."

Five months of throwing up and the woman would waste away to nothing, Bowie thought. She was thin to begin with.

"Competitive though you are, that doesn't necessarily have to be you," he told her.

Marlowe gave him a look.

"That's not exactly something I'm aspiring to, either," Marlowe replied.

SEVERAL TIMES DURING that day Bowie had found himself observing Marlowe. Whenever he did, he forced himself to look away, trying his best *not* to watch her. Trying to get his mind on something else.

Anything else.

He had never been even mildly interested in marriage or in having a family. The idea of having a baby actually unnerved him, and he had always liked to think of himself as fearless. Until this child had suddenly come into the picture, he would have said *nothing* scared him— although having someone out there trying to kill him had come pretty close.

As far as his resistance to having a family went, part of the problem was that he had no model to emulate, nothing to even remotely give him a home base. His own father had hardly ever been home, and even when he was home, he really wasn't. His mind was always elsewhere, calculating and refiguring things that had already been done.

Franklin Robertson was the epitome of a workaholic. Bowie knew that their relationship was tense, and Bowie wanted nothing more than to prove to the demanding man that he had it in him to take over the company when that day came.

A baby didn't figure into any of that. Especially not a baby whose lineage was half Robertson and half Colton. He was certain that his father would go absolutely ballistic once he found out that little tidbit.

While he wanted Marlowe to know that the baby's future would always be secure, Bowie didn't want her thinking that what the two of them had between them would ever develop into something more than what was there already.

They were outside the cabin at the moment, looking at the peaceful sky and just enjoying, as much as they could, the night air.

But because the stillness was getting to be too much, and he didn't want to risk saying something that might lead them to far more dangerous territory—like the bedroom—Bowie reiterated what he'd already said to her before.

"You know, I meant what I said earlier, about my being there for you and the baby."

"I know, because your word is your bond. Did I get that right?" she asked with a touch of cynicism, parroting what he had told her the day before.

"Yes," he answered, pretending not to notice the shift in her tone. But he really didn't want to take a chance on misleading her. That wouldn't be fair to Marlowe. He needed to be clearer, he decided, so there would be no mistakes made. "Maybe I should also mention that I've always been sort of a lone wolf."

"Are you trying to tell me that you howl whenever there's a full moon out?" she asked sarcastically.

"No," he answered impatiently. "I'm trying to tell you that with my being a lone wolf, well...marriage isn't in the cards for someone like me," he said bluntly, then quickly added, "but that doesn't mean that I would shirk my duty toward the baby."

Her tone grew icy. "That's very nice of you, but you don't have to concern yourself about doing your *duty*,"

Marlowe told him. "I am more than capable of taking care of and providing for my baby," she concluded flatly.

"You mean *our* baby," Bowie corrected her.

Her eyes narrowed as she looked at him. "The last I heard, possession was nine-tenths of the law," Marlowe informed him, her hand moving to protectively cover her as-of-yet exceptionally flat belly.

She'd clearly had just about enough for one night, she thought. "If you don't mind, I think I'll just turn in early."

She didn't wait for Bowie to respond. Instead, she turned on her heel and walked back into the cabin. Once inside, she went straight to the bedroom in the back, slamming the door in her wake.

Damn it, he hadn't meant to do that, Bowie thought, upbraiding himself. His only intention was to spare her from entertaining any false hopes about their future.

He frowned, looking back toward the cabin door. In getting his message across, he had somehow managed to scare her off altogether. That wasn't what he was trying to do.

This was all damn confusing. He was really attracted to her, probably a great deal more attracted than he had ever been to any other woman before her. But a wife and baby were just not in the cards for him, he silently insisted. RoCo was everything to him, and he had to focus on the company, not on the daughter of his father's archenemy—as melodramatic as that had to sound, he thought, mocking himself. More than likely, she felt the same way about Colton Oil.

With a sigh, Bowie decided to call it a night himself and went into the cabin. Closing the door behind him, he made sure that locks were all secured. Satisfied, he started to go toward the back bedroom, wanting to apologize. But he stopped himself before he got halfway there.

It was better this way.

He couldn't afford to pursue Marlowe, or to allow the attraction he felt for her to get the better of him, beyond being a good dad. For all he knew, if he said anything at all about being attracted to her, she'd laugh at him. Or she might tell him that even though they'd had one good night together, that didn't mean anything in the long run.

Marlowe was married to Colton Oil for the long haul; she had all but told him so. He needed to stop letting his emotions rule his head and get his priorities straight and *keep* them that way once and for all.

BOWIE SPENT AN even more restless night this time than he had the previous night when he had intentionally stayed awake.

Come morning, he had made up his mind about what to do next.

"We can't hide here indefinitely," Marlowe told him early the following morning. "I think it's time to go back. I know I have work to do and I'm assuming so do you. If I stay here for another day, I'm going to go stir-crazy."

Bowie smiled, nodding. At least they were in agreement when it came to this, he thought. "Yeah, me, too."

"Maybe Callum, who's a bodyguard, can help keep

an eye out. I guess we have some things in common," Marlowe told him.

Without thinking, his eyes ran over her body. He felt himself reacting before he shut down. "Yes, we do," he responded.

THE TRIP BACK to Mustang Valley was fairly tense. Bowie kept looking over his shoulder, as if he expected their unknown stalker to pop up at any moment, while Marlowe was very quiet. Her mind was busily trying to figure out just what her connection was to the killer who was after Bowie—and perhaps her, too. Was Bowie right that this had all begun after he left her room that night, or was that all just a terrible coincidence? Or could one of Colton Oil's clients feel that their investment money was being misused because they found out she was looking into making the company green?

She was fervently hoping that she would be able to think more clearly once she was back at work. Back in familiar surroundings.

Going to the cabin had ultimately been a bad idea. She hadn't been able to shake the feeling that she was a sitting duck, waiting for some invisible villain to get off a kill shot. And having Bowie around was just a bitter reminder of the mistake she had made six and a half weeks ago: Bowie thought of himself as a lone wolf. Wolves didn't settle down; they prowled around, she thought.

Well, he was free to do that once they got back to town. She certainly had no intentions of standing in his way.

As a matter of fact, the way she felt right now, she would be more than happy to *push* him on his way, and good riddance.

As BOWIE PULLED his vehicle up in front of the Colton Oil building, he noted the rather strange, contemplative expression on her face.

"Everything all right?" he asked her, setting the hand brake and shutting off the engine.

"Just peachy," she replied with what sounded like false cheerfulness. "You don't have to get out," she told him. "I can just get out here."

"No, I'll walk you in," Bowie said firmly. Not giving her a chance to protest, he told her, "I'll carry your suitcase for you."

Her shoulders grew rigid. "I already told you, Robertson," she said, opening the passenger door, "I'm perfectly capable of carrying my own suitcase."

Bowie began to answer, then closed his mouth. Everything was a fight with her ever since he'd said something to make her angry last night. He was tired of fighting.

"Fine," he declared. "Have it your way."

Plucking the suitcase from the back seat, she pulled it out. "I usually do," she replied, sounding deliberately smug.

He should have his head examined, getting mixed up with this bullheaded, stubborn she-devil, Bowie upbraided himself angrily.

Still, rather than pull away, he continued to sit where he was, watching Marlowe as she walked up to the building entrance and then went inside.

MARLOWE WAS THINKING SIMILAR, equally critical thoughts about Bowie as she rode up to her office and swept in. Parking her suitcase off to the side, she sank down behind her desk and let loose with a long, deep sigh of relief.

This was more like it.

She was back in her home territory. She knew what was expected of her here, what she needed to accomplish. Being alone in that cabin with Bowie had jumbled up her brain for a little while, made her entertain thoughts she had absolutely no right to entertain.

She— Marlowe froze as she saw the large package that was placed in the middle of her sofa. She didn't remember ordering anything.

Maybe someone had sent her a gift, she decided. Rising from her desk, she crossed over to the sofa. Sitting down beside the package, she picked it up. She turned the box around, examining all six sides of it. There was no return address.

An oversight?

That was odd, she thought. But maybe whoever had sent it didn't want to call attention to him or herself. There was undoubtedly a card inside, probably meant for her eyes only.

Going to her desk to get a letter opener, she used the sharp object to rip through the wrapping paper around the package so she could get to the box underneath. When she did, she still had no clue who had sent it.

Ordinarily, she would have thought the package had been sent by a secret admirer. But the strange events of the last three days, especially her one interaction with the mysterious shooter who had fired at both her *and* Bowie, well, that had changed the way she viewed things like a package.

She was being silly, Marlowe told herself. This was probably some harmless gift, or maybe even some promotional gimmick meant to get the attention of the president of Colton Oil.

Having calmed herself down to an extent, Marlowe gingerly opened the cardboard box.

She found a profusion of tissue paper covering a sweet-faced stuffed teddy bear that could easily be placed in any baby's nursery.

Pulling the stuffed bear out, she also managed to pull out a card.

Finally, she thought, wrapping one arm around the bear to hold it in place. Mystery solved, she told herself, opening the envelope and pulling out the card that was inside.

Congratulations on your baby. Wish it was mine.

The scream that escaped her lips came totally unbidden. As was her reaction as she threw the stuffed bear to the floor.

Her assistant came running in immediately, looking as if she didn't know what to expect when she opened the door. "Is something wrong, Ms. Colton?" Karen asked breathlessly.

Marlowe struggled to get herself under control. The last thing she wanted was to be seen as a hysterical woman, even though everything inside of her was shaking. Who could have sent this?

"Did you see who left this, Karen?" she asked her assistant.

Seeing that the threat was just a stuffed teddy bear,

Karen relaxed and seemed a little calmer as she ventured forward.

"Oh, how adorable," she said, her face softening and forming a smile as she looked at the gift.

"Did you see who left this?" Marlowe repeated, this time more sharply.

Karen shook her head, looking somewhat nervous again. "No, Ms. Colton. Whoever left it must have come in before I did."

Marlowe looked at the teddy bear as if it was the enemy. "So it was already in my office before you got in? What time did you come in?" she asked, her uneasiness growing.

It was obvious that it took Karen a minute to think. "I was here by seven," she remembered. "I had some paperwork to catch up on. Whoever left this for you had to have done it before seven. Is something wrong, Ms. Colton?" she asked.

Marlowe didn't answer the assistant directly. Instead, she instructed the woman in an urgent voice, "Call Security and tell them to come in here, Karen."

Karen blinked, her eyes widening as she looked at her boss. "Security, ma'am?"

"Yes," Marlowe answered, keeping her eyes on the teddy bear. "I want them to examine footage to see who dropped this off and check this thing out completely, just in case it's wired for explosives."

Chapter Eleven

She had to concentrate to keep her hands from shaking as she stared at the note she had taken out of the package. *Congratulations on your baby. Wish it was mine.*

All sorts of half-formed thoughts were ricocheting around in her head.

Who had sent this?

Why?

Did she have some creepy stalker tracking her after all?

Had someone followed her into the drugstore and watched her buy the pregnancy test? And even if that was true, how could this stalker have possibly known the results of that test?

Or was he just guessing? After all, there was a fifty-fifty chance of being right. But to what end? And why?

She was back to her first question: Who was doing this to her?

Marlowe could feel herself becoming nauseated again. She closed her eyes and *willed* her stomach to settle down. Willed it to cease its bitter-tasting rise up into her throat and mouth. She pulled her fingers into tight fists. This wasn't the time to let her body dictate to her.

She needed to think, to *do* something, not just be a sitting duck.

Marlowe drew in a deep breath and then let it out slowly, then did it over again.

Security had come in and taken possession of the possibly lethal teddy bear a few minutes ago, so at least she didn't have to worry about the damn thing exploding and harming anyone. That was something, she thought, silently consoling herself.

Marlowe took out her phone. Her hands were still shaking.

She started texting Bowie, wanting to tell him about this newest development in what was quickly becoming a very complicated saga. Before she had gotten to the third word, the company phone on her desk rang, making her jump.

She really needed to get a grip on herself, Marlowe thought.

Blowing out a tense breath, she yanked up the receiver and all but barked, "Hello?"

"Marlowe?" It was Ace's voice on the other end of the line. He sounded as tense as she felt, she thought. "Good," her brother was saying. "You *are* back, then. I need you to come into the boardroom right now. Ainsley just got the DNA test results back. She wants to tell us the results all at the same time. The rest of the board is already here."

Of course they were, Marlowe thought impatiently. This was getting to be the story of her life. The last one in.

"Did she tell you what the result of the test was?"

She heard her brother laugh, but there was no humor in the sound. "You know Ainsley. If the result is supposed to be a secret until everyone is gathered together to hear it, then she intends to keep it a secret—even from herself—until then," Ace told her. "She hasn't even opened the envelope herself. So hurry up and get here. This suspense is killing me."

"I'm on my way," she promised, quickly hanging up the phone.

With all this craziness going on in her life, the pregnancy, the shooter and now this stalker, she was embarrassed to admit that she had completely forgotten about Ace and the DNA test. Marlowe felt almost guilty that she had.

But it wasn't as if Ace needed her to boost his morale, she silently insisted. Of course the DNA test was going to show that he was a Colton. To think that anything else could possibly happen would be absurd, she told herself, hurrying to the boardroom.

The results were going to be positive. They *had* to be, Marlowe insisted.

Even so, her heart felt like it was racing to the tune of "Flight of the Bumblebee" by the time she walked into the boardroom.

The five other members of the board were already assembled in the room, just the way they had been when that bombshell of an email had been sent. Looking quickly around, she noted that their expressions all looked just as hopeful as hers did.

All except for Selina, Marlowe thought. Selina's expression was that belonging to a woman who was anticipating *her* version of good news.

"Nice of you to join us," Payne said sarcastically, the moment that Marlowe crossed the boardroom threshold. And then the man shifted his eyes toward Ainsley. "All right, Ainsley, go ahead. Open the envelope and read the results out loud."

Ainsley flashed an encouraging smile at Ace, then ripped open the side of the envelope. She took out the lab results. Pressing her lips together, Ainsley scanned the single sheet of paper in her hand.

"I said out loud, Ainsley," Payne repeated sharply, raising his voice so that it all but thundered through the room.

Ainsley's expression turned grim.

This couldn't be good, Marlowe thought, hoping against hope that her instinct was wrong.

Ainsley read the results out loud. "It says that there is less than zero chance that Ace Colton is a Colton by blood."

"What?" Rafe cried, stunned.

"There has to be some sort of mistake," Marlowe insisted. "It can't say that."

"That can't be right, Ainsley!" Ace declared, looking like someone who just had a land mine explode right in front of him. "There must have been a mix-up at the lab. We need to have the sample retested, this time by another lab."

"Dad," Rafe spoke up, coming to Ace's defense. "Marlowe's right. A mistake has been made."

All their voices were blending together in a cacophony of noise, each voice drowning out the others. Payne himself looked as if he was in a state of shock, and for once in his life, he was speechless.

Of all of them, only Selina looked pleased. *Really* pleased.

"Payne, remember, the bylaws are the bylaws and they have to be obeyed." Her smile deepened, verging on almost malicious. "You know what you have to do," she told him, looking at her ex-husband expectantly. "Go ahead," she urged. "Do it."

"I want no one to speak about this." Payne's dark eyes swept over every face at the table, almost as if he was looking into their very souls. "The public can't get wind of this. This stays in the family. Am I making myself understood?" he demanded, looking at each and every one of them again.

"Payne," Selina said in a patronizing tone.

Payne blew out an angry breath. Marlowe knew that what he was about to say gave him no pleasure. If Ace, or this person who had grown up in front of him with Ace's name, wasn't a Colton, then the man had no business being the CEO of Colton Oil. He needed to step down.

"She's right, boy," Payne said, his voice flat and cold, "you can't be part of the board of directors and you most certainly can't be the CEO now that we know the truth."

Ace stared at the man he had thought of as his father for his entire life. How could some piece of paper, most likely faulty, negate forty years, just like that? As if they had never happened at all?

"Dad, you can't really be serious," Ace protested, stunned, hurt and angry. "I don't care what that paper says, I'm still your son—"

"No, that's just it. You're *not*," Payne retorted, his voice growing in volume. "I don't know who you are, and I certainly don't know who switched you with my son at birth, or why they did, but you are definitely *not* my son, and that means you can't be the CEO of Colton Oil," he repeated, all but shouting the words.

Ace shouted back. "You can't do this!"

Payne's eyes grew cold. "I just did," he informed Ace flatly.

Fury entered Ace's eyes. Visibly stunned and reeling, Marlowe imagined he felt as if the very rug had been pulled out from under his feet and he was struggling to get his bearings. After all, his whole life had just been declared null and void by his own father, a man who was obviously incapable of even an ounce of sympathy or compassion. Surely he had never felt so abandoned and alone before in his entire life.

"You're going to regret doing this, *Dad*!" Ace promised.

Ace stormed out of the room, leaving his disoriented siblings to try to comprehend what all this meant for the company as well as for them.

Marlowe was also wondering why their father had allowed himself to be manipulated to agree with Selina, a woman *none* of them even remotely liked.

Was she behind this somehow? Marlowe couldn't help wondering.

Meanwhile she was also experiencing regrets again. She regretted having told Bowie about the email and that Ace being related to the rest of them had consequently been in doubt, so a DNA test had been initiated. The bottom line was that the results had caused

Ace to be ousted by their father. She could just imagine that this would have the Robertsons beside themselves with joy, although she doubted that Bowie would feel that way. She was beginning to feel that he wasn't such a bad guy, all things considered.

She should have just kept her mouth shut, Marlowe upbraided herself. Desperate to have something to blame, she zeroed in on her condition. If it wasn't for this stupid pregnancy, causing her to be soft as well as weak, she wouldn't have said *anything* to Bowie about Ace.

Well, no more, Marlowe promised herself. From now on, she was going to be as closed off and as tough as she used to be, she vowed.

Marlowe looked at her father, disappointed beyond words at the way he had handled all of this. Disappointed, too, that the man she had looked up to, despite everything, had given in to Selina, of all people, rather than override the witch.

Not for the first time Marlowe wondered if the hateful woman was holding something over her father's head. Something that would make Payne jump through hoops and turn his back on the rest of his family.

There was no other explanation for her father's actions.

It had to be something really big, she decided. Otherwise she was certain that Payne Colton would have sent that woman packing, her tail between her legs, a long time ago—immediately after their divorce, Marlowe thought. Instead, she'd watched her father, never a patient man, keep treating the wretched woman like she was some sort of trusted confidante instead of the hateful, poisonous viper that she was.

Only the look in his eyes, when he occasionally let his guard down, told Marlowe otherwise.

What is it, Dad? What does Selina have on you that keeps you in line like this?

"Okay, everybody, settle down," her father ordered, raising his voice. It wasn't a request, it was a flat-out demand, and they all knew better than not to obey. "With Ace gone, someone is going to have to take over as the company's CEO."

Marlowe stiffened, praying that her father was not about to appoint her to this post. There was just too much going on in her life right now for her to maintain a clear enough head, let alone the entire Colton Oil company. She liked to think that she was up to any challenge, but this would have been just too much for her.

"So, for the time being," her father was saying, "I'll take over the position. It's my old job, anyway," he said with a resigned shrug, as if part of him had always known it would come down to this eventually. "So, unless there are any objections—" his tone indicated that he didn't assume that there would be as he looked around the table again "—meeting's adjourned. Go do your work, people," Payne ordered.

The others filed out of the room, but Marlowe hung back. She and Ace were not as close as they used to be, although they did work together on the board. But she really felt for him because of what he was going through now. That made her feel that she needed to say something to her father about the explosion that had just happened between the two men.

Payne pulled a few papers together, then raised his eyes when he saw that Marlowe hadn't left yet.

"You got something to say, girl?" Payne addressed her gruffly.

He must have assumed that she was going to ask for his forgiveness for the mess she had gotten herself into with the Robertson kid.

"Yes, I do," she told her father. "Ace didn't mean it, Dad."

Payne's forehead furrowed into a mass of wrinkles.

"What?" he demanded.

Her father had a gold medal in intimidation, but Marlowe refused to back down. Instead, she forced herself to push on.

"Ace was just upset," she told Payne. "His whole world has just come crashing down all around him, and he wound up turning all his anger on you. But you have to know that he didn't mean what he just said."

Payne grew angrier.

"What goes on between Ace and me is none of your damn business, missy, so back off, you hear me?" he shouted at her. "And you're in no position to give me any kind of advice!"

Marlowe struggled to hang on to her own temper. She supposed that her father was upset by the news himself and this was his way of dealing with it. But she wasn't in the mood to make excuses for her father or put up with his bad temper or his even worse personality.

"Sorry," she said sarcastically. "I guess I forgot my place."

"Damn straight you did. Well, don't forget it again, you hear me?" he warned. "You might not like the consequences."

Her father was treating everyone as if they were annoying interlopers. There was just no getting through to him today, she thought, annoyed clear down to the bone.

Turning on her heel, Marlowe left the boardroom as quickly as possible, wanting to get away from the man before she said something cutting and surly.

That, she knew, would make her no better than her father—and she didn't have the sort of surly outlook to carry it off.

She was about to return to her office when she caught sight of Ace. He looked both angry and lost at the same time.

Impulsively, she hurried over to the man she had always regarded as her oldest sibling. Because they had two different mothers, Ace was actually her half brother, a fact that her father always emphasized for reasons known only to him, but she had never thought in those terms. Ace was her brother, pure and simple. And the DNA results, along with what had just happened back in the boardroom, didn't change anything.

He was still Ace to her, just as she intended to be still Marlowe to him. She couldn't live with herself if she didn't say something to Ace in an attempt to make him feel better.

"Ace," she called out to him. When he kept walking, she tried again. "Ace!"

Reluctantly, Ace stopped walking and turned around to face her. The look on his face was defensive and surly, as well as hurt.

"What?" he said bitingly.

"I just wanted to tell you that I don't care what some DNA report says. You're still my brother, Ace Colton, as far as I'm concerned, and I just wanted you to know that you have my full support, no matter what you decide to do. This was a terrible blow, but I know you. You're going to pick yourself up, dust yourself off and find a way to come back from all this."

He looked at her as if she were talking nonsense. "Excuse me, but have you *met* our father? Sorry, I mean *your* father?" He tersely pretended to correct himself. "The man doesn't bend or give."

"Yet. He hasn't bent or given *yet*," Marlowe pointedly insisted. "But there's always a first time, Ace. And I know it's going to happen."

Ace laughed shortly. "I appreciate the Pollyanna pep talk, Marlowe, I really do," he told her. "But right now I think that I just want some space from everything, if you don't mind."

Humoring Ace, she raised her hands as if to symbolically give him that space.

"You've got it, big brother. Just promise me that you won't let that space turn into something that winds up becoming insurmountable."

"Okay, I promise," Ace said in an offhanded manner as he left. There was no conviction in his voice.

With all her heart, Marlowe really wished that she could believe her brother meant what he said.

Chapter Twelve

"Mr. Robertson, there's a Ms. Colton asking to see you." Bowie's administrative assistant, Gloria Kennedy, who had been with the company since its very beginning, peered into his office. Looking like everyone's kindly grandmother, the woman entered Bowie's office only after knocking first and being told to come in. "Shall I tell her that you're in a meeting?"

"But I'm not," Bowie told Gloria, although he appreciated the fact that she was attempting to guard his privacy.

What was Marlowe doing here? he wondered. He assumed it had to be Marlowe, because why would any of the other Colton women have a reason to come to see him? Something must have happened, he thought. But what?

"I know, sir," Gloria answered patiently. "But it is a Colton, sir, and…"

Gloria's voice trailed off as if that lone fragment was enough to explain why she had kept the woman cooling her heels in the outer office.

Bowie didn't bother debating the matter with his assistant. He normally trusted Gloria's judgment implicitly, but this was an entirely different matter. Without saying another word, he strode into the outer office.

He was just in time to see Marlowe going to the outer door, leaving.

"Marlowe, wait," he called out, crossing quickly over to her.

Visibly annoyed at the way she'd been treated by Bowie's assistant, Marlowe made no effort to stop walking out of the office.

Bowie was quick enough to catch up to her, and he placed himself directly in the way of Marlowe's escape route. He was now convinced that something had to be terribly wrong for her to come into what he knew she considered enemy territory to see him.

Had someone made another attempt on her life? The very idea left him cold.

Catching hold of her arm, Bowie physically stopped her exit. "Marlowe, what's wrong?"

Because he had her arm, she was forced to stop. It was either that or create a scene, and while he knew she had no qualms about doing that if the situation warranted it, for the time being, it didn't.

Tossing her head, Marlowe looked up at him. "You mean other than the fact that your assistant over there could benefit from a crash course in manners?" she asked, casting a disparaging look in the older woman's direction. Gloria stood, looking formidable, frowning at Marlowe.

Right now, his attention was focused on the large box Marlowe was holding. He curbed his immediate desire to ask her about it.

"Yes, other than that," Bowie answered dismissively.

He knew without turning to look in Gloria's direction that the woman was taking in every syllable. The assistant was exceedingly protective when it came to him. "Why don't you come into my office?" he suggested. "You can tell me why you've ventured into enemy territory." He expected at least a small smile in response, but when Bowie peered at her face, Marlowe continued to look like the very definition of anger. "Nothing?" he asked. "This is bad, isn't it?"

Rather than answer his question, Marlowe said, "Let's go into your office like you suggested—as long as your fire-breathing protector doesn't object."

Bowie felt like he had to come to the woman's defense. "Gloria was just doing her job, Marlowe," he told her, leading the way back to his office. "There are a lot of people trying to get to talk to me for one reason or another."

"Really?" she said. "That must be really rough on you."

Bowie closed the door behind them. Once it was shut, he turned to look at his unexpected visitor. She really looked upset, and he didn't think that he was the reason for that.

"All right, Marlowe. Let's stop waltzing around. What happened since I dropped you off? Why are you here?" he asked. And, since she hadn't volunteered the information herself, he nodded at the box she was holding. "And what's that?"

She placed it on top of his desk. "That was waiting for me in my office when I got in this morning. When I asked my assistant who left it there, she didn't know. She said it must have been put into my office before she got in. The woman regularly gives roosters their wake-up call, as a sideline."

"So whoever dropped that thing off either came into the office incredibly early, or he knew your assistant's routine," Bowie surmised.

"And if it's the latter, that suggests that whoever did leave this gift works at Colton Oil," she told him. "Otherwise, how could he possibly have known Karen's routine?"

Bowie inclined his head. She had a good point there, he thought. "And just what did this mystery man drop off?" he asked, his curiosity finally getting the better of him.

Marlowe had been doing her best to distance herself from the implications that this "gift" brought with it, not to mention what it indicated about the person who had given it to her. She had just gotten the bear back from Security, which had found the stuffed animal to contain nothing harmful. A lot they knew, she thought.

Telling Bowie about the bear brought those feelings back to her in spades.

Pulling the teddy bear with its note out of the box, she put both on his desk.

"This," she declared.

"A teddy bear?" he asked, as if not quite certain why she seemed to be so shaken up by the gift. "It's a little strange, but I don't—"

"Read the note that came with it," she insisted. "And then we'll talk."

Picking up the card, Bowie quickly read it. His expression became grave. "I see what you mean."

"It appears that I've got a hostile admirer," she told

Bowie. She could all but feel the hostility emanating from the card. Restless, Marlowe began to pace back and forth in front of his desk. She wasn't accustomed to not handling problems, and yet, with no one to focus on, there wasn't anything she could do about this.

Bowie nodded thoughtfully. "That would explain why the attacks on me started after I left your hotel room that morning. It points to the fact that this admirer of yours is jealous."

Marlowe tried not to shiver, but she failed. "My admirer is crazy," she corrected.

"Well, yes, that goes without saying," Bowie agreed. "Can you think of anyone you've turned down recently?"

Marlowe shook her head. "I haven't turned down anyone," she protested. "I've been so busy, nobody's even approached me on a social level. It's been all about work," she told him.

"Okay, have you noticed anyone staring at you lately—worshipfully or otherwise?"

"No to both questions," she told him. She drew herself up. "But I know one thing for sure."

"And what's that?" he asked.

"Whoever this so-called admirer is, it has to be someone who works at Colton Oil, because I spend *all* my time at Colton Oil," she told him.

Bowie showed just the barest hint of a smile.

"Well, not *all* your time," he told her, his eyes moving down to Marlowe's waist and lingering there for the briefest of moments.

Marlowe sighed audibly. "All right, except for that one anomaly," she allowed. "Which wound up with me getting pregnant, as well as getting my very own creepy stalker—and someone trying to kill both of us," she said in disgust.

"The least I can do is get you a bodyguard," he offered Marlowe as he reached for the phone on his desk, drawing it closer.

Marlowe quickly stopped him from lifting up the receiver. When he looked at her quizzically, she said, "Like that won't be at all conspicuous," she told Bowie, vetoing the idea. "Look, if I wanted a bodyguard, I'm perfectly capable of getting one myself," she informed him.

"But you won't," he guessed. The woman was too stubborn for her own good.

She shrugged off what she knew he was implying. She wasn't being stubborn; she was being practical. "A bodyguard will only get in my way," she informed him.

"Yeah, well, so will a bullet," Bowie countered matter-of-factly. "What if Callum kept an eye out for you?"

But she shook her head. "I really don't think this guy is out to kill me," Marlowe told him. "You, maybe, but not me."

Bowie laughed shortly. "Well, that's reassuring," he said sarcastically. "Would you stop pacing?" he asked her. "You're making me dizzy."

"Cold-blooded killers generally don't leave cute teddy bears as their calling cards," Marlowe pointed out, telling him the conclusion she had reached now that she'd had time to think about the situation. "And before you ask, I had Security take this guy apart to see if maybe he'd been wired with explosives or something else equally as lethal. Turns out that the teddy bear was just an ordinary teddy bear. Whoever left this," she lifted up the bear again, "was either just trying to get my attention, or at the very most, to unnerve me."

"You can't take that for granted. If he's playing games like that, it could easily escalate," Bowie told her. "Look, I'm going to get that bodyguard for you, so you might as well stop arguing with me. I can either do it with your permission, or behind your back. It's up to you, but one way or another, you need to wrap your mind around the fact that you *are* going to get extra protection. I am not about to look back at this down the line and regret the fact that I didn't go with my instincts, and because I didn't, you and our child are no longer part of the equation."

"So now we're part of some equation?" Marlowe questioned, clearly trying to goad him into an argument.

"Don't change the subject, Marlowe. I *am* getting you that bodyguard. And don't worry, he'll be totally vetted. His only job will be to look after you and keep you safe. That means that he's not going to give a damn about whatever company secrets you might be harboring and could divulge. He's just going to be there to watch your back—just in case."

He knew Marlowe's suspicions wouldn't be entirely put to rest, but she was going to have to trust someone, and it might as well be him.

"I've got your word on that?" she asked.

He was surprised at her phrasing. If she was being serious, that meant that they were finally making some headway, he thought, pleased.

"Are you willing to take my word?" he questioned, watching her face for any telltale signs that she assented.

She raised her chin and her eyes held his. "Yes," she answered stoically.

"Then yes, you have my word on that," he told her.

When he saw the smile that slowly bloomed on Marlowe's lips, it hit him just how worth it all of this had been. Even though he tried to seal himself off, her smile really got to him.

Marlowe's phone buzzed at that moment. Forced to glance down at the screen, she read the text that had come in for her.

It was from Callum, inviting her to come with him to Mustang Valley General Hospital. He intended to try to find out just who had been on duty that fateful night that the person they had come to know as Ace had been switched with the "real" Ace.

We're going archive hunting, the text told her. Want to come help?

"More bad news?" Bowie asked, looking at Marlowe's expression.

That was when she remembered that she hadn't told Bowie about the results of the DNA test—and the subsequent fallout that bombshell had had.

But that was a story for another day, she decided. She didn't want to get into it right now, nor did she really have the time to try to field any of his questions, legitimate though they might be.

"No," she answered. "No bad news. Possibly good news," she continued, keeping her response deliberately vague. "I really won't know until I actually get there." She tucked away her cell phone as she started to go for the door. "Oh, Bowie," Marlowe said, turning around to face him just before she opened the door and walked out, "about the bodyguard…"

Because she was standing at the door, he had a feeling that she was going to tell him that she'd changed her mind about having one. Bowie braced himself for an argument. A knock-down, drag-out one if it came to that, because he wasn't about to have her out there, possibly a moving target, without some sort of protection.

"What about it?" he asked.

Her expression softened into a smile. A smile that managed to curl up in the pit of his stomach. "Thanks."

He would have wanted to accept her thanks at face value, but he'd come to know that nothing, when it came to Marlowe, was that easy.

"But?" he asked, waiting for her protest or refusal of the offer.

"No but," she told Bowie. "Just thanks."

Despite her initially trying to tell him that having a bodyguard wasn't in the cards for her, Bowie had remained steadfast and pushed because he was concerned. Marlowe couldn't help but compare that to her father's reaction. Payne Colton knew that she had been the target of an attack at her apartment, but he hadn't said anything about getting her a bodyguard or even acted concerned that the attack had happened.

She knew that her father, by definition, was not a demonstrative man. As far back as she could remember, he had expected his children to take care of themselves, handle their own problems. Time and again, he had said that it "built character." He obviously expected that it would do that for her, as well.

But it was obvious to her that Bowie didn't subscribe

to that sort of philosophy. Or, if he did, he still wasn't about to take any chances with the life of the woman who was carrying his child.

There were all sorts of ways to view his insisting on a bodyguard for her in a bad light, but Marlowe chose not to go that route. Instead, she just wanted to enjoy the fact that someone cared enough about her well-being to stand up to her and do what he felt was necessary.

His stock definitely went up, as far as she was concerned.

Bowie grinned then, as if relieved he wasn't going to have to fight her on this after all.

"Don't mention it," he told her.

"Just let me know when your guy starts to do his job," she told him. "Otherwise, his head will end up mounted as a trophy on my father's wall. My father has a way of shooting first and asking questions later," she added.

Bowie laughed dryly. "I'll keep that in mind," he told her.

"You should," Marlowe agreed, nodding. "For your own peace of mind, as well as for my future bodyguard's well-being."

"Hey," Bowie called after her as she opened the door and began to leave. "Aren't you forgetting something?" he asked.

She had no idea what he was referring to. "Like what?" she asked, a trace of suspicion reentering her voice.

In response, Bowie indicated the teddy bear that was still sitting on his desk.

Strangely relieved that this wasn't going to be something that could escalate into an argument between them, Marlowe laughed and shook her head. "I didn't forget. He stays here," she told him. "Think of him as your new little friend." Her mouth curved a little more. "He'll keep you company."

And with that, she walked out.

As was her habit, Marlowe drove back to Colton Oil with a lead foot, stepping hard on the gas to zip through yellow lights that were about to turn red. She admitted to herself that she was not known for her patience, and her patience was in exceedingly short supply when it came to wasting time being stuck in traffic, waiting for lights to turn green.

She calculated that her method enabled her to save both on time and gas, and although saving gas meant nothing to her as a member of Colton Oil, time was something she had always valued a great deal.

Zigzagging through the small, homey streets, she got back to Colton Oil's headquarters even quicker than she had anticipated. Marlowe really hoped it was an omen of how things were going to go in her hunt through the archives.

"You slowing down these days?" Callum asked when she pulled up. He was down in the parking garage, waiting for her, and she'd arrived later than he'd anticipated.

"Hardly," she retorted, getting out of her vehicle.

Her twin knew better than to continue teasing her.

Chapter Thirteen

Mustang Valley General Hospital was a large, inviting, five-story brick building that had been built back in 1925. It had gone through several renovations by now and could currently boast being a total state-of-the-art hospital. But it had become so only over the last fifteen years, thanks to endowments funded by Colton Oil.

Located at the far end of downtown Mustang Valley on its own well-manicured five-acre plot, the hospital was on the tail end of a winding road down which Callum was currently driving himself and Marlowe. He pulled his car up as close as he could to the front entrance of the building. Because of its large parking lot, finding a spot wasn't an issue.

"Why do I get the feeling that we're about to embark on a wild-goose chase?" Callum said to his twin as he got out from behind the wheel.

"Could be because behind that handsome, rugged exterior, you're a born pessimist," Marlowe answered. "Do what I do. View this in a positive light." She closed the passenger door. "Just think of it as unraveling a mystery for Ace."

"Except that he's not Ace anymore," Callum said as

they crossed the parking lot and made their way to the hospital's front entrance.

Almost a foot shorter than her twin, Marlowe hurried to keep up. There was no way she was about to ask him to slow down. "Well, that's the name that he's responded to for the last forty years, and as far as I'm concerned, he'll always be Ace to me."

"Yeah," Callum agreed. "Me, too. But Dad doesn't see it that way," he pointed out as they came up to the entrance.

The hospital's electronic doors drew apart and they walked in.

"So we'll work on Dad until we convince him," Marlowe said. "After all, there's two of us. We outnumber him."

It had been a while since either of them had been here, but the layout was still the same. There was an admission's desk on the left and a desk for outpatients to register on the right. Comfortable love seats were scattered for people to use throughout the lobby.

"Not the last time I checked," Callum answered. "One Payne Colton outnumbers six offspring, especially when one of the biological ones turns out not to be the real deal."

"You're impossible," Marlowe complained. Zeroing in on the woman sitting at the admission's desk, she physically pointed her brother in that direction. "C'mon, put that gorgeous face of yours to use," she told him in a lowered voice. "Charm the lady behind the desk into giving us the information we need," Marlowe instructed, all but giving him a push in the right direction.

Walking up to the woman's desk, he cleared his throat. "Excuse me," Callum said, speaking up.

"Be with you in a moment," the woman behind the admissions desk, whose name tag read Irene Ryan, said curtly. She continued typing data into the computer that was on her desk, keeping her eyes on the monitor.

Finished, she looked up. The moment she did and saw the man who was looming over her, her features instantly softened. Irene's voice almost sounded melodious as she asked the man, "What can I do for you, sir?"

"This is going to sound a little strange," Callum said, prefacing what he was about to ask. "But we're—" he glanced back at his sister as if for backup "—looking for information about births that took place at the hospital forty years ago. Specifically, births on Christmas morning."

The young admission clerk's smile faded, replaced by a look of confusion. "Is this some kind of joke, or a prank?" she asked Callum. It was obvious that she was growing defensive.

"No, ma'am," Callum politely assured her, "it's not a joke."

Marlowe spoke up, moving closer to her brother. "We're really trying to find any information we can about those births."

Irene paused to think for a moment, then shook her head. "That's way before the hospital began digitizing its data. My guess is that those records, if they're still around, would have been placed in the batched files stored in the basement. I'm really sorry," the young woman said, addressing her words to Callum rather than to the both of them, "but we don't have the resources or the time to just drop everything and go digging through files that are more than a quarter of a century old." She sat up a little straighter in an attempt to sound more official. "I'm afraid that you're out of luck," she told Callum.

"Are you sure you can't just—" Marlowe began but got no further before the admissions clerk cut her off.

"Yes, I'm sure I can't," Irene said curtly, sparing Marlowe a quick, dismissive look and acting like this was her kingdom and she was the first line of defense.

"Ms.—" Pausing, Callum glanced down at the nameplate sitting on the desk in front of the woman. "—Ryan," he said, attempting to create a bond between them by using her name. "In the heat of the moment, I completely forgot to introduce my sister and myself. I'm Callum Colton and this is my sister, Marlowe Colton."

The woman looked as if she had suddenly been fed a rock and was desperately trying to get it to go down. "Colton?" she repeated uneasily.

"Yes," Marlowe confirmed, abandoning all pretense of attempting to be nice to the woman. "You might have seen it written on some of the dedication plaques scattered around here in the hospital."

It was easy to see that Irene was a mouse, easily intimidated by authority. Placing her palms on her desk, she pushed herself up to her feet. Marlowe noticed that her hands were shaking.

"Um, yes," Irene answered nervously, her eyes now as large as saucers. "Wait right here…let me go get Anne Sewall. She's the hospital's administrator," the young woman told them, stumbling backward as she tried to make a graceful exit—and failed. "I'll be right back," she mumbled under her breath.

Marlowe turned toward her brother, putting a look of satisfaction on her face. "I knew that pretty face of yours would get us results," she told Callum.

"I tend to think that it was hearing our last name that got Miss Would-Be Efficiency moving as if there was a fire lit directly under her," Callum contradicted. Marlowe knew he wasn't the type who needed or wanted to have his ego stroked.

"Hey, I'll settle for whatever works," Marlowe replied with a laugh.

She crossed her fingers, hoping that one way or another, they would wind up getting the information they were after. Forty years *was* a long time, she readily admitted. Who knew what kind of state those old records would be in, once they were found? *If* they could even be found.

"Uh-huh, looks like it's showtime," Callum whispered to his sister as the admissions clerk returned to her desk.

"Mr. Colton, Ms. Sewall will see you now," the young woman told Callum. Her voice had taken on a formal cadence. "You, too, Ms. Colton," she added, as if suddenly remembering that she hadn't addressed the woman standing next to Callum. "Her office is right down the hall. Step that way," Irene added, pointing in the direction she had come from.

"One step closer," Marlowe murmured to her brother as they passed the desk and retraced her steps to an office where Anne Sewall waited.

Anne was a tall, thin woman in her early sixties

with a blond bob, wire-rimmed glasses and a heavyset face. She gave the impression of being overworked even when she was sitting down and not moving a muscle.

The woman rose to her feet the moment that Marlowe and her brother walked into her office.

"Ms. Colton, Mr. Colton, this is a great honor," she gushed, shaking first Marlowe's hand and then Callum's. She made Marlowe think of a lapdog that was desperately trying to gain favor. "Please, sit, sit," she cried, as if repeating the word somehow made the request that much more urgent. She gestured toward the two chairs in front of her antique desk.

Once Callum and Marlowe had both sat down, Anne took her own seat, sliding forward and sitting on the very edge like a bird waiting to take flight at the slightest provocation.

Her brown eyes darted back and forth between her two visitors, as if she didn't know whom to address first.

"What is it I can do for you?" Anne asked eagerly.

Callum took the lead. "We need to take a look at your hospital records, Ms. Sewall. Specifically, we're interested in records about a baby or babies born in the hospital on Christmas morning forty years ago."

The administrator looked somewhat puzzled and uncertain. "Did you say forty years ago?" the woman asked.

"Yes," Callum answered.

"May I ask why?" Anne asked.

"We'd rather not go into the particulars right now, Ms. Sewall," Marlowe told the other woman.

"But we assure you that there is nothing underhanded going on. The records concern our brother, Ace. He was born here on Christmas morning," Callum explained, then repeated his request again. "May we see those records, please?"

Anne continued to look nervous and uncertain. "I'm afraid that's impossible," she told him.

Marlowe sighed. "We know about the privacy issues," she interjected. "But the records have to do with Ace's birth. If we could just take a look at those records—"

"That's just it. There *are* no records," the woman informed them.

Callum scowled. "How is that possible?" he asked. "My father witnessed his wife giving birth to his first child. All of that has to be documented somewhere—"

"I'm sure what you're saying is all very true. However, I'm afraid that there was a fire in the maternity ward that very morning and it destroyed all the recent records regarding all the births that had taken place in that time frame, not to mention the names of the hospital staff who were on duty the night before as well as that morning. It also destroyed the nearby nurse's station. I'm sure everyone was grateful that the fire was contained and gotten under control before it could do any more damage, and fortunately, the infants were never threatened.

"Like I said," the administrator told them, her voice sounding a little strained, "this was all before records were kept on a computer and archived."

She flashed them a contrite look. "I am really sorry, but I don't have anything to show you." The woman looked almost eager to usher them out of her office. "I will do everything I can to shed some light on how the fire started and if anything at all survived the isolated blaze. But as for the information you're looking for, I'm afraid that it just no longer exists," she told them with finality.

"If I hear of anything, though," she went on, "I promise I'll give you both a call."

That was clearly their signal to leave, Marlowe thought. Callum rose to his feet, as did Marlowe. "I guess we can't ask for more than that," Callum told the administrator. "Thank you for taking the time to see us," he said.

"Of course, of course," Anne said, shaking each of their hands again. "I'm just sorry I couldn't have been of more help," she added, looking genuinely contrite in Callum's opinion.

"WELL, THAT WAS awfully convenient, don't you think?" Callum asked his twin as they walked out of the hospital. "A fire breaking out just after the real Ace and our Ace were switched?"

"I suppose it could have happened," Marlowe allowed. "But you're right. It just sounds like much too much of a coincidence. If you want my opinion, the person who switched the babies most likely set the fire," she concluded.

"No argument," Callum agreed. The same thing had occurred to him. "Now what?"

The entrance doors closed behind them and they began to walk toward the parking lot and Callum's car.

"Now we keep digging," Marlowe answered. "Maybe we can find out who was working at the hospital around that time. If we're lucky, maybe someone saw something but didn't know what they were seeing at the time. There had to have been a great deal of pandemonium and panic during the fire, what with everyone rushing around, trying to save the babies and their mothers."

"I don't know about that." Callum didn't seem so sure about the scenario she had just verbally sketched.

"What do you mean?" Marlowe asked.

"Dad would have mentioned something like that at some point. Maybe the fire was purposely a very small, isolated one," Callum theorized. "Just big enough to destroy the records, but not big enough to threaten anyone else, including the babies."

"Sounds like a good theory to me," Marlowe agreed. The more she thought about it, the more likely it sounded to her.

"We just need to find someone who worked at the hospital in the maternity ward at the time to confirm that," Callum said. He made it sound simple, but she knew it was anything but that.

Marlowe said it out loud for both of them. "Easier said than done. But then," she reflected, "what fun is easy?"

Callum shook his head. "You do have a very unique way of looking at things."

"I'm a Colton," she said as they got into his car. "I was born unique."

"And humble," he said with a laugh, putting his key into the ignition. "Don't forget humble."

"Never," she replied with a straight face. "I wouldn't forget that." And then Marlowe's expression became serious. "I think we need to call the board together for another meeting so we can tell them what we found out—or didn't find out," she amended. "Maybe one of them has a better idea of what to do next."

"Are you saying my idea wasn't good?" Callum asked, pretending to take offense.

She slanted a look in his direction. "I'm saying that the more ideas we have to work with, the better our chances of resolving all this are. Besides, I think it's time we get everyone involved in searching for any and all hospital personnel who worked at the hospital forty years ago. This isn't a job for just one or two people, not with all of us having our own set of responsibilities when it comes to running Colton Oil."

Callum sighed. "Yes, there is that." Rather than race through a light the way Marlowe was wont to do, he slowed down as it turned yellow, then red. "There's also another factor."

Marlowe shifted in her seat to look at her brother. "Which is?"

Callum took his time in responding. When he did, what he said wasn't anything that she'd expected. "How are you feeling?"

Nauseated as hell, she thought, but since she'd managed to keep everything down, she wasn't about to say anything about it to her brother.

"Okay," Marlowe answered. "Why?"

"Why?" Callum echoed incredulously.

"Yes, that's what I just asked, Callum. Why?" Marlowe repeated.

"Because you're pregnant."

Marlowe rolled her eyes. She was trying to get away from talking about her condition, not dwelling on it. She thought he would have understood that. He was her twin, and there were times when each knew exactly what the other was thinking. "C'mon, Callum, don't you start."

"Hey, I'm just worried about you. I've seen you turn green a couple of times in the last few hours, and green is *not* your natural color. Are you getting enough rest?"

"I am fine, Callum," Marlowe insisted.

He tried again. "Okay, what did the doctor say?"

She kept her face forward, not wanting to make any eye contact. "What doctor?"

"You haven't been to see your doctor yet?" he cried. "Hell, what are you waiting for?"

"Um, in case you haven't noticed, I've been a little busy, with my oldest brother suddenly not being my brother and some crazy person taking a shot at me *inside* my condo. That doesn't exactly leave much time for me to go sashaying off to my ob-gyn's office to read two-year-old magazines while I wait three hours for a consultation with her—*if* she doesn't cancel at the last minute because she's been called away to make a unscheduled delivery."

"Not good enough, Marlowe. You know you're just making up excuses," he told her. "You need to see your doctor."

"Fine," she said from between gritted teeth. "First spare minute I get," she told him.

"Make an appointment or I'll carry you there myself," he told her.

"You need a woman, Callum. Someone you can drive crazy other than me."

"Until that happens," he informed her, "you're stuck with me."

She slid down in her seat, staring through the windshield. "Terrific," she muttered. But deep down, she did appreciate the thought.

Chapter Fourteen

"Looks as if the board meeting has to be postponed,"
Marlowe told her brother as they got back to Colton
Oil headquarters. Just before they'd left the hospital
parking lot, she had sent out messages to all four of the
other members on a group chat. It had seemed strange
to Marlowe to delete Ace's name from the list of included members, but for the time being, for the sake of
peace, she knew it had to be that way.

Three of the texts that she had sent out were answered before Callum pulled up.

"Why?" Callum asked. "Who can't make the meeting?"

She slipped her phone back into her pocket. "Dad,
Rafe and Ainsley are all busy for the rest of the day."

"I'm sure one of them is available, right?" Callum
said.

"Oh no, we're not having a meeting with just her,"
Marlowe declared with feeling. "I might be tempted to
hold a meeting if the other three are there and dear old
Selina wasn't, but there's no way in hell that we're going
to have a meeting with *just* her at the table." Taking out
her phone, she looked at her schedule for the next day.

"Ask them if tomorrow at ten works for them," she said, getting out of the car. "If not, we'll keep pitching different times until we find one that works for everyone."

"Including ex–Stepmommy Dearest?" Callum asked sardonically.

Marlowe sighed. "Yes, her, too," she answered, although not happily.

Marlowe felt her phone buzz. She took it out, paused to look at the screen and saw she had a new text.

"Someone letting us know that they've changed their mind?" Callum guessed.

"No." Marlowe quickly read the message. Several emotions wafted through her simultaneously as she tried to figure out just how she felt about the text from Bowie. "This has nothing to do with the meeting."

Callum tilted his head, peering at his sister's face. "Robertson?" he guessed.

Marlowe looked up sharply. "Since when did clairvoyance become part of your makeup?" she asked.

"I'm not clairvoyant," Callum denied. "But if I were you, I'd really try to work on my poker face," he advised. "Your whole countenance changed when you looked at your phone screen. You lit up."

"You're imagining things," Marlowe insisted dismissively. Getting out of Callum's car, she shut the passenger door.

"No, I'm not," he said. "Hey, do you have feelings for this guy?" He quickly added, "Because it's okay with me if you do—that is, if he's treating you right."

Oh no, she was not about to get into this with her brother. She loved Callum dearly, but this was none of his business—especially since she wasn't 100 percent sure just what she was actually feeling when it came to Bowie.

"Callum," she told him, "the last thing I need right now is to play Twenty Questions with you."

"Okay," Callum said, retreating and raising his hands as if in surrender. "But you're going to have to figure it out sooner or later—for your own sake," he underscored. "Not for Dad, not for Mother or for anyone else, but for your own sake," he insisted firmly.

She knew he meant well and that she was being decidedly far too touchy about the matter. "Yes, O Wise One, I know." Smiling at Callum, she stood up on her tiptoes and brushed her lips against his cheek. "Now go and try to coordinate the troops while I see what this wild card in my life wants."

"You," Callum told her as if there was no question about it. "That would be my guess."

If she were being perfectly honest with herself, Marlowe didn't know if that was what she was afraid of, or what she was hoping for. So she said nothing. Instead, she hurried off, leaving her brother in the lobby. When she called Bowie, she wanted to be able to talk to him in private.

That privacy turned out to be available only in her office.

The minute she walked in, she closed the door. Rather than call Bowie, she crossed to her desk, sat down and proceeded to text him back. The message she sent read: I'm back in my office. What did you want to tell me?

In less than a minute after she had hit Send, her cell phone rang. She didn't have to look at the caller ID.

"Hello?"

"Are you planning on staying put?" Bowie's deep voice rumbled against her ear.

A warm shiver danced through her in response to his voice. She needed to get that under control, she told herself.

Rather than answer Bowie one way or another, she had a question of her own. "Why?"

"Because I need to see you." As if realizing how that had to sound to her, Bowie added, "I've got someone I want you to meet."

Now what? she wondered. She wasn't exactly feeling very social. "Listen, now's not a very good time," she began, getting ready to put him off.

As if he'd anticipated this move on her part, Bowie deftly blocked it. "No time is a very good time with you," he commented. "Stay put," he ordered. "I'll be there in twenty minutes."

She didn't like being told what to do—she never had, not even as a child. She could feel her back instantly going up. "Listen, I—"

"—can stay put for twenty minutes," he informed her, managing to predict what she was about to say.

Marlowe stared at her phone screen. The connection had been terminated. She could feel her temper rising quickly. For a second, she fought against the urge to throw her phone against the wall. Taking in a deep breath to help her get hold of her escalating impatience, Marlowe told herself there was no reason to take her anger out on her phone when she could just as well wait for Bowie and take it out on him in person.

Two more deep breaths later, she buzzed for Karen. The petite assistant was inside her office almost immediately.

"What can I do for you, Ms. Colton?" Karen asked.

"Bowie Robertson will be coming to see me. Bring him in as soon as he gets here," Marlowe instructed.

Although she was obviously surprised, Karen did a good job of hiding her emotion. "Very good, Ms. Colton," the assistant replied. "Anything else?" She stood by the door, awaiting further instructions.

"Not as far as I know."

She knew that it was a vague response to her assistant's question, but at the moment Marlowe wasn't feeling all that focused. On the contrary, her mind felt as if it was spinning around here, there and everywhere. A little like a sparrow caught in a storm, searching for somewhere to land before being helplessly blown completely off course.

About to withdraw from Marlowe's office, Karen looked at her boss over her shoulder.

"May I get you some tea, Ms. Colton?" her assistant offered. "You look a little pale, if you don't mind my saying so."

Mind? Why should she mind having an employee tell her that she looked like death warmed over? Marlowe thought.

She realized that her hands were clenched. She was flying off the handle again, Marlowe thought. What was going on with her, anyway? Her assistant was just trying to be kind, not criticizing her.

"Herbal tea would be very nice, thank you, Karen," she agreed. "Cream, no sugar."

"Cream, no sugar," the young woman repeated. "Got it." Karen said it almost happily, appearing glad to have something specific to focus on.

Marlowe leaned all the way back in her chair and closed her eyes, trying to think.

Why was Bowie actually coming here? They'd just seen each other this morning.

And then she remembered that he had said something about getting her a bodyguard, as well as having someone look into trying to track down the source of that awful email she and the others had all received. Could that be it? Had he found out something important and was coming to tell her in person because he thought the phone lines were being bugged? Was the person who had uncovered all this for her the person he wanted to introduce her to?

Or should she be worrying about something else entirely?

Not for the first time, part of her really regretted ever having gone to that energy conference. If she hadn't gone, then none of this would be happening and she could focus on the drama surrounding Ace's case instead of feeling so scattered right now.

But then, if she hadn't gone to the conference, she wouldn't have spent that spectacular night with Bowie and she wouldn't be...

She wouldn't be wasting her time sifting through possible scenarios and practically talking to herself like some loon, Marlowe thought, completely annoyed with herself.

A light rap on her door had her back snapping into place, rigid and alert. Her eyes immediately darted toward the door. But when it opened, it was only Karen coming in with a large steaming mug of tea.

"Here you go, Ms. Colton," she said, putting the mug down on the desk in front of Marlowe. "Herbal tea, cream and no sugar." The young woman began to withdraw from the office. "I'll let you know when Mr. Robertson arrives."

"You do that," Marlowe murmured.

Almost without thinking, she wrapped her hands around the large mug. The warmth that seeped into her was oddly comforting. Closing her eyes, she let herself drift for a moment.

But the knock on her door a few moments later had her eyes flying open.

"They're here, Ms. Colton," Karen announced, opening the door.

"They?" Marlowe questioned. Who exactly were *they*?

The next moment, Bowie came in, followed by what could have very possibly been the largest man she had ever seen. He wasn't fat, just very, very wide and solid looking. The man had shoulders broad enough to double as a landing field, encased in a navy blue sports jacket that the giant seemed oddly comfortable wearing. But instead of a button-down shirt, he had on a gray turtleneck sweater. Casual, yet refined.

But just who was this man, and why had Bowie brought him into her office?

Turning her chair in his direction, Marlowe began to frame her question. "Bowie...?"

Way ahead of her, Bowie made the introduction. "Marlowe Colton, I'd like you to meet Wallace Bigelow." He smiled. "Your new bodyguard."

It took effort not to have her mouth drop open. She really hadn't expected Bowie to act so fast. "My what?"

"Your bodyguard," Bowie repeated. "We talked about this, remember?"

She had just assumed that Bowie had forgotten about that. Or would at least take his time.

Getting up from her chair, she moved over to the side, indicating that Bowie should move with her. When he did, Marlowe said, "I remember *you* talking. What I don't remember is my agreeing to this."

"Well, you did," he informed her, "and here he is." Bowie moved back to the center of the room, next to the man he had brought with him. "Bigelow, this sunny, smiling woman is Marlowe Colton. I want you to guard her with your life and make sure that absolutely nothing happens to her. Understood?"

"You have my word, sir." Wallace's deep voice seemed to practically rumble through the entire office like thunder.

Okay, this really wasn't going to work, Marlowe thought. "No offense, Wallace, you seem like a very nice man, but I don't need a bodyguard," she told the giant, then turned toward Bowie. "I don't," she insisted.

Bowie's expression didn't change. "Would you like me to drag out exhibit A, that giant teddy bear you brought into my office? Or maybe exhibit B, the card that came with him?"

She knew when she was looking down the sights of defeat. What she needed to do now was gain some concessions.

"All right, all right, you've made your point. But shouldn't a bodyguard be, well, you know, a little more inconspicuous than, say, a skyscraper?" She turned toward the giant of a man in her office. "Again, no offense, Wallace."

For such an intimidating figure, Wallace had a very nice, winning smile. "None taken, ma'am," he assured the woman he had been told to guard.

"Ma'am," Marlowe echoed. She couldn't help wincing. The label made her feel as if she was ancient. "Okay, if this is going to have a prayer of working, he can't call me *ma'am*," she told Bowie.

Bowie grinned. "I think it's in his DNA," he confided. "But Wallace doesn't have to call you anything, do you, Wallace?" The man shook his head in agreement. "He just has to *be*," Bowie told her.

"Don't worry, you won't even know I'm there," Wallace promised her.

That was impossible, she thought. "I highly doubt that," she told Wallace.

"Unless you need me," Wallace added pointedly, his soft blue eyes looking at her.

"He really is very good at his job," Bowie told her. "And besides," he said, getting to what, in his mind, was the important part, "this is nonnegotiable."

Marlowe looked at Bowie. Ordinarily, she would have been spoiling for a fight. But there was something annoyingly endearing about how adamant this man, who hadn't been part of her life a mere two months ago, was about keeping her safe. Not because he wanted something from her, not because he was getting anything out of it, but just because he…cared?

The thought hit her with the force of a six megaton bomb exploding in her brain.

"What?" Bowie asked. "You just got a really strange look on your face. Like something frightened you. Is something wrong?"

She looked at him, not certain how to process this newest thought that had suddenly cropped up in her head. "I'm not really sure," Marlowe told him honestly. "I'll let you know when I figure it out."

"Okay," Bowie agreed, backing away from the subject, "but as long as we're clear, Wallace stays," he told her.

Marlowe pressed her lips together, then nodded her head. Resigned. "Wallace stays," she said. "But he stays restricted."

"Meaning what?" Bowie asked.

To her it was self-explanatory. "He can't venture into any areas that might contain restricted company secrets."

Was that all? He could respect that, Bowie thought. "Fair enough," he agreed. "Wallace is being paid to be your bodyguard, not my spy. Besides, in case you've forgotten, our companies have slightly different approaches toward producing energy."

"No, I didn't forget," she told Bowie. Her mind went back to that evening at the conference, when everyone else had left and they were still talking, at first trying to convince the other of their stands and then…well, then they weren't standing at all. "Yes, I remember. I remember that debate we had at the conference that night."

"Okay," he told her. "I've got to be getting back for a meeting, but Wallace is going to stay with you 24/7. I'll call you later and check in," he told the bodyguard.

"Wait, what?" Marlowe cried, stopping Bowie. "I thought he was only going to be around during working hours."

She should know better than that. "Crazy people don't punch a time clock," he told her. "That includes stalkers who leave oversize gifts in your office. Just because he left this for you at work by no means guarantees that this guy won't pop up anywhere else—and that includes your condo."

"We have security at the house," she informed Bowie. That went without saying.

"Well, now you have a little more," he told her, trying to be reassuring. "It's just until we catch the guy, Marlowe," he promised.

"And when will that be?" she asked.

She expected Bowie to say something, but it was Wallace who answered her question. "Soon, ma'am. Very soon."

"Not soon enough for me," she couldn't help adding.

"I'll call you later," Bowie promised. His eyes took them both in. "Both of you."

Then, before she knew what was happening, he pulled her into his arms and kissed her deeply and thoroughly before releasing her just as abruptly.

And with that, he was gone.

Chapter Fifteen

"I'm sorry, Ms. Colton. She insisted on seeing you," Karen apologized as Selina Barnes Colton pushed her way into Marlowe's office.

"Oh, stop your whining, you useless waste of space. I am part of Colton Oil's board of directors. That gives me a perfect right to see anyone I damn well please in this building, and I don't need permission to do it," Selina informed Marlowe's assistant in her high-handed manner.

To Marlowe, hearing Selina's voice was tantamount to hearing nails being slowly drawn across a chalkboard. It took everything she had not to wince.

"I'll thank you not to talk to my assistant that way, Selina," Marlowe told the woman coldly. "Karen was only doing her job." Her eyes narrowed as she looked at the attractive woman she and the rest of her siblings thought of as a venomous snake. "Now what's so important that you have to come barging into my office like this, disrupting everything?"

But Selina's attention was diverted to the man she saw standing in the background.

"And who is this?" she asked Marlowe. Her eyes

slowly appraised everything about the wide, imposing bodyguard. Finished, Selina's eyes shifted back toward Marlowe. There was a smirk on her full lips. "He's a little old for you, isn't he, dear? Has your father met him yet?"

Not waiting for an answer, Selina continued her biting monologue. "I bet Payne hasn't, and when he does, there will be hell to pay, you do realize that, don't you, dear?" Selina laughed to herself, as if enjoying her own private joke. "It's rather ironic. Your father doesn't really take an interest in any of your lives," she said pointedly, "except whenever something one of you does might reflect badly on the company."

Not giving Marlowe a chance to respond, Selina sidled up to Wallace Bigelow and gave him another once-over, doing it up close this time.

"My, but you're a big one, aren't you? But if you think you've got yourself a meal ticket in little Marlowe here, think again," she advised maliciously. "Her father's going to have you out on your—"

She had had just about enough, Marlowe thought. She raised her voice and broke in, wanting to put an end to this and to rescue Wallace from Selina's tongue, as well.

"Not that it's any business of yours, Selina, but Wallace happens to be my bodyguard," she told the infuriating woman.

"Your bodyguard?" Selina repeated in a mocking voice. "Oh, is that what they're calling it these days?" She batted her long lashes at Wallace. "Care to do a little moonlighting on the side, sweetie? You might find it interesting."

"Don't proposition my bodyguard, Selina. It's beneath you, and he hasn't had his antivenom shots yet," Marlowe said, rising to her feet. Wallace was much too polite. In his place, she would have told Selina to get lost a long time ago. But he had merely stood there, enduring the woman's close scrutiny. "Although I'm starting to think that absolutely *nothing* is beneath you," Marlowe told her father's ex.

"What a clever turn of phrase, dear," Selina retorted to her ex-husband's daughter, her tone nothing if not belittling. "Did it take you long to come up with that?" Selina mocked. "Anyway, I came to find out what, if anything, you and that brother of yours learned at the hospital about how your fake brother wound up going home with your father and that mouse of a first wife of his. Anything?" she prodded.

Marlowe instantly took umbrage for the person she had known all of her life as Ace. "You'll find out with the rest of the board when we convene tomorrow," she informed Selina.

"You're planning on drawing this out, are you?" Selina surmised.

Marlowe didn't bother to hide the loathing she felt for the woman. "I don't think it's fair that you know something before the others do," she said, deliberately being vague. She knew that it would get under Selina's skin.

Selina laughed at her. "You're bluffing. You have nothing. If you did, you'd tell me just to put me in what you deem is my place," she concluded.

Marlowe was up on all of her tricks. She viewed them as rather pitiful. "You're not going to goad me into saying anything, so you might as well just drop this," she told Selina.

Wallace finally spoke up, stepping forward. "Is this woman bothering you, Ms. Colton?"

"Every day of my life, since the first time I ever met her," Marlowe replied with feeling. "But that's all right, Wallace. She was just leaving, weren't you, Selina?" she asked solicitously.

Selina drew herself up. There was pure hatred in her eyes. But she kept her temper. "For now," the woman replied haughtily.

Turning on the heels of her exceedingly expensive designer shoes, Selina walked out.

"Sorry about that," Marlowe apologized to Wallace.

"No need to apologize, ma'am," the bodyguard told her, returning to his initial post. "Almost every family has one of those in their number."

"Doesn't make putting up with her any easier," Marlowe said with a sigh. "I can't shake the feeling that she's like this sleek vulture in a designer suit, waiting for one of us to drop in front of her so she can feast on the carcass."

It suddenly hit Marlowe that she was sharing bottled-up feelings with a man who was, by definition, a virtual stranger to her. It wasn't something she normally did—ever.

"I'm sorry," she began. "I shouldn't have…"

Wallace seemed to understand her discomfort. "That's all right, ma'am. Talking to me is like talking to a piece of furniture. You don't have to worry. Whatever you say to me won't go anywhere."

Marlowe couldn't help laughing at herself and the entire scenario. "You were right," she told him.

"Ma'am?" he asked.

"You really do blend in," Marlowe said.

"Yes, ma'am," he answered agreeably, smiling broadly at her.

Maybe this wouldn't be so bad after all, Marlowe thought. And she had to admit, having this behemoth around to protect her did make her feel a great deal safer. Finding that teddy bear sitting there in her office this morning had made her exceedingly jumpy. That wasn't a feeling that she welcomed. Though she wasn't about to admit it out loud just yet, she appreciated having Bowie caring for her and their unborn child.

"You know," Marlowe said thoughtfully a few hours later as she finished up the proposal she had been working on, "that woman is always trying to stir up trouble between us."

"Between you and her, ma'am?" Wallace asked, deftly trying to pick up the thread of conversation where it had been dropped earlier.

"No, between all of us. All of my father's offspring," Marlowe clarified. "Not to mention that there were more than a few times when she subtly tried to get us to turn not just against our father but against each other, as well.

"And," she said, continuing with her thought, "I have no doubt that Selina has whispered in my father's ear and tried to get him to turn against us wholesale again." She didn't know if it was another wave of morning sickness or thoughts of Selina that were making her stomach suddenly churn, but she was feeling sick again as she shook her head. "I have absolutely no idea why he insists on keeping that woman around." She frowned as she looked at her new confidant. "Dad says she's good at her job, and I have to admit that she is," Marlowe said honestly.

Being honest was almost a curse at times, she thought darkly. But Selina Barnes Colton was not exactly a wizard. If she wasn't there tomorrow, someone else would come along to fill the vacancy and do just as good a job—if not better—without secretly attempting to pit them against one another.

The benevolent giant looked at her thoughtfully. "Perhaps there is something that Mrs. Colton is holding over Mr. Colton's head. Blackmail is a very powerful, dangerous tool in the wrong hands," he told Marlowe.

The point had already crossed her mind more than once. She remembered saying as much to Callum when they had discussed the power Selina seemed to wield over their father.

She closed her eyes. Something else to worry about, Marlowe thought.

TRUE TO HIS WORD, Bowie called Marlowe to check in on how she was faring with his bodyguard the moment that his own meeting was over.

"Would you mind if I dropped by?" he asked Marlowe.

The very sound of his voice had her brightening. She tried to upbraid herself for her reaction, but it had no dampening effect on the way she responded to him. The plain truth of the matter was that hearing his voice made her smile. She called herself a fool, but it didn't change anything.

"When?" she asked.

"I was thinking now," he answered.

She could feel her heart racing and called herself an idiot. She was acting like a simpering teenager, not the president of a high-powered oil company.

"Sure. I've still got a few things to finish up." It was a lie, but it was all she could come up with on short notice.

"Be right there," he promised. When Bowie arrived at Colton Oil within the half hour, he got right down to business. "So, is everything going all right?" he asked Marlowe, clearly referring to Wallace.

"Well, I hate to admit it," Marlowe told him, "but it's going better than I thought it would."

"Then I was right?" he asked innocently, glancing over toward the bodyguard. "Bigelow is blending in, becoming part of the furniture?"

Deliberately turning her chair away from Wallace's general direction so that her voice didn't carry, she told Bowie, "He's a little too big to be an ottoman, but yes," she said, giving Bowie his due, "you were right. Wallace does seem to have a knack for blending in."

Bowie all but beamed. "Told you."

The man was obviously pleased with himself. That made her a little leery. She didn't want him thinking that she was handing him free rein over her.

"Oh no, you're not going to be one of those men, are you? The ones who say 'I told you so' every chance they get?" she asked. Marlowe was only half kidding.

"Only if the situation calls for it," he told her with a grin. "All right, I won't say it—this time," he added after a beat.

"You know, I've been thinking," Marlowe went on to say.

"Good thinking or bad thinking?" Bowie asked.

"Well, I don't know how you're going to view this. What I do know is that to implement this I'm going to have to leave Wallace behind," Marlowe told Bowie, warming up to her subject.

He cut her off before she could say any more. "Not doable," Bowie replied.

Marlowe pushed on, curbing her very strong impulse to inform Bowie that he was *not* the boss of her and she was only going along with his providing her with a bodyguard because it suited her purposes. At the moment, however, it didn't, and she wasn't going to allow Bowie to stop her from doing what she felt might be the only course of action available to her.

She talked right over him as if he hadn't said anything. "I want to follow dear old Selina the next time she leaves headquarters, and I can't do that with Wallace shadowing my every move. Selina will see him coming from a mile away, and whatever I'm hoping to catch her doing won't happen. I have to go alone," she insisted.

"No," Bowie contradicted her calmly, "you don't have to go alone."

Marlowe could feel her temper fraying, just like that. "Look, Robertson, I'm not going to argue about this," she informed him.

"Good, because I don't want to argue—and before you get your second wind and launch into another all-out attack, trying to shoot me down, I just want to tell you that you're right."

Marlowe's mouth dropped open, the words she was

about to say dying before they ever emerged. He'd caught her completely off guard.

"I'm what?" she asked.

"You're right," Bowie repeated. "From everything you've told me, Selina doesn't have your family's best interests at heart, and I wouldn't be surprised if we found out that she was at least partially behind what's been going on to undermine the company with Ace."

We. He had said *we.* As if they were a set, two parts of a whole. Ordinarily, she would rebel against that, saying something snide because she felt that he was trying to order her around or just take over.

But for some reason she couldn't begin to explain to herself, this time the fact that he thought that way just warmed her.

She could only think that this pregnancy was playing havoc with her mind as well as her emotions. What other reason could there be for her reaction? She wasn't willing to admit that she was falling for the father of her unborn baby, at least, not yet. Even though, deep down in her gut, she already knew the answer to that.

"So you agree with me that I should follow her the next time she leaves the building unexpectedly. See what she might be up to," Marlowe concluded. She didn't expect it to be this easy. He had to be up to something, she reasoned—or did he just really care for her?

"I agree with everything," Bowie told her, "except the part about you following her on your own."

"Robertson," she began, frustrated because they seemed to be going around in circles.

But Bowie pushed on as if she hadn't just said his name. "Which is why I'm going to tag along when the time comes," he told Marlowe, then turned toward the bodyguard. "When that happens, consider yourself relieved, Bigelow."

"Yes, sir."

"Wait, what just happened here?" Marlowe asked, feeling railroaded.

"I just agreed with you," Bowie replied simply.

"The *other* part," Marlowe stipulated from between clenched teeth.

"The other part?" Bowie repeated innocently.

That only managed to fan her anger. "Yes, the other part. The part about you taking Wallace's place and coming with me while I follow Selina to wherever she plans to go."

"Seems to me like you have a clear understanding of that part," he told her. And then he grew serious. "Look, Marlowe, there's someone out there who clearly has it in for Colton Oil in general and maybe you specifically. In either case, I have no intentions of taking a chance on you getting hurt—or worse."

"*You* have no intentions," she echoed.

"Then we understand each other," he concluded, evidently hoping that would be the end of it.

Marlowe drew herself up. "Since when did you get to figure into this equation?" she demanded.

Bowie's eyes looked into hers. "I think you know the answer to that," he informed her in a low voice that was only loud enough for Marlowe to make out.

"Oh, and having you with me won't set off any alarms with Selina?" She laughed at the very idea.

"I thought the idea was to follow the woman discreetly so she could lead you to whoever she's working with—if she *is* working with anyone," he qualified.

Marlowe blew out a breath. She was defeated and she knew it. Bowie had just shot her down, and he was right. She would be safer with him along—not that she'd mind having him by her side. She had no doubts that Selina was vindictive enough to do something drastic if she set her mind to it.

"All right, you win," Marlowe told him. "When I follow Selina, I'll let you know."

He looked at the man he had hired to be Marlowe's bodyguard. "Bigelow?"

The big man knew what was being asked of him. "I'll call you and let you know, sir," he promised.

"My word isn't good enough for you?" Marlowe questioned, looking at Bowie.

"You might get caught up in the moment and forget to call," he explained innocently. "While Bigelow here has only one thing to focus on—your safety," he told her.

"You have an answer for everything, don't you?" Marlowe said curtly.

"That's why they pay me the big bucks at my company," Bowie replied.

Chapter Sixteen

Everyone who filed into the boardroom the next day was aware of the conspicuously empty chair at the conference table.

Ace's chair.

Marlowe could see by the looks on her siblings' faces that they all felt as awful about Ace's absence as she did. Oddly enough, she had the feeling that her father felt the same way that the rest of them did.

All of them except for Selina, of course. Her father's haughty ex looked like the cat that had eaten the canary—and had enjoyed every bite.

Selina leveled her gaze at Marlowe, looking at her expectantly. "Well, go ahead, tell us what you learned, Marlowe," she urged. As if she and that woman had a close relationship, Marlowe thought, rather than the antagonistic one that existed between them.

"We didn't learn anything," Marlowe informed Selina coolly.

"Well, that doesn't sound right," Selina commented. The woman cocked her head, as if trying to understand. "Why not?" she asked.

Marlowe fought the really strong desire to scratch

the woman's eyes out. She had a feeling that Selina already knew the answer to that.

Taking a breath, Marlowe managed to get her temper under control. Going down to Selina's level wouldn't accomplish anything or lead anywhere, Marlowe told herself.

Deliberately turning toward the other people who were around the table, she said, "According to the hospital administrator, the day Ace was born, there was a fire in the maternity ward. All the records there at the time were destroyed in that fire."

"A fire?" Ainsley repeated, surprised. "I don't remember ever hearing about a fire breaking out at the hospital before."

Marlowe nodded. "From what Callum and I could piece together, it was just a small fire, and it was quickly gotten under control before any lives were threatened," Marlowe told the group.

"But not before the maternity records were destroyed," Rafe concluded.

"No, not before then," Marlowe said, knowing how suspicious that had to sound to them. It did to her, as well.

"That sounds awfully convenient to me," Selina said to the other board members. There was more than a trace of sarcasm in her voice.

"Yes, it would seem that way," Marlowe was forced to agree. It was obvious that she was far from satisfied with this outcome. "But I'm not giving up until we get to the bottom of this—and to an explanation of what sounds like a Christmas miracle."

Her siblings exchanged looks. Marlowe had lost them with her last sentence.

"How's that again?" Ainsley asked.

"Dad, didn't you say that when he was born, Ace was very frail and sickly. So frail and sickly, the doctors didn't expect him to live through the night. And yet, he not only lived, but he actually went on to thrive, almost overnight. The night after his birth," Marlowe specified.

Remembering, Payne smiled sadly. "I thought those were just the Colton genes, coming to the forefront and taking over," he told the rest of his children.

"Or," Marlowe suggested, "it could be someone switching babies that night, substituting a healthy son for an unhealthy one."

Marlowe knew that, on the outside, it sounded preposterous. "But why?" Ainsley asked. "Why would someone do that? Who stood to benefit from the switch?"

"Well, from where I'm sitting, *that* sounds like the million-dollar question," Rafe told the others.

"So you all think we should go looking for the real Ace—provided he survived his sickly infancy." The statement came from Payne and surprised everyone. He was not in the habit of asking anyone for advice, least of all his children.

Ainsley put her two cents in. "I think we should look for the real Ace, but we should check him out before we risk telling him who he really is," she told her father. "You don't want to take a chance on bringing in someone who was shortchanged in the morals department. We have no way of knowing what sort of influences the real Ace had in his life while growing up.

For all we know, he might have turned into some kind of serial killer."

Payne was shaking his head.

"Blood or not, the Ace we knew was—*is* my son," Payne insisted, clearly upset by the discussion, despite the fact that he had been the one who had ousted Ace from the boardroom to begin with. It was obvious to Marlowe that for the first time in his life—as far as they knew—Payne regretted something that he had done.

"Well, you can always ask our Ace to come back on the board," Ainsley told her father.

"People." Selina raised her voice to get their attention. "You are forgetting about the bylaws. You can't just go against them like that because it suits you to do so," she informed the others sitting around the conference table.

Payne looked as if a gathering storm was about to break. "I can if I want to," he informed his ex-wife angrily.

"Payne," Selina countered, looking at him squarely. There was a warning note in her voice as she told him, "I beg to differ."

Marlowe saw the expression on her father's face. He was struggling to get himself under control. That wasn't his style. He was a volcano that blew on a regular basis.

There was something else going on here, Marlowe thought, not for the first time.

Because it was what she thought he wanted, she decided to try to buy her father a little time. "Why don't we hire a very good, very discreet private investigator to try to locate the so-called real Ace? And while he's at it, maybe the detective can also locate *our* Ace, who as far as I know seems to have taken off. He's not at home, and he's not at any of his regular haunts." Nor was he answering her calls when she tried to check up on him. She had left a total of five messages and received no answers. She hoped that he wasn't doing anything drastic, just giving himself a little space and taking a breather from all of this for now.

Rather than talk over them, Rafe raised his hand to get the others' attention. "Why don't I look into that for us?" Of all of them, he, as an adopted son, surely knew better than any of them what Ace had to be going through at the moment. "I've got a couple of ideas on how to follow up on this," he told the others.

Selina looked as if her interest had been suddenly piqued. "Just how do you plan to proceed?" she asked.

Rafe looked at the woman, unmoved by her question. "I'll let you know when and if I find something," he said her.

Miffed, for once Selina turned toward her ex. "You know, I get the feeling that your children don't trust me, Payne."

Payne's eyes narrowed as he looked at the woman who had been a thorn in his side for years now.

"There's a lot of that going around," he replied cryptically.

That was not what she was expecting. Selina shot her ex a very cold, dark look. Caught in the cross fire, Marlowe could hardly keep from shivering.

Payne drew himself up, looking even more formidable than he usually did. "Well, if there's nothing else, this meeting's adjourned," he declared. "I've got a meeting to get to with some possible investors." He glanced toward Rafe and Marlowe. "Keep me apprised of any progress you make. And definitely call me if you locate Ace—our Ace," he specified. "Tell him he and I need to talk." He took a breath, then added, "I feel bad about the way we left things."

Well, this was new. Marlowe exchanged looks with her siblings.

"Dad?" she said hesitantly. "Are you feeling all right?"

"Why?" Payne challenged gruffly.

On the spot, she knew she had to push on even though she wasn't up to a shouting match. "Because you don't usually feel the need to, well, apologize," she told him.

Payne's complexion went through several changes in color. "Yeah, well, sometimes things need to be shaken up," was all Payne seemed willing to say. "I've got to go," he repeated, removing his all-but-overwhelming presence from the boardroom.

Marlowe exchanged looks with her siblings. "Who was that man?" she quipped, only half in jest.

Rafe raised his broad shoulders in an exaggerated shrug. "Beats me."

Turning to pick up the notepad she'd brought in with her, Marlowe suddenly became aware of another empty seat at the table. She looked around the room to no avail. "Where's Selina?"

Turning to answer Marlowe, Ainsley said, "She's— gone." It was obvious that was *not* what she thought she was going to say when she'd started her sentence. "I didn't see her leave, did you?" she asked Rafe.

Annoyed with herself for not noticing the woman

slipping away, Marlowe said, "No, but she probably just slithered out. You know how vipers are."

Marlowe's mind was racing ahead, weighing several possible answers to that question. Possibly Selina had just gone back to her office to lick her wounds. Or perhaps she had slipped out to meet with someone. She still couldn't shake the feeling that her father's ex-wife was somehow involved in sending that anonymous mass email that had started all of this turmoil. For that matter, she could be even further involved in all this. Maybe she had even known about the switched infants and had helped with the switch—but Selina would have been a child herself when Ace was born.

Her head began to hurt.

She needed help with this, she thought. Impartial help. That ruled out her siblings for now. They all viewed Selina in the same light that she did. If her intent was to be fair, she needed someone outside the circle so that she could be sure she wasn't allowing her own intense dislike of the woman to color her outlook or taint her conclusions.

She left the boardroom quickly.

Wallace was waiting for her in the corridor. At her request, he had remained outside the boardroom because, with everything else going on, she didn't feel like having to explain his presence to her father. Wallace had agreed only after he had checked out the boardroom and was satisfied that the large room was accessible only through one set of double doors.

The moment she emerged from the boardroom, he was right at her side.

Marlowe got right to what was on her mind. "Do you

think your boss is out of his meeting yet?" she asked the bodyguard.

"You're my boss," he responded in his quiet, authoritative voice.

Marlowe sighed. "Your *other* boss, Wallace," she specified.

Wallace looked at his watch. "Yes. Unless it ran over," he qualified.

That was all she wanted to hear. "Thanks," she murmured.

It amazed her how quickly she recalled Bowie's cell number. She'd started dialing it before she realized that she hadn't had to pull out Bowie's business card this time.

He answered on the second ring. "Hello?"

She felt the hair on the back of her neck curling in response to the sound of his voice. This was getting worse, she thought, not better.

"Are you available?" she asked.

She heard him chuckle softly. "Well, you'll have to buy me dinner first, but, yes, I'm available."

"Very funny," she said dismissively, then got down to the reason for her call. "I really need to follow Selina."

"So you said."

"I know," she said impatiently, "but I think it might be more urgent than I initially thought. I'm fairly sure that she's got something big on my father. Something that has him practically twisting in the wind and jumping to obey her slightest whim." She paused, looking for the right way to phrase this. "I might be totally wrong about this, but I think that it might have something to do with Ace being switched with a healthy baby at birth." She realized how that had to sound to Bowie. "According to my father, when Ace was born, he was really sickly. They didn't think he'd even make it through the night, and suddenly, not only did he make it, but he was thriving."

"And no one noticed?" he questioned.

"From what I gather, my dad and his wife at the time chalked it up to being a Christmas miracle," Marlowe told him.

Bowie was quiet for a moment, thinking. "Well, best guess, Selina might be trying to bring down Colton Oil," he suggested.

"No, that's more your father's style," Marlowe said. Then, suddenly realizing what she had just said, she tried to backtrack and apologize. "Sorry, that just came out. But anyway, Selina would have no reason to bring down Colton Oil. It's far more to her advantage to have the company bringing in money. That way, she gets to continue living in the lifestyle that she's grown accustomed to enjoying. That woman will never have enough money."

That made sense, but blackmail wasn't always about making sense. "It could just be her way of getting revenge," Bowie brought up. "You know, because your father divorced her all those years ago."

"According to the story, the divorce was Selina's idea. And even if it wasn't, wouldn't she have done something to undermine the company long ago, not waited all these years to make a move?" she asked Bowie. That only made sense to her.

"Ah, but revenge is a dish best served cold," he said.

There was that, she supposed, but she wasn't convinced. "Maybe," she agreed. "But right now, I just want to be sure that the viper isn't going to do something awful to foul up Ace's life."

"Which Ace?" Bowie asked.

"The Ace *I* know," Marlowe snapped. The next second, she instantly regretted her reaction. "Sorry. My temper keeps spiking." She blamed it on stress and the pregnancy. The latter was in part Bowie's fault, but she couldn't allow herself to go down that path. There was no future there.

Marlowe heard him chuckle again. The sound all but undulated through her, sending goose bumps all along her body.

"Yes, I noticed," Bowie said. "Okay, I'll be there in the next forty minutes."

She sighed. Forty minutes might be too long to wait. She needed to be ready to take off at a moment's notice. "That's all right, I can just—"

"Okay, hold your horses. How does twenty minutes sound?"

"Better," she told him. "Fifteen would sound even better than that."

He laughed. "Only if I learn how to fly."

"I thought you already had that superpower," she deadpanned.

"Very funny. Look, I just need to wrap something up and I'll be there as quick as I can. Wait for me." It wasn't a request, it was an order.

She didn't like being given orders, even if she was asking him to come. She struggled to make light of it. "Or what, no dessert?" she asked him.

Another one of his chuckles rippled through her. "Okay, if you want to call it that."

Was he talking about sex? She could feel herself responding to the very suggestion and abruptly shut down. That was what had gotten her into this mess to begin with, she reminded herself.

"Robertson, if you don't get down here in the aforementioned fifteen minutes, I will be gone by the time you *do* get here," she warned.

"Cool your jets for a few minutes, mama. I'll be there."

Mama.

Marlowe felt her back go up. "Don't call me that," she retorted.

"Don't worry, you're not going to lose your identity. But you are going to be someone's mama—aren't you?" he asked.

"Just get here, Robertson. We can have that other discussion some other time," she informed him.

She had already made up her mind about the baby. But she didn't want Bowie thinking that he could just bend her will and turn her into some obedient, subservient human being.

Maybe she shouldn't have called him, she thought, terminating the call.

She didn't need this further aggravation.

Chapter Seventeen

It had been almost a week that she and Bowie had been conducting their surveillance on Selina. Six days of discreetly sitting in his car near the guest house where Selina resided on the Colton ranch.

It had gotten them no closer to any answers about her former stepmother. Nor had they gotten more information about the attempts on their lives or the mysterious email sent to the board.

Selina was either determined to keep a low profile now that the wheels of her plan had been set in motion, or "she didn't have anything to do with that email about Ace that went out to all of you," Bowie concluded on the sixth evening. After sitting in the car, night after night, he was beginning to feel as if his legs were permanently cramping up. "And this is all just a wild-goose chase."

Bowie had parked his car well in the shadows, confident that Selina couldn't detect them.

From their present location, Marlowe couldn't even see the main house, and after being out here, night after night, she was beginning to get a little antsy, not to mention really stir-crazy.

Added to that, she felt much too close to Bowie, and she didn't need that added stimulus.

Glancing toward Bowie, Marlowe sighed in response to his last comment. "I'd hate to think you were right," she admitted.

"Don't get me wrong," he qualified. "I am perfectly willing to sit in this car with you for as long as you want, but wouldn't you feel more comfortable sitting in a secluded booth in a restaurant?" Bowie asked her. "If nothing else," he shifted, doing his best to get comfortable, "there's more leg room in a booth."

Marlowe looked toward the guest house again.

Nothing.

Selina had gone inside the house a little more than two hours ago, and the lights throughout most of the house had been out for the last forty-five minutes. "She's got to be up to *something*," Marlowe insisted. She felt it in her bones, even as she noted to herself that no further attempts had been made on their lives.

"Oh, no argument there," Bowie agreed. Selina was far too devious a woman to just sit around and do nothing. "But right now I'm not so sure what that something has to do with Ace."

Marlowe sighed. Bowie was right. This was just a waste of time—just as the other five nights of surveillance that had come before tonight had been.

"You're right," she told him. "Drive me back to Colton Oil headquarters and we'll call it a night."

He turned on the ignition and slowly retraced his route, quietly driving away from Selina's home until he got to the main road.

"Why don't we shake things up a little?" he suggested once they were headed away from the ranch. "Instead of you going back to the office so you can pick up your car *and* Bigelow, why don't you give him the night off? You and I can get a late dinner, and then I'll bring you home to the Colton compound afterward. You did say the place had security, right?" he asked, making sure that wasn't something she'd said just to get him to back off when he'd suggested getting her a bodyguard.

"I did and we do," she told him, adding, "but I don't think dinner's such a good idea."

He slanted a look in her direction. "Still afraid to be seen with me out in public?" he guessed.

Marlowe drew herself up. "I am not afraid of anything," she informed him.

"Right. I forgot. You're fearless," he said. "So then why this reluctance to be seen out in public with me?"

"It's not you," she said, "it's dinner. There's no point in paying for a fancy meal when all I can keep down these days are crackers and tea—and I consider even *that* a victory," she added.

"Still getting sick to your stomach?" Bowie asked her. He'd thought that would have passed by now. Obviously not.

Just talking about it made Marlowe feel queasy. "That's putting it mildly, but yes, I am."

There was sympathy in his eyes as he looked at her again. "I'm sorry."

She almost believed he meant that, but then that night they had spent together came back to her like a blaring movie trailer. "It's not your fault. Oh, wait, yes it is—and mine, too," she deliberately corrected herself.

There was no point in arguing over this part of it. He

just wanted to take her to get something to eat, whatever she could successfully keep down.

"We can stop at a restaurant and get you tea," he told her.

There weren't that many places to eat in Mustang Valley. She was acquainted with all of them. "No restaurant is going to want to serve their customers just tea," she told him.

"Oh, I don't know about that," Bowie contradicted. "They might be willing if they know that there's a fifty-dollar tip coming."

"A fifty-dollar tip?" she questioned. "For *tea*?" That sounded absurd to her.

The absurdity of that didn't seem to bother Bowie because he said, "That's right."

"For tea," she repeated in disbelief.

He nodded. There weren't many cars out this time of night. They were making good time. "That's what I said."

She shook her head. "It's a wonder you people have any money if you spend it like water."

"Not water—tea," he corrected with a straight face. "So, what do you say? You willing to go out and get some decaf tea and crackers and anything else that you might be able to keep down?"

The man was going to keep hammering away at this, talking her ear off until she agreed, Marlowe thought. With a sigh, she surrendered.

"Oh, all right. Let's go and get some tea," she told Bowie, giving in. Her stomach was really acting up and threatening to give her a hard time. Maybe having some tea would make her feel a little more human.

"Better?" Bowie asked her fifteen minutes later.

They were sitting in a small booth in Lucia's Italian Café, and Marlowe was sipping a cup of tea very slowly. In between the sips, she was taking small bites of the plain crackers that were arranged in a small circle on her otherwise empty plate.

Marlowe nodded in response. She had to give him his due, she thought. "Better. Thank you," she added after a beat.

"Hey, like you pointed out, this was all my fault," he said, glancing toward her waist. "The least I can do is get you tea and crackers to make your stomach feel a little better."

That made her feel guilty. Bowie had put up with her recriminations and her mercurial shifts in mood these last few days when he didn't have to. Anyone else would have told her to get lost and then left. But he hadn't. He was a good man—one worth a woman's time and affection. Even if that woman wouldn't be her...

Marlowe looked at him for a long moment.

"What?" he asked, glancing down at his chest. "Did I spill something on my jacket?"

"No," she answered quietly and then forced herself to say what she was thinking. "You're not such a bad guy," she acknowledged.

Surprise filtered across his face. And then Bowie said, "Careful. You don't want me to get a swollen head now, do you?"

Marlowe frowned slightly. She was attempting to apologize, and he was making jokes. For a second, she thought about just abandoning the whole thing, but she was too stubborn not to continue. "I'm trying to say I'm sorry," she said, exasperated.

For a moment, Bowie grew serious. "I know," he said. "And I'm trying to let you know that you don't have to," he countered. And then he turned his attention back to the turbulent condition of Marlowe's stomach. "Now, how are the crackers?"

She looked at what was left on the plate. They weren't exactly tempting, but at least she wasn't throwing up. "Flat."

"Are you talking about their shape or their taste?" he asked her, curious.

She didn't even have to think about her answer. "Both."

Bowie found her response encouraging. "Well, at least your sense of humor is alive and well—such as it is."

She wasn't sure if that was a put-down or his idea of a compliment. Most likely the former, she thought. "Sorry I'm not up to your stand-up comedian standards."

"You're forgiven," Bowie deadpanned. And then he decided to get down to business. "Seriously, what does your doctor have to say about this?"

"My doctor?" Marlowe repeated, momentarily confused by the question.

"Yes, about your morning sickness," Bowie stressed. Finished, he wiped his fingers and put aside the napkin. "Surely he or she must have a better remedy for what you're going through than just tea and crackers. That was the solution of choice back in my grandmother's day. Seeing all the progress medicine has made, they have *got* to have come up with something better than that in this day and age."

In response Marlowe merely shrugged and looked away, avoiding Bowie's eyes.

For once, Bowie evidently decided that he wasn't going to drop the subject. "What's that supposed to mean? They haven't come up with anything better?" he questioned.

Why was he hammering away at her like this? "I have no idea what they've come up with," she retorted.

"You haven't asked the doctor?" he guessed, somewhat surprised.

She sighed. "No, I haven't *gone* to the doctor," she answered, exasperated.

Bowie stared at her, stunned. "You haven't gone to the doctor?" he repeated incredulously.

"Well, there's nothing wrong with your hearing," she retorted.

"Which is more than I can say about your common sense," he informed Marlowe. "Why haven't you gone?" he demanded.

She could feel her temper beginning to spike and had to struggle in order to keep from telling him what he could do with his questions. She knew he was concerned, but it annoyed her that he was treating her as if she didn't have enough sense to think for herself. Why did she have to go to the doctor? She knew what was going on. She was pregnant. As far as she knew, she was healthy, so there was no rush to submit herself to having her doctor poke and prod at her, right?

Why did people keep nagging her about seeing a

doctor? First Callum, now Bowie. Didn't anyone have anything better to occupy their lives with than *her* life?

She felt as if she was spoiling for a fight. "Maybe you haven't noticed this, but I've been a little busy lately."

"That's no excuse," Bowie informed her quietly so that they wouldn't attract any undue attention from the handful of other people dining at the café. "You make time for the doctor." His eyes held hers as he went on to tell her, "This is important, and you're not the only one involved here, Marlowe."

"Meaning you?" Marlowe asked, ready to tell him what she thought of his interference in her life.

"Meaning the baby," he told her.

That took the wind out of her sails, effectively deflating them as well as embarrassing her. Damn him, he was right. For the baby's sake she should have already gone to the doctor just to make sure everything was all right. Except for this awful morning sickness, she felt she was healthy. But what if she wasn't? What if she was overlooking something important, or hadn't realized it yet? And even if she herself *was* healthy, she needed to take prenatal vitamins and get checkups— for the child's sake.

Marlowe pressed her lips together. This was not easy for her. She forced the words out. "You're right," she told him grudgingly.

"Does that mean you're going to make an appointment with your doctor?" He evidently wasn't convinced that she wasn't merely paying lip service, just telling him what he wanted to hear.

"Yes," she fairly hissed.

She wasn't off the hook yet. "When?" he asked.

"Well, I can't very well make it now, can I?" she pointed out. "It's after eight and her office is closed for the day."

Bowie nodded, accepting the excuse. "When?" he repeated, his eyes on hers.

She really wanted to shout at him, but she managed to keep herself under control because there were people around.

"Tomorrow," she told him, gritting her teeth. "I'll call the doctor tomorrow. Is that good enough for you?" she demanded.

He inclined his head. "Ask me again *after* you make the appointment."

Marlowe rolled her eyes. He was really pushing it, she thought. "You are the most infuriating man," she told him.

To her surprise, Bowie flashed an almost blinding smile at her. "But I'm growing on you, aren't I?" he asked her.

She was tempted to tell him a number of things, none of them flattering at the moment. But she refrained. "I reserve the right to remain silent," she answered.

She saw the way he smiled at her and knew he had her number, no matter *what* she said to the contrary. What he said next confirmed it.

"You don't have to," Bowie told her. "That says it all." He looked at the nearly empty plate and her teacup. "If you've had your fill of tea and crackers, I'll take you home."

She rose from the table, surprised when he drew the chair back for her. She had to admit, the man had some very good inherent traits. And he might very well make a good father—or husband…

"Take me to the condo instead," she told him. "I don't feel like answering any questions, and if I go home to the ranch, with a bunch of people wandering around, I'm bound to run into someone, and they'll ask questions. I'd rather just have some solitude."

"All right, I'll just give Bigelow a call," Bowie began to say.

"No, don't," she said as they walked out of the restaurant and to his car. "Give the poor guy a break. I'll be all right for one night," she assured Bowie.

He rolled over what she'd said in his mind as he got into his vehicle. "I'm not going to take that chance," he informed her.

Anticipating that he was about to take out his cell phone, Marlowe caught hold of his hand. "Wallace has probably made some plans for the evening. Even if he hasn't, let him just enjoy some peace and quiet for a change. I don't need a babysitter. I'll be fine," she assured him.

He left his phone in his pocket and instead started up his car. "Yeah, you will be," he agreed, surprising her. "Because for tonight, I'm going to be your bodyguard."

She thought of the last time they had been together for the duration of an evening and her mouth curved in an ironic smile. "That didn't exactly turn out well the last time, now did it?"

He drove toward her condo a short distance away. "If you recall, I wasn't your bodyguard then," Bowie reminded her.

No, he wasn't. He was something totally different,

she thought, remembering that night. The next moment, she shut the memory away.

WALKING INTO HER condo a few minutes later, Bowie looked toward her living room. "I see you got the window fixed," he commented.

"It's January, and even though this is Arizona, the temperature can still drop down into the thirties at night," she reminded him. "That's more than a little brisk."

"I was just making an observation," he told Marlowe. "You know, not everything's a criticism. You really have to stop being so defensive."

She opened her mouth to respond, then closed it again. Lord, she hated it when he was right, but she knew she had to admit it.

"Sorry, you're right. This whole situation has me feeling really uptight. Not to mention that I haven't really been myself lately."

"Take a few deep breaths and just focus on calming down," he told her.

"So, now you're a life coach?" she asked, then instantly regretted it.

But Bowie apparently took no offense. "I can be if you need one," he offered. He sounded so genuine that she regretted being so flippant.

"What I need is a drink to help me unwind." She saw him opening his mouth and beat him to the punch before he could say it. "I know, I know. The baby. I know I can't have one."

She looked so despondent, he wanted to do something for her. And then he thought of something. "Got any cans of chicken soup around?"

Of all the things she might have expected him to say, that was not one of them. "Why?" she asked. What did he want with soup?

"It's comfort food," he told her. "It shouldn't really bother your stomach and it might just help settle it."

"Guess we'll never know. I don't have any cans of chicken soup in the pantry." She saw him taking out his phone. Had he changed his mind about Wallace taking over bodyguard duty? "Who are you calling?"

Bowie held up his hand to stop her flow of words because someone had picked up on the other end of the line. "Yes, this is Bowie Robertson. Let me speak to Lucia, please."

"Lucia? You're calling the owner of the restaurant we were just in?" she asked, surprised.

"You want something, always start at the top," he told her.

Before she could say anything, he was talking to someone on the other end of the line again. It took her a second to realize that he was ordering food to be delivered to the condo.

"I'm fine," he said to the person on the other end. "Yes, I was there earlier tonight. We were discussing your wonderful meals and the lady I was with had a sudden craving for some of your wonderful chicken soup. Would you mind having someone come by and deliver? Oh, about five servings should do it. Wonderful. Here's the address." And then Bowie rattled off the address to the condo for the owner of the café.

Marlowe listened to him, in awe of the way he could

make people jump through hoops and still not resent him for it.

She was beginning to understand how he had managed to come as far as he had. And how he might just be the man she'd never known she'd needed in her life.

Chapter Eighteen

Marlowe sat across from Bowie at her dining room table, looking at the overly large container that had just been delivered. There was still steam rising from the soup, and oddly enough, the aroma that rose up to greet her was very tempting. Food hadn't smelled good to her for a very long time now.

She raised her eyes to Bowie. "Am I supposed to eat this or swim in it?" she asked.

"That's up to you. Whatever you feel like doing," he told her. "But personally I think that eating it might be the better way to go. Where are your soup bowls?" he asked, looking around the small, exceptionally neat kitchen.

"In the cabinet above the counter," she answered. She still couldn't believe that Bowie had actually had the soup delivered. That was exceedingly thoughtful, and it didn't match the image she had of him—but that was beginning to change, she realized. Drastically. "I didn't even know that Lucia's Italian Café delivered."

"They don't usually," he said in an offhanded manner, setting the two bowls he had found in the cabinet down on the table.

"But they just did for you," Marlowe pointed out.

"Let's just say that's because I'm a very good tipper," he told her with a wink. Finding a ladle, he brought that over as well, then looked at Marlowe. "We should eat this while it's still hot. What do you think?" he asked.

Marlowe shrugged. "Go ahead," she told him. She watched as Bowie used the ladle and distributed equal measures of the soup into her bowl, then his. A great deal more of the liquid still remained in the container. She picked up her soupspoon, paused and then placed it back down.

"What's wrong?" Bowie asked. She looked as if she was bracing herself for a huge ordeal, not just a bowl of soup.

"I'm still not sure about this," Marlowe confessed.

Bowie realized that he was hungry, but he wasn't about to eat anything until Marlowe did. His spoon remained suspended above his own bowl. "What's the worst thing that can happen?" he asked her.

Well, that was easy enough to answer, Marlowe thought. "I could throw up."

He nodded as if conceding the point while not really thinking much of it.

"If that does happen, I'll hold your hair back so you won't get it dirty while you're purging your stomach," he told her pragmatically.

She looked at Bowie. Most men wouldn't take something like that in stride; they'd do their best to get away from it. She looked at him more closely. "You're serious," she said in surprise.

"People usually know when I'm kidding," he assured her. "I have this telltale smile that gives me away. Go ahead," he urged, nodding at the bowl of soup sitting in front of her. "Take a spoonful." He saw the leery look that came over her face as she stared at the steaming bowl. "It's soup, Marlowe, not poison," Bowie reminded her.

Hoping for the best even as she feared the worst, Marlowe dipped her spoon into the steaming liquid and brought it up to her lips.

To make her feel more confident, Bowie did the same, taking in a spoonful of soup at the same time that she did. He watched her the entire time, probably holding his breath and mentally crossing his fingers—not for himself but for her. In his opinion, Marlowe really needed to get something more solid into her stomach than just the crackers she'd had earlier.

When she realized in surprise that she seemed to be able to hold down the first spoonful, she attempted a second one. And then a third. Her stomach remained in a dormant state.

"Everything okay?" Bowie asked, peering closely at her face.

The smile on her lips bloomed very slowly, hesitantly, then went on to coax out just the tiniest bit of a relief. She looked almost afraid to say anything because if she did, she felt that she might just wind up jinxing everything.

He saw the small battle that was going on within her. "Marlowe, are you okay?" he pressed, concerned.

"I am...very...okay," she told him, sounding out each word and really happy to relate that message. "The soup seems to be...not wanting to come back up," she declared in surprise.

Looking pleased to hear that she *wasn't* experiencing yet another bout of nausea, Bowie nodded.

"That's really good to hear," he told her. "But don't overdo it," he advised. "Your stomach is probably still wondering what all that warm liquid coming in is. From what I've gathered, you and food haven't exactly been on the friendliest of terms, so let yourself get accustomed to this by degrees. That way you won't lose the ground you've gained."

"You don't have to baby me," she told him, feeling he was talking down to her.

"I'm not," he protested. "I'm just in training so that when this little person finally gets here, I'll be ready for her or him."

She frowned. "I didn't think you wanted to hang around for that. You made it clear that commitment wasn't your thing," she reminded him.

"I don't know," he said honestly. "Maybe it is. I'm taking this one step at a time, seeing where it goes," Bowie told her. "But I was serious about being there for you and the baby," he insisted. "I have no intention of running out on you, Marlowe. And," he went on, "I want you to believe that. I might not have a clue how to be a great dad—I was shortchanged when it came to the role model department."

An ironic smile curved his mouth. "My own father was hardly a good model. But the one thing I do know is that I really wanted my father to be there for me, to be around when I wanted him to watch me compete in a sport or beam with pride when I walked across the stage to collect my college diploma. That much I can do for my kid. I figure I can wing it when it comes to the rest of it. The thing I know for certain is that I never want my kid—"

"*Our* kid," she deliberately corrected. Her heart warmed at Bowie's words, though.

"Our kid," Bowie continued without missing a beat, "to feel that his father doesn't care." And then he raised his eyes to hers as another thought hit him. "I don't want you to think that I'm crowding you, or dictating terms regarding this baby, but—"

"Stop talking," Marlowe told him.

That came out of nowhere, and she had managed to completely catch him off guard. He stared at her now. "What?"

Marlowe was on her feet and rounding the table to get closer to him. Everything he had done and said tonight had abruptly knocked down all the walls she had so very carefully constructed around her heart in her effort to keep from getting hurt. Everything he had said had made her heart soften to the point that she had allowed herself to feel what she had been trying so hard *not* to feel: an exceedingly strong affection for this man, which she had allowed to sneak into her heart without truly realizing it.

Now, as she came up to where he was seated, she slipped her fingers into his hair and around both sides of his face. She tilted his head just a little, and brought her mouth down to his, kissing him with all the energy, all the unbridled emotion she could feel pulsating through her veins.

When Marlowe finally drew her lips away from his, Bowie looked at her, making no effort to hide the fact that he was stunned. He looked like it took him a second to regain the use of his brain and another second to remember how to form words. She could feel that heart continuing to beat fast enough to take off on its own.

"Was it something I said?" he asked her.

The breath she released was shaky. "It was *everything* you said," she told him.

There wasn't a drop of alcohol in her system, and yet it felt as if her head was spinning madly like a runaway top.

Lord, she had missed this, she thought. Missed the feeling of being utterly intoxicated, not on alcohol, but on the man who had already made her throw all caution to the winds once and was now making her want to do that all over again.

She desperately wanted to feel that way again. To feel as if the very world was at her fingertips just waiting for her to do something. To feel as if she could soar above the clouds.

She wanted to feel invincible, and she realized that only he could do that for her.

As she kissed him over and over again, she could feel him weakening, feel him giving in to the strong wave of desire that had washed over both of them.

But then, just as surprisingly, just as she had pushed his jacket off his shoulders and down his arms while he had begun to undress her, too, Bowie abruptly stopped.

Stunned, bereft, she looked at him, confused and hurt. Was he rejecting her? Didn't he want her? Marlowe wanted to flee, to hide, but instead, she made herself stand her ground.

"What's wrong?" she asked him in a shaken voice.

He wanted her more than he had ever wanted anything. More than he wanted to breathe, but he couldn't just consider his own needs in this.

His eyes searched her face. "Marlowe, are you sure about this?"

For a moment, she was speechless. And then the sunshine slowly returned.

"Do you want me to fill out an application?" she asked him.

"I just don't want you to regret this in the morning," he told her.

"What I'll regret in the morning," she told him, "is if you stop now."

He searched her face again, looking for the flaw in her statement. He found none. She was being serious, and everything inside of him lit up.

"Then let's make sure you have no regrets," he told her in a low voice that instantly seduced her.

The time for words was over. Now there were just very deep-seated emotions finally rising to the surface, seeking release. Seeking validation after being suppressed for what felt like an eternity.

Within seconds, it felt exactly the way it had that night at the conference. Except this time, there would be no gaps waiting to be filled in, no spaces that needed something to complete them.

This was all happening just the way it was meant to happen.

The hunger seemed to rise up suddenly, coming from his very toes and sweeping over him in a breath-stealing rush. It was making demands that had him all but shaking inside.

He hadn't admitted to himself just how much he had

wanted her. How much he wanted to hold her, kiss her and, most of all, make love with her until he was just too tired to breathe.

Bowie hadn't wanted to admit it because something within him felt that admission would somehow undermine him, shackling him to something he didn't want to be shackled to.

But he wanted this.

Wanted her.

The moment he allowed the thought to form in his mind, Bowie suddenly felt as if he was free. Free to finally be himself and to enjoy this all-too-fleeting revelry that was throbbing so hard throughout his entire body.

"Are you all right?" he asked, looming over her and eager to continue. But he wanted to be very sure that he was taking nothing for granted, wasn't allowing his own needs to blind him to any possible discomfort on Marlowe's part.

Marlowe blinked, perplexed. "Why wouldn't I be?" she asked.

"Your stomach, the baby…" he said, letting his voice drift off in case he had left something else out.

Her eyes smiled at him. "My stomach, thanks to the chicken soup from Lucia's, feels wonderfully calm for the first time in a while. As for the baby, it's cheering you on," she told him with a laugh. "So whatever you do," she said, her voice dropping to an enticing whisper, "don't stop."

"Then I won't," Bowie told her, his words gliding along the hollow of her throat.

His smile seemed to burrow right into her, lighting up her very soul.

His lips and hands seemed to be everywhere at once, touching her, pleasing her, making her ache for more. And all the while, she couldn't help wondering how she had managed to go so long without this after having sampled it that very first time the night their baby was conceived. She felt like a giant jigsaw puzzle that had just been put back together after an endless wait.

Although she wanted nothing more than to enjoy this, to absorb every touch, every single nuance of his fingers glancing along her skin, she just couldn't lie back and have this happen without some sort of reciprocation on her part.

Marlowe eagerly slipped her hands beneath Bowie's shirt, opening buttons, moving aside the fabric and all the while yearning for the next exciting moment.

And the next.

A moment filled with reverence, with kissing. With fire.

His breath along her skin excited her beyond all measurable scope, and she desperately wanted to make Bowie feel what she was feeling. Determined to try, Marlowe returned his kisses with a frenzy that she had never experienced before, fueling a fire that burned to unimaginable heights within him.

Bowie felt his heart pounding, and while he wanted to experience the rush that came with ultimate release, he was determined to prolong what was happening between them for as long as was reasonably possible.

Capturing Marlowe's hands to keep them still as well as from causing him to reach the peak of their experience, Bowie kissed her slowly, deeply, his passion increasing with each passing moment until Marlowe all but melted into a puddle right beside him.

A hot, contented, bubbling puddle.

She bit her lower lip as she felt his mouth branding every inch of her body with hot, achingly slow, arousing kisses.

Unable to remain still, she began to twist and turn beneath him as she tried to absorb each imprint, each arousing pass of his hands gliding along her throbbing skin.

He was making her crazy.

Shifting, she reversed their positions, and suddenly, she was the one who was leaving hot, moist trails along his heaving body; she was the one making him ache for her instead of the other way around.

Marlowe was working him up to the point that he was afraid, any second now, he was going to wind up wanting her *too* much and lose the control he was exercising over his body.

"Who would have ever thought that underneath that beautiful, cool exterior was this churning volcano of molten lava about to erupt and shower its fire all over me?" Bowie said with a laugh.

"That has to be the best-kept secret in Arizona," he added, his eyes shining as he looked at her again.

And then there was no more time for talking, no more time to continue to keep feeding the fire. The fire they had lit was now hot enough to consume them both.

Bowie shifted his body, moving along hers until he was directly over her. His eyes all but devoured her, holding her prisoner.

Lowering his mouth to hers, he captured her lips and then moved to enter her.

At first he did so slowly and then with more feeling, moving so that the dance that was within their souls suddenly bloomed and became very much a reality.

Marlowe caught her breath as a shower of stars exploded within her. By the way he moved, she knew he'd been captured in the fallout, as well.

With all her heart, she wanted to hold on to this feeling forever, even though she knew that really wasn't possible.

But at least she had now, which meant a great deal to her and made her heart sing. As for the rest of it, she would deal with that later.

Chapter Nineteen

She knew her bed was empty the second she woke up, even before she opened her eyes the next morning.

Marlowe was reluctant to actually open them, because then she would know for sure, and until she did, she could continue to pretend she was wrong. That Bowie was still here beside her.

Oh, grow up, Marlowe. You can't just spend the entire day in bed with your eyes shut, in a state of denial.

That wasn't who she was, she told herself. Denial was not the way she operated, anyway.

Bracing herself, she opened her eyes.

The emptiness hit her harder than she would have ever thought it would.

He was gone.

So what? Marlowe upbraided herself angrily.

After all, she knew what she was getting into, right? Bowie Robertson had turned out to be an honorable man, saying that he would step up when the time came, but he had made absolutely no promises to her about their future together in the traditional sense. When it came to that, he hadn't said any of the things a woman wanted to hear with the sole goal of getting her into his bed.

As a matter of fact, if she were being honest about it, she thought with a sigh, Bowie hadn't tried to get her into bed at all. *She* was the one who had made the first move. She had kissed him and made it abundantly clear that she wanted to make love with him last night.

If anything, Bowie had even tried to get her to back away, pausing right at the beginning and asking her if everything was all right. If she had suddenly backed away at that point, she knew he would have let her.

He might not have been happy about it, but he would have definitely let her.

No, she thought, tossing off the covers and looking around for her robe, last night had been a wonderful, *singular* experience—well, all right, *two* experiences, she amended with a smile. But right from the beginning she certainly knew that he had no intentions of turning that into their way of life from here on in.

If things wound up working themselves out, there might even be a few repeat performances of last night, but there was nothing on the drawing board to suggest it would turn into something permanent, and the sooner she wrapped her head around that, the better off she would be.

Besides, she had enough complications in her life right now. She certainly didn't need anything more.

The main things on her mind right now should be finding who had targeted her and Bowie previously. And Ace and who had switched him for her so-called real brother that night. Also she needed to find out why they had done it. For all she knew, the person who had switched those two babies could have even been her own father.

The more she thought about it, the more it sounded like it could have been something he would be capable of. After all, the image of a sickly first son was not exactly in keeping with the kind of legend Payne Colton would have liked to project.

C'mon, Marlowe, up and at 'em, she silently ordered, sitting up. Seeing her robe, she pulled it over and put it on.

Last night was in the past—as was Bowie, she insisted. Time to face a new day. All she needed was to grab a quick shower and get dressed, and she could be on her way—that thought stopped her. Her car was still back at Colton Oil's headquarters. Unless she felt up to a long walk—and she didn't—she needed a ride.

Callum, she decided. She'd give her twin a call. He wouldn't mind driving her in to work, and he wouldn't ask her a lot of unwanted, pesky questions while he was doing it. Callum, thank goodness, knew when to mind his own business. He—

Marlowe stopped abruptly. Was she imagining things? Because right now she could have sworn she smelled…chicken soup?

But that was impossible. She was positive that Bowie had put the remainder of the container of soup into the refrigerator before things had heated up between them last night. If it was there, how could she smell it now?

Curious, she went into the kitchen to investigate. Startled, Marlowe stifled a scream. But it was still loud enough to have Bowie almost drop the pot he had just finished warming up and was now about to transfer to the counter.

He put the pot down just in time. "Hell, Marlowe, you just made my heart stop," he told her. "And not in a good way," he added, as if remembering last night.

She glared at him. If there was one thing she hated, it was acting afraid in front of an audience, even an audience of one.

"Well, that makes two of us. I thought you'd left," she accused, taking a deep breath in an attempt to calm down her galloping pulse. "What are you doing here?"

"Not exactly the most welcoming tone of voice I've heard, but I'll answer that I said I was taking Bigelow's place as your bodyguard. That would include this morning until I get you back to the office and under his watchful eye. Don't you remember?" he asked.

Marlowe shrugged. The only thing she had thought of this morning was that he wasn't there. "I just assumed when I woke up and you weren't next to me…"

"That I had folded my tent and disappeared into the night?" Bowie guessed. Had he caught a glimmer of disappointment in her eyes when she'd screamed? Perhaps that thought made him smile, although he clearly did his best to maintain a straight face.

"Something like that," Marlowe admitted, hating just how happy the sight of him made her feel.

His being here didn't change anything. He'd practically told her as much. He was just being honorable and living up to his word, but that didn't mean he was about to turn over an entirely new leaf and become a new man. He was a commitmentphobe, and that wasn't about to change.

"Well, you assumed wrong," he told Marlowe.

So it would seem, she thought. Desperate to change the subject, she nodded at the pot on the counter. "What's with the soup?"

He turned toward the counter, grateful to have something else to focus on. "Since you tolerated it so well last night, I thought maybe you could have some more soup for breakfast, too—until you can eat other food," he explained. Then he looked at her more closely. "How's your stomach this morning?"

"Well, I haven't thrown up yet," she answered, then added philosophically, "but then, the morning's still young."

"Ever the optimist," he commented. And then he smiled encouragingly. "Maybe this is a sign of things to come," he told her.

"Maybe," she allowed, although she wasn't nearly as confident as he was. She was still holding her breath, waiting for her stomach to rebel against her.

"I've got water boiling for herbal tea just in case," he told Marlowe. "But since the soup's all warmed up," he said, taking the ladle and putting just a small serving into a bowl, "why don't you try sipping some of that first?"

"You don't have to do this," she insisted.

Being on the receiving end of all this fussing from someone who wasn't being paid to dance attendance on her made her feel uncomfortable. Having him wait on her like this put her in his debt, and she didn't like the way that felt.

"I know," Bowie answered. "Maybe I'm just trying to explore my domestic side," he told her, a grin twitching his lips.

"Heating up chicken soup and boiling water for tea isn't exactly going to turn you into the next Julia Child," she informed him.

"Another dream shattered," he quipped. And then he indicated the bowl he'd placed in front of her. "Just eat the soup, Marlowe."

She frowned. She didn't want to be beholden to him in any manner, and yet here he was, serving her and keeping her company while she ate.

"I can call a cab, you know," she told him, "or have one of my brothers come and pick me up." She looked at him almost accusingly. "You don't have to hover over me like this."

He patiently refuted her arguments. "Number one, I'm not hovering." He had taken a seat opposite her. "Number two, I already told you, I'm taking Bigelow's place until I get you back to him. And number three, if I didn't have such a thick hide, thanks to my father, I would have said that you trying to get rid of me like this is hurting my feelings. Now eat your breakfast."

He was talking down to her, she thought, leveling an annoyed look at Bowie. But she grudgingly did as he told her to.

Picking up her spoon, she raised it, then dipped it into her soup. "Anyone ever tell you that you're a dictator?"

"Yes," he answered simply. "It's one of my better leadership qualities." He waved at the bowl. "Now stop stalling and eat. I've got another meeting to get to this morning."

"Then go," she all but ordered him. "No one's keeping you."

Bowie frowned at her. Being with this woman required a great deal of patience, he couldn't help thinking. "Were you always such a slow learner?" he asked. "I just said I wasn't leaving your side until I turn you over to Bigelow. Now stop arguing with me and eat!"

"You know, maybe you should take lessons from Wallace," she informed Bowie.

"I'll be sure to let him know that. It'll make him happy," he said. "Now are you going to eat your soup, or am I going to have to feed you?"

She raised her chin, almost spoiling for a fight. "Go ahead," she challenged.

He'd never been one to back away from a challenge. "All right, I will." Picking up the spoon, he dipped it into the bowl and then proceeded to say, "Open up, Marlowe. Here comes the airplane heading straight for the hangar."

He said it so seriously, she couldn't help but laugh. And once she started, it was hard for her to stop. When she finally did, Bowie picked up the spoon again, filled it and brought it up to her lips once more as if nothing had happened.

What he hadn't counted on was the act of feeding her like this, of keeping his eyes on her as he slipped the spoon in between her lips, aroused him.

As it did her.

Bowie managed to get exactly three spoonfuls into her mouth like that and then the spoon, as well as the pretense of feeding her, were abandoned. He rose to his feet, bringing her up with him. And then he took her into his arms and kissed her.

She felt his smile against her lips. "You know," Bowie told her, "at this rate, you're going to wind up starving to death."

"Well, if that happens, I'll die with a smile on my face," she told him, her eyes never leaving his.

"Yeah," he agreed. "Me, too."

"ARE YOU GOING to be late now?" Marlowe asked Bowie nearly an hour later.

Bowie was finally taking her to Colton Oil headquarters after first calling Wallace to alert the bodyguard that he needed to be there to take over. Bowie was not about to just leave her at the building and take off. He took his responsibility very seriously.

"I'm the one conducting the meeting. They can't very well start without me, although I really wasn't planning on being late," he told her.

And he hadn't counted on wanting her so much after they'd already made love twice the night before. He was beginning to think of Marlowe as an addiction that he couldn't seem to shake.

"That's what you get for trying to be nice," she told him.

"Trying?" Bowie echoed. "I thought I was pretty successful in that department."

"I was talking about being nice," she informed him, "not the other part."

He grinned at her, even as he warned himself not to get drawn in again. He didn't have time for entanglements or for getting caught up with the daughter of his father's archrival…even though they were now having a baby together.

So why was he having so much trouble convincing himself to leave her alone?

"So was I," he told her, his grin getting under her skin.

It occurred to Marlowe that he was driving awfully slowly for a man who was supposed to be in a hurry. This was a sports car, for heaven's sake.

"Can't this thing go any faster? You're not the only one with meetings to get to," she told him. "I've got one scheduled for half an hour from now, so step on it," she urged.

"Five minutes isn't going to make a difference," he told her. "It's not just your life you'd be risking by speeding. You're going to have to start thinking more like a mother, Marlowe."

She really didn't take well to being lectured to. "I am thinking like a mother," she informed him. "An impatient mother. Now make this car go faster!"

Her eyes widened as she felt the car slowing down, not picking up speed. Looking at the speedometer, she saw that she was right. Bowie *was* slowing down.

"What are you doing?" she demanded.

"Making you take a breath." He wasn't kidding anymore. Bowie was deadly serious. "If you're not careful, you're going to wind up giving yourself preeclampsia," he told her.

She stared at him. He was making that up, she thought. "Say what?"

"That's where you wind up with high blood pressure, swollen ankles, and a lot of other unpleasant symptoms and side effects, which in turn will force you to spend the duration of your pregnancy laid up in bed, something I have a feeling that you *really* wouldn't like," he concluded. "So stop being such a rebel and just take it light, all right?"

"How do you know all this?" she asked, still not certain if she believed the man in the driver's seat or not. She wouldn't have put it past Bowie to have made that word up.

"Since you told me about our pending bundle of joy, I've done a lot of reading up on the subject," he told her. "Preeclampsia is also something you would know about if you made that appointment with your doctor." The look on Bowie's face told her just what he expected her to do next.

"Fine," she told him, rolling her eyes. "I'll make that appointment with my ob-gyn. Now can you *please* get me to my office, or do I have to flag down a turtle to get me there?"

"No offense, but I don't think you'd fit on the back of a turtle," he told her, clearly doing his best to keep the smile off his face. "Besides," he said as he slowed down and pulled over to the curb on the next block, "we're here. And here's Bigelow, right on time." He brought his car right up to where the bodyguard was standing and waiting for her.

With a welcoming smile, Wallace leaned in and opened the passenger door for Marlowe.

"Good morning, Ms. Colton," the bodyguard said brightly. He presented his elbow to her, waiting for her to take it.

Marlowe deliberately ignored his elbow as she swung

out her legs and rose to her feet. "I can still get out of a car on my own, Wallace," she informed the bodyguard stiffly.

"Never said you couldn't, ma'am," the bodyguard replied politely. He still watched her every move carefully—just in case.

Bowie leaned over inside the car toward the passenger side to get a better look at the bodyguard.

"I'd say you've got your work cut out for you, Bigelow. As you can see," Bowie told the man on his payroll, "Ms. Colton left her sunny disposition at home this morning."

Wallace flashed his employer a smile. "I'm sure everything will be fine, sir," he said, glancing toward Marlowe.

"Just get me away from Mr. Personality here," Marlowe said from between clenched teeth. "Before I say something he won't appreciate."

"As you wish, ma'am," Wallace said, making certain that he was only half a step away from her at all times as he escorted Marlowe toward the building's entrance. Reaching it, he held the door open for her.

Bowie remained where he was until he saw Marlowe walk into the building. Then he gunned his engine and pulled away.

Hearing the sound the car made as it left, Marlowe muttered under her breath, "I *knew* that sports car could go faster."

"Yes, ma'am, it really can," Wallace agreed, following her inside the building.

Chapter Twenty

Pausing, Marlowe rotated her shoulders and then rubbed the bridge of her nose.

Her head was killing her and her vision was getting really blurry, making the words on her computer screen look as if they were shimmering and moving about as they went in and out of focus.

Marlowe sighed as she looked at her watch. She had been working on this new proposal and telling herself "five more minutes" now for the last hour and a half. Every time she thought she was finally finished, something else would occur to her and she would have to stop and rework what she had written previously to make it jibe with what she had put down a few minutes ago.

She hated to admit it, but maybe she was pushing herself too hard.

It was getting to the point that things were beginning to spin around in her head. Even Wallace had grown completely quiet. He had adjourned to the outer office, leaving her alone. He'd done it undoubtedly in hopes that it might just help usher her along and get her to finally finish what was ultimately going to be a rough draft of the report she was going to be finalizing tomorrow.

The report that she was going to present to the state energy commission.

Marlowe bit her lower lip. This had to be just right, and at the moment, no matter how much she reworked it, she really didn't feel that it was.

Marlowe sighed again.

Where had all this insecurity come from, she asked herself. Ever since she'd gotten pregnant, it was as if up was down, down was up and everything felt as if it was skidding sideways. Her confidence had always been her best asset, and now...

Now she needed to straighten up and fly right, Marlowe sternly told herself.

And that, she realized, was *not* going to happen until she took control of herself, went home and got a decent night's sleep.

Her days of running on fumes were definitely over. She hated to admit this, even to herself, but this, perforce, was going to be a brand-new chapter in her life.

"Okay, Wallace," she announced, raising her voice so that it would carry into the next room, otherwise known as her administrative assistant's office. Wallace would avail himself of that area whenever Karen had gone home and he felt that she needed a little space to finish up whatever she was working on. "Your wish has come true. We're going home."

While her bodyguard wasn't exactly the most talkative man in the world—there were times when he was downright quiet, almost eerily so—he did always answer her when she addressed him. Even if he wasn't in the room, he would come back in and then answer her because he didn't believe in shouting.

But Wallace wasn't answering her now. He wasn't making a sound.

Had he fallen asleep? No, that didn't seem possible, she thought. The man ran on batteries.

"Wallace, did you hear me?" she asked, raising her voice a little louder. "I said I'm packing it in and you can take me home now."

Still no answer.

Curious now, she pushed her chair away from her desk. Maybe Wallace had gone to the men's room, although in all their time together, she couldn't recall the bodyguard having availed himself of that facility even once. It had gotten to the point where she had begun to think of the man as a human camel.

"Wallace, are you there?" she asked, an uneasiness beginning to spread through her. Why wasn't he answering? If he had suddenly started to feel sick, wouldn't he have said something to her? He usually checked in with her if he was going to do anything out of the ordinary.

Marlowe was fairly certain that Wallace wouldn't have just gone off to get a breath of fresh air. The man was the most self-contained person she had ever met. He didn't eat or drink on the job, and she was beginning to think that Wallace was the closest thing to a self-propelled robot she had ever encountered.

Growing a little concerned now, she called out, "Wallace, where are you?" as she walked out into Karen's office.

Still there was no answer.

The outer office was fairly dark, and she didn't see him.

Not at first.

And then, staring into the darkness, Marlowe realized that she could make out a form.

Her knees went weak.

Wallace was over in the corner, lying on the floor, partially hidden behind Karen's desk. Rushing over to him, she saw that there was a bloody crease across his temple. Stunned as well as worried, Marlowe fell to her knees beside the man, feeling for a pulse.

At first, she couldn't find one. Forcing herself to calm down, she tried again and finally detected a faint beat. Wallace was alive.

She almost cried.

"Oh God, Wallace, you gave me such a scare," she told him, addressing the unconscious man as if he could hear her. She had no idea what had happened to the bodyguard. All she could think was that he had to have tripped on something and wound up hitting his head on the corner of the desk when he went down.

But whether that did or didn't happen didn't matter right now. There was a far more immediate problem to be handled.

"We've got to get you to the hospital," she told Wallace as she took her cell phone out of her pocket.

But before she could even hit the number nine, a voice came out of the darkness and said, "I wouldn't do that if I were you."

Startled, her heart pounding almost wildly, she got up quickly and turned around toward the voice. She saw an average, nondescript man stepping out of the shadows and coming toward her.

As he came into the light, she realized that the man was holding a gun.

It was pointed right at her.

For the last several days now, she had had this strange, uneasy feeling that she was being watched. A feeling she couldn't shake, even though no one had shot at her or Bowie in over a week. With effort, she had managed to convince herself that the only one watching her was Wallace and that she was being paranoid.

But now she saw that she'd been wrong.

There was something definitely wrong with this man, she thought, but she couldn't let fear get the better of her. Wallace needed medical attention, and she was the only one who could get it for him.

"He needs an ambulance," she insisted, beginning to dial her cell phone.

"He doesn't need anything," the stalker told her darkly. When she continued to dial, he barked, "Put the phone down. Now!"

Afraid he would harm Wallace further, Marlowe did as the stalker told her, never taking her eyes away from the man.

"What did you do to him?" Marlowe demanded, doing her best to use an authoritative tone.

"What did you do to him," the stalker parroted, mimicking her voice and making it sound high-pitched and singsong. "It's always someone else who has your attention, isn't it?" he snapped. "Never me. Well, now I have your attention, don't I?" he asked, mocking her. His eyes narrowed, resembling small laser beams. "Now you have to pay attention to me, don't you?" he asked—and then he swung the gun toward Wallace, aiming it at the man's head. "Because you know I can snuff your friend out. Just. Like. That. Right?" he taunted.

"Don't!" she cried before she could get hold of herself. "Please don't. You have my attention, my complete attention. I swear it," Marlowe told the man with feeling. "Just don't shoot him."

The man sneered as he looked at her contemptuously. "You don't even know who I am, do you?" he demanded. He looked familiar, but only in a vague sort of way. For the life of her, Marlowe couldn't recall where she had seen him before, or even *if* she had seen him before or was only imagining it. But she sensed that if she said that to this man, it could send him over the edge or have some other dire consequences. She wasn't ready for either Wallace or her to pay that price.

So she lied.

"Of course I do," Marlowe told him in her warmest, friendliest voice.

For just a split second, she could see that her ruse was working and he believed her. But then his expression transformed into an ugly mask of pure hatred and, his face turning red, he shouted, "Liar! You *don't* remember me. I've been in love with you for over two years now but you never even gave me the time of day. Never even knew I was alive," he shouted, his face growing even redder.

"That's not true," Marlowe insisted, even as she racked her brain trying to remember seeing him somewhere. Desperate, she came up with an idea. "Of course I knew you were alive. But you know how it is, how my

father is," she told him. "If I let my father know about
you, about how I *felt* about you, he would have made
your life a living hell." She lowered her voice, as if con-
fiding information to her stalker. "He doesn't want me
paying attention to anything—or anyone—except for
the oil company."

Though it sickened her, she drew closer to the man,
playing up to him. "I pretended not to notice you so that
you could go on working here." She was making it up
as she went along, praying that she had guessed right
with this wild stab in the dark she was making.

The man's pale, gray face lit up, really pleased. She
had guessed right, she thought triumphantly. The stalker
did work here in some capacity.

But where?

Marlowe thought back, remembering that uneasy,
really creepy feeling that would come over her unexpectedly. He had to work somewhere in the company
where he could see her with a fair amount of regularity. Maybe even daily.

Whom did she have daily contact with but didn't
notice?

She tried to think, but it was almost as if her brain
was suddenly paralyzed. Frozen.

Nothing came to her.

His smile faded as the truth came to him. "You *don't*
remember me," he shouted. "You only have eyes for
that Robertson man. Ever since I saw you two at that
conference…"

"Oh, but I do, I do," Marlowe told him with feeling,
trying to convince him. "It's just that you're waving

that gun around and you're scaring me, so I'm having trouble thinking."

Anger creased his forehead as he glared at her. "You'd like me to put the gun down, is that it?" he asked her.

Her eyes met his, and she did her best to stay calm. More than anything, she needed to get him to listen to her. "Yes, please."

His eyes grew even colder. He raised the gun, aiming it at her. "You must think I'm really stupid," he accused her with a sneer.

"No, no, I don't think you're stupid at all," she denied adamantly. "I think you're smart. You were just biding your time, that's all. That was your plan all along."

Marlowe kept talking, but she could see that she wasn't getting through to this man. She was beginning to think that he was totally crazy. She could feel her heart starting to sink.

Her phone had already gone off once since her stalker had come on the scene, menacing her. And now it rang a second time.

Her stalker cocked his weapon, taking aim at the offending cell phone.

"Turn that damn thing off or I'll turn it off for you with my gun!" he all but shrieked.

"All right," she told him in a soothing voice as she reached for her phone, "I'll turn it off."

"Use your left hand!" he ordered sharply. This time the stalker shifted the gun so that it was pointed at Wallace. "Or so help me, I'll finish him off right now," he threatened.

The last of her hope withered and died within her. Marlowe drew in a shaky breath. She had no choice but to do as he said.

DAMN IT, BOWIE THOUGHT, Marlowe wasn't picking up, either. Now he *knew* something was wrong.

It had become his habit to check in once an hour with Wallace. But the bodyguard hadn't picked up his cell phone in the last hour, even though he'd called Wallace a total of three times.

And then he'd called Marlowe, but she wasn't picking up. He'd had his assistant check to see if there was a dropped signal, but all systems came back up and running.

Bowie tried again without success.

If the system was up, why weren't Bigelow or Marlowe answering their cell phones?

He could feel a knot tightening in his already twisted stomach.

Something was very, very wrong.

Racing to his car, he drove over to Colton Oil headquarters at top speed the entire way, thinking that Marlowe would have enjoyed feeling the rush of cold air against her skin.

The sports car had barely come to a stop when Bowie leaped out, running all the way into the building. All he could do was pray he wasn't too late.

The elevator wasn't there. He didn't have time to wait for it. Instead, he took the stairs, racing up the steps and taking them two at a time.

His lungs were burning by the time he reached Marlowe's floor.

Running to her office, he nearly came to a stop right then and there when he saw Wallace on the floor, unconscious and bleeding.

Half a dozen scenarios played through his head, each one worse than the one that came before. "Bigelow, where is she?" he demanded.

For one awful moment, he was afraid the big man was dead. But then he heard the bodyguard emit a low moan. Relieved, he knew he couldn't waste any precious time trying to make the man regain consciousness. He had the very sick, uneasy feeling that seconds counted and he might have already gotten there too late to be able to save Marlowe.

"Marlowe!" he shouted, scanning the area. "Where are you? Are you all right?"

There was no answer, only the sound of his own voice echoing back at him.

"Marlowe, say something! Anything!" he pleaded, fear all but closing his throat.

And then Bowie heard it. It sounded like a muffled cry. Like someone, he realized, whose mouth was being covered to keep her from crying out.

Scrambling back up onto his feet again, he called, "Marlowe, I'm coming!" It was more of a promise than a declaration. "Just hang on—I'm coming!" he cried, racing toward the sound of the muffled cry.

Bowie ran into her office and saw someone at the far end of the room brandishing a gun and dragging Marlowe into the stairwell that was located at the very far end of the wide office.

Her private stairwell, he remembered. He wasn't sure where it led, but he had the awful feeling that if the stalker was able to drag her inside, he could barricade himself and Marlowe in there. The very least that could happen was that the stalker might wind up harming her—and their unborn baby.

Bowie knew he couldn't let the man succeed in getting in there with her.

Exerting practically superhuman effort, he all but flew through the room, cutting the distance between himself and Marlowe and the stalker at an incredible rate. With one giant surge of effort, he leaped up and then *into* the man, tackling him before the man could succeed in making off with Marlowe.

Marlowe tumbled backward, but the shock of the blow he'd sustained when Bowie crashed into him had the stalker dropping her hand.

Backing up, Marlowe watched Bowie battling her would-be kidnapper. Despite his slighter build, incensed with fury, her stalker was able to match Bowie swing for swing. Desperate to help, Marlowe looked around the immediate area, searching for something—*anything*—to use as a weapon so she could knock the other man out.

Feeling half-crazed, she saw the commemorative statue of an oil rig her father had given her. Grabbing it, she intended to swing it at the stalker the very first clear shot she got of the man.

But the stalker and Bowie kept switching positions as they grappled for the weapon.

And then suddenly, the gun went off.

Marlowe screamed, terrified. Her heart froze. Who had shot who?

For one long, horrible moment that seemed all but suspended in time, she couldn't tell. Both men looked ashen.

And both men, she realized one awful, awful moment later, had blood on them.

Finally, Bowie staggered up to his feet. With a sob, Marlowe threw her arms around him.

"Are you hurt? Did he shoot you?" she cried, running her hands all over his upper torso, searching for the bullet wound. "Tell me he didn't shoot you," she begged Bowie.

But he didn't have to.

At that moment, the man shrieked, and then his body crumpled, falling to the floor. That told Marlowe all she needed to know: he had been the one to catch the bullet, not Bowie.

"I'm all right," Bowie told her, pulling himself together. "What about you?" he asked, quickly scrutinizing every inch of her. "Are you hurt? Did he hurt you?" he cried, searching for some telltale sign of an unseen wound.

"I'm fine," she assured him, leaning her head against Bowie. "He didn't hurt me."

Chapter Twenty-One

Once Bowie placed the call to the police station, Chief Barco and one of his people, officer James Donovan, arrived at Colton Oil headquarters within minutes of the call.

When the two men walked into Marlowe's outer office, Wallace was just trying to get to his feet. But Bowie placed his hand on the man's wide shoulder, making the bodyguard stay where he was.

"Don't get up," Bowie ordered him.

Any half-hearted protest Wallace was about to express died on his lips without a sound in deference to Bowie's authority.

"Everybody all right here?" the chief asked, concerned. His kind green eyes swept over the three people he knew in the room.

Bowie spoke up. "I am, but Bigelow here needs an ambulance to take him to the hospital." He turned toward Marlowe. "And it might be a good idea to have Ms. Colton checked out, as well."

Marlowe immediately vetoed the suggestion. "No, I'm fine, really," she assured the chief, who looked as if he was ready to whisk her off to the hospital himself. "Or I will be as soon as you get that man out of my office and into a jail cell." Her eyes were filled with loathing as she thought of all the harm her stalker could have done if he had fired his weapon.

Barco turned his attention to the bleeding, semi-conscious man on the floor. "I take it this is the man who took a shot at you in your condo," the chief said. "Cuff him, Donovan," he ordered.

The officer eagerly produced a set of handcuffs and quickly complied.

"If you check the bullets that were gathered up in front of the hotel when someone took a few shots at me, as well as the bullet that killed my personal body-guard," Bowie told the chief, "I think you'll find that they all match this man's gun." Hysterical, the stalker had confessed to Marlowe and Bowie after he'd been shot. He nodded at the stalker as Donovan was dragging the man up to his feet. Marlowe had told him all about the man stalking her and it was all he could do to keep from strangling the man with his bare hands.

The chief's eyes narrowed as he glared at the prisoner. "Get this scum out of Ms. Colton's office, Donovan."

The officer nodded. "With pleasure, Chief," he told his boss.

Fully conscious now and in pain, the stalker began to yell. "You can't get rid of me that easily," he shouted at Marlowe.

"I wouldn't bet on that, you bastard," Bowie said with loathing.

"But we were meant to be together. We were!" the stalker insisted, a frantic look entering his eyes. "Tell them, Marlowe. Tell them we belong together and that they're standing in the way of true love!" He was practically shrieking now.

Seeing the maniacal look on the stalker's face was when it suddenly hit her. She knew who her stalker was. "Edward Jones," she cried, moving forward past Bowie. "You work in the mail room!" Marlowe recalled how uncomfortable the man's intent stare made her feel whenever she had occasion to be anywhere near the mail room.

She could feel her flesh creep now.

Jones took her recognition to be an omen. "See?" he cried, trying to yank away from the officer who was leading him away. "She remembers me. She knows we're supposed to be together! Get these cuffs off me, you stupid ape!" he ordered hysterically.

"Yeah, right. In your dreams," Donovan said. "Keep walking."

Jones was still shouting as Donovan led him outside to where the police car idled, waiting.

Meanwhile, the chief had glimpsed Marlowe's face as her stalker was being led out.

"Don't worry, Ms. Colton," Barco reassured her. "I am personally going to lock that scum up and throw away the key." The chief looked from Marlowe to Bowie. "He won't be bothering either one of you anymore," he promised. "And whenever you're feeling up to it, come by the station and I'll take down your statements." He tucked away his cell phone. "Right now my advice to you is to go home and put all of this behind you."

"That's good advice," Marlowe agreed. "But I'm

not about to do that until I see Wallace get the care he needs."

"It's just a scratch, ma'am," Wallace told her. He obviously didn't want to be a burden to her.

But Marlowe frowned as she looked at the man's bloody forehead. "You could have bled to death from that scratch if I hadn't found you when I did," she informed him.

"But, ma'am—" Wallace began to protest.

Bowie stepped in, interrupting the bodyguard. "Just say yes, Bigelow. Trust me, I'm telling you this for your own good. It's a lot easier than trying to win an argument—any argument—with her."

Marlowe pinned Bowie with an almost lethal look. "And when did you *ever* win an argument with me?" she asked.

Bowie laughed under his breath. "The key word here, Ms. Colton," he said, addressing her formally, "was *trying.*" Hearing a siren in the distance gradually growing louder, Bowie looked at the man he had hired to keep Marlowe safe. "Sounds like your ride's here, Bigelow."

Minutes later, two attendants came in pushing a gurney between them.

"No need to ask who the patient is," the taller of the two attendants said. "Don't worry," he said to Wallace, "they'll have that stitched up and you'll be good as new in no time."

"Make sure that he is," Marlowe told the attendant.

"Yes, ma'am," the other attendant replied.

Wallace looked at Marlowe after the attendants had helped him get onto the gurney. "I'm sorry, ma'am," he apologized.

"For what?" she asked.

Wallace appeared genuinely distraught. "For not being able to protect you."

Although his hand was far larger than hers, she picked it up and squeezed it. "He got the drop on you. It could have happened to anyone," she insisted. "And it all turned out well in the end, which is all that really matters, don't you think?"

"If you say so, ma'am," Wallace responded.

"You do what the doctor tells you, big guy," Bowie instructed. "I'll be there to check in on you in the morning. Meanwhile, I'm just glad you're all right," he added with sincerity.

The chief had been standing by quietly while all this was taking place. Once the ambulance attendants had left with Wallace for the hospital, Barco turned toward the two people who were still in the room.

"Well, if there's nothing further, I'll be going, too. I've got to book that SOB," he told them. Then he confided, "I'm going to be looking forward to having the judge throw the book at him for all the emotional grief he caused, not to mention that he killed your security guard."

Bowie nodded. "I think that makes three of us," he told the chief.

Bowie waited until the chief had finally left to join Donovan before he slipped his arm around Marlowe's shoulders.

"It looks like it's finally over," he told her. And then he looked at her, surprised. "Marlowe, honey, are you shaking?" She knew he was aware how much she didn't like having attention drawn to any display of weakness, but her reaction had apparently caught him off guard. "What's the matter?" he asked Marlowe. "We got the bastard. He can't hurt you—or anyone else—anymore."

Because she had always come on like gangbusters, he evidently had no idea how to handle this new, vulnerable side of Marlowe.

"I don't know," she cried, upset and self-conscious over her behavior. "I guess it's just a reaction to everything."

She had managed to hold it together while it was happening, but now that it was over, now that she thought of how close she had come to being kidnapped or even killed, how close Bowie and Wallace had both come to the same fate because of her, Marlowe just couldn't get herself to stop shaking. Her baby's life had been in danger, too—and she had nearly lost Bowie forever.

"I'm sorry," she apologized, turning away and waving her hand at the whole thing. "This isn't me."

Bowie put his arms around her, drawing her close as he held her. "Well, until the real you turns up, I'll just hold on to the fake you if you don't mind. Just until she stops shaking."

Marlowe made a disparaging, self-conscious noise. "That may take a while," she confided. She was still avoiding looking into his eyes.

Bowie spun her back around gently and, placing his index finger beneath her chin, forced her to look at him.

"That's okay," he assured Marlowe, stroking her hair. "I don't have any place to be—except the ER while the doctor checks you and the baby out."

"I already told you, I'm fine," she insisted.

"I'd like a professional opinion confirming that," he told her.

"But—"

"Shh," he told her as he ushered her toward the door. "Humor me. That baby is half mine."

BECAUSE HE FELT that Marlowe could benefit from being in familiar surroundings, when they finally left the ER, Bowie took her to her condo in the city rather than to his own place.

Though she tried to disguise it, she still seemed rather shaky to him. He spent the night doing his best to comfort Marlowe and reassure her that at least *this* threat was over, even though the larger, more involved mystery involving Ace was still ongoing.

They talked about a variety of things until, exhausted, she finally fell asleep.

WHEN MARLOWE OPENED her eyes the next morning, the first thing she saw was Bowie's face. He was lying in bed beside her, awake and watching her sleep. She had the impression that he had been like that throughout the whole night.

"Were you able to get any sleep at all?" she asked Bowie, feeling both guilty and yet touched at the same time.

Bowie shrugged off her concern. "I dozed off and on," he told her.

"Mostly off," she guessed.

He smiled at her. "I never needed much sleep, not even as a kid." Peering more closely at her face, he asked, "How do you feel?"

That caused her to stop and think. The first thing Marlowe became aware of was her arm. She realized that it ached and felt as if it were on fire. That was thanks to her stalker, who had twisted her arm behind her back as he tried to drag her into the stairwell.

"Like I've been run over by a truck," she said honestly.

Bowie sat up instantly. That was when she'd realized that he was still dressed, as was she. Nothing had happened between them. Bowie had been serious about guarding her, she thought.

The man had been a total gentleman.

Bowie looked guilty about being remiss. "I knew I should have made you stay at the hospital just in case," he told her, berating himself for failing to do that. "Let's go—I'll take you back now."

Marlowe grabbed hold of his arm, making him stay where he was. "Take it easy," she told him. "My shoulder hurts because that crazy man yanked it. He didn't break it. Besides, we already went to the hospital to make sure the baby was all right. Everything is fine." She took a breath, centering herself as she tried to think. "If you want to take me some place, take me to the police station so I can give my statement and hopefully get that sick SOB locked up until the turn of the next century."

Bowie laughed shortly. "Amen to that. But first," he qualified, "since you seem to be able to keep food down now, you need to have something to eat."

Marlowe rolled her eyes. "You're being a mother hen again," she complained, trying to redirect his attention. She didn't want to eat; she wanted to go down to the station and give her statement now that she was no longer shaking.

"Mother hen?" Bowie repeated, pretending to be insulted. "I'm just making sure you keep your strength up, that's all," he insisted. "Now get ready, and I'll see about making you some breakfast."

She looked at him, puzzled. Something wasn't jibing. "I thought you said you couldn't cook."

Bowie frowned. "Beating two eggs with a fork and then pouring the results on a hot frying pan isn't cooking," he told her. "It's called survival."

Marlowe laughed to herself as she shook her head. "You have a very unique way of looking at things, Robertson."

In response, Bowie just grinned at her. It was a grin that was really beginning to get to her, Marlowe thought. Rather than becoming immune to it, she found that each time she saw the corners of his mouth curving, the defensive walls that she had spent so many years building up to protect herself from feeling anything just became thinner and weaker.

At this point, they had turned into tissue paper and were close to shredding away.

If she wasn't careful…

Marlowe shut the thought away before it solidified and became reality.

"So?" Bowie asked.

Having changed her clothes, Marlowe had returned less than twenty minutes later, ready to go out and face the day. Bowie had placed a plate in front of her, making her sample his efforts.

Marlowe didn't answer him at first, thinking it prudent to take a second forkful before she said anything. As the second mouthful made its way down her throat and into her stomach, she found her opinion didn't change. She had to give Bowie his due.

"It's good," she pronounced. "Surprisingly good." Marlowe looked up at him as he watched her. "Are you sure you don't cook?"

"On the rare occasions when I don't send out for food or stop off at a local restaurant—wherever I happen to be—I dabble with whatever I have on hand." When she looked at him uncertainly, he explained, "I don't like being helpless in any given situation."

"So you learned how to cook," she concluded. In her opinion, that put him in a class by himself.

"I learned how to wing it," Bowie corrected. "I've seen enough people frying an egg to know what to do with said egg on my own."

Nodding, Marlowe took in another couple of forkfuls. "Well, whatever you did with it," she told him, "this is very good."

She hadn't said it, but he sensed that she was about to say "but." He decided to coax it along. "So, what's wrong?"

"Oddly enough, nothing," she answered. But it was obvious, even to her, that her response wasn't 100 percent the truth.

"But?" he asked, waiting for the rest of her statement.

Looking uncertain, Marlowe laid down her napkin. "I'm still waiting for my stomach to reject the breakfast you made. No offense," she qualified. "It's not a reflection on you. It's just that since this little guy moved in," she said, placing her hand over her abdomen, "a living hell has been going on inside my stomach."

"Maybe you're over the worst of it," Bowie theorized.

She closed her eyes, afraid to allow herself to even begin to entertain that idea because of the disappointment attached to it if she turned out to be wrong.

"Oh, if only that were true," Marlowe responded wistfully.

Bowie seemed determined to have her think positively. "Maybe it will be," he told Marlowe. "Tell me when you're ready to go," he said.

Within five minutes, finished with the meal Bowie had made for her, Marlowe retired her fork and pushed away her empty plate.

A small smile quirked her lips. "I'm ready," she declared.

"And you're sure you want to go in to the police station to give your statement?" Bowie asked.

Marlowe nodded. "To the police station and then to work. You can just drop me off at Colton Oil," she added. "I think it might be better if I face my family alone and tell them what happened." Knowing how her father thought, she didn't want any possible fallout to hit Bowie.

He could guess what was on her mind. "I'm not afraid of your family, Marlowe," Bowie said.

"I didn't say you were, but I think it just might be better giving them the details on my own. Having you there would only be a distraction."

Wanting to lighten the moment, he asked, unable to keep the smile from his lips, "You mean for you, or your father?"

"For now," Marlowe answered, "let's just say both. But you know what will be nice?"

He was game. "I'll bite—what?"

"Going into work and *not* having to look over my shoulder every few minutes." It had taken her the entire length of the night, but she had finally managed to allow Bowie to convince her that her stalker no longer posed a threat to either one of them, that he wouldn't suddenly reappear in her life.

Chapter Twenty-Two

The moment that Marlowe walked off the elevator and approached her office, members of her family began to appear, converging and surrounding her. They all but swallowed her up as they fired their questions and concerns at her.

Her father outdid them all. He came storming down the hallway as soon as he was alerted that Marlowe was in the building.

Payne Colton's eyes met and held his daughter's. "Where the hell have you been?" he demanded loudly, frowning at her.

Confronted with her father's harsh greeting, it made Marlowe regret that she had turned down Bowie's offer to come with her to her office. He would have definitely been her buffer.

No, she thought, she was a big girl, a mother-to-be. She could fight her own battles.

Marlowe searched her father's face, doing her best to try to read between the lines. Had he heard about the stalker? Did he even care? She didn't have a clue.

"And hello to you, too, Dad," she responded cryptically.

What happened next took her totally by surprise. Her

father threw his arms around her, embracing her and giving her what amounted to a bear hug.

"Dad?" she asked uneasily, utterly stunned by his action. She could count on less than five fingers of one hand just how many times her father had demonstrated this sort of affection for her. Holding her breath, she waited for an explanation.

Releasing her, Payne drew back his shoulders. "Chief Barco stopped by the house late last night to notify us that he arrested a lunatic stalker working in the mail room and that lowlife had tried to kidnap you. Barco scared your mother half to death," her father informed her in an accusatory voice. "That poor woman must have called you more than a dozen times." He demanded, "Why didn't you pick up?"

"I turned off the phone," she explained, trying to subdue the wave of guilt she felt. "After what happened, I just wanted to put the whole thing behind me and try to get back to my old self."

Her father frowned. "I understand all that, but you still have an obligation to the family," he reprimanded. "When you didn't answer, we didn't know what to think. You could have saved us all that grief."

"I'm sorry, Dad," Marlowe apologized.

But one of her brothers took offense at the way their father was badgering Marlowe. "C'mon, Dad, give Marlowe a break," Rafe chided.

She didn't like being defensive, but she liked being blamed for having a normal, understandable reaction even less.

There was no such thing as being cut any slack when it came to her father. "That homicidal maniac almost succeeded in kidnapping me," she stressed, repeating what her father had already acknowledged.

"But he didn't," Payne said, pointing out the obvious. And then normal curiosity got the better of him. "How did you stop him?" he asked.

"I didn't," Marlowe answered, then told her father something she knew he didn't want to hear. "Bowie did."

Payne's salt-and-pepper eyebrows drew together, forming a single squiggle. "The Robertson kid? What was he doing in your office after hours?" he demanded.

"Oh, I don't know," Marlowe answered her father, deliberately sounding nonchalant, "saving my life when he didn't get an answer from the bodyguard he hired to watch over me."

"He did what?" Payne demanded. His face turned a bright shade of red as he tried to come to terms with what his daughter had just told him. "What the hell is Robertson doing hiring bodyguards for you?"

"Bodyguard, Dad, not bodyguards. There was just the one," she emphasized. "And to answer your question, Bowie hired a bodyguard for me because he was *worried* about me. For good reason."

That was clearly not a winning argument in Payne's estimation. "We Coltons can take care of our own," he said bitingly, throwing back his shoulders.

"Apparently we're not very good at it," Marlowe contradicted, "because if Bowie hadn't come to check on his man, we might not be having this conversation right now. Just admit it, Dad," she retorted, losing her patience. "Bowie did a good thing."

"Yeah, after he did a bad thing," Payne declared, deliberately staring at his daughter's still flat stomach.

Disgusted, Marlowe threw up her hands. "There is just no talking to you!" she cried, completely exasperated.

"Well, you're going to have to, missy," he informed his daughter. When she looked at him quizzically, he explained his comment. "As our new CEO, you'll be reporting directly back to me."

She had been expecting this ever since he'd let Ace go, and it had been weighing heavily on her mind. "About that," she began, since her father had given her an opening. "I don't know if I can handle being a CEO *and* an expecting mother."

The look on Payne's face told her that he harbored no such doubts. "You underestimate yourself, Marlowe," her father said. "I have every confidence that you'll rise to the occasion."

"But," Marlowe began, feeling that her father was not being realistic, "I'm going to be a new mother in a few months," she stressed. And that opened up an entirely new, unknown world for her. A world she knew nothing about and one she felt she needed to focus on, in order not to shortchange the baby, herself—or Bowie.

That argument was not a deterrent for her father, however. "So, you'll find a good nanny. Hell, I'll even pay for one," Payne told her, then declared, "There, problem solved."

"Not really," Marlowe told him. He was being far too simplistic. "And even if finding a good nanny did solve *my* problem, what about all the other mothers who are working for Colton Oil?"

Her father looked completely lost. It was obvious that he wasn't following her. "What about them?" he asked.

Marlowe sighed. "Does Colton Oil even *have* a day care center?" She knew it didn't, but she was trying to make a point.

Payne looked at her blankly. "What?"

She did her best to patiently explain what she was thinking. "I feel awful that I never even *thought* about that until it suddenly affected me directly."

Her father scowled at what he felt was convoluted thinking. "Why should you?" he asked her. "I certainly didn't."

"That's just the problem, Dad," Marlowe insisted. Couldn't he see that?

It was obvious that Payne was losing his patience with this discussion. "Marlowe, maybe you *should* take a few more days off," her father told her. "You're not thinking clearly."

"No, Dad," Marlowe contradicted, "for the first time in a long time, I *am* thinking clearly. We need to set up a day care center right here on Colton Oil's premises."

Exasperated, Payne exchanged glances with Rafe. "So now you're saying we need child labor?" her father asked sarcastically.

Marlowe tried again. "No, Dad, I'm saying we need a day care center on the premises. If I want to be close to my baby, other mothers, other parents," she corrected herself, widening the circle to include fathers, too, "should have the same option, as well. How about it, Dad? Can we set one up here?"

Payne didn't like being put on the spot like this, especially since it wasn't his idea to begin with. "I'll think about it," he told her evasively.

But Marlowe shook her head. Her father's answer wasn't good enough to satisfy her.

"You need to do more than just *think* about it, Dad," she insisted. And then she looked at her brother. "Back me up here, Rafe."

Rafe said simply, "I think she's right, Dad."

"Oh, you do, do you?" Payne asked his adopted son in a mocking tone.

The tone was meant to make Rafe back off, but the latter surprised him by digging in. "Yes, I do."

Payne looked at him in disgust. "And just who is going to foot this bill?" he demanded.

"Oh, come on, Dad," Rafe answered in disbelief. "You're pinching pennies now? Having this day care center on the premises will buy you more goodwill than you can possibly imagine," Rafe assured the overbearing head of Colton Oil.

Payne frowned. He really hated to be forced to admit it, but he had to say that Marlowe and Rafe did have a valid point.

Although he wouldn't come right out and say it, he demonstrated his agreement by retreating.

"All right, you two handle it," he told the pair. "I'll underwrite the day care center. Now let's move on to more pressing problems," he said authoritatively to the duo.

Marlowe and Rafe both knew their father was talking about trying to locate the real Ace, as well as finding the one whom they had thought of as Ace for all these years. There would be no peace until both of the Aces were found and the mystery surrounding their unorthodox switch was solved.

"I'm already looking into that, Dad," Rafe reminded his father. "I still think the idea of hiring a private investigator is a good one. Think about it," he said before Payne could protest. "If it's our PI, we get to control what news is released and what is kept secret until such time as all the pieces of the puzzle come together."

Marlowe nodded her agreement. "Rafe has a very good point," she told her father.

Payne looked from his daughter to his son. "So now the two of you are tag teaming me?"

Marlowe wasn't certain if her father had just made a joke. But for the first time since she had entered her office that day, she smiled at the larger-than-life man.

"Is it working?" she asked.

"Maybe," Payne answered evasively. And then he finally conceded. "Yes," he said. "But don't let that go to your heads. Odds are that you've got to be right at least once in a while," Payne conceded.

"Thanks, Dad," Marlowe said. "Coming from you those are glowing words of praise." His daughter was only half kidding.

Payne looked at her for a long moment, thinking.

"Seriously," he began in a tone that was extremely subdued from the one he usually used. "Did that bastard hurt you? The stalker, I mean," he added in case he hadn't been clear.

"I know who you mean, Dad, and no, he didn't. Thanks to Bowie," she stressed, wanting Payne to acknowledge that she was here due to Bowie's efforts.

Payne frowned as he cleared his throat. "Yeah, well, tell the boy I said thanks," he mumbled.

"Wow. More praise," she marveled in surprise. "I'll pass that along, too," Marlowe told her father, clearly impressed by this magnanimous side he was displaying.

"Yeah, you do that," Payne said in a low, less-than-enthusiastic tone of voice.

It was clear that uttering kinder words like this made the older Colton completely uncomfortable. Payne was far more in his element when he was shouting at people and ordering them around than when he was dispensing any sort of praise, no matter how much the other party might deserve it.

"Well," Payne said, looking from one of his children to the other, waiting. "Anything else that we need to discuss?"

"Not that I can think of at the moment," Marlowe answered. She turned toward Rafe. "You?"

"Nope," Rafe answered. "I'll let you know how things are progressing once I've hired that PI. I've got a number of candidates I want to vet first."

Payne nodded, his thick salt-and-pepper hair falling into his eyes. He combed it back with his fingers out of habit.

"I expect nothing less," Payne informed his adopted son.

"I know," Rafe replied, well aware how his father operated.

"And you…" Payne turned toward his daughter, belatedly beginning to take on the role of a hands-on father, a role that wasn't exactly second nature for him and didn't suit him, either. But he was trying his best.

Surprised by her father's attention, she asked, "What about me?"

"Your doctor say that you're okay to go back to work?" he asked. "You and the baby?" Payne added after a beat.

Marlowe could only stare at her father. This was a first. A whole new side to her father that she had never seen before and she wasn't sure how to react. He had never been a concerned father unless there was something about a particular child's behavior that could be seen as reflecting badly on the company. Then he would make his displeasure known.

"Well?" Payne pressed. "I know you can talk, girl. You damn near can talk the ears off a brass monkey," he declared. "Why aren't you talking now?" Always one to anticipate the worst, Payne stared at his new CEO, waiting to hear the news. "The doctor say something bad?" he asked.

"No." At least that much she could say honestly, Marlowe thought.

"Then he said it was all right to come back to work right after what you went through?" Payne pressed, watching her face intently.

He was like a dog with a bone, Marlowe thought. Once he latched onto something, he was not about to let it go until he was good and ready to. When Marlowe said nothing, his eyes all but burrowed into her.

"Well? What did he say, girl?"

Marlowe had never lied to her father. She thought of lies being in the same category as quicksand. Once she stepped into that territory, there was no getting out of it, and she didn't want to have to go through the ordeal if she could possibly avoid it. Because she knew in her soul that no matter how finely crafted the lie would be, somehow, some way, her father would find out that she had lied to him, and then all those years she had spent building up and cultivating his trust would be lost to her in a single second.

"Well?"

"She didn't say anything," she finally said. She was very aware that not only her father was looking at her but Rafe was, too. She really wished that lies could come rolling off her tongue with ease, the way they did whenever Selina talked. But she lacked that particular talent, and most of the time, that was all right with her.

The next second, she berated herself for wanting to be like Selina in any manner, shape or form.

"Why not?" her father asked.

"Because I didn't schedule an appointment with an ob-gyn yet," she answered in exasperation.

Her father looked surprised, then thought her answer over. "I appreciate you being tough, but this isn't just about you, it's about—the baby you're carrying," he forced himself to say, although she knew it wasn't easy, since the child in her belly was half Robertson. "You have a responsibility to it."

She never expected to hear her father say anything remotely like that. To acknowledge her condition and even be concerned about her state. Especially since he was aware of the fact that the baby was Bowie's—*and* the grandchild of his archenemy. A grandchild that would very possibly force the two families to come together.

"Point taken," she told her father.

"So finish whatever you have to do," he instructed, "And then call your doctor. Tell her what happened yesterday. Don't leave anything out," he said harshly. "And then do whatever she tells you to."

"And if the doctor tells me to stop working?" she challenged.

"We'll deal with that when the time comes. Now I've got a meeting to go to," he announced. Looking at Rafe, he said, "Let me know when you find a private investigator," he ordered.

And with that, Payne walked out, leaving his two children flabbergasted in his wake.

Chapter Twenty-Three

"Mind if I walk you home?"

Marlowe looked up from the assessment estimate for the proposed day care center she had been working on for the last few hours. She was surprised to see Bowie standing in the doorway.

Belatedly, his unusual question registered in her tired brain, and she looked at him as if his words weren't computing.

He found her bewildered expression endearing. "What?" he asked innocently as he came in. And then he gave up his ruse. "Sorry, that's my impression of me the way I might have sounded as a teenager."

That cleared up nothing for her. "Why?"

"Well, since we didn't travel in the same circles back then, I thought I'd pretend to go back in time to see what it might have been like if we did the typical, universal things, you know, like my walking you home after school, things like that." Reaching Marlowe's desk, he bent over to brush his lips against hers.

She found the taste of his lips exceedingly arousing as well as comforting. Without thinking, she sighed with pleasure. And then she laughed softly, warning herself not to slip into that trap.

"You're crazy, you know that?" she asked Bowie.

He didn't bother pretending to take offense. Instead, he merely grinned at her. "Yeah, maybe a little. All right." He feigned thinking the matter over. "I'll drive you home instead of walking."

It didn't seem right to have him chauffeur her around, even though she could easily let that become a habit.

"My car's still parked here," she reminded him.

"And it'll still be here tomorrow," he answered. "I'm sure the parking structure attendant won't let anything happen to Ms. Colton's car if it stays here for another night." Bowie dealt any argument she was going to come up with a death blow by adding, "Your father will have his head."

Getting up out of her chair, Marlowe gathered her things together. "My father's not all that bad," she informed Bowie, feeling it was her obligation to come to her father's defense, especially after this morning.

Bowie just gave her a very dubious look. "Hey, legend has it that Payne Colton eats interns and new hires for breakfast."

"Bowie—" she warned as she picked up her briefcase.

Bowie relieved her of the case, taking her other hand in his.

"Okay, I'll stop," he conceded, leading the way toward her doorway. "But that means you have to let me take you home."

"Whose home?" Marlowe asked. "Yours or mine?"

He paused next to a coatrack, took the lone coat

hanging there and slipped it onto her shoulders. Bowie kissed her again as he began to close her buttons for her. "Your choice."

"Seriously?" She thought he'd have had this all plotted out at this point.

"Hey, I'm just trying to be accommodating." Finished buttoning her coat, he picked up her briefcase again.

"Speaking of being accommodating," she said, thinking of what she had spent her afternoon working on. "Guess what my father agreed to do this morning?"

They began to head toward the elevator. "That was *not* where I thought this conversation was going to go," Bowie admitted playfully. There was no doubt about it. She brought out the lighter side of him. "Okay, I'll bite—what did your father agree to do this morning?"

Marlowe announced the news proudly. "To open up a day care center here for the employees who have very young children."

He saw the pleasure in her eyes. Bowie caught himself thinking that Marlowe could even make work seem adorable. "Let me guess—your idea?" he asked her. He held his hand up between the elevator doors to keep them from closing before they got on.

"Yes, but that doesn't matter," she said, waving that part away. "He actually agreed to it. He wouldn't have a few months ago."

Bowie pressed for the ground floor. "A few months ago, he didn't have a daughter who was going to make him a grandfather," he pointed out.

"Be that as it may," she continued, "it doesn't change

the fact that he's becoming more human, more sensitive to what people need."

Heralding Payne Colton didn't sit quite well with him. "Maybe he doesn't like falling behind and realizes that he needs to keep up with the times," Bowie told her. The elevator stopped and its door yawned open. He waited half a beat to allow her to get a step ahead of him.

"My father doesn't keep up with the times, he blazes trails," Marlowe informed him.

Leading her back to where he had parked his vehicle, Bowie took her words in stride. And then he smiled at her. "Maybe he should consider having you doing his PR for him."

About to say something curt, Marlowe realized that she was becoming unduly defensive. She curbed that. "I guess maybe I did come on strong," she admitted.

Reaching his car, Bowie opened the passenger door for her and waited for Marlowe to get in.

"Just a tad," he agreed. "But your loyalty is one of your more admirable qualities," he told her.

Closing the door again, he rounded the hood and got in on the driver's side. Buckling up, he asked, "So, have you decided?" Then, when Marlowe gave him a puzzled look, Bowie prompted. "You know, have you made your choice? Where you want me to drive you tonight?" he added.

"To your place," she answered.

"Good choice," Bowie said with approval. Starting up his car, he waited until he pulled out before asking, "So, how was your day?"

"I just told you the highlight," Marlowe said. "Otherwise, my day was filled with everyone stopping by, asking me how I was doing and if they could get me something." She shrugged, not comfortable about having everyone being so solicitous toward her. "But I suppose that is only to be expected, since I am the boss's daughter—and the new CEO—and this just might be their way of trying to butter me up."

"You're forgetting the most important part," Bowie told her. He could feel her looking at him, waiting for him to continue, so he explained, "You're a terrific person."

"Now who's doing the buttering up?" she asked, trying her best to suppress a grin.

"I can't give you a compliment without an ulterior motive?" he asked Marlowe innocently.

A smile played on her lips. "I don't know, can you?"

"Absolutely," Bowie told her.

Marlowe suppressed a sigh. He was making her feel things, want things.

Want him.

She knew she needed to change the subject before she went with her impulse and asked him to pull over to the side of the road so she could give in to those feelings. The overwhelming warmth she was experiencing was liable to make her do things she didn't want to be caught doing out in the open.

But it was getting harder and harder to bank down those feelings.

"How's Wallace doing?" she asked Bowie without any preamble.

That caught him by surprise. "Wallace?"

"Yes, you know, the man whose head was used as a

football while he was doing his best to guard me?" she reminded Bowie.

"I know who Wallace is," he told her, "although I tend to think of him by his last name. I was just surprised that you're asking me about him out of the blue like this."

"Not out of the blue," she protested. "I've been thinking about him all day."

He slanted a glance in her direction. "Should I be jealous?"

"No, you idiot," she retorted, curbing the strong impulse to hit him, "you should be relieved that I'm not this self-centered woman whose only focus in life is herself."

He hadn't seen her in that light for weeks now. "I realized you weren't like that when we slept together at the conference."

His response surprised her. "I thought you said that you didn't remember anything about that night," Marlowe told him.

"Oh, but how could I have possibly forgotten you?" Bowie asked teasingly.

He pulled his car into a driveway and then turned off the engine.

For a moment, she thought he was reading her mind, then she realized that they were in front of a condominium. He had arrived at his home.

"Wallace is doing fine," he answered. "He's not here," he continued, anticipating her next question, "because I told him to take some more time. I thought with your stalker safely locked up in jail and out of the way, you didn't need a full-time bodyguard anymore.

Just maybe a part-time one," he added, then flashed a smile at her. "I could fill that position," he told her. "Actually, I'd *like* to fill that position." He turned toward her. "Ready to come in?"

Marlowe looked at him uneasily, responding to his tone. "You make it sound like I should be bracing myself for something."

"Maybe," he allowed. And then, with what she could only term as an impish grin, he said, "I'll tell you a secret."

"A secret?" she echoed, a little bewildered. What kind of a secret could he possibly be sharing?

"Yes. I'm not exactly the world's neatest housekeeper," he told her, then confessed, "Actually, I'm pretty bad at it."

She laughed, relieved. From the nature of his tone, she had been expecting him to say something so much worse. "Nice to know you're not perfect. And that so-called vice of yours, well, it can easily be rectified with a cleaning crew coming in maybe once a month. Or maybe less," she added.

Bowie unlocked his front door, and she walked in ahead of him. She looked around at the opened room. "Or, maybe more," she amended.

It wasn't the last word in cluttered, she thought, but it was definitely close to it.

Bowie had never liked the idea of a stranger pawing through his things.

"I'll think about it," he told her. "But right now," he continued, closing the door behind them and then locking it. "But right now," he repeated with renewed energy, "I've got something more important than a cleaning crew on my mind."

Marlowe's breath caught in her throat as she looked up into his eyes.

"Funny, me, too," she told him just before she turned her mouth up to his and melted into his kiss.

The moment she did, she wrapped her arms around his neck and kissed him again.

And again.

In absolutely no time at all, he had her blood rushing and her heart pounding, going faster than a hummingbird's wings.

In less time than it took to think about it, Bowie was carrying her up the stairs and into his bedroom. Once there, they made slow, languid love the first time around. Then, catching their collective breath, they did it all over again, but faster and more intensely the second time.

Finally, when it was over, Bowie pulled himself up onto his elbow and looked at Marlowe. "You know, I think you could get to be very habit-forming."

He said the word *think*, but in reality, he already knew that she was. Deep down, his cautious nature wouldn't allow him to state the fact flatly because, more than anything, he didn't want to set himself up for rejection just in case she didn't feel the same way he did—or didn't *want* to feel the same way that he did.

"Could get to be, huh?" Marlowe said, repeating the words he had just used.

It just proved to her what she had feared all along. That Bowie was not the type of man to commit, even though he had promised to provide for their child. She didn't *need* him to provide for this baby; she could do that on her own and do it well. She didn't need his money, and she didn't need him, not if she had to twist his arm like this.

"Well, I wouldn't want you to get any bad habits on my account," she told him, her voice rising as she threw off the sheet and started to get up.

Seeing the way Marlowe had just thrown off the covers, he stared at her. "Where are you going?"

"I'm getting dressed, and then I'm going home. To *my* home," she emphasized.

But Bowie caught hold of her wrist, anchoring her in place. "Hold it—did I just say something to make you do a U-turn like this?"

"No, of course not," she answered sarcastically. "You didn't say anything. Anything," she emphasized with feeling.

Still holding her in place, his eyes looked into hers. "I'm sensing hostility," he told her.

"Very perceptive of you," she replied bitingly. "Now if you'll just let go of my wrist, I can get dressed and leave you to whatever it is you want to be left to."

"Marlowe, calm down," he told her sternly. "We need to talk."

"No, what I need to do is have my head examined for actually thinking that we—" Her phone rang just then, distracting her. "I need to have my head examined," she repeated, upbraiding herself for being so naive and stupid.

She got no further because her phone rang again. Exasperated, Marlowe looked down at the screen. It was her mother.

Talk about bad timing, she thought.

"I have to take this," she snapped. "It's my mother, probably calling to make sure I haven't been abducted again." Blowing out a breath, she swiped her phone on and declared, "I'm fine, Mom," before her mother could say a word.

And then she realized that her mother wasn't able to say anything. Her usually composed parent was sobbing almost hysterically.

Feeling guilty, she said, "Mom, please, calm down. I'm fine, really. There's no reason for you to cry like that."

But Genevieve Colton didn't seem to be able to take any comfort from her daughter's assurance. For a moment, she couldn't speak at all. And then, still sobbing, her mother managed to get out a few words.

"Mar...lowe. You...you have...to...come..."

At a loss as how to deal with her mother's very obvious distress, Marlowe tried to figure out what her mother was trying to tell her.

"All right, Mother, if it means that much to you, I'll come home to the ranch."

"No..."

The words her mother was trying to say seemed to get caught in her throat.

That didn't make any sense to Marlowe. "Wait, you *don't* want me to come home?"

"Your father..." Genevieve gasped, trying desperately to catch her breath and be coherent.

Marlowe tried hard to fill in the blanks and guess what her mother was trying to tell her. "My father's worried about me, too?"

"No!" her mother sobbed, frustrated.

"He's *not* worried about me?" Marlowe asked.

None of this made any sense to her. If her mother was this hysterical, she suspected that her father had to be involved in this somehow. Maybe her father had fed her mother details that the chief had given him and that was what had made her mother so beside herself like this.

"What is it?" Marlowe asked, desperately trying to unscramble what her mother was trying to tell her.

"Marlowe…your father… He's…he's been…shot," her mother finally managed to get out.

Marlowe was on her feet instantly, reaching for her scattered clothing, her outstretched hand trembling.

"How?" she demanded. "When? Is he… Is Dad…?" She couldn't get herself to ask the question, fearing the answer she would hear.

Listening to her end of the conversation, Bowie was already getting into his own clothes, throwing them on while never taking his eyes off Marlowe.

Ace was now on the phone, having taken it from his mother. "Marlowe, it's Ace. Dad's at Mustang Valley General Hospital. The police brought him here. The whole family's here, and we're not sure if he's going to pull through," Ace told her. He sounded totally shaken. "You need to get here as fast as you can."

"But what happened?" Marlowe cried urgently. "And where were you? When did you—"

Her questions went unanswered. Ace had ended the call.

Chapter Twenty-Four

Marlowe was trying very hard to keep from being over-whelmed by the shock that vibrated through her. Still, the phone slipped from her fingers.

She looked in Bowie's direction, hardly seeing him. "My father's been shot," she cried, dazed.

Bowie bent down to pick up her phone and handed it back to her.

"I heard," he said gently. He couldn't imagine what she was going through right now. "Do they know who did it?"

Numbness all but saturated her, stealing away her very breath. Marlowe shook her head in response to his question. "I don't know."

More than anything, he wished he could take her pain away. "But he's still alive, right?"

He saw Marlowe's eyes fill up with tears. "For now," she whispered. Looking around the room, trying to focus, she said, "I've got to get to the hospital."

"Get dressed," Bowie told her. "I'll drive you over there."

That was when Marlowe looked down and realized that she still hadn't put anything on. She was still nude.

"Oh. Right," she mumbled. Her brain felt as if it was stuck in first gear.

Moving quickly, Bowie picked up her scattered clothes and laid them out for her on the bed. His heart ached for Marlowe. She looked so stricken, so lost, it was as if she was moving through a fog, searching for her footing.

"Do you need any help getting dressed?" There was nothing sexual or seductive implied in his offer. All he wanted to do right now was somehow help her get through this.

"I can manage," Marlowe told him. She could barely squeeze the words out. They felt like shards scraping against her throat.

Bowie's eyes, full of sympathy, met hers. "I know you can," he said, doing his best to sound encouraging.

She was dressed in seconds.

"Ready?" he asked.

"Ready," she blurted out.

They were back in his car and on the road to the hospital in less than two minutes.

IN RESPONSE TO the attempted homicide, the hospital corridor directly outside the OR was crowded with people, drawn there by concern. They were all keeping vigil.

A quick scan of the immediate area told Marlowe that, just as Ace had said, her whole family was already there, even Ace, who had been conspicuously missing ever since the flare-up had happened between him and their father.

Marlowe's siblings—even her older half brother Grayson, who didn't work at Colton Oil and was not close to their father—were all surrounding Genevieve Colton. Another brother, Rattlesnake Ridge Ranch foreman Asher, stood next to their mother, who looked frightened and terrifyingly frail and brittle. She gave every indication of a woman who was on the verge of falling apart.

Even Selina was there, hovering around along the perimeter. She gave Marlowe the impression of a vulture ready to pick the anticipated carcass clean the moment the last breath was drawn.

Deliberately ignoring her father's ex-wife, Marlowe crossed to her mother and threw her arms around Genevieve, hugging her.

"Oh, Mother, how is he? Does anyone know what happened?" she asked, embracing the woman.

A little more composed now than when she had called Marlowe, Payne's distraught wife gave their daughter what details she could, the same details that she had finally managed to give to the chief.

"The cleaning lady called me from your father's office," she said in a shaken voice. "She was the one who heard the shot."

"So someone did shoot him?" Marlowe questioned, wanting to get straight as many details as she could. But just saying that sounded so incredible to her. *Someone had shot her father.*

Her mother pressed her lips together to keep from sobbing again. She wanted to get through this once and for all for Marlowe's sake without breaking down.

"Payne was working late again," she told her daughter. "The cleaning lady said she heard what she thought was a gunshot, followed by the sound of someone running away, and then a stairwell door being shoved open, then banging shut again. After that, she said there was nothing but silence. The brave woman ran toward the sound of the gunshot.

"Thank goodness she did," her mother continued with feeling. "because she found your father lying on the floor, bleeding profusely from the wound in his chest. She immediately called the police. If she hadn't done that, your father could have died without the proper medical attention." Her voice hitched, and she pressed her fisted hand to her mouth, stifling another sob. "He still might," she said, her voice breaking.

"Shh, don't think that way, Mom," Marlowe chided. "He's going to pull through. Dad's tough. He's going to be all right," she insisted.

Genevieve Colton was crying again. Marlowe could feel her mother's muffled sobs against her shoulder, seeping into her clothing.

"I'll take over, Marlowe," Callum offered quietly, drawing their mother away from his twin and over toward him.

"Does anyone have any idea who did this?" Marlowe asked, looking around at her siblings to see if *any* of them could give her more information.

Murmured voices blended together in what seemed like non-answers. And then Ace's voice rose above the rest. "The police said they were checking the security footage to see if it caught anyone in the vicinity of Dad's office," he told her. "But so far, all they know was that Dad was shot twice in the chest."

"That's either revenge or the killer was a damn poor shot," Rafe said.

Marlowe closed her eyes. "Oh Lord, I thought once Bowie caught that disgusting stalker, everything was going to start going back to normal. But this is just too awful," she declared, her eyes filling up with tears again.

She felt strong arms going around her shoulders and knew that Bowie was trying his best to comfort her, literally offering her a shoulder to cry on.

Marlowe struggled to pull herself together, but for now, she just let him hold her and did her best to rally for her mother's sake, if not for her own.

BOWIE REMAINED WITH Marlowe and her family until Payne's surgeon, Dr. Jonathan Bohan, came out to tell them that the operation had been successful. The bullet had not hit any vital organs. Currently, he was in the recovery room.

"When can we see him and talk to him?" Ace asked.

"You can see him in an hour once they bring him to his room. Talking to him, however, is going to be another matter," Dr. Bohan told them.

Instantly suspicious, Ainsley asked, "Why do you say that?"

"Because," the doctor said heavily as he delivered the news, "Mr. Colton slipped into a coma."

"A coma?" Rafe questioned. "How long is that going to last?" he demanded. "When's our father going to wake up?"

"I'm afraid that is anyone's guess," the surgeon said. "It could be in the morning, could be in a few weeks."

Ace looked up sharply, disturbed by what he was hearing. "Or it could last forever?" he questioned.

"It could," the surgeon agreed matter-of-factly.

"In other words, anything is possible," Marlowe said, hating to even entertain that idea, but it seemed that was what they were being told.

The surgeon exhaled heavily. "I'm afraid so," Bohan answered.

"But he could wake up tomorrow," Bowie hypothesized, speaking up for Marlowe's benefit in order to give her something to hang on to.

Bohan nodded his head. "We can only hope that," the surgeon told the family members.

Somberness gripped the Coltons even tighter.

BOWIE REMAINED WITH Marlowe for a few more hours, doing what he could to bolster her morale. He congratulated himself on achieving moderate success with his efforts.

When Marlowe appeared to be doing a little better, he decided that he could leave her for a while in order to take care of something that had been preying on his mind. Watching this drama unfold before him the way that it had, having something so traumatic happening without any warning, convinced Bowie that he needed to square things with his own father.

This had shown him that there weren't endless opportunities in which to take care of things, to square them away and make them right. There was only now. Tomorrow might never come.

Time was mercurial and fleeting.

He almost hated to disturb her, but he knew he'd never forgive himself if he let this matter go and something happened to his father the way it just had to hers.

Leaning over toward Marlowe as they all sat in the waiting area, Bowie whispered in her ear, "You'll be okay for a while if I run an errand?"

Marlowe was touched that he actually cared enough about her to ask if he could leave her side for a while. "I'll be fine," she assured him. And then, because she wasn't sure if he was going to leave permanently, she asked, "You're coming back here?"

On his knees if he had to, Bowie thought. But he didn't want to crowd her at a time like this. "Unless you don't want me to," he qualified.

She hesitated, wanting to tell him that she didn't need him to stay with her, that she could get through this on her own. But then she thought, Who was she kidding? "Come back," she told him.

Bowie knew that took a lot for Marlowe to say. It was, in effect, exposing herself. "As fast as I can," he promised. "Call me if you need me to come back faster than that," he added, concerned.

"Go do whatever you have to do," she told him, sending him on his way.

THE DRIVE BACK to the Robertson Renewable Energy Company offices went by both quickly and slowly. Quickly because it was over before he was even aware of the trip taking place, and slowly because he kept reviewing and rehearsing what he was going to say to his father once he got him alone.

None of the words sounded right to him, but they were all he had.

And then he was there, and there was no more time to rehearse.

"Is he in?" Bowie asked Jeannie, his father's administrative assistant, as he quickly walked past the woman's desk.

"Yes, but he's on his way out," she warned, calling after him as she half rose from her desk.

"He's always on his way out to somewhere," Bowie answered. Reaching his father's office, he knocked on the door and opened it without waiting for Franklin to give him permission to enter.

His father was in the middle of packing his briefcase and he looked up, surprised. "Didn't think I'd see you today," Franklin commented. It was clear that his father was preoccupied and wasn't about to remain.

Crossing to his father's desk, Bowie put his hand on top of the papers, causing his father to stop putting the papers into the case.

His father looked at him quizzically.

"Dad, we need to talk," Bowie told him.

"Sure," Franklin's tone was carelessly dismissive. "When I get back."

"No, Dad. Now," Bowie insisted.

Stunned, Franklin looked his son. "What's this about, Bowie?"

"About a few years overdue," Bowie told his father quite honestly. He could see that his father didn't understand. He tried a different tact. "I want you to hear this from me, Dad."

"Hear what?" Franklin asked impatiently.

"You're going to be a grandfather," Bowie told him.

Several emotions seemed to sweep over the older Robertson's face. And then he said, "Well, I suppose you were bound to slip up sooner or later. Will the woman listen to reason?" he asked.

He knew that his father meant, Could she be bought off? He contained his temper. "I'm going to marry her, Dad," Bowie said.

Franklin's eyes opened wide. "Oh?"

Bowie couldn't quite read the expression on his father's face, but he pushed on. "It's Marlowe Colton."

"What?" Franklin shouted, stunned. "Payne Colton's daughter?" His face was red now. "What the hell were you thinking?"

"That Marlowe Colton is the woman I've been looking for all my life," Bowie answered simply.

"That's a bunch of horse manure!" Franklin declared. "You can't be serious," he insisted.

"Actually, Dad, I am *very* serious," Bowie told him. "So serious that I'm willing to walk away from the company I love and believe in because my priorities have totally changed. I intend to be the husband and father that Marlowe and this baby both deserve and are entitled to, and I'm not about to allow anything to get in the way of that."

Franklin stared at his son in disbelief. "You really mean that?"

"Yes, I do," Bowie told him. "I know I don't have an example to follow, but that wasn't your fault," he added quickly, absolving his father of any blame for being absent for all those years. "You were busy building the company for the family. However, I fully intend to be a good father and husband to the best of my ability. I'm sorry to be so blunt, and if I hurt you, Dad, I don't mean to, but—"

"No, you didn't hurt me, Bowie," his father was quick to assure him. And then he took him totally by surprise by adding, "I only wish that I had been half the man that you are. And, if you want to marry her, you have my blessings, Bowie. But please, don't leave the company," Franklin implored. "I need you, and I can't do this without you. RoCo needs you," he emphasized. "Stay. Whatever else you want to do is fine with me. I won't stand in your way, but please, stay."

Bowie hadn't expect this, not in a million years. He grinned at his father, relieved beyond belief. "I will, Dad."

"And tell the Colton girl she's a lucky woman," Franklin said, calling after his son as Bowie left his office.

Bowie knew his father meant that sincerely.

"I will. But I'm the one who's lucky, Dad," he said by way of parting.

BOWIE FOUND MARLOWE just where he'd left her, still at the hospital, sitting in the waiting room. He came up behind her and gave her a quick hug.

Surprised, Marlowe turned around to look at him. "You came back," she said, smiling at him.

"I said I would." Rafe made room for him and Bowie sat down next to her. "How's your father doing?" he asked.

Marlowe smiled bravely. "The same, but at least he's still breathing. Get your errand taken care of?" she asked, wanting to change the subject.

"Yes, I had to clear up something with my father," he confessed.

He hadn't mentioned that. "Your father?"

"Yes." He grinned. "I wanted to tell him that he was going to be a grandfather. And that I wanted to marry you," he added, his eyes now searching her face for a sign that he hadn't frightened her off. "If you'll have me."

She looked at him, stunned and almost speechless. "Wait, back up," she cried. "What?" She was certain she was hearing things.

"I said I want to marry you and be a father to our baby," he repeated as if it was an everyday occurrence.

The words still weren't sinking in for her. This was Bowie, the commitmentphobe. Was he actually saying what she thought she was hearing? It didn't seem possible.

"Seriously? You want to settle down? You, Mr. I Want To Be Free, is talking about putting down roots?" she asked incredulously.

"Suddenly being free isn't all that appealing anymore," he told her. "So, what do you say?"

Did he think she needed help? Was that why he was saying this? "This is the twenty-first century. Women don't need to get married to have a baby."

"I know that," he told her, "but I need to marry you."

She looked at him suspiciously. "Why?"

He laughed and shook his head. Leave it to her to over-examine this. "Because I love you, Marlowe Colton, despite that sunny, easygoing personality of yours."

She started to laugh then. "Good answer," she said to him, beaming with approval.

"How about you?" he asked. "Do you love me?"

"I guess I could put up with you for a while." And then she laughed again, throwing her arms around his neck. "Yes, I love you, you big idiot."

He considered her response. "Not the most romantic answer," he decided, "but I guess it'll do." She finally realized that Bowie was a man of his word—he wouldn't leave, and they were going to be a family together.

"Well, it'll have to," she informed him just before she kissed him long and hard, with all the feeling she had been trying so hard to bury.

Bowie was not about to disagree.

Epilogue

Wrapping her fingers around Bowie's hand, Marlowe crossed over to where her mother was sitting in the waiting area with Callum.

"Mother," she spoke up, getting her mother's attention, "I know this is a very difficult time for all of us right now, but I have an announcement to make." Marlowe's eyes swept over the members of her family. All of them were still determined to keep vigil over her father for as long as they were able—or until such time as Payne Colton regained his consciousness and recovered.

"Now, Marlowe?" her mother questioned. It was hard to tell what Genevieve was thinking as the woman looked at Bowie intently.

Marlowe smiled at her mother. "I thought this might provide a little shelter in this storm we're enduring." At least that was her hope. "Bowie just asked me to marry him—" she glanced at Bowie "—and I said yes."

For a moment, the silence in the room was almost deafening, and then Callum rose to his feet and clapped Bowie on the back by way of congratulations.

"Well, it's about time!" her twin declared, moving on to Marlowe. He gave his sister a bear hug. Looking over toward their grim-faced mother, Callum said, "This is a good thing, Mother."

"I know," she replied. "I realize that. I just wish that this news came at a better time," she told her children sadly.

"It'll be better soon," Rafe promised, squeezing the older woman's hand before he moved on to shake Bowie's and hug Marlowe. "Congratulations," he whispered into Marlowe's ear, genuinely pleased for her.

Ace was just adding his own voice to the congratulations when Marlowe, facing the doorway, stiffened slightly. She saw a tall, slender woman entering the room where they were all gathered.

Marlowe had a bad feeling.

"Can I help you?" Bowie asked, stepping forward. This was not the time to bother Marlowe's family, he thought, acting as a buffer. He had noticed the uncomfortable look on Rafe's face when he saw the woman walking in.

The redhead walked over toward Bowie. "I'm Detective Kerry Wilder," she said, introducing herself. Next to her, Rafe noticeably stiffened. Marlowe wondered why.

Marlowe instantly reacted. "Do you have any information to tell us about my father?" she asked eagerly.

"No, not yet, I'm afraid. We're still looking into all the possibilities." She turned toward the men in the waiting area. "Which one of you is Ace Colton?" she asked.

Ace stepped forward, moving around Grayson. "I am," he told the detective.

She nodded, as if she already knew which of the

men he was but wanted to see if he would volunteer the information.

"Would you come with me, please?" she requested.

"Where are you taking him?" Grayson asked, clearly ready to protect his older brother. Like Marlowe, he had never stopped thinking of Ace as that, no matter what his father had said about switched babies.

"To the police station," Kerry answered. "There are some questions that need clearing up."

It was apparently all that the detective was willing to say at this time. Putting her hand on Ace's arm, she began to usher him out of the room, leaving the others to exchange looks and wonder what was going on.

"Are you arresting him?" Ainsley asked.

But the detective didn't answer. That left everyone wondering: *Did* Ace shoot his father? Was this what Ace had meant when he'd told the older man that he would be sorry for having thrown him off the board?

Marlowe refused to entertain that thought, but it certainly looked that way.

She was determined to find out as soon as possible for everyone's sake—most of all for Ace's, even as she looked forward to her own future with Bowie and their child.

* * * * *

COMING SOON!

We really hope you enjoyed reading this book. If you're looking for more romance, be sure to head to the shops when new books are available on

Thursday 9th January

To see which titles are coming soon, please visit

millsandboon.co.uk/nextmonth

MILLS & BOON
MEDICAL
Pulse-Racing Passion

Set your pulse racing with dedicated,
delectable doctors in the high-pressure
world of medicine, where emotions run
high and passion, comfort and love are the
best medicine.

MILLS & BOON

True Love

Romance from the Heart

Celebrate true love with tender stories of heartfelt romance, from the rush of falling in love to the joy a new baby can bring, and a focus on the emotional heart of a relationship.

MILLS & BOON
Desire

Indulge in secrets and scandal, intense drama and plenty of sizzling hot action with powerful and passionate heroes who have it all: wealth, status, good looks… everything but the right woman.

MILLS & BOON

HISTORICAL

Awaken the romance of the past

Escape with historical heroes from time gone by. Whether your passion is for wicked Regency Rakes, muscled Viking warriors or rugged Highlanders, indulge your fantasies and awaken the romance of the past.

LET'S TALK
Romance

For exclusive extracts, competitions
and special offers, find us online:

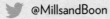 facebook.com/millsandboon

🐦 @MillsandBoon

📷 @MillsandBoonUK

Get in touch on 01413 063232

For all the latest titles coming soon, visit
millsandboon.co.uk/nextmonth